THE PLEASURE
GARDEN

THE PLEASURE GARDEN

EROTIC TALES·OF CARNAL DESIRE

·AMANDA McINTYRE·
·CHARLOTTE FEATHERSTONE·
·KRISTI ASTOR·

THE PLEASURE GARDEN

ISBN-13: 978-0-373-60554-5

SACRED VOWS
by Amanda McIntyre
page 7

PERFUMED PLEASURES
by Charlotte Featherstone
page 129

RITES OF PASSION
by Kristi Astor
page 237

SACRED VOWS
by
Amanda McIntyre

PROLOGUE

THE MAY QUEEN, THEY SAY, WAS BEAUTIFUL beyond compare—men were drawn to her irresistible charm and grace. She was betrothed to the Winter King, ruler of everything cold and dark, a man whose reputation spoke of a demanding, relentless lover who took what he wanted in order to satisfy his needs. And while she did bear some affection for her betrothed, she did not desire him. Would she survive his ardent attentions, she wondered, with no fire in her heart for him?

Conflicted, she retreated to her refuge—a garden that exists in neither place nor time, but in another realm hidden far away from mortals' prying eyes. Set beside a deep, dark wood and shaded by a copse of trees, the garden is a veritable oasis, its walls protected by magic. There the May Queen spent her days in quiet contemplation, the trees rustling above her head, the fountain gurgling beside her. Flowers in every hue bloomed in abundance, perfuming the air, and birds sang gaily to one another while the queen pondered her future.

The Green Man, wild and reckless, ruler of all that is warm and light, took pity on the poor queen's plight.

Watching her night after night in the secret garden in which she hid, he found his pity soon turned to lust. He requested permission to enter her verdant hideaway, and, drawn to his warmth and earthy sensuality, the lonely queen admitted him. Taking him into her confidence, she confessed that because she felt no fire for the man she was meant to marry, she feared that none existed within her. Challenged by her confession and overcome by her great beauty, the Green Man coaxed forth her passion like honey from a bee, sampling her lips with reckless abandon. The resulting sparks ignited a fire that neither was able to control. Their lovemaking was erotic and passionate, and time seemed to stand still as they hid away from the rest of the world, giving in to their carnal pleasures again and again. There in the secret garden, the lovers professed their eternal devotion, and the queen promised to break off her engagement to the Winter King.

But before she was able to do so, the Winter King discovered the secret affair. In a fit of rage, he denounced their forbidden love, publicly humiliating the queen, and cursed her beloved garden. Challenged to a duel, the Green Man fought valiantly for his lover's reputation, but was defeated by the Winter King, who cast him to stone and imprisoned him in the garden. The despondent queen, unable to live without her lover's touch, took her own life within the garden walls, taking all of its beauty and vibrancy with her. There in the now-barren garden, the Green Man was forced to forever witness the death and destruction his wanton passion had wrought.

Though darkness prevails, the Green Man knows that with the awakening of passion, the fires of love can burn bright once more. Indeed, if he can summon three pairs of lovers into his garden—lovers who possess the same passionate intensity that he and his queen once shared—the curse will be broken. The garden will once again flourish, and he and his lover will be reunited in another realm for all eternity.

It is said that on the eve of Beltane—a time for celebrating new beginnings—you can hear the Green Man's voice on the wind, singing his tale of woe.

I am the wind, softly caressing her hair
the breath near her ear
whispering words of passion she yearns to hear

I am the hand cradling gently her breast
awakening inside what others cannot,
I not so humbly confess

I am the sigh as she offers me all
and with no reservation,
I answer her call

Reborn in her passion, but faced with remorse,
she turns from my arms,
and faces her betrothed

A duel, says he, as I dust off my hands
and comply with his challenge
for her reputation to stand

I am the fire burning bright in my quest
ridding the cold, dark of winter,
winning my May Queen's breast

Yet before Darkness is finished, he utters one final warning,
and to his bride now banished
claims her death come the morning

You shall remain imprisoned in this dead withered place
as atonement for your sins,
and then to me he did face

No one will admire your seductions, kept hidden beneath
the vines
until thrice over you awaken
stone hearts and cause passion to entwine

1

FORBIDDEN. THE POSSIBILITY THAT HE AND his friend Gregory could be held in high treason by the English king was the last thing on Edmund's mind as he stared at the lovely creature walking through the crowd toward them. Fair-skinned with luxurious red hair, she sauntered with ease, greeting vendors, charming all with whom she came in contact, offering them a smile from lips that Edmund found himself wanting to taste. He watched as the object of his attention accepted an apple from an old man and bit into it. She closed her eyes at the pleasure of its taste, and Edmund licked his lips in response. She curtsied to the old man in thanks and he offered her a toothless smile before waving her on.

Not before this moment had Edmund ever seriously doubted his future in the priesthood, a future designed by his parents without discussion. Nonetheless, he questioned it now, for his next breath hinged on capturing just one glance from this fair beauty. Edmund was mesmerized.

"Aha, now there is a flower ripe for picking, eh, Edmund?" Gregory slapped him on the shoulder, biting into his own apple with a noisy slurp. "Good enough to eat."

Edmund jabbed Gregory in the ribs to end his annoying gibberish. With every step he took, the air seemed to pull in as though the center of his world were closing around him. His heart pounded against his ribs. "On my oath, she is no common woman. Are you blind? Do you not see how the magic surrounds her? She is the envy of all she passes."

"Oh, my boy," Gregory said with a chuckle, "it is by magic you are smitten, of that there is no doubt." His friend huffed. "But do you see her escorts? Am I the blind one, then? Surely, were she as respectable and fine a woman as you say, she would not be left unattended." His gaze flitted from one maiden to another in the crowd. "And to remind you, my friend, may I say our purpose in coming here today was to merely sample only, not to find a wife." He chuckled again.

It was midday and dark clouds had rolled in, playing hide and seek with the sun, casting long shadows over the lush spring valley. Here, beyond the newly imposed barricade barring the Gaels from the English, the ancient rites of spring were being celebrated. Plentiful food and drink mingled with mirth and promiscuity were the reasons Edmund and Gregory chose to ignore the new Statutes of Kilkenny imposed by the paranoid English king. Not easily enforced, they served to keep the Gaelic influence from swallowing the small English contingency in Ireland. Gregory's and Edmund's fathers, involved in the English governing bodies in Dublin, placed both them and their families at great risk of prosecution by the crown.

All of which was inconsequential as Edmund stared at the Gaelic beauty walking toward him.

"Shall we draw straws, then, to see who shall try to win her favor?"

Edmund glanced at his friend in amicable warning.

Gregory's eyes glistened with mischief, but he smiled. "Very well, there are countless such flowers waiting to be plucked today." He shrugged.

Edmund's body reacted to her of its own accord and he panicked at his discomfiture, unused to the protocol of approaching the fairer sex. That was Gregory's specialty—the wooing of women.

"What shall I say?" Edmund mumbled from the side of his mouth.

"Let her see you are interested, but do not reveal your intent. Make her come to you," his friend calmly advised.

In a hazy fog of virginal ecstasy, Edmund found the advice fading into oblivion, leaving only her beautiful face and dancing brown eyes meeting his as she passed. He sucked in a breath, unable to speak, certain that he'd met his destiny.

"Good day." She offered a quick curtsy and journeyed on, but then favored him with a glance over her shoulder. Edmund swore her cheeks were flushed. Or was that his imagination?

He held his hand to his heart, finally finding his tongue. "God forgive me. Surely I will die and be cast into hell for my thoughts," he whispered aloud, without care for who might hear him. His eyes were pinned on the gentle sway of her hips, his cock straining to follow her.

A harsh slap on his back woke him from his carnal trance. He gave Gregory a startled look. "Was she not the most beautiful maiden ever to grace the earth?"

His friend rolled his gaze upward. "Go after her then. You've not taken any vows of celibacy yet, my friend. I should think that God would prefer you purge yourself of your carnal demons now rather than later, wouldn't you agree?" Gregory winked at a young maiden who caught his eye. "Oh, my brother, I do not envy you your future. You are far nobler than I, to have the strength to give up such earthly pleasures—more to the point, women."

Confused as much by the battle warring between propriety and the reaction of his body below his belt, Edmund was dismissed by his friend with a jaunty wave. "Go on, enjoy yourself. I'm going to find a bit of shade and a drink for my parched throat." Gregory sauntered off and soon struck up a conversation with two maidens.

Edmund chuckled and turned, immediately stumbling over two pairs of legs protruding from a makeshift tent. He righted himself, ready to make his apologies, but the loud groans from within caused him to stumble backward again, realizing the pair likely hadn't been disturbed. Edmund took in the sights and sounds of the festival, searching for a tankard of mead, trying to avert his eyes from the public displays of carnal pleasures going on around him. He found drink and settled himself on a knoll, content, if need be, to stay away from temptation. Within moments a crowd began to gather nearby to watch a small acting troupe. He sipped his mead and listened as the story unfolded, involving the betrothal of the lovely May Queen to the cold and ruthless Winter King. He'd heard bits and pieces of the tale before, but never from a Gaelic perspective. He was enthralled, drawn up in the slow thrum of the music and the pleasant buzz from the need forming in his head. His attention, riveted to the sensual dance of the May Queen for her secret lover, the Green Man, left a disturbing awareness inside him, causing him to shift his legs to hide the protrusion in his brocs. Finally consummating their love, the queen straddled her lover's lap. Their realistic acting skills were not lost on the crowd as cheers and whistles encouraged the actors to portray the forbidden lovers. Edmund stared in fascination that this carnal behavior was not only publicly permitted, but also encouraged. His gaze landed on the scowl of the actor portraying the betrayed Winter King, his frustration increasing even as Edmund's erection became *his* frustration. The woman's soft cries brought his attention back to the couple, acting out the mating ritual with determined fervor.

Edmund's cup slipped from his hands and rolled down the hill, and he stood to retrieve it. Over the heads of the enamored audience his eyes met with those of the lovely maiden he'd seen earlier. The sounds of the play and the intense desire he felt swelling pushed him through the crowd, seeking an escape from the seduction of the play. He found a space beyond the crowd and took a gulp of air to settle his nerves.

"Come in here, boy. I have what you need." A woman called to him from a tented sanctuary across the road. She pulled down her bodice, exposing her plump breasts.

Edmund turned away, needing time to think. He hastened toward the outer edge of the festival and came to rest near a grove of trees. Deep fingers of purple began to stretch across the pink horizon. Passion surrounded him, wanton and sensual. Not exactly the kind of place for a young man about to go into the pastoral life. But his parents had given him no choice. The priesthood would bring both wealth and social stature to him and his family. He was torn—torn between what they wanted and what he wanted, right now. He was a young man in his prime; should he not be allowed a little taste of life's pleasures?

His eyes were drawn to a flickering light in a clearing beyond the trees. He entered the wood, aware of how the sounds of the festival grew faint, and curious to know what lay ahead. He emerged to find a small stone abbey, and nearby, the crumbling shell of a castle with one tower still standing as sentinel over what appeared to be a dormant garden.

A movement caught Edmund's eye as a brown-robed monk began lighting the tall torches that hovered a head above him. As the flames began to illuminate the area, Edmund noted the path of a massive circular maze made of small stones. Surely this was part of a pagan ritual, but the purpose of the maze intrigued him.

"Do ye seek quiet fer yer soul, my son?" A lilting voice came from beneath the monk's hood.

Edmund stared down at the man, unable to see the monk's face, but feeling the heat of his words as much as the torch that he held. "It is true, Father, my soul is unsettled."

"Aye, I sensed as much. Passionate men quite often find themselves lost in their purpose. You must walk the labyrinth, my son. Let the silence speak to you. Listen to your heart. It will lead you to your destiny." The monk turned and walked away.

"But how will I know what is the truth?" Edmund called after him.

The bow-backed man looked over his shoulder. "If it is truth you seek, then the truth you shall find. You need only listen."

Edmund frowned, and looked about him, searching for anyone else nearby, but there was not another soul around. "Is it always so desolate here?" He turned back to the monk and found himself alone.

Though he didn't take to heart the old man's word, he decided the solitude might help his perspective. He stepped inside the ring and methodically followed its narrow path.

Determined, Edmund tried to empty his mind of the soft moans he heard through the trees, reminding him of the sinful lust occurring within the woods. He turned his mind to his family, and the hopes they had for his future— one that would bring them better social and political connections with the king of England. He was to leave in a few days to begin his teachings, and yet it seemed an eternity away.

A twig snapping nearby caught his attention, and he searched the twilight shadows, thinking perhaps that the old man had returned. Instead, his eyes locked with those of the beautiful maiden he'd seen at the festival, and all previous thought ceased to exist.

Cara Ormond's heart pounded in her chest. Her father's wary concern flashed in her mind as she remembered how she'd begged and pleaded to attend the festival. Only when her older sister, Kiernan, agreed to let her accompany her and her betrothed to the faire did their father relent, but with a stern warning to both daughters. "Do not think I am unaware of what goes on at the festival. The two of you stay together and be wise of trouble."

No sooner had they arrived at the celebration than Kiernan kissed her sister, bidding her farewell. "Mind ye, Cara, stay away from trouble. You heard Da."

"And the same to you. Where are you off to, then?"

Her sister smiled impishly, squirming in her lover's tight embrace. "We'll be a-mayin', of course. Be good." And Cara had watched them run into the woods. She was happy for them, and true, they were within a few weeks of wedding, yet Cara couldn't help feel a twinge of melancholy. Things were changing, and she felt restless, yearning for someone special herself.

She pushed aside the concerns of her family, pondering for the span of a heartbeat the wisdom of her actions here at the abbey. She'd sensed something different about this young man, with his broad shoulders and hair the color of straw, from the first. He'd stared at her as though she were a ripe peach. He did not speak as she'd passed him at the faire, though his friend smiled with blatant admiration. A backward glance confirmed the blond man's interest, and he'd smiled as he held her gaze until she turned away, her cheeks aflame. Cara had tried to forget the episode, finding delight in watching a skit retelling the Gaelic tale of the forbidden triangle of the May Queen, the Winter King and her lover, the Green Man. However, the torrid affair, played well by the acting troupe, did little to quell her curiosity about the gray-eyed man or her lustful thoughts of him. After sampling some wine and wandering about the festival she saw him enter the woods, and she'd followed, hoping he wasn't going to meet a maiden. Cara had no idea where he was from, though she suspected him to be English, given that she would have certainly remembered him from any of the nearby villages. And if that were so, despite that her da called the new edict "cow dung," he was at risk for breaking the orders sent down from the English crown, mandating separation between Gaels and the English settlers in Dublin.

But as Cara watched him silently from the shadows, she felt certain the Mother Goddess had fashioned this meeting and so, drawing a deep breath, she took a step forward, a brittle twig breaking under her foot revealing her presence. Despite his lingering glance, Cara averted her eyes, stepped onto the path and followed the maze. She focused on the sound of her leather slippers brushing over the soft earth. This was a sacred place, respected for private meditation, and with no talking permitted within the perimeters, she could not even ask his name.

The longer they walked, the more Cara sensed the powerful magic of the labyrinth and the festival, calling to her to listen to the whispers of her heart. Around the circle, passing close but not touching, they moved in silence. Cara chewed the corner of her lip, aware of her nakedness beneath her kirtle, where she'd not thought of it before. A delicious shiver slithered between her thighs as she swerved, following the path that led back to the center of the maze. It was odd, this dance she found herself in with a handsome stranger, yet it stirred her emotions, urging, demanding.

Her throat grew dry. Gooseflesh rose on her arms, and she found herself sneaking glances at him, only to find him doing the same. Her fingers fisted the fabric of her gown, holding up her hem so she could see the path. She quickened her steps, noting how he stumbled slightly when they met side by side on their separate walks. Her eyes were drawn to the tented hood of his brocs and she caught her breath, smacked with a powerful jolt of desire. Cara battled the war between it and her father's insistence that a woman's purity was her most precious gift and should not to be given to just anyone. In the distance, the sensual sound of the *bodhran* drum kept beat with the increasing thrum in her chest, seducing her, coaxing her to follow her desires.

Forbidden.

The word served more as an enticement than a warning. Cara scanned the area, the idea of being alone with him festering in her brain. Aware of the tension mounting between them, she felt her sensitive breasts tighten, responding in arousal to her thoughts. She wanted to embrace her first Beltane in the same manner she'd seen so many others do today, free of rules and restrictions, celebrating the earthly pleasures that life has to offer. She'd sampled the wine, the food, the entertainment, and now she wanted to take the next step, proving that she was no longer a child, but a grown woman.

She spied a small grove of fruit trees, and beyond, what appeared in the flickering light of the torches to be a shriveled up hedge with a wooden gate. Glancing over her shoulder, she lifted the hem of her gown again and hurried toward it, hoping the man would follow her. Whether prompted by the goddess Mother Earth, too much wine or her own desire, she was not afraid to lose her maidenhead. And who better to do so with than a complete stranger?

She pushed through the gate, letting her eyes adjust to the change from torchlight to the ghostly illumination of moonlight. She'd heard of the crumbled shell of a castle, with its lone tower, abandoned long ago by the Romans. The druid priests who later settled here had built a small stone gathering place and created the labyrinth for contemplation. The heavy wood gate slammed behind her and Cara clutched her gown, determined to follow through with her quest. She moved cautiously forward, noting that the once royal garden now showed very little signs of life within its walls, filled now with dry brambles and brush. Not allowing her brain to second-guess her desire, she searched for a perfect spot where they could be together, for the first time wondering if he was any more experienced in the ways of the flesh than she was.

She pressed forward and found herself in what had perhaps been a small courtyard. A stone fountain, set among some overgrown vegetation near the tower, stood as its focal point, embellished with the sculpture of two lovers entwined in an intimate embrace. Cara stopped at its base, staring at the man and woman, seeing the moon reflected in the water left from a recent rain. As she studied the woman's face, the fragrance of roses seemed to waft in the air, and a chill ran up Cara's arms. She hugged herself, wondering if she was mad to be flirting with something so dangerous. What if she'd imagined the fair-haired man's interest, and even now he was off to find his friend? She bent down, dipping her hands in the cool water, splashing it against her heated cheeks. Perhaps he thought her foolish for running off as she had. Would he bother to try and find her? Cara closed her eyes, seeing him in her mind, wanting to taste those lips—just once. She lifted her arms over her head and gazed up the star-sprinkled night.

A gentle voice whispered on the breeze. *I am the wind, softly caressing your hair, the breath near your ear. Whispering the words you long to hear.*

Cara's body surrendered to the sound of ancient music and she began to sway, lost in its seductive rhythm. She danced around the statue, celebrating the couple's union, wishing for a lover of her own.

2

EDMUND SQUEEZED HIS EYES SHUT. THIS GIRL had done nothing to encourage these rebellious emotions, but had appeared innocently as angel and temptress both, causing him to break out in a feverish sweat. Reason bade him to turn and walk away, go find Gregory and head back to Dublin, none the wiser about how her lips might taste, how soft her skin might feel beneath his hands. What was happening to him? Was it some pagan magic luring him to sin, or the seedlings of his own wayward desires—prompted by Gregory's insistence to enjoy himself before taking his vows?

The old monk's words pervaded his thoughts: *If it is truth you seek, then it will find you. You need only listen.*

Fists clenched at his sides, Edmund felt the seeds of a higher truth begin to sharpen in his mind. What if this was the truth? Perhaps fate had brought them together. The possibility existed that he was trying to justify his carnal thoughts. Of course, what else could it be? Surely this could not be love, for it was folly to think that love could be conceived from a single look.

The deafening silence only made Edmund's attempt at

denial worse. It was as though he heard her heartbeat and felt the softness of her breath on his skin. Or was it the wind and the pounding of his heart deluding him? He was not like Gregory, able to catch a woman's eye, and with nothing more than a smile, have her freely offer him favor. That was Gregory, unashamed and without fear of consequence.

Edmund swallowed with difficulty. The more he searched for a reason to avoid giving in to his reckless thoughts, the louder the voice of seduction became.

Contemplation. Redemption. Purification.

"You're no better than a savage," he muttered quietly, verbally flogging himself for the way he'd watched her breasts sway gently with her determined gait. His fingers itched as he imagined the weight of them in his palms, brushing his thumbs over their pert tips. Edmund licked lips gone as dry as his throat from his perverse musings. In a few days he was to begin a journey of devotion and self-denial to the ways of the flesh, and yet he found a shred of justification for his thoughts. Was there anything more pure, more beautiful than the consummation of two hearts?

He came to a stop, realizing that he could die before morning without having known the joy of being in a woman's arms, or of sacrificing his life in servitude. Was it not his right to understand the great mystery between a man and woman, so that he might use his experience to guide his future flock?

It was all clear to him now. *This* was the truth he sought, the truth he was meant to find.

Edmund drew in a deep breath. Having seen her disappear among the trees near the castle tower, he quickened his pace, fearful that he might lose her without ever knowing her name. His heart thudded against his ribs as he trotted the length of the glen, then paused to peer into the dusky shadows among the fruit trees. A flash of white caught his eye, vanishing through a wooden gate flanked by a tall hedge of tangled growth. He hurried forward, then stubbed his toe against something nestled in the thick grass. He stooped down to pry it loose from the earth, and, brushing away the dirt, held it up to the dim light of the rising moon.

Edmund stared at the object. It was a mask. The eyes hollow, surrounded by ornately carved leaves. He recognized it as part of the costume of the Green Man in the play. The grin on the stone face seemed to be poised in a playful smirk, as though about to wink at Edmund's pursuit of the maiden.

Though the hedge bore no leaves, no fragrant blossoms of any kind, Edmund was surrounded by the alluring scent of roses in full bloom. His gaze moved from the mask to the gate, where he spied a crude nail, and hung the mask upon it. His heart thrummed as he reached out to break off a vine, and sensed the mask watching him, waiting. With a shove, Edmond pushed open the gate and stepped through, peering into the shadows. The moon shone down through the tangled branches, illuminating patches of the yard. Cautiously, he moved forward, scanning the garden void of the life that even now blossomed beyond the dormant hedge walls. He took another step, his eyes scanning the private space, and hoped the old monk would not suddenly reappear. Were they found, an Englishman with a Gaelic woman, there was no telling the punishment that might befall them.

He saw a movement in the shadows and found her standing next to a large fountain. Some of its grandeur had crumbled, falling in disrepair, but a statue of lovers in a passionate embrace remained intact. For a moment Edmond watched her, again debating whether to stay or take his leave. She bent down, her long hair swinging forward to cover her face, and dipped her hands in the fount. Enamored, Edmund envied the water as it splashed over her eyes and mouth, watching as it cascaded down the gentle curve of her neck. Her hands followed, as did his gaze, as she smoothed her palms over her throat, letting them trail down over her breasts. Was it his imagination that she'd followed him to the labyrinth, or that she'd led him here in hope that they would be alone?

He braced his hand against a tree to steady his nerves, but the sound of his labored breathing belittled his efforts. She raised her arms in the air and began to sway to the steady beat of the distant drums. He'd seen bonfires begin to dot the hillsides, and heard music whose magic stirred in his soul.

She was beautiful, his pagan queen, lost in her sensual dance. He remembered the actor portraying the May Queen, and how she'd performed for her lover, finally consummating the desire that would not be denied. Raw and passionate, they had celebrated their union, dispelling the darkness.

Edmund blinked, watching her move freely, so blissfully unaware of anyone else. Or did she know of his presence, this Gaelic seductress who'd stolen glances at him throughout the day? It was then he realized he'd been the one living in darkness, but forced by his parents to enter the religious life. As the third son, he had no right to his father's estate, nor had he the desire to make the military his life, like his other brother. For Edmund there was little choice other than the priesthood. And there was no question that his alliance to the king in matters pertaining to Rome would be a boon to his father's position. Edmund was resigned to them, all of them—his parents, the king and his petty rules and decrees—always doing what he was told, doing what was right.

This maiden was a light come to dispel *his* darkness. It all seemed so clear to him now. No longer afraid, he moved forward, careful not to startle her. Everything inside him seemed to resonate with certainty.

He saw the lifelike figures of the lovers at the center of the fountain, in what might have once been a beautiful garden. The male statue, missing one arm, held tight to his lover with his other, his face turned to hers as though declaring his love.

Edmund emerged from the shadowy arbor into the open, where the fountain stood at the base of the massive tower. He had no idea what he would say, or if she would be able to understand his words. How could he make her understand that she held him by some magical spell, and that only she had the power to set him free?

A feather-light hand touched her shoulder. Startled, Cara backed away, but the stranger's fingers caught her wrist. Her heart beat wildly, as she saw it was the handsome man from the labyrinth. And though she had wished for this moment, now that it was reality Cara was filled with mixed emotions.

"I mean you no harm," he said softly, inching forward as she moved away, until her back met the tower wall.

His broad shoulders blocked the moonlight as he stood in front of her. He held her hand, threading his fingers through hers. Cara felt the heat of his body through his clothes. He smelled of wood smoke and night air, a potent combination.

She would not succumb to her fears of what her father might say, of what might happen if they were caught. She wanted this. She'd wanted him from the moment their eyes met. "I am not afraid," she told him.

He touched her cheek, tracing her lips with the pad of his thumb. She held his gaze, his eyes glittering in the moonlight as he lowered his head, lightly brushing his lips to hers. She welcomed his hungry mouth. He held her arms pinned to her sides, and the frustration of not being able to touch him heightened her desire. Insistent yet gentle, he left no doubt that she was not alone in her lustful thoughts. At last he released her arms, holding her face to his. She slipped her arms around his neck, pulling him close, savoring every kiss as though she might awaken from this dream.

Desperate to touch him, she tugged his shirt free, and he smiled, drawing it over his fine torso. He closed the gap between them, capturing her mouth again as though they were lost lovers needing to satisfy a desire too long denied. She smoothed her hands over his heated flesh, in wonder at the delight of touching a man's body.

He pulled his lips away at long last, leaning his forehead against hers, and she watched the rise and fall of his broad chest. "See what you do to me?" he whispered, and took her hand, placing it over the swell at the front of his brocs. His breath caught and he leaned forward, his sighs fanning across her face, intermittent with his burning kisses, as she caressed his length.

Cara's senses spun in sensual bliss. She felt so empowered that she could coax such a reaction from his body.

He pushed forward, pressing into her hand with another audible sigh.

"I need..." His voice trailed off, ending with a kiss that threatened to set her skin on fire.

She had not a reasonable thought in her head. All she could think of was being close to him, as close as her body would allow. "Yes," she replied, and began to tug up her gown. His hands covered hers, helping her to bunch the gown around her hips. A cool breeze circled her bare legs and his hand moved between her thighs, coaxing a sigh from her lips. Cara closed her eyes in abandon to the dark and smoky sensation of his long fingers teasing her maidenhood. His mouth claimed hers in a searing kiss, barely giving her time to take a breath. Her body grew hot, her skin damp. Her emotions spiraled out of control as a need built inside her. "Please," she muttered incoherently.

Everything stopped, including her heart, as he stepped away and moved swiftly to free his swollen cock. He kissed her thoroughly, lifted her into his arms and, bracing her against the stone, pushed into her ready virgin sheath. His kiss ignited the smoldering fire inside Cara, and she held on tight, crushing his mouth to hers as the quick stab of pain turned to liquid heat. She cradled his neck, his eyes meeting hers as he withdrew from her partway, reentering deeper each time, stretching her until he filled her completely.

"So beautiful," he whispered, nuzzling his lips to hers, rocking his hips gently and letting her body adjust to his. His fingers kneaded the sensitive flesh of her thighs as he seduced her with slow, thorough kisses. Cara laced her fingers in his hair, pulling him close, riding the fluid motion of his increasing thrusts. Lost in a haze of magic, she turned her face to the heavens, pressing him to her chest.

The moon shone down, causing her to gaze in wonder at its remarkable beauty. She could barely breathe for the dizzying feelings imprisoned inside her, desperate to be freed. Cara teetered on the verge of sensual madness, needing relief and yet not wanting this to end. A gentle breeze whirled around them, lifting her hair, brushing across her fevered skin. The scent of roses grew stronger, as her body broke free in a blinding rush of pleasure. The sound of his low groan brought her attention back to him as he pushed deep, his body shuddering with his release, spawning another wave of ecstasy in her body.

Cara clung to him as though her life depended on it. Then she leaned her head back and took a gulp of cool night air. As she did so her eye caught the profile of a shadow leaning out the window above. A slice of moonlight washed over the face, and her breath caught in her throat. Concerned by her gasp, her lover set her feet on the ground, and Cara smoothed down her kirtle. Her body still thrummed from the experience, yet save for the soreness betwixt her legs, reminding her she was no longer a child, she felt no different inside.

She watched him dress, this stranger she knew nothing about, who, unknowing, had taken more than her virginity. She'd given him a piece of her heart, but hadn't expected to feel more alone than she had before.

Cara wrung her hands and waited until he finished and raised his eyes to hers. "Are you well? Pray, tell me that I was not too rough." He took her hands in his, searching her face with what seemed genuine concern. Cara guarded her true feelings, careful of giving too much of her heart to this Englishman. No, though he hadn't admitted it to her yet, it wasn't hard to discern.

"I think there is someone in the tower, watching us." She pointed to the window.

He stepped back and peered into the darkness. "I think perhaps it is nothing more than a carving in stone."

"How can you be sure?"

"Well, there is only one way." He took her hand and tugged her through the open door and up a spiral stone staircase. Partway, he stopped, and in the pitch blackness, she felt him squeeze his body next to hers. His breath on her face alerted her to how close he stood.

"My name is Edmund. What is yours?"

"I am Cara. You are not Gael, are you?"

"Does it matter?" he asked.

Cara felt his hand brush through her hair. "If we are caught—"

His finger touched her lips, silencing her. "We won't be."

"You are a man sure of himself."

"Have not I proved myself on that point, milady?" His teeth shone in the dark stairwell when he smiled. "Now I shall prove that no one is in this tower."

He stepped around a wood door sagging on its hinges, and held her hand as she followed him.

"See, there is no one here." A swathe of moonlight illuminated the small interior, revealing a plain chair, a small wood table and a pile of straw piled against one wall. A blanket most likely left behind by a traveler lay in a heap on the floor.

Edmund leaned out the window and Cara hurried to his side. He twisted his body, having no fear that he might lose his balance.

"Look here, just as I thought. It is but the carving of

a face in stone. Come, see for yourself." He pulled back inside and ushered her forward.

Cara didn't want him to know she was skittish about heights, so she leaned on the window ledge and craned her neck as best she could to catch a glimpse of the carved face. She drew back in turn and closed her eyes, taking a breath before reopening them.

"Do you believe me then?"

"Aye, it is as you said." She thought of the statue of the lovers below. "It is the Winter King looking down on the forbidden lovers." She gazed out at the bonfires glowing on the horizon. Edmund came to her side and they shared the view together in silence.

"You mean the Green Man and the May Queen," he said, brushing her hair over her shoulder. The simple, sweet gesture brought a tear to her eye, and she blinked it away.

"When the king discovered they'd betrayed him, he placed a curse on them, and every year the Green Man has to fight the king to bring the May Queen out of the darkness she is in. It is the legend of our Celtic seasons."

"And you believe this legend is real?"

Cara looked at him then and saw something in his eyes that she'd never before seen—adoration. "We are like them. We should not be talking. You should not be here." She touched his face. His expression was full of naive promise, just as she felt, deep inside. But the reality was that they couldn't stay in this secret place forever.

He softly grazed her cheek with his knuckles. "Let me worry about the English king, who is far away from here and cannot order what my heart can and can't feel."

Cara looked out the window, leaning her hands on the ledge, wishing it were so easy to dismiss the English king.

But she'd heard enough of her father and mother talking to know he was a man who always found a way to get what he wanted.

She felt Edmund's arms encircle her waist.

"Do you suppose that your secret lovers wasted one moment of the time they had together?" he murmured, nuzzling the back of her neck.

She laid her head against his shoulder, bewildered that she should feel so at home in his embrace. "Nay, I would say they did not."

He eased aside her hair, pressing his lips to the back of her neck. The now familiar signs of desire smoldered, her body heating to his touch. His nimble fingers stroked the curve of her throat, turning her face to meet his mouth. Cara marveled at how well he knew what her body craved—when to be gentle and when not to be. She smiled as he loosened the ribbons holding the back of her gown together, making adequate room to slip his hand beneath her bodice. His fingers caressed, weighing one and then the other breast, rolling her nipples between his fingers as he kissed her senseless. He turned her to face him and, checking for her response, slid the gown past her shoulders, until it hung at her elbows, her firm breasts exposed to him. Cara accepted another kiss, her breathing growing rapid as his mouth left hers and slid over the sensitive tip of one breast. Her fingers trembled as he caressed her, tormenting her with teeth and tongue. Every moment with him she learned more about herself, what gave her pleasure. She let out a shuddering gasp when he suckled her, sensing the wet heat trickling down her leg.

"That pleases you?" He glanced up at her with a raised brow and an ornery grin.

"Aye, and you are wearing far too many clothes." She

tugged the gown from each arm and let it pool around her feet.

She watched him take her in as she stood in the moonlight. Cara had never been naked in front of anyone but her ma and her sister. She was unprepared for how deliciously wicked it made her feel to have this man's heated gaze on her.

She stepped forward and, licking her lips, helped to draw his shirt over his head. She pressed her body to his, hugging him tight, lifting her face for another of his blistering kisses.

"Do not move." He quickly fluffed up the straw and covered it with the old blanket, then turned and eased his brocs down his muscular legs. He stepped from them and looked at her.

He was beautifully built, his body young, muscular, solid as stone. And his enlarged cock…here in the bright moonlight, she could see it jutting proud from his finely honed body. He held his hand to her and she went willingly, unashamed of their nakedness, taking what he offered in his tender kisses, his whispered words. He held her hand and she lay back on the blanket, looking up at him, her heart full of how Mother Earth had smiled on her tonight. He dropped to his knees, covering her body with his, and Cara melted into him. Fervent sighs, hot wet kisses… Cara grew dizzy, unable to get enough of him. She rolled him to his back and knelt over him. He grinned, capturing her breast with one hand, and with the other found the spot between her legs that nearly left her undone. She looked at him with a fierce need, feeling his velvet tip near her entrance, and held his hardened length, sliding him into her heat until he filled her entirely. Cara pressed her palms to his chest, the gooseflesh of anticipation rising on her bare skin. The sensation was glorious, freeing, and she cupped his face, kissing him soundly, and then straightened, drawing her arms over her head, delighted yet again in being with him.

"You are more beautiful than any May Queen," he said, caressing her thighs. His hands guided her hips, moving them forward and then back until she captured the natural gait. Reality blurred. Her throat dry, she looked down at him watching her, and smiled as another tear escaped from her eye.

"My beautiful Cara," he sighed. His brow crinkled and he closed his eyes, lifting his hips, slowly pushing deep. "My sweet, beautiful Cara."

Frosty and pale was the moonlight washing over their bodies. Cara did not know what the dawn would bring, only that the gods and goddesses had given them this moment. With a soft cry, her body surrendered to her release, and soon after, Edmund followed.

She lay exhausted across him, hearing the beat of his heart. He stroked her hair, her back, and kissed the top of her head. Neither of them spoke. Finally, Cara rested her arms on his chest and looked into the eyes she swore the universe had fashioned just for her pleasure. She took note of his face up close, the gentle look in his gaze, the scar that creased his brow. She'd never felt this way in her life, so whole, so complete.

"Edmund? Edmund, are you in there?" A loud voice boomed from down below. "There was an old man out here, though for the life of me, I cannot find him now. He described you and said you'd been here, along with a young woman. Well done, Edmund. That is, if you're not cowering in there alone." Raucous laughter followed.

Edmund shifted, lifting Cara from him, and began to

put on his clothes. "He's drunk. I better go to him before he makes a scene and gets us all killed." He pulled on his brocs. "He can be a bit of an ass, but it's his nature to be slightly pompous."

"This is your friend that you came with?" she asked, searching for her other slipper. Edmund reached down and plucked her shoe from the shadows, dangling it from his fingers as he offered it to her. He pulled it back just as she reached for it, and leaned down, placing a tender kiss on her mouth swollen from his kisses.

"Time to go home, my friend. Dawn is not far off and the guards will be changing soon," Gregory called out quietly.

In haste, Edmund helped to tighten the lacing of Cara's gown. She sensed his concern. "Do you regret what has happened between us, milord?" she asked, her stomach beginning to knot with worry. Could she have misread the look in his eyes?

"Not one moment." He turned her to face him, and clamped his hands around hers. "Do you?"

"Nay, Edmund."

"I like hearing you say my name." He kissed her again.

She pulled her hands from his. "But in truth, what future do we have? You know as well as I do the English law put in place to keep our people apart."

"It is a ridiculous law," Edmund fumed.

He hurriedly drew his tunic over his head. "I will think of a way to make this work, Cara. Until then, promise me that you will wait for my return."

She looked at his pleading eyes. "Edmund."

He held her face, kissing her and then drawing her so close she could scarcely breathe.

"There is no question now. I will speak to my father. I

will make him understand. Things have changed, Cara. They will have to listen to me. I am a man now. I can make my own choices."

She knew what it would be like in her family were she to her approach her father in a similar fashion. There would be no discussions, no compromises. Was his father any different?

"We will make an oath, one to another. If you feel as I do, Cara, then let this be our private handfasting."

She knew that he wanted things to be different, but the truth was that he would have to leave her on this side of the barricade, leave her here in the private world they'd created. Edmund rested his cheek on the top of her head. "You'll wait for me then? By your oath?"

He did not pause for her answer. "Come, I want you to meet the one man who will have no quarrel about us being together." He tugged on her hand.

She held her ground, pulling her hand from his. "I have not given you my word, Edmund. Besides, what is he talking about? What does he mean about the guards?"

Edmund turned back, clamping his hands on her shoulders. "There is nothing fret over. It's only a few villagers placed along the barricade. They nap most of the time."

"Perhaps it is not wise that your friend know we've been together—at least for now."

Edmund grinned. "Gregory can be trusted. I want you to meet him. He is my dearest friend." He grabbed her hand, pressing his lips to her palm. "If you can see past his drunken state, he is a good man."

She followed him out of the tower to the garden gate. When he yanked it open the mask rocked precariously on its narrow peg.

His friend, Gregory, stood on the other side, dangling

a wineskin over his face, aiming for his mouth. The red liquid ran in rivulets down his chin. With a bleary-eyed start, he lowered the skin and wiped his jaw with his sleeve. He gave them a slobbery grin.

"So it is true. There you are, with your lady fair, Sir Edmund. I trust the two of you have been discussing politics?" His eyes roamed over Cara, visually feasting on her from head to toe. Edmund drew her protectively to his side.

"It is true we should be getting back, but if Edmund..."

Gregory reached out, brushing his hand over Cara's arm. "I might be persuaded to find time for one more frivolous rite before taking our leave. The name is Gregory, milady." He bowed, stumbling awkwardly toward them. Edmund caught his shoulder and righted him, with a gentle nudge pushing him away from Cara. Gregory eyed the two, his mouth lifting in a smug grin.

"Perhaps, Edmund, we should let the lady decide what she prefers?"

"Now you've gone too far, Gregory." Edmund lowered his head and drove it into his best friend's gut with full force, knocking them both to the ground in a tangle of limbs.

Cara watched in horror as the two men flailed their fists blindly at one another, now and again making contact with a loud smack. "Stop it, please, before one of you gets hurt." She grabbed Edmund's tunic, tugging with all her might. Finally, he pushed to his feet, bringing a weary Gregory with him, then took one last swipe across Gregory's jaw, sending him to his backside.

"Have you gone mad?" the man shouted angrily, rubbing his jaw.

Edmund grabbed Cara's hand and dragged her through

the trees to the open glen. The labyrinth was covered in a fine morning mist; the silvery gray dawn was beginning to light the sky. He pulled her close, wrapping her in a warm embrace. She wanted to tend to his wounds, to check his eye, which was beginning to swell now from contact with Gregory's fist. He shook his head as she ran her fingers delicately over his face.

"I must take my leave. But I promise you this—I will return."

He cupped her cheek, kissing her with such certainty that she almost believed him. She fisted his shirt in her hands, memorizing his taste, his scent.

"Come on, then," a voice stated. It was Gregory, a sullen expression on his bruised face. Blood trickled from his nose. Cara backed away from Edmund, hugging herself, averting her eyes from Gregory's dark, piercing gaze. He made her uncomfortable despite what Edmund wanted her to believe. She glanced at Edmund, finding him studying her, the struggle between leaving and staying evident in his stormy eyes.

"You'd best be on your way, then. My father will be looking for me and my sister soon."

"There's another one like you at home? Younger or older?" Gregory asked with a cocky grin that didn't reach his eyes.

"Soon to be married," she answered quickly.

Edmund stepped forward, taking her hands in his. "You remember what I said?"

Cara's gaze slammed into Gregory's dark orbs just beyond Edmund's shoulder. His moody friend stormed past them, heading in the direction of the woods. "I hope your friend is not angry."

"Not to worry, my love. We've had other scuffles, far

worse. It will pass. It always does." He leaned down, leaving a soft, lingering kiss on her lips. "Wait for me, Cara," he whispered. "It may take some time to convince them, but I will."

She smiled at him, wishing she could remember where she'd left her shawl, for she felt a sudden chill that seeped deep into her bones.

3

"YOU TOLD HER WHAT?" GREGORY RUBBED
his jaw and stared at Edmund in disbelief. "Have you gone
mad? Take my word for it, Edmund. Stop thinking with
your cock and start thinking with your brain, unless perhaps they are one and the same." He continued to walk,
reaching down to yank a shaft of long grass to chew on.
Safe now across the barricade that separated them from the
Gaels, they walked a little slower toward home.

Edmund looked at the pinkish hue of the sun creeping
over the hillside. The world suddenly looked different. He
saw things with greater clarity.

"Regardless of what you think, I am going to go back
for her. I cannot help the feelings I have for her. Feelings
that well may be love, Gregory." Edmund smiled, hearing
the words aloud.

"As your friend, it is my duty to remind you that you
would be throwing your life away on that girl. It goes
against the king's edict even to be uttering such ideas out
loud," Gregory stated, pointing an emphatic finger at him.
"Your family, I'm quite certain, will not favor this idea.
Your life is set, Edmund. You leave for Rome in a few

days. Did you forget?" Edmund followed slowly behind, pondering Gregory's words. He could not refute the truth of them, and yet part of him wondered if his friend's lack of support stemmed from honor to the crown or jealousy. Gregory had never before been a model for keeping rules.

"This is because she would not give in to your wishes, isn't it?" He hurried to Gregory's side, slamming his hand down on his shoulder.

The friend he'd known since childhood whirled to face him, his eyes ablaze with a fiery hatred. Edmund stared at him in shock. He'd never seen him so angry.

"You think I care about bedding your Gaelic wench? I had my fill, Edmund—more than enough, thank you— and I assure you none of them was any less special than your Cara. What makes you think she is any different? How many others were there before you? Did you bother to ask?"

"I did not have to ask," he retorted without thinking.

Gregory's expression went from anger to puzzlement, then to shock. "She was a virgin? Good God, Edmund! What have you done?"

Edmund stormed ahead, entirely uncomfortable talking with Gregory about this any longer. His stomach roiled with the potential consequences of his actions. "Swear on our friendship you will not breathe a word to anyone of this." He tossed his friend a side glance, and when Gregory gave no response, Edmund grabbed his arm, stopping him again.

Gregory stared at Edmund's grasp, and then pried loose his fingers, shoving his hand aside. "Very well, if you promise me that you will go on with your life, Edmund. Do what you are destined to do. You owe your allegiance to your family, your country and your king." Gregory's eyes bored into his, waiting for his answer.

Edmund's heart raced, thrumming hard in his chest, caught in a stranglehold between what he wanted and what was right. He squeezed shut his eyes and nodded. "I will consider all sides before I make a decision. Until then, swear to me that you will speak to no one."

Gregory turned away, and for a moment Edmund was not sure he would agree to his request. "Swear on our friendship, Gregory." He punched his shoulder.

Those dark eyes turned back to him slowly. "Do not ask me to lie, Edmund. You think only of yourself, but you forget that you place me in danger as well for harboring your secret."

Edmund stared at his childhood friend. "Were you not the one who suggested we sneak into the festival?"

"I could as easily admit that I was going with you to keep an eye on you."

"Bollocks. No one in their right mind would believe that," Edmund responded, curious why Gregory would be so stubborn about this. Was it the fight? Had he been humiliated in front of Cara? "You're the one with the reputation for misconduct. Your own father knows it."

"Even so, it is you making claims that you're going back for a Gaelic woman. What did you intend, Edmund? Marriage? You and your family could be hanged for treason to the king. Hers, too. The truth, while I feel it may be distasteful to you, my friend, is that I have little choice in this matter, and my troth to stay silent or not will have little bearing on the outcome, only perhaps its expediency."

The truth hit Edmund, causing his knees to buckle. He dropped to the grass, his head in his hands. His own neck was one thing. But he'd not thought of his family or hers.

He was blinded by his emotions and selfish in thinking only of himself and his desire for Cara. He felt Gregory's hand clamp down on his shoulder and squeeze it with brotherly affection.

"There now, Edmund. In a day or two, you'll not remember her name."

He felt as though he'd been slashed wide open. Bile rose in his throat. As much as he despised the truth, Gregory was right. However cruel the Fates, Edmund had to accept it. But on one point, Gregory was incorrect.

He would never forget what had happened this night or his beautiful maiden.

Edmund was jolted from his dream of Cara's body shuddering beneath his, and only had time to brace his hands in front of his face before he was tossed to the floor from his bed.

"Did you think to keep your indiscretion a secret from your family? What in God's name were you thinking, boy?"

Still groggy from the wine he'd drunk the night before, trying to forget Cara, Edmund pried open one eye and saw the dark scowl on William Collier's face. He combed his hand through his hair, each word from his father's mouth stabbing at his brain.

"I do not know what you speak of, Father," he mumbled, his mouth feeling akin to a quagmire. Edmund pushed himself upright, cautious of the wave of nausea assaulting him. He sat still, deciding it best not to move from that spot for perhaps the rest of the day.

"Do you deny it?" his parent bellowed, standing over him with clenched fists. "Do you deny that you went to the Beltane festival and had carnal relations with a Gaelic woman?"

Well, there it was. He knew, and if he did, so too did Gregory's father—Edmund would stake his life on it. Better to face his demons now.

"You make it sound like she is a disease." Edmund looked up at his father through bleary eyes. "What if I told you I want to marry her?"

William's eyes, already wild, widened further. "That is out of the question!" he snapped, with the ferocity of a leather whip.

Defiance pushed the words from Edmund's lips before he had time to consider the ramifications. "The truth of it is I am in love with her and I intend to marry her." He tried to stand, but his stomach churned precariously, causing him to stay put. "Father, I have no desire to be a damn priest," he mumbled, rubbing his hand across his face to jostle himself awake.

His father's hand came too fast across the side of his head for Edmund to dodge. The blow jarred him and left a residual ringing in his ears.

"That is the last time I will hear you take the name of a religious man in vain, boy! Indeed, if for no other reason than to teach you humility to your God, to your king, I have made arrangements on a merchant ship bound later today for Italy. You sail at sunset, and you will be on that ship if I have to tie you to the masthead myself."

Edmund held his face, his flesh still stinging from the blow. "What have you against me?" he demanded. Though his head was on fire, he met his father's dark, piercing gaze with a challenge. In matters of discipline, William had often said taking the strap to his children's hide was for their own good. By now Edmund should be

filled with good; he had the scars on his back to prove it.
But he stood every bit as tall as his father now. His shoulders were as broad, his strength equal to William's, if not
more so. Still, Edmund could not refute the love he knew
his father had for him.

William sank down on the edge of the bed, his hands
folded over his knees. "It is not hatred that drives this decision, Edmund. It is to save your life. It was the only choice
I was given. I was told that I must send you away, as an
example to those like you who might defy the statutes. I
was told you needed to be disciplined. The alternative was
imprisonment for treason."

"But Gregory—"

His father's upturned hand stopped him.

"It does not matter. You sail tonight. That is the end of
it. Now, you won't need much. Your vows will strip you
of all worldly possessions at first." His father stared blindly
across the room, lost in his thoughts.

"Do you find them a farce?" Edmund asked.

"What, the statutes?" William shrugged. "It is not for
me to say, whether to believe in them or not. We are here
to serve our king. What he decrees, we must follow."

"And what if, all those years ago, his decree meant that
you could not have married my mother. What then would
you have done?"

His father sighed, searching Edmund's face before responding. "It was not the way of things before, and it may
not be so again one day. But for now, it is the law, and we
will abide by it."

Edmund sat with his head in his hands. He seethed with
hatred. What bloody deity would allow Cara to come into
his life when there was no future to be had? He leaped to
his feet, taking his father by surprise, and paced back and

forth across the room. Perhaps they could run away. He turned abruptly, an idea popping into his head. "Then I will wait for that day."

"And you would expect this girl to also wait? What good would come of destroying two lives? See reason, my son. Let this go and move on with your life. For her sake and yours. Hurry now, your mother will want to spend time with you before you sail."

His hands were tied, and there was more at stake here than his own happiness. Edmund only hoped that one day Cara would understand, and perhaps, in time, forgive him.

4

Three years later

CARA DID NOT MIND THE WALK TO HER SISTER'S house. It kept her away from her father, at least. Every day she saw the disappointment in his eyes, endured his silent glances. But the sun was brilliant on this late summer day, and the path she walked well worn by the weekly visits she paid to her sister and brother-in-law. Today, she was off to help her with their growing brood of children. Kiernan and Conner had produced three children over the years and had become parents to one more not their own. Every week, with twin emotions of gratitude and guilt, Cara made the trek. Today she made it with a heavy heart, given the disturbing news her father had given her. It was yet another of his decrees in the past three years that had served to tear apart the close relationship they'd once shared. Cara's mind drifted back to the day her life had changed forever.

Cara backed away, seeking safety in the shelter of her mother's protective arms. Kiernan and Conner had been married for several months, already attempting to expand their family. Cara, no longer able to disguise her predicament beneath her loose kirtles, decided it was time to tell her parents the news. She had anticipated they would not be pleased, but it was her father's temper that she dreaded the most.

"You? Having a child? How is that possible, daughter?" her father roared. Still seated at the table after the morning meal, he slammed his fist down, knocking over his cup.

Cara's hand trembled as she cradled the small protrusion of her belly. She could not look either of her parents in the eye. She was no better than one of the village whores. Her lip trembled and she bit it, forcing herself not to fall apart. There was enough chaos in the house as it was.

"Who is it? Is it a lad from our village? I'll go have a talk with his da. We can get things squared away before the child comes. It will be a quiet ceremony." He pushed himself from the chair, pacing the floor, lost in his thoughts of how to resolve the destruction she'd brought upon his house.

Cara swallowed, wanting to sit down, but afraid she wouldn't be able to escape his wrath when she told him who the father was. She'd only ever been with one man in her entire life—Edmund.

Her father's wild red hair exaggerated the fierce look in his eyes. He glanced up, pinning her with his angry gaze. "Daughter? I am waiting on your answer."

Nervously, she uttered the first thought that came to her mind. "He is dead." The words tumbled from her mouth like pebbles rolling down a hillside, preceding a rockslide.

Her father stared at her, burning with frustration. "He's *what?*" His green eyes narrowed, penetrating her soul, defying her to repeat her lie.

Cara blinked, summoning her courage, relying on reason, since she had little else. It was, after all, not a complete untruth. To her and her unborn child, Edmund was dead. He'd left without a word and broken his promise. "He is dead," she repeated with greater confidence.

Her father scowled as though unsure whether to believe her. "How did you find out?"

Cara's throat went dry. She felt dizzy. It came back to her that it had been nearly eight months or better since Edmund had left. "How...did I find out...what?" She grabbed her belly, grimacing as an excruciating pressure gripped her middle. The pain radiated to her lower back and tightened with such force that she thought she might pass out. "Mother," she managed to gasp before she fell to her knees.

"How did you find out that the boy had died?" Her father's gruff tone added to the pain assaulting her body. "Is she going to have that child here?" His voice softened a bit.

Cara's mother helped her to bed, easing her over onto her side, propping her belly with a blanket. "Go fetch the midwife," she calmly ordered her husband, brushing the damp hair from Cara's face.

"It hurts more than I can bear.... Am I going to die?" Cara had no control over the pains that came and went like the tides. She curled herself into a ball, gritting her teeth against the next wave.

"Nay, Cara. I suspect you are getting close to your time. But you must tell me the truth, now that your father is gone. Who is the father of this child?"

Tears streamed down Cara's cheeks. She welcomed the freedom of telling someone the truth she'd been holding inside for so long. "It was an English lad I met at the Beltane festival."

Her mother's eyes grew wide. "Does he know?" She held her hand to her heart.

Cara shook her head and squeezed her eyes shut against another rolling wave of pain clamping her midsection.

"Did he force himself on you, Cara, that Englishman? Your father may kill him when he finds out what he did to you. I feared something like this would happen. I should not have let you go. Pray, child, why did you not tell us that night that you had been violated?" Worry shone in her soft blue eyes.

"Nay, it was not like that," Cara said, then was overtaken by another cramping pain. She sucked in a breath and pushed out the words. "I wanted to be with him as much as he wanted to be with me. I loved him, Mother." Her tears poured in earnest, between the pain attacking her body and her heart.

Her mother dabbed her face with a cool wet cloth, then placed it on her forehead. "It will not be long now, Cara," she said soothingly.

"What will happen?" Cara thought of Gregory's words, the plans he'd shared that had taken Edmund so far away from her.

"Your father will need to speak to the boy's father. We will have to see what can be done."

Cara grabbed her mother's arm, looking up at her, true fear striking her heart. "The statutes! No, you mustn't. They will take my child. I will never see her again."

"The boy must know that he is a father," she insisted, patting Cara's hand.

Cara shook her head. "He is gone, Mother. Truly, he is

dead to my child and me. By now he is in Italy, in his apprenticeship."

"Apprenticeship? For what trade?"

Her mother rubbed her hand up and down Cara's back, and the pain subsided. She shut her eyes, exhausted, wanting to sleep. "I have heard that he is bound to take his Holy Orders."

"Did you know this when you met him at festival?"

Cara slowly shook her head, fatigue sweeping over her. "Nay, he did not mention it afore the time we were together. He said that he planned to speak to his parents and that he would come back for me. He told me he cared for me, that he wanted us to marry." She opened her eyes, noting her mother's sorrowful expression.

"Oh, Cara," she sighed, and looked across the room, lost in her thoughts.

"I am sorry for what I have done to you and Father."

Her mother gazed down at her, a soft smile playing on her lips. "It will be well. Sleep now. You'll need your strength in the days to come."

Cara nodded, her body and soul racked with weariness. She fell asleep and dreamed of Edmund holding his child.

She awoke sometime later to the sound of her father's angry voice.

"I'll not have a bastard child of an Englishman in this house." His words rocked off the walls of the small dwelling.

"But, Galen, we cannot turn our daughter out," her mother pleaded in Cara's defense.

Cara pushed herself from the bed and stood in the doorway to the main room. Her father and mother stood toe-to-toe, arguing over her.

"Then she will have the babe at her sister's house, and

if they agree to it, they will raise the child as their own."
Her father spoke as if she was not there, but he spotted her
then, pointing his large finger at her. "No one is to know
about this. You have brought shame to this house, Cara.
You are fortunate that I do not cast you out."

She said little as she packed her belongings the next
morning. Her father took her to Kiernan's, where Cara
was made to explain her situation and ask for her sister's
mercy. Gratefully, Connor agreed to take her in and, after
the birth, to raise the child.

So it was that Cara bore her daughter and lived for a
time in the same house, not as little Moyran's mother, but
as her aunt. It was her mother finally who saw the pain it
caused Cara to live with the child, unable to acknowledge
her as her own. She interceded, convincing Cara's father
to allow her to come back home. Only in the past year had
things between her and her father begun to return to what
they once were.

This fine morning, Cara spotted her daughter's fiery red
hair glistening in the sunlight as she played.

"Aintin Cara!"

The little girl came running to greet her. Cara scooped
her into her arms and hugged her tight, never tiring of her
sweet outdoor scent. The child loved being out in nature
and was curious about herbs and potions, and all the ancient druid ways. But Kiernan had little time for such
things, as she seemed to be constantly with child.

Cara studied the girl's excited expression, a pang of
hurt pricking her heart when she looked into her stormy
gray eyes. "What have you discovered today, my dearest Moyran?" Cara placed her on the ground and took
her hand, walking with her toward the wooden fence

surrounding the thatch-roofed house. Kiernan was hanging clothes in the yard, her belly round again, her baby due in the next few weeks, if the midwife's timing was correct.

"I can make a flower crown, to wear in your hair."

The young girl's face was radiant. Cara smiled, grateful that she was a happy child, and grateful that at least she'd been able to be a part of her upbringing. "You'll show me then, in a bit? I want to visit with your mother and see how she fares, all right?"

The child nodded, wisdom much older than her years shining in her eyes. She gave Cara a peck on the cheek and, spotting her brother, ran off to play.

Kiernan looked over and offered Cara a weary smile. "You are a sight for sore eyes, to be sure. My back is aching today, more than usual. I could use help with the rest of the wash, if you've a mind to."

Cara took the wet laundry from her sister's hand. "Go on now. Find a place to sit out of this sun." She watched her waddle to a small bench in the shade of a giant oak, then shook out a wet shirt, preparing it for the line. "Where is Conner?" she called over her shoulder. Kiernan's time was at hand and Cara wondered at the wisdom of his absence.

"He's gone to the village with Jacob, to do some trading. They left early, so they should be back before long."

"Mother will ask me if you are eating well. I hear about her concerns for you on a daily basis, you know." She finished hanging the clothes and went to sit at her sister's feet. Moyran reappeared and plopped unannounced in Cara's lap.

"Mother says I got the color of my hair from Grandda. It's the same as yours. We are lucky, as we are the only ones who have hair that looks like it's on fire. That is what

Da says." She focused on weaving the flowers together in her chubby hands. Cara glanced up at her sister and saw the look of pity in her eyes.

"Have you had any nibbles?" Kiernan asked. Cara knew that she worded the question so the child would not catch her meaning.

"Scoot now, Moyran, I have a few things I need to visit with your mother about. We'll go for a walk in the woods a bit later."

Unaffected at being shuffled off, the little girl gave Cara a grand smile, hopped from her lap and ran to a rope swing that Conner had fashioned for the children.

"Father has arranged a marriage for me, Kiernan."

Her sister sat silent for a moment, searching Cara's face. "A good man, yes?"

Cara's eyes welled. "Aye, I suppose for a used daughter, it is. He is a widower, nearly Father's age. But he swears he will be good to me, and he would like many children surrounding him in his old age." Tears rolled down her cheeks. Her sister reached out, drawing Cara's head to her lap, stroking her hair.

"It could be worse, to grow old alone."

"Do you think he would allow me to bring Moyran with me?" Cara considered wistfully. An older man might appreciate a ready-made family.

"She is safe here, Cara, and happy. Are you sure that is what is best?"

Cara lifted her head, her eyes stinging. She wiped her cheeks. "What is best?" she huffed. "Isn't it obvious that I've much to learn in that area?"

"Dinna be so hard on yourself, Cara. What happened is in the past. You are older now and able to make your own judgments."

Cara thought for a moment and nodded. "I wish Father thought as much."

"'Tis unfortunate that your choices are what they are," Kiernan remarked.

Cara caught a movement from the corner of her eye and turned to watch Moyran at play. Would she have done anything differently had she been able to?

5

LOST. DAY AFTER DAY, FOLLOWING THE SAME routine, Cara felt no more comfortable being cast as the wayward daughter, estranged from her own parents in their house, than she was in not being able to be a mother to her own child. She found herself spending more and more time alone, taking long walks through the woods between the two households, seeking solace for the loneliness inside her. Today, on her way to Kiernan's, she'd chosen a path less traveled closer to the edge where the English and Gaelic boundaries met. Nestled deep in the woods, she discovered a secluded pond and paused to rest her weary form in the arms of the grassy bank.

"Imagine meeting you again, after all this time."

Cara opened her eyes, startled to find Gregory leaning against a tree, watching her. She bolted upright from her nap.

"I did not wish to disturb your sleep. You looked so peaceful," he stated with a pleasant smile.

The last time she'd seen him had been that fateful night three years ago. It seemed an eternity now. The thought crossed her mind that he might have stayed in contact with

Edmund. She stood, brushing the grass from her gown, aware that she'd perhaps strayed too far off course this time. "My apologies, is this your land? I was walking and must have wandered too far."

Gregory tossed a twig into the water. "It's quite all right. My father's land, really, that of Dublin castle, meets against this line of woods. But you've no reason to be alarmed. I'm glad to see you again."

Cara was aware from listening to her father speak about the English that it was Lord DeVerden who lived in Dublin castle. "You are Lord DeVerden's son?"

He gave a short laugh. "Guilty as charged." He bowed low and came up smiling. "I've never given my position much thought, to be truthful, Cara."

She eyed him, uncertain whether to believe what she remembered about him. He did appear more like a man, and certainty as to his physical features...

Cara looked away, suddenly aware that she'd been staring.

"The years have been kind to you, Cara. You are still as beautiful as I remember."

Overwhelmed by his presence and mindful of his social position, she held her tongue, unsure what power he welded. She watched a dragonfly skirt along the water's surface. A fish leaped from the water, snapping the bug in its jaws before disappearing into the dark depths.

"Cara, I can understand why you would not be able to find it in your heart to look at me, much less speak to me. I behaved horribly to you when last we saw each other. You are well, then?"

His questions, too intimate, unnerved her. "I am well, thank you." She bent down to retrieve her shoes. "If you will excuse me, sir, I must be going."

"Must you?" he asked, taking a step toward her. "You have not even asked how I am, or about Edmund."

Cara's heart stopped at the mention of Edmund. "Forgive my manners, milord. I hope you are well, but I must take my leave. My sister will be expecting me."

"Ah," he said with a look of resignation. "Then you still carry feelings for him."

She met Gregory's steady gaze, stopping herself before she could blurt out that Edmund was, after all, the father of her child. She had no reason to believe she could trust this man to get word to him that he had a daughter, despite the fact that Gregory was her only connection to him. But the urge was powerful, just the same, to reveal her secret. "He is taking his orders?" she asked instead. Time had dulled the pain of his leaving, and Cara had finally resigned herself that he'd come to his senses, seeing the danger of fighting the law and betraying his king.

"It was strange," Gregory responded. "The last I knew from Lord Collier, Edmund was living in a monastery in the French mountains. They live very stark lives, giving away everything to the poor, living off the land. His family, of course, was furious. His father all but disowned him for abandoning the more profitable priesthood."

Cara was not surprised somehow that Edmund might find a way to quietly defy his family. She raised her eyes and met Gregory's dark brown gaze. There was no malice nor mischief in them as before; in fact, there was very little sign of the boy she'd met at the festival.

He picked up another stick, aiming it toward the pond. "If I know Edmund, he's created a sanctuary for every living thing in need of help." Gregory tossed her a side glance. "He was always better with people than was I."

A rumble in the rolling gray clouds above caught her

attention, and Cara looked up just as the rain began to pour. Gregory beckoned for her to join him under the shelter of the tree.

"Nay, I should be going," she called above the din of the torrential downpour.

"It will be over soon. Quick, before you get soaked to the skin." He offered his hand.

Cara looked down at her gown, seeing it was already sticking to her body. Reluctantly, she took his hand and joined him beneath the dome of leafy branches.

"There now, that's not so bad, is it?" He smiled and plucked a wet strand of hair from her cheek, tucking it behind her ear.

His gentle kindness surprised her in a way that she found admirable. Perhaps he'd changed from the egotistical young man she once knew. Cara remained on guard about his intent, just as she did around all men.

"Do you believe in fate?" he asked.

He was standing close enough that she could feel the warmth from his body. What alarmed her was her own body's reaction. Was it fear or something else that made her heart beat wildly in her chest? It was not as though she held any wistful thoughts about romance anymore. "Nay, I believe we decide our own fate."

He ran his knuckle softly down her cheek. Cara's eyes met his.

"In that case, I cannot tell you enough times how sorry I am for how I behaved in my youth."

She averted her eyes, wishing the rain would cease, yet confused why she should let that prevent her from leaving. "There is no need for you to make your confession to me, milord."

"I know I have not given just cause why you should

listen to me, but I hope in my heart that you will." He paused, placing his fist to his mouth, as though deep in thought. "Edmund was—and is, no doubt—a better man than me. Unselfish, full of love for his fellow man. God knows he was more than tolerant of me when we were young."

She glanced at him. "I thought this was about you."

His finger touched her chin, drawing her eyes back to his. "Edmund made his choice." Gregory searched her eyes. "And did what he had to do."

One question had burned in her mind all these years, and unable to ask Edmund, she chose to ask his friend. "Did he love me?" she blurted without thinking.

The corner of Gregory's mouth lifted with a sad smile. "I believe that he *believed* he loved you."

It was not the answer she had hoped to hear. After years of imagining what it would be like to have Edmund return and see the three of them as one happy family, Cara realized suddenly that she'd painted an unrealistic picture, just as Edmund had done that night.

"I would never have left you, Cara."

She frowned, jarred from her thoughts. "My apologies, what did you say?"

Gregory gently cupped her face between his hands, and Cara's feet froze where she stood. "From the first moment I saw you at the festival I was lost."

She studied his face. What was this? "What is your meaning?" She could barely breathe, staring into his intense brown eyes, eyes that seemed able to look deep into her soul and see her painful loneliness.

He lowered his head, watching for her response as his lips hovered over hers. "I lost my heart that day, Cara. But

Edmund was certain that he would have you. What could I do? He was, after all, my friend."

His lips, cool and moist from the rain, touched hers, sliding over her parched mouth. He did not press any further than she wished, but hesitated, his breath warm, waiting for her to choose her fate. Need pushed her to her toes. It had been so long since she'd felt the heady pull of desire, the taste of a man's lips. Cara gave in to her curiosity little by little. Could another man's kiss affect her as Edmund's once had?

Tender yet insistent, Gregory's hungry mouth coaxed her lips until she opened willingly, letting her tongue mate with his. Cara's hands dangled lifeless at her sides, lost as she was in his rapturous kisses. He lifted her arms around his neck and deepened the kiss. His palms drifted down her back, cupping her bottom, drawing her close, leaving no question of his arousal.

This was all too surreal. Perhaps it was a dream, a strange dream of him nuzzling the warm spot below her ear, eliciting pleasured sighs from her. Making her feel sensations she hadn't felt in years. The image of the Green Man on the garden gate emerged in a sensual fog in her brain. Her fingers twisted into his shirtsleeves as a rush of cool air washed the shoulder where he'd tugged down her dress. His mouth left fire in the wake of his hot kisses.

"Why are you doing this?" she gasped. She was breathless with wonder at how desperately she missed the touch of a man.

He slid his fingers down the front of her gown, pushing away the fabric, lifting her soft mound in his palm. He closed his mouth over the sensitive tip, causing her blood to heat with desire. His unshaved cheek rubbed against her tender skin.

"I have never forgotten you, Cara," he breathed against her rain-soaked flesh.

Three years? What was she doing? Cara moved her hand over her breast, halting his ministrations, and stepped away. She lifted her bodice back in place and forced herself to look at him. "Are you telling me that in the time since we met, you have never taken a wife?" she asked incredulously, distancing herself as best she could under the confines of the tree. Something didn't seem right.

"I found no one to compare to you, Cara. It is true. Please, it pains me to see the look of mistrust in your eyes."

"But you are Edmund's friend."

He nodded, raking his hand through his hair. "One of the reasons I waited so long to find you, I'm afraid. I wanted to be sure Edmund had made up his mind."

"And how did you find me?" she asked.

Gregory smiled. "I was preparing to ride to your father's house in the next few days, but in truth, I am glad that fate gave us this opportunity to speak together first."

She shook her head. Surely she was dreaming this. "Visit with my father? About what? What about the statutes? You should not even be here."

Gregory cast a look to the heavens. "The statutes?" He gave a short laugh. "They've weakened to nearly nothing. Even the man who proposed it has left parliament, in a quandary to its validity, nay, its necessity. Not only have they not been able to enforce it, there have been countless unions made between the Gaels and English. You didn't know?"

Cara would not believe him. "Nay, and why should I believe you?"

His face registered surprise. "I assure you, milady, it is the truth. Why would I speak otherwise?"

A swirl of mixed emotions filled Cara's heart. "And what is the truth, milord?" she retorted. "Which of you, Edmund or yourself, has had the heartiest laugh at my expense?"

"Ah, I see now how it is. You think that I am telling you these things in order to win a quick romp. Here is the truth then, Cara. When my father dies, I stand as his heir to inherit everything. I can take care of you. Give you everything you want, all you deserve."

Cara could not believe her ears. Of course, he didn't know about her child. That bit of news would no doubt sour his amorous intentions.

"Cara. You must believe me," he said, reaching out to touch her, but drawing away at the look on her face.

"Why should I? Three years. You don't know me. You don't know what I have been through, what sacrifices I have made."

He regarded her with an inquisitive look. "Tell me everything, Cara. If I can help, I will. I want you to believe me."

He took a step toward her, but she eased away. She held up her hands to keep him from touching her, and backed out from under the tree. The rain came down in torrents, pounding her body. "Leave me alone," she said, grabbing her shoes and running through the downpour to Kiernan's house.

Cara stared out of the window of the room she'd once shared with her sister. The episode with Gregory the day before had left her confused, and then to come home and hear her father extolling the praises of the fifty-year-old widower farmer he'd hope she would marry was too much for her. She'd gone directly to her room, refusing the evening meal, and now breakfast. Cara thought of how many times she'd lain in her small bed and dreamed of the handsome young man she would marry one day. How passionate would be their love and how they would gracefully grow old together, surrounded by their grandchildren. But all of that was but the dreams of a naive young girl, a girl who no longer existed.

A soft tap on the door brought her out of her reverie, and she found her mother, hands clasped together excitedly, standing in her room.

"Ye need to come out here, Cara. There's a most handsome gentleman whose come a-callin'. He speaks of marriage."

Cara searched her mind for the handful of young men in her village not already betrothed. Gregory's words sparked in her mind and she stood, peeking around the door to see him seated at the family table, speaking with her da. Her eyes widened and she slinked back into the room, her mind reeling over what to do. Had marriage been what he'd meant when he told her he was coming to see her da? Cara hugged her arms.

"Cara, you should make yerself presentable to your guest," her mother suggested.

"I cannot marry him," she whispered, trying to control the panic playing in her head.

Her mother eased the bedroom door shut and settled on Kiernan's old bed. "Listen to me, child. I canna say what misgivings you have about this man. But he is of sound stock and has promised many good things to yer da in exchange for your hand and your dowry."

Cara studied her mother's eyes. "My dowry?"

"Aye, as our only child yet unmarried. Yer da has offered part of his land to the lad now, and the rest upon his death. He's added a part of our cattle, as well, and a shared seat in the village administration."

"That's too much. Why would he offer an Englishman so much of all he has in this world?"

Her mother rose and came to her, touching her cheek. "Because in spite of what you think, yer da wants to see you happy. This young man apparently has impressed him as being one to provide that. Things are not the same as they once were, Cara. Our way of life grows smaller each day. Yer da knows this and is trying to see to it that you and Kiernan will be cared for."

Cara paced, considering her options. "Does Gregory know about Moyran?"

Her mother shook her head. "I think Galen is leaving that in your hands. Moyran is safe and happy as any child could be. It is possible the lad would take her in, but he may also want to be startin' a family of his own."

Cara took a deep breath and looked up at the simple thatch roof she'd lived under her whole life. How would she fare in the elegance of an Englishman's house? How could she marry Edmund's best friend?

"Then again, there is always the option of Theron Harrington's hand." Her mother gave her a pointed look.

The idea of suffering through life with an old man whose teeth were nearly gone turned her stomach. And as Gregory had pointed out, Edmund had chosen his life. Now she must choose what was best for her. Not all marriages began because of love. She could learn to love Gregory, and at the very least, she knew she might enjoy his bed.

Cara followed her mother. Gregory and her da both

stood when she entered the room. Cara etched in her mind the look of desire on Gregory's face and tucked it away. "It is with humility that I accept your proposal."

6

EDMUND LOOKED DOWN AT THE ROUGH SCARS crisscrossing his hands, evidence of his work in tending the gardens of the remote mountainside monastery. He hadn't taken much notice before now. The letter he'd received had caused him to face the ghosts of his past—the reality that a world truly existed beyond the safe walls of this simple abbey. Since the arrival of the invitation three days ago, sent via his mother, a part of his life that he'd managed to tuck away, denouncing its importance as part of a reckless and rebellious childhood, had been reopened. And it drummed up emotions that he'd set aside long ago in favor of servitude and self-denial. His parents, of course, were angry that he'd abruptly ended his studies toward becoming an entitled member of the priesthood. Even more so, when he instead chose a path that many would find difficult, if not impossible to walk. But he'd chosen it as a sacrifice, a way to rid himself of his past mistakes, to empty himself entirely of every gain—material or title— and exist in a cloistered world where he would serve only God in silent humility.

Edmund shifted on the stark, backless bench, waiting

for the abbot, who had summoned him to the abbey's administrative quarters. The heat from the sultry autumn day pooled between Edmund thighs. His palms sweated. His plain white linen robes were comfortable enough out of doors, but inside, where little air circulated, his body was suffocating. He pushed himself to his feet, crossing his arms over his chest as the old man entered the room. Edmund bowed out of reverence, accepting the lord abbot's hand, placing a kiss on his ring.

"Peace to you, Edmund. Please sit. This heat is almost unbearable, but we can't complain. The crops enjoy the sun well enough to give us good harvest."

Edmund sat, as did the abbot, across the plain table that served as his desk.

"You seem to be doing well here, Edmund. I trust the monastic life agrees with you?" The abbot did not look at him, only shuffled some papers, peering at them with a frown, before he picked up his spectacles and adjusted them on his nose.

"I am, Your Reverence. It is a good life, serving God in this way," Edmund responded.

The old man, his face covered with a snow-white beard, nodded, drawing his hood down around his neck. Edmund noted how the abbot's thin white hair barely covered the top of his sun-burnished head. He glanced at his hands again, noting how dark his complexion was in comparison to when he'd first arrived.

"Our work keep us busy." The abbot chuckled. "The Lord's work is never done."

"Yes, milord," Edmund replied, wondering why he'd been called here. He was anxious to get back to the fields and finish the weeding before evening vespers.

"You have news from home, I understand?" The abbot gave him a brief glance before looking again at his papers.

Edmund felt the folded sheet he'd tucked in the pocket of his robe. He'd not yet had the chance to write and tell his mother he wasn't coming home. He pulled it out and handed it to the abbot.

The old man dismissed it with a wave of his hand. "I have read it, my son. It is why you have been called here today. I understand this is your best friend who is to be married?"

Of course, Edmund thought as he slipped the paper back into his pocket. All communications—ingoing or outgoing—went through the high clergy. Still, Edmund wasn't sure why he would have been called in because of the letter. He'd made no request for special permission to leave. He had no intention of attending the wedding. Edmund waited, not wishing to show disrespect by asking what was the point of this meeting.

"What do you intend to do?" the Abbot asked calmly, his gaze resting on Edmund.

"*Do?* Milord, I am not certain I understand the question," he responded.

Edmund looked at his mentor, the man who saved him three years ago when he collapsed on the monastery steps, destitute and hungry. He never arrived at the Roman seminary, instead setting forth on a journey of his own, searching for a greater purpose to his life, perhaps in an attempt to abolish the guilt of disobeying his parents and breaking his promise to Cara. He wandered village to village until the day he stumbled upon the steps of the remote abbey in eastern France. Nursed back to health, Edmund felt he'd found his calling, to serve faithfully alongside those who had helped him in a time of need. Not once had he ever questioned the abbot's most puzzling methods of testing his faith.

"So I ask you, what are your plans? Is it not an invitation to return to your village and attend the springtime wedding of your childhood friend?"

Edmund shrugged. "He will have to understand that my work here at the abbey is more important."

The old man propped his fingertips together, his shaggy gray eyebrows drawing into a frown as he spoke. "This is your third year with us, is that not true, Edmund?"

"Yes, your Reverence."

"And you have twice made your vow to serve God according to the Byland brethren."

Edmund nodded, shifting again from the warmth permeating his flesh beneath his robes. His thoughts raced back over the two years since he'd decided to seek admission into the monastic life. Years as a novice, twice reaffirming his vows. It had been a wise choice, Edmund felt, using hard work to replace the guilt of disappointing his family, of defiling a woman, of forbidden desire.

"This is your third year. Soon you may request to take your permanent vows and receive your full orders." The abbot's gaze narrowed on him. "You are our youngest candidate, Edmund, a young man in his prime. And yet you are certain that this is the path that is best for you?"

Edmund swallowed hard and stared into the eyes of wisdom. "Forgive me, milord. But has there been some cause to doubt my dedication?"

"No, no, Edmund, you are a most welcome addition, and I have no doubt that in time you would be an asset to our order."

It did Edmund good to hear the affirmation, since, having received the letter from home, he found his mind filled with the memories and images he'd tried with great determination to remove. His body had yearnings that he'd not experienced in a long time. He'd lain awake at night, unable to sleep, haunted by visions of walking through the labyrinth, the full moon high overhead, the drums drifting through the night air, mingling with Cara's sighs as he rode her to completion. He could not look in the abbot's eyes. "Thank you, milord."

"You are a humble and noble man, Edmund."

His eyes darted to the old man's steady blue gaze, sparking with wisdom.

"However ready you may feel you are to join our abbey, I must ask—have you resolved the issues of your past? You once told me that you had parted ways with a good friend, over a disagreement. Is this man that friend, by chance?"

He could not deny what the abbot had already concluded. "Yes, milord. We were once as brothers, inseparable."

"Yet you have not spoken to him since the day of your disagreement?"

Edmund nodded.

"Edmund, the path to serving God is not a smooth one. Like the gardens you so love, it, too, can grow cluttered with stones, overgrown with weeds. And we are the tenders of that garden. Only we can clear the path, so that the growth of God's goodness is not hindered by obstacles."

Edmund stared at the old man.

"Do you understand what I am saying?" the abbot asked.

Though he wanted to deny it, he couldn't. There were aspects of his life that had been left unresolved. They needed to be made right, so that he could move on with a clear conscience. He'd wrestled with the demons of his past for too long, and now he had to make peace with them, before he could be at peace with himself.

"You are telling me that I should attend my friend's wedding. Isn't that what you're saying?" he asked.

The abbot smiled. "No, my son, I am suggesting that you should make your vows with a clear conscience and whole heart. While it is true that God is our refuge, we do not wish to have to hide behind his robes in the face of adversity."

Edmund nodded. "I'll pack my things at once." He rose and knelt next to the abbot, kissing his ring.

"May God go with you on your journey, Edmund, and we look forward to your return. Go now, in God's peace."

He nodded, unsure if he'd ever truly felt God's peace, or if he'd deluded himself all this time in hiding behind what he thought was right. It would be good to have things between himself and Gregory harmonious again. Even if his life in the abbey took him far away from home after this, he would be better for this slight deviation in his plans.

7

IT WAS JUST AS HE'D LEFT IT. LITTLE HAD changed in Dublin since Edmund sailed from its shores three years ago, except now he noticed traces of Gaelic influence had seeped back into the predominantly English village. Celtic music played freely in the courtyard of a pub, and in the din of voices on the wharf, he'd heard snippets of the ancient Gaelic tongue. His mother had kept him abreast of the changes, explaining that parliament was weakening its stand on keeping the two cultures separate, for they were already so tightly woven together.

His mother had also noted that Gregory's betrothed was the daughter of a Gaelic leader of great influence with his people, and so of great value to what alliance he would bring to the crown. Edmund considered that news of Lord DeVerden's—Gregory's father's—recent knighthood by the king may well have played into the union, as England rarely did anything that didn't also bring them greater political power.

Given what he knew of Gregory, Edmund found it hard to imagine him settling down with one woman. She must be quite special. The thought of marriage seemed so foreign to Edmund now. Though he still had the desires of any man, he had sacrificed his hope for a wife and family long ago, out of self-preservation. His first year away from home, away from the only woman he would ever give his heart to, had been torture, and yet in some perverse way it was the memory of Cara and their short time together that got him through his darkest hours. Eventually, his dedication to their love turned to a greater love—one that required selflessness. The abbot knew, even as Edmund knew, deep inside, that it was good he should come home to test himself, his priorities.

Edmund took his time walking home. It was a beautiful late winter afternoon, just days before the return of spring...Beltane. The street vendors displayed their wares, and the mingling of familiar scents, of raw fish and baking bread, made Edmund's mouth water. His heart had a sudden yearning to remain here in the familiar surroundings of his childhood home. But his life had changed, and so, too, had Gregory's. Edmund was here to make amends so that he could go with his life and give his blessing for Gregory to go on with his own.

Edmund's family estate was situated near the grounds of the main castle. Compared to the poor villages he'd worked in, it was a palace. He paused at the front door with its austere lion's head knocker. He reached for it, then, having second thoughts, opened the door and walked in. He was greeted by the sight of his mother standing at the base of the great curved staircase. She wore a stern expression, which explained the scrambling of the servants around her.

"Mother," he said. He dropped his tattered sack of worldly belongings by the door, dismissing with a wave of his hand a servant who tried to pick it up. Edmund opened his arms in greeting, but his mother offered nothing more than her cheek for him to kiss.

"You arrived early. How wonderful." She gave him a stony smile. "You must be hungry." She motioned to one of the servants. "Prepare something for my son to eat. And bring him some fresh milk and cheese." She looped her arm through his and escorted him to the front room. "Good heavens, Edmund. You are nothing but skin and bone."

"Where is Father?" he asked.

She gave him a quick glance. "He is with Lord De-Verden."

"Just as well. It will give us some time to catch up." He patted her hand.

"Not until you bathe, Edmund. I'll not have you at my table. You smell akin to a fish barrel."

In short order a tub was brought to his room and made ready with hot water. He couldn't deny the pleasure of sinking into it and lathering himself with the French soap his mother insisted was best for the skin. One of the solemn-faced servants returned twice with fresh hot water.

"Lady Collier has requested that I remind you that your meal awaits and is getting cold, sir."

Edmund had planned to shave, but decided it was better not to keep his mother waiting any longer. The servant picked up his dusty, brown robe. "You can leave that."

The man held it between his fingers with a disparaging look. "It won't take any time at all to place it with the daily wash, sir. We will have it to you fresh by morning, then?"

Edmund knew it was pointless to argue. His mother would steal his clothes away in the dead of night if need be. "Very well." He smiled, wondering whether to show up at his mother's table in the suit God had given him.

"Lady Collier also suggests that you will find extra clothes, preferred for dining, in the wardrobe."

"She thought of everything," Edmund mused aloud.

"She always does, sir," the elderly servant muttered. "Will you require my assistance with your clothing, sir?"

"I've been dressing myself for quite some time now, thank you," Edmund responded. He stood in the tub. "That did feel glorious... What was your name again?" Baths at the monastery were taken in the crystal cold lake.

"Bentley, sir."

"Ah, Bentley, if you'd be so kind as to hand me that towel and tell my mother I will be down straightaway."

He nodded once and left Edmund to ponder what clothing choices his mother had provided.

Edmund picked through the wardrobe and settled on a shirt, long breeches and a pair of his old boots, but it felt strange, almost decadent, to be wearing ordinary clothes. He entered the dining hall and found his usual chair ready for him. His mother clapped her hands, summoning a flurry of servants, who lined up one at a time to offer an array of culinary delights on silver platters. Edmund eyed the feast and smiled at his mother. "I could no more eat this much food in a week. At the abbey we have but two meals a day."

She waived away the servants and eyed him with a tolerant sigh. "What title are you given at this...abbey?" She passed him a basket of bread. "Are you sure you want nothing more?"

Edmund chuckled as he broke off a piece of homemade bread. "I'll take one of those apples." He gestured to the bowl containing the red fruit he suspected was meant for display rather than eating.

His mother rested her hands in her lap. watching him from where she sat but he sensed she might as well have been miles away. She didn't understand his vows of poverty. Edmund could only hope in time that her disappointment would lessen. "Well, to begin with, Mother, I will always first be your son."

Her mouth dropped open in surprise. From the look on her face, Edmund could see she was preparing to lecture him about his choices, and how they'd caused them insurmountable grief. He'd received such comments in the letters they'd sent in the beginning, when they thought they could change his mind. Still, with such a short time before he must return to the abbey, he did not wish to argue. He stood, taking a sip from the fine goblet before him.

"I'm still your Edmund, Mother. I've not yet taken my vows." His need to see his old friend and make things right between them weighed on his heart. "I think I'll go visit Gregory. Let him know I've arrived, in case he needs my counsel, or perhaps just a willing ear." Edmund leaned down and kissed his mother's cheek, finding the chalky taste of her face powder still the same.

She didn't look at him. He knew that she didn't approve of his disobedience, but over the years, he'd managed to get past the guilt of his family's disappointment. Now it was a matter of hoping they would accept him, if not his choices. "I will be back soon, and hopefully, with Father. If I know the two of them, he'll need an arm to steady himself after partaking of Lord DeVerden's port."

"Edmund?"

He paused at the arched entrance and looked back, noticing concern on her face.

"Be careful, Edmund. It has been some time since you and Gregory parted ways and, as I recall, not on cordial terms. Though I have him to thank, I suppose, that you are not rotting in some English jail. Remember that because of his father's knighthood, he, too, has a position of great influence over our family."

Edmund knew what she meant was be careful and don't cause a public spectacle. "Thank you, Mother, for your concern. But I imagine since it was Gregory himself who invited me to this happy occasion, it would indicate that he is willing to place the past where it belongs—in the past. And I wish to do the same. It is better for both of us to do so." He offered her a short bow and departed for Dublin Castle.

Cara had never seen anything so grand. The walls of the castle were as high as the cliffs standing over the sea, and washed with bright colors. Massive paintings hung high and low on the walls, set in exquisitely ornate frames. Upon her arrival she was taken immediately to her room, where she was told she needed to prepare properly before meeting Gregory's parents. She'd been given a maidservant, who waited dutifully at her side while Cara gawked at the size of her quarters. She was astounded by the opulence and wealth, more of it displayed within these two rooms alone than the entirety of her village back home.

"May I pour your tea, milady?" The young servant girl moved to the table and picked up the fine teapot.

"That would be lovely, thank you," Cara responded, remembering every manner her mother had taught her.

The young girl ushered her to a seat, snapped open a cloth and lay it over her lap. She handed her a cup and saucer, folded her hands in front of her and looked at Cara with a no-nonsense look in her eye.

"After tea, you are to rest. Your bath is scheduled at five. You are to be dressed, and then meet Master DeVerden in the formal dining hall promptly at eight."

Cara cradled the fragile teacup with the care she'd use gathering the hens' eggs back home. She had much to learn about the new life she was about to marry into. The saving grace to many of her concerns was a promise by Gregory that after they were wed, he would arrange for her whole family to be brought to the castle to live. She was glad to see that the tradition of family ties was as important to him as it was to her.

She had not yet told him about Moyran, but still pondered what her mother had said about him wanting to have his own children. Still, it did her heart good to know that she would have a greater say in offering her daughter a quality upbringing if she was under the same roof.

The maidservant stood silently next to the table, her gaze focused straight ahead. Cara made the mistake of glancing at her over the rim of her cup.

"Yes, milady?" She straightened abruptly.

Cara wondered if the poor girl ever smiled. "I have all I could possibly need. Surely you have other things you must do."

Puzzled, the young girl shook her head. "No, milady, my duty is to serve you."

"Then I give you permission to take your leave, as I am about to rest."

She curtsied. "I will wait outside should you need me."

Cara began to protest, but stopped herself, not wishing to create any disruptions for the girl. "Thank you," she replied, and realized it was going to take her some time to get used to being waited on at every turn.

Once she was alone, she explored her chambers, testing out the luxuriously thick mattress, big enough, she was certain, for five people. Cara plucked at her dusty clothes, wanting to change into one of the lovely gowns that hung in her wardrobe. But she dared not do so before her bath. She lifted back the heavy red drape and looked below at the bustling courtyard full of horses, footmen and peasants, all crisscrossing paths, going about their chores. She leaned her head against the cool window glass. In a few days it would be Beltane—and her wedding day. It had been at Gregory's insistence, as that was the day he'd first seen her.

Her eye caught sight of a lone man, his stride determined, his face obscured partially by the courtyard shadows. There was something familiar about him, about the unruly wave of his wheat-colored hair hanging to his shoulders.

The air was sucked from her lungs as she studied his purposeful gait. As he paused at the door and looked up, a shaft of afternoon sunlight swept across his face. Her heart stilled.

Edmund.

Cara grabbed the edge of the curtain and moved quickly away from the window. She couldn't breathe. Her mind launched into a flight of questions. Why would he come back now? A squeak of laughter bubbled from her throat. Why wouldn't he? Of course he'd been invited to the wedding; that only made sense. But why was he not in his vestment robes? Surely by now he'd have taken the first of his vows. Cara pushed open her chamber door, startling the young servant dozing in a chair outside the room.

"Milady, I will accompany you—wait!" the girl called

after her. But Cara did not slow down. If anything, she quickened her pace, pushed by a nameless force. She hurried down the wide marble steps, being careful not to stumble as she navigated the many stairs. At the bottom, she searched right and left, unsure of which way to turn. The maidservant, out of breath now, appeared at her side, her hand clutching the curved gold rail.

"Which way to the entrance from the courtyard?" Cara asked, taking the girl by the shoulders.

She looked at Cara as though registering her request, then pointed her finger to the left, down a long hall with an arched, vaulted ceiling.

"Take me there," Cara ordered, hoping the urgency of her request didn't border on desperate. She took the girl's arm and fairly dragged her down the hall.

"No, milady, this way." The girl tugged at Cara, causing her to lose her footing on the slick tile.

"There now, be careful...."

Strong, capable hands caught her and kept her from taking a nasty spill. She looked up, her eyes meeting a familiar pair of gray-green eyes the color of a stormy sea.

"Cara?" Edmund spoke her name in a whisper.

She could not respond. Her tongue would not permit it and her brain had not a rational offering.

"What are you...why are you here?" he asked, and then it didn't matter why. He smiled, and joy crept into his eyes.

"Ah, finally! Edmund, my dear friend!" Gregory's voice boomed across the hall. "I had hoped to present the news more formally at dinner this evening, but since you have already been reacquainted, allow me to introduce you to my betrothed. Cara and I are to be married on Beltane. Fitting, would you not agree?"

Edmund's face fell as his eyes turned to Cara. She saw him swallow hard, recovering from the obvious shock. Gregory had not told him whom he was to marry. Edmund forced a bright smile and bowed, kissing the back of her hand. "My sincere prayers for your complete happiness, milady."

Gregory brushed by her, grabbing Edmund in a show of brotherly affection. Cara stood by, silently observing the two friends, curious why Gregory would not have mentioned her name. Edmund's eyes rose to hers over Gregory's shoulder. A flash of hurt slid across his face before he pulled back and held Gregory at arm's length, offering a sincere smile. "Congratulations, my friend. I wish you all of God's richest blessings."

Gregory laughed and slapped Edmund on the back. He placed one arm around his shoulder and drew Cara toward him with the other.

"Together again, after all these years and—" he laughed, punching Edmund playfully "—who has the girl now? What is it you once said, my dear? We make our own fate." He uttered a happy sigh. "It is good to have you home, my friend." He looked from one to the other. "Now, I must check on Father and see to a few last minute arrangements for the celebration tonight. You'll stay, won't you, and dine with us?"

Edmund shot Cara a quick glance. "I'm afraid I've other plans."

"Nonsense, change them. Your father has already agreed to stay. I insist." He hugged Cara to his side. "Don't you agree, my dear, that Edmund should join us for our family celebration?"

Cara felt nauseous, but forced a smile and nodded.

"Then it is settled." Gregory started down the hall.

"Perhaps I may be of some service?" Edmund called after him.

"Still taking care of the needs of others? Bless you, my friend. Perhaps later. For now, I will show you where you can freshen up before supper." Gregory snapped his fingers, gaining the attention of Cara's maidservant. "Take my beautiful bride to her chambers, where she might ready herself for the evening."

The servant curtsied and waited patiently for Cara.

This was not how she'd imagined their reunion would be. Cara wanted desperately to speak with Edmund, to see how he had fared all these years, to ask him the one question that she'd been carrying, buried deep in her heart. But was it wise now to even bother dredging up the past? She gave thought to these questions, deciding that despite everything, he should know at least that he had a daughter. One day, when Moyran noticed she was different from her brother and sisters, she would ask questions, perhaps wish to meet her father.

Cara allowed herself to be returned to her chambers. She sat at the writing desk and penned a simple note. She folded it carefully, tied it with a ribbon and tucked it in her maidservant's hand. "See to it that you deliver this in private to Mr. Collier. Be quick and stop for no one." She paced the floor, hoping the girl would loyally perform what she'd asked.

Finally, Cara lay down to nap, but found sleep eluded her. She was restless, with images of her and Edmund and the passionate night they'd shared. She'd given Gregory her troth to marry, but she had yet to give him her heart, in hope that one day she would grow to love him. But after seeing Edmund, just looking into his eyes one more time, she found her thoughts becoming twisted. Was it

possible she still loved him? Despite what he'd done, despite the years that had passed?

Where was that girl?

Other servants came and went, bringing in an ornate
tub and filling it with warm water. Still there was no word
from her maidservant. Cara proceeded with her bath alone,
hoping the girl would show up in time to help her dress
for the evening meal. The warmth of the water soothed
her tension some, but there was little water could do to
ease the way her body ached for Edmund. She shut her
eyes, feeling a whirlwind of guilt, scolding herself for her
wicked thoughts, which betrayed Gregory and lusted after
a man of God.

"Milady, Master Collier to see you," the maidservant
suddenly announced. A gasp escaped the young girl's lips
when she realized she could not stop Edmund's purposeful
stride into the room.

His gray eyes went wide, and for a moment, he stared
blatantly at Cara, then spun on his heel, facing away from
her. "My apologies, milady."

The now frightened maidservant hurried to Cara, offering her a robe. She stepped from the tub and covered her
nakedness, then nodded to the girl. "Leave us."

The servant opened her mouth to speak, her eyes darting toward Edmund.

"It is quite all right. Master Collier and I are old friends,"
Cara explained.

Hesitant still, the girl bowed and left the room, but Cara
knew she would be outside the door.

Cara walked over and closed it quietly. What she had to
tell Edmund she didn't want all of Dublin to know.

8

"I WOULD BE MORE THAN HAPPY TO WAIT OUT-
side while you dress." Edmund kept his attention focused
on his feet, his back still turned. "I must tell you, I do not
feel it is wise for me to be here. Are you in some kind of
trouble? Your note—"

"Edmund, look at me."

He raised his head and met her lovely green eyes, not
expecting that she would affect him as powerfully as she
did. Her beautiful hair, wet at the ends, clung in provoca-
tive tendrils against her neck. Edmund pushed away the
thought of that glorious red hair sweeping across his bare
flesh.

"I am fine. You have been working in the sun, I see. It
suits you," she said.

He raised his hands, noting the nicks and scars crisscrossing his skin, the calluses from holding a sickle. Edmund
shifted the conversation away from himself, purposely
keeping his gaze anywhere but on her. "This is a lovely
room. It suits you, Cara," he said quietly.

She stared at him, holding the brocade robe together

with her clasped hand. It was the only thing standing between him and paradise….

Edmund mentally reprimanded himself. Had he been deluding himself that he'd forgotten her, that he was able to put aside the deep stirrings it had taken him so long to get past? He had to find his perspective, his peace in facing her again, and in accepting that she was about to marry his best friend. "You, uh, said in your note you need me?"

"Yes, Edmund, I do. Please sit down." She sat across from him, carefully tucking the robe around her legs.

Edmund eased back into his seat and cleared his throat. His gaze strayed to where her robe gaped open, revealing not the young girl's small breasts he remembered, but a woman's—full and lush. His throat went dry and he fought to ignore the heat that flashed through his body. "Cara, if this is about Gregory or the wedding, you owe me no explanation."

Following his gaze, she realized the problem, and remedied it, clutching the two pieces of fabric together, hiding her flesh. A quiet sigh followed. "I had not thought this would be so difficult." She glanced at him, her cheeks stained with a pale blush.

"I want you to know that you have no reason to be uncomfortable around me, Cara. In truth, it is I who should be asking your forgiveness."

She looked down, twisting her fingers in her lap. He leaned forward and took her hands, trying to make her understand. "I did not keep my promise to you." He lifted the corner of his mouth in a half smile. "I had sound reason, of course, but little choice in the matter."

"Because of the statutes?" she pressed.

"Yes, in part," he responded.

"And what about now?"

The murky water he found himself wading into just got murkier. He looked down and shook his head. "Cara, you are to be married in a few days."

"All the more reason, Edmund, that I deserve to know," she said, searching his eyes. God in heaven, he'd forgotten how beautiful, how expressive they were. He had a difficult time imagining her in Gregory's bed, and the heaven of waking to her face each morning. What did it matter now? Edmund looked at their hands, clasped as they had been the night he'd left her. The night he'd vowed to return for her. She could have been his, had he followed through with that promise, if he'd listened to his heart and stolen her away that night. But fate had other things in store, and now so much had changed. "What is it that you need to know, Cara, so that you can move on with your life? If I have answers to those questions, then I am happy to give them."

Being with her face-to-face reminded him how easily they'd been able to talk with one another, how quickly they'd bonded. In some ways, it felt like only yesterday that they had parted. Perhaps it was the possibilities that plagued him—the thought of what might have been.

"Have you taken your vows, Edmund?"

He rose, walking to the fireplace across the room, distancing himself from her. The question posed a disturbing reality that he was not prepared to face. The one that had hit him in the stomach the minute he'd seen her in the hall today, and his body had reacted of its own accord. Even now, he struggled with the dark smoke of desire swirling inside him.

He leaned his hands on the mantel and stared at the crackling fire, welcoming the distraction of the colored flames.

"Edmund?"

Her hand gently touched his shoulder, and he turned to her, his eyes stinging.

"Are you crying?" she asked, studying his face.

"No, it is the smoke from the fire."

"If I've hurt you by my question, I am sorry. I understand the choices you've made. But I had to hear from you." She searched his eyes. "To be sure."

Edmund looked at her sweet face, the one he'd dreamed of so many nights. "How could you possibly bring me pain, Cara? I will always cherish the short time we had."

"I know, I feel the same." She threw her arms around his neck and hugged him tight, her breasts pressed against his chest. God forgive them both. He found her mouth, finding the easy rhythm he remembered, the give and take. A small groan crawled from his throat and he thought of nothing else but gathering her into his arms and satisfying what he'd denied himself for these past years. He parted her robe, his hands caressing, his callused fingers touching her satin-smooth skin. Eager, driven by her insistent kisses, he explored every curve, each tightly pebbled peak, the sweet warm valley between her thighs.

"Oh," she sighed, capturing his mouth in a heated kiss as he coaxed her, slipping his fingers into her slick warm heat. She crooked her hand around his neck, her thighs parted, not taking her eyes from his as he fanned the need building between them. He told himself that this was against everything he'd worked so hard to accomplish, and yet it was worth every moment, hearing her breath catch.

"You do still care for me," she whispered, and slipped the robe from her shoulders, letting it fall to the floor.

She gripped his hand, backing up until her legs touched the settee, and she lay back, inviting him with her eyes, her arms, her moist, pink flower awaiting him. Edmund closed his eyes, fighting the hardening of his cock. He did not want to weigh what was wrong and right; he wanted only to feel her tight around him, as he'd dreamed of so many times. He freed himself and knelt on the cushion before her. Lifting her thigh, finding just the right angle, he pushed deep as she sighed. She looked up at him, her eyes bright with adoration, lifting her hips to meet his fervent thrusts. There was no time for sweet words, no time for gentle caresses. She deserved much more, but his body, determined to rid itself of this dark lust, slowed, driving deeper. All the time he watched her expression, seeing her body ascending to that state of bliss. How many times he'd imagined this moment, not in secret, but in wedded union with her. Fluid heat filled him, and his hips moved in blind freedom. Only one question plagued him now—one that he fought to ignore.

Did he love her still?

Her quiet gasp was followed by her spasms that caressed, encouraged him. Biting back a loud groan, Edmund grabbed her hip and held tight, giving in to his own exploding release. Then he backed away, pulled up his breeches and dropped to his knees with his head in his hands. The implosion of regret attacked him. What had he done? My God, whether he cared for her or not, what good was it now? She was to be married to another in two days' time, to a man who could care for her in a proper manner. And worse, Edmund had just sentenced himself to a lifetime of torture, coveting another man's wife. "I'm sorry, Cara. I did not mean for this to happen. I didn't know you were Gregory's betrothed. If I had known, I would have stayed away, for this very reason."

"No, Edmund." She sat up, the sweet, musky scent of

sex wafting toward him, arousing him once more. She stroked his head, gently forcing him to look at her.

Oh, God, how could he be thinking of wanting her again?

"Edmund, we still feel the same as we once did. There is no shame in that. What would be a shame would be to ignore such a gift and pretend it did not exist."

He pushed himself to his feet, turning his eyes from her beautiful body—a body he had no right to. He bent down and draped the robe around her shoulders, covering her tantalizing flesh as much as possible. "I have made my choice, Cara, as you have. Your life with Gregory will be far better than anything I can offer you. Think of what he can give you, your family. He can take care of you in ways that I cannot."

"But it is not Gregory I love, Edmund. Are you so blind you do not see that?" she pleaded. "Look at me." Her voice rose, and Edmund feared they would be heard. He took her face in his hands, not knowing how else to calm her.

"Look at me and say that you have no feelings for me."

He could not lie to himself or to her. "It does not matter how I feel. You are to marry another, and that is the way of it. We are not the wide-eyed children of three years ago, Cara. There are matters of greater importance now and we must accept that." Despite the bravado of his words, Edmund strode from the room, knowing if he looked back, he would crumble.

"Edmund, we have a child," she said after he'd gone. Why didn't she tell him? Cara grappled with guilt that she hadn't come out and told him about Moyran. But she'd needed to know first how he felt about her. She didn't want to saddle him with the guilt of a child, if he no longer cared for her. She closed her eyes, her body heating even now, remembering the way he'd looked at her, the passion shining in his eyes as he made love to her. She could not be mistaken in this. He did still care for her, but his pride and loyalty blinded him to the fact.

She changed back into her clothes and gathered what few possessions she'd brought with her. It was impossible for her to marry Gregory now, not with the knowledge that Edmund still carried feelings for her. Perhaps she was a fool to think he might change his mind. That he would see the sacred gift the gods and goddesses had bestowed on them. Such passion could not survive both time and distance, if not for a higher purpose.

She paced the room, weighing how best to explain her decision to Gregory. It occurred to her that it could even be called a change of heart, for she had never really loved him, not in the way she loved Edmund. Cara stopped, taking a deep breath as her gaze fell on the settee. Gregory needed to know, and the best way, the most kind way, would be to speak with him face-to-face.

She opened the door and her maidservant leaped to her feet. Cara noted, however, that she would not look at her directly. "I need your help," she said, hoping that she could appeal to her compassion. "I need to speak to Master DeVerden."

The young girl's eyes lifted to hers. "Yes, Mum. I know he was to meet with his father before the evening meal. In his study is where the master has his family meetings."

"Will you take me there?"

She nodded, and they set off down the stairs in silence.

After reaching the main level, and following a number of corridors, the maidservant stopped and, with her eyes cast to the ground, spoke. "I am allowed no farther, madam. No woman is permitted in this hall."

Cara peeked around one of the great marble columns that lined either side of the hall. At the far end was a wide door and standing sentinel was a lone guard. She eased back and swallowed, clenching her palms, which were clammy from anxiety. How would Gregory and his family react to this news? What consequences might there be for her family? Or would he assume that her refusal had something to do with Edmund's return?

The sound of a latch turning caused Cara to push the young girl into the shadow of one of the massive columns. She heard the voices of two men in conversation as they made their way down the hall. Becoming aware that she'd clamped her palm over the girl's mouth, Cara released her hand and placed a finger on her lips. Much to her relief the maid nodded, seeming to understand her request. Cara considered stepping out before they reached the turn at the end of the hall, as though they'd been on a casual walk about the castle, but the dialogue between the two men, one of whom she recognized as Gregory, gave her pause, and she listened closer.

"Once you have her dowry, it will be easy enough to do away with the village. A simple grass fire from one of their incessant bonfires ought to take care of removing those Gaelic pains in the king's ass."

Her breath caught in her throat. What was she hearing?

"Does the girl suspect anything?" Gregory's father spoke, and the sound of his voice on the opposite side of the column stuck fear in Cara's heart. She held her breath, mentally searching for the easiest route out of the castle.

"No, she is far too enamored with my promise to bring her family to live here at the castle to think of much else. There may be one problem, though his naivety still astounds me—that is Edmund."

How could she have been so blind not to see that the English king would somehow have his hands in this union? Cara wondered. But the extermination of her people? And they called the Gaels barbarians! Had she really been so naive to think that she'd found someone who cared for her as she'd once believed Edmund did?

The two men had stopped near where the two women were tucked in the dark shadows. Cara reached down and slipped her hand around the servant's, squeezing it. To her good fortune the girl seemed to be on her side.

"Collier?" Gregory's father snapped matter-of-factly.

"Yes," Gregory replied, though his tone smacked more of annoyance than concern. Cara's jaw ticked as she held back the urge to tear his eyes out. "But if my suspicions are correct, my dear friend's honor and allegiance to his sanctimonious religious life will be my greatest ally, just as it was three years ago, Father. It worked in our favor then, keeping Edmund's father where you needed him, and I have no doubt it will work again for our purpose now."

"And if that Gaelic tart is able to persuade him differently?"

Gregory's low chuckle sent a chill up Cara's spine. "Then there any number of accidents that can happen while two good friends are taking a walk in the woods."

She closed her eyes, angry that she'd fallen for his scheming lies and that she'd led her family and her people right into this English snare. She waited until the men had moved on down the hall before she took her next breath. It was imperative that she warn her family and Edmund.

She looked at the young girl and knelt in front of her. "What is your name, child?" Cara asked. The girl could not have been more than a dozen years, if that.

"Anne," she replied, blinking her soft blue eyes.

"I need you to return to your post outside my chambers, and if asked, say you have not seen or heard from me since leaving me to rest. Will you do this for me?"

"May I speak freely, milady?" the young girl whispered.

Cara nodded. "Of course. Are you concerned for your well-being?"

"Not for myself. My concern is for Master Collier. He was always kind to me when he frequented the castle with Master DeVerden, as I swear on my oath that Master De-Verden was not. I suspect the young master and his father are not to be trusted. To that end I give you my troth." She took Cara's hand. "Where will you go, milady?"

Cara shook her head. "I can say no more. So you will do this?"

The girl nodded.

Cara hugged her tight.

"Go down the last hall to a spiral stair that will take you into the storage chambers for winter food. Follow the hall to the end and you will find a door that takes you into an alleyway of the village, outside the castle wall. From there, you are on your own."

"Thank you," Cara replied, releasing her. She checked the hall to be certain the way was clear.

"Milady?"

Cara looked over her shoulder.

"Do you wish for me to give Master Collier a message?"

The young girl was wiser than her years and had likely heard the goings-on in Cara's chambers. Still, Cara could not risk giving the girl any more information. She'd already asked too much of her. "No, Anne. What will be will be. I leave it in the hands of the gods and goddesses now."

9

EDMUND LOOKED UP FROM HIS SOUP, WATCH-
ing as the steward bent to whisper something in Gregory's
ear. Guilt assuaged him when Gregory's dark eyes darted
to the empty chair that presumably was Cara's. He then
looked at Edmund.

"Milord, is there a problem?" Edmund wasn't certain he
truly wanted the answer to that question.

"It is Cara. It seems she is not in her room and her maid
cannot find her. You wouldn't happen to have any idea
where she might be?"

Edmund shook his head. "Of course not, but if I may be
of service…"

Gregory eyed him. "She may be in the castle, but she
may also have decided to explore the gardens. She may
have fallen and twisted her ankle." He tossed his napkin on
the table. "Excuse me, miladies and milords…" He bowed
and left the table.

Edmund excused himself and followed him into the
hall. "Is there something I can do?"

Gregory whirled on his heel and pinned Edmund with

a dark look. "Oddly, I would say that you know her nearly as well as I do. Where do you suppose she has wandered off to?"

Edmund could not dismiss the underlying tone of his question. Despite his guilt, and his curiosity over Gregory's sudden jealousy, Edmund's chief concern was for Cara's safe return. He hoped that her disappearance had nothing to do with what had happened earlier between them, though his gut told him it did. "If you would like, I could take a horse and search the woods near the gardens." He knew Gregory would recognize the area. It was where they'd tromped many a time in their youth, the very place, in fact, where they'd sneaked into the Beltane festival.

"Ah, yes, the old abbey tower," Gregory said, almost as an afterthought. "Good idea. I will organize a search party of the castle. And be sure to check her father's house. Perhaps she has had second thoughts."

Edmund smiled and patted Gregory on the back. "She would be a fool to do that."

"Indeed, my friend. Indeed."

Edmund continued down the hall toward the stables, hoping that he could find Cara and talk some sense into her.

"Pssst, Master Collier."

Edmund heard the soft voice of a girl coming from inside a dark room. A hand reached out and motioned to him. He checked over his shoulder and slipped inside, easing the door shut. "Who is this?" he stated in a hushed whisper.

"It is Anne, milord. Milady Ormond's chamber maid."

"Anne, of course, but you're much older now." Edmund wished he had some light to see the child's face.

"Aye, milord, eleven now. She asked me not to speak to anyone. But you have never given me reason not to trust you."

"Thank you, Anne. Your faith means a great deal, please, if you know what has happened to Lady Ormond, tell me quick. We've not much time."

"Milady has run away."

His worst fears confirmed, Edmund reached out and found the warmth of the girl's arm. "I mean you no harm, but you must tell me where she is."

"She would not say, milord. Only that she cannot marry Master DeVerden."

Edmund did not wish to waste more time in trying to find out why. He already knew that. "Very well, return to your station and say nothing of this to anyone," he cautioned. He slipped back into the hallway and called to the guards. "You two, follow the riverbank. You two check the Gael village. I will search the tower and abbey grounds. Check everywhere."

The last dredges of sunlight deepened the shadows as he urged his horse across the open valley that separated the English Pale from the rest of Ireland. He thought of that fateful night when he'd met Cara. How beautiful she was! But he could not think of one moment in that night when Gregory had ever mentioned he might have feelings for Cara. She was nothing to him, any more than any other women he'd bedded before. A strange, disturbing realization began to dawn in Edmunds head, making him question Gregory's friendship. Being of true English birth, and Edmund of Norman, or Old English blood, the two had never allowed political obstacles to affect their friendship. Only now, Edmund questioned whether it was still the case.

The tower, showing signs of decay, stood tall in the waning light. Edmund dismounted and held the torch high to light his path through the meadow with its labyrinth, now nothing more than an overgrown field. Only a handful of the orchard trees remained. But the garden, surrounded on three sides by a tangled mass of shrubbery and dead branches, remained just as he remembered it that night.

Cautiously, Edmund started to open the gate, then jerked his hand back abruptly. Flashing the light over the spot, he discovered the garish grin of the Green Man mask, left where he'd hung it years before. Edmund chuckled at his skittishness. "Hello, old friend. It's been a while," he said quietly. He swore one of the eyes winked, then reasoned it was only a play of the shadows. The gate opened with ease and he was surprised that by now it wouldn't have fallen into disrepair. Inside, a cool breeze met him, filled with the scent of a fresh meadow after a rain on a beautiful summer night. Did he imagine the heady scent of roses?

"Cara?" Edmund called into the darkness. He did not relish being out here alone. Not that he believed in such things as ghosts and magical spirits, but this place brought back memories he'd fought too long to erase. His foot kicked something in the grass, and he knelt down, finding one of Cara's slippers.

She was here.

"Edmund?" Her familiar voice issued from the door leading to the tower room.

He moved quickly toward where he remembered the fountain, crouching low to avoid the growth of brush and tree limbs. "Cara?" he called, keeping his voice low.

"Tell them you could not find me."

"Cara, you must see reason. You cannot stay out here. It is too dangerous. Even now, the guests are beginning to arrive. We have talked about this, and I beg you to do what is best for all."

"Nay, I will not." Her voice now came from behind. Edmund turned on his heel, finding no one.

"Enough of these games, Cara. Sometimes God's ways are not our own. Sometimes we must obey, even though we may not fully understand."

"No, Edmund. You don't know everything, and I don't believe in your English God."

"Cara, if necessary, I will take you back by force," he warned, moving through the brambles toward the tower doorway.

"Do you smell the roses?" Her voice issued over his left shoulder, and he turned, careful not to set the brush afire with his torch.

"Come, Cara, it's getting cold and late."

"I smelled them that night. The night you pledged to come back for me."

Edmund frowned, remembering his broken promise. The light of his torch passed over the statutes of the two lovers, frozen forever in each other's embrace. Was this a spirit of the place, taunting him? He squinted, peering as best he could through the shadows.

"There is good reason for my choice, Edmund. You must trust me." Her voice seemed to float on the breeze.

"Then come out, tell me, and let us return home and confront him together." Edmund grew frustrated.

"That is not my home, Edmund."

He shoved a weary hand through his hair, wondering what to tell Gregory. "How do I know this is not a spirit speaking? If it is you, Cara, why not show yourself to me?"

"Milord Collier?" a deep voice shouted from the other side of the gnarled hedge.

"Come tomorrow, Edmund. I give my oath I will tell you everything," she called in a whisper, her voice melding with the breeze. "Promise me."

"Milord, are you in there?" The man spoke with greater urgency.

"Very well," Edmund replied in a low voice, looking once more around him. "Yes, I am here. Nothing but a mass of brambles and twigs. She's not here," Edmund called to the guard. He tossed Cara's shoe into the dry, leaf-filled fountain.

Edmund yanked open the gate and met the bewildered look of the soldier on the other side.

"I thought I heard voices in there." The man peered over Edmund's shoulder.

"I quite often pray aloud when I'm alone." It wasn't a complete lie.

The man lowered his eyes, dutifully humbled. "Of course. My apologies, milord."

Edmund shut the gate behind him and felt a jolt against his back. Curious, he leaned down, his torchlight picking up the secretive smile of the mask, laying on the ground looking up at him. He picked it up and hung it again on the peg, remembering when he had done so the first time. This time, he would not break his promise to return.

Cara woke to the sound of thunder rolling overhead. It took her a moment to remember where she was. She'd chosen this place for its isolation, thinking that when they discovered her absence, they would first go to her father's household. She pushed herself up from the bed of straw she'd gathered the night before, and peered out the open window. The view offered the lush green of the valley beginning to blossom with spring, and gray ominous clouds rolling in, darkening the skies. What little sleep she'd had was restless, fraught with the choices she must make, and with wondering whether Edmund would indeed return. His determination to marry her off to Gregory plagued her, her heart refusing to believe that he didn't still care for her. If she listened, and married Gregory, it would mean the certain destruction of her family and her village. If she refused, the repercussions could be worse. The dark, stormy clouds wiping out the clear blue sky matched her mood as she turned from the window. She appeased the gnawing in her stomach with a few bites of stale biscuits she'd snatched while escaping through the food storage tunnels. They offered little comfort to the riling of her stomach, and Cara cupped her hands, retrieving enough water to cool her parched throat.

The shrill neigh of a horse caused her to draw away from the window. Fear struck her heart. What if Edmund had told Gregory where to find her? Was he so determined that she'd be better off with his old friend? Cara summoned her courage and peeked around the edge of the window, relief flooding her when she saw Edmund striding across the brown lawn. She turned and heard his purposeful steps on the tower stairs. He walked into the room, and she could not contain her joy that he'd kept his promise. She ran to him, curling her arms around his neck. But he stood stiffly, not returning her exuberant embrace. Confused and more than embarrassed, she stepped away and looked at him. His face was drawn, his cloak and clothing soaked. It appeared as though he'd had little sleep.

"I am here as you requested. I have stated that I was coming to speak to your family, to check if they have seen you. Gregory shows great concern, Cara. I beg you tell me what it is that causes you to run away from a marriage that stands to give you and your family the best of all possible futures."

Dumbstruck, Cara searched his eyes and stepped away from him. Had she been fooling herself that he still cared?

"I brought you some water," he said, rummaging through his bag.

Cara could only watch how matter-of-fact he was acting. How detached he was compared to yesterday.

"I wasn't sure if you had eaten." He untied his cloak, draping it over a broken chair. "I brought an apple and some cheese."

"I do not need your charity." She returned to the window, letting the soft rain brush against her heated face.

"Cara, I do not know what more you want from me."

She smiled, though her heart was bitter. Indeed, what she'd thought he wanted was *her*. She looked down at the tattered, dry garden below, recalling the story. "Do you remember the tale of Beltane?"

"Scarcely, but enough, I think," he responded.

"The story says that the garden died when the May Queen died. She could not love the man who had chosen her as his queen, and she could not have the man she truly loved." The reality of the queen's heartbreak—legend or not—Cara now understood intimately. How she must have suffered. "The man she had given both her body and heart to did not possess the same commitment beyond his desire for her." Cara's chest grew tight, a sense of hopelessness building with the sorrow in her heart. Her eyes were drawn to the craggy stones below, imagining the queen's lover finding her broken body.

Cara jolted when Edmund's hands cupped her shoulders.

"Is that what you think? That I cared for you only in the carnal sense?" he asked quietly.

She shrugged, her shoulders burdened already, without his pity as well.

"I did love you," he stated.

His confession, meant to appease, instead stabbed at her heart. "Did?" she repeated, jerking away from him. "'Tis a great comfort to me to know that now," she said, her voice filled with anger.

"Cara."

He started toward her and she stopped him with an upturned hand. Was there any reason now to tell him about his daughter? With the eyes of her heart at last opened, she would no longer pine away with silly romantic notions. "I would like to know, Edmund, in these past years, was there never a time you thought about us, how it was between us? And yesterday...I thought—" She shook her head. "Tell me that what happened yesterday meant nothing."

He looked away, a painful scowl marring his handsome face.

"Say it," she demanded, tired of being the only one who believed in what she felt even now, as much as three years ago.

A cold rush of wind swirled through the open window, picking up bits of straw and debris in its wake. The strong scent of roses grew intoxicatingly thick. Her desire for him blurred reality. She slipped her gown from her shoulders and stood in naked challenged before him. If lust was all they had between them, then she needed to know.

His head snapped up and his eyes roamed over her body, heating her blood.

"Is that why you came back? To satisfy your need once more, before I am wed? Why not admit it to me and to yourself? You dinna care for me, you've made it clear. What else is left?"

His lips pressed together in an angry line. "That is not fair, Cara. It is not your body I came for."

She laughed. "Then perhaps it is your noble intent to save the poor pagan girl you tarnished all those years ago? Who, in a weak moment, tempted you beyond your control?"

He was upon her in two strides, grabbing her arms. "Stop it," he growled. His eyes flashed with frustration, but something more.

"But I ask why anything should have changed? You never intended to come back for me, did you?" She thought all her tears had dried, but having him close, seeing the confusion in his eyes, renewed the pain.

"I did intend to return that night," he muttered through clenched teeth. "I wanted to. They threatened to harm you and your family, as well as mine. I did not leave quietly. My father would have chosen to keep the entire incident quiet, but Gregory admitted to his parents everything about us sneaking into the festival."

Cara searched his face, unsure if she could risk that he might be telling her the truth. "Would that not reveal Gregory's true character?" she asked.

"I was young, Cara. The statutes back then would have found us all in treason to the king. What I did was for the good of all. I wish you could believe me." His eyes filled with frustration, pleaded with her to understand.

Edmund's hands trembled as they touched her face, and

his stormy eyes held hers. "I prayed that one day you could forgive me. But yesterday, when you sent for me, it was as though time had stood still."

He drew her into his arms, hugging her so close Cara could barely breathe. His lips touched her bare shoulder. She felt his warm breath skitter across her flesh.

"God forgive me, I have always loved you, Cara."

She turned her head, meeting his hungry eyes. "Love me now, Edmund."

His manner, patient this time, aroused her in new ways. Thorough in his quest, he nuzzled the curve of her shoulder, brushing his mouth along her flesh, unhurried in his journey to her mouth. Needing to touch him, she drew his rain-soaked shirt over his head, revealing the hard, bronzed body of a man who worked in the sun. She ran her fingertips over his flesh, delighting that he welcomed her exploration. He threaded his hands through her hair, capturing her head as she leaned forward, leaving kisses on his chest, his throat, his chin.

"It is useless, Cara. I can no longer deny my love for you."

His mouth came down on hers, seeking, probing. She grew wet, restless, feeling his hard length beneath his breeches pressed against her stomach. "My Edmund," she whispered breathlessly, succumbing to another of his fiery kisses.

He knelt with her on the blanketed straw, nudging apart her thighs. His kisses snatched away every thought, creating a desperate ache inside her. Another breeze wafted through the room, bringing with it the promise of spring, of new life. Cara held him to her breast, closing her eyes as she savored his gentle touch.

He trailed hot kisses across the curve of her stomach, his

mouth brushing over the sensitive spot between her thighs. Her fingers kneaded his hair, the teasing of his tongue drawing her up, sending fire through her veins. He rocked back long enough to free himself, then covered her body with his, pushing his swollen cock deep into her ready warmth.

"Don't leave me," Cara sighed, drawing her knees upward, relishing the ease of their lovemaking. He withdrew, then pressed deeper, filling her.

"I am here, Cara. I am here."

She could not get close enough. She wrapped her arms around him, feeling his muscles bunching, flexing beneath her palms with each thrust. A sound escaped her lips as her body exploded in a burst of light and her soul was reunited with his, drawn together in a powerful release. Her fingers gripped his shoulders, helplessly drawn upward with his insistent frantic drive. Her body broke free once more and her soft cry joined his as he followed her. Cara held him close, welcoming the weight of him joined to her, wishing they could remain always as they were now.

Reality reminded her that was not possible.

He stood, drawing up his breeches, and took her hand, pulling her into his embrace, kissing her slow and tenderly. Then he sighed and stepped away. Cara hugged her arms around herself, chilled at his absence. He found her gown and held it out to her. "Though I question the wisdom of putting this on, for I am bound only to remove it shortly, I do not want you to catch a cold."

"Edmund." With his assistance, Cara tugged the gown over her head. "I must speak with you about a matter of great importance."

"Indeed, my love. You must get something to eat and then we must find a way out of this predicament." The corner of his mouth lifted in a grin. He rubbed his knuckle softly down her cheek. "You can tell me anything, Cara."

There was no easy way to convey her news, but if they were to start a new life together, he needed to know the truth. "We have a child, Edmund."

10

EDMUND STARED AT HER, LETTING THE WORDS register in his mind. "What did you say?" He was certain his ears were playing tricks on him.

"A child, Edmund. It was the night of the festival that she was conceived."

His arms went limp at his sides; he'd lost the ability to speak. Three years. A child of his would be three years old. He found his tongue and pushed through his confused thoughts. "What do you mean 'she'? I have a…a daughter?" An image of a blond-haired child flashed in his mind. "Why did you not write and let me know?"

"And who would I have trusted with such news, do you think? Your family? Your best friend, Gregory, perhaps? She'd have been taken from me, Edmund, and I would not have it. Besides, until this day I didn't suspect that you cared enough to want to know."

Edmund rested his head on his hand, his thoughts spinning. And yet they kept returning to one illuminating fact—he was a father. "Does your family know I am the father?"

She looked at her feet. "Nay, I told my mother you were to become a priest."

He felt a little nauseous. "I need to sit down." He realized that Cara was waiting, silently watching how he was taking the news. He reached up, drawing her down beside him. "Tell me everything, Cara. I want to know everything that I've missed."

"At first I denied the possibility for as long as I could, but when my body had changed to the point where I could no longer conceal it, I had to tell my family." She smiled as though lost in her thoughts. "I used to sit in my room and talk to her, tell her about her da. What a kind and generous, handsome man he was."

Edmund squeezed her hand. "Go on. How did your father take it?"

"As you might imagine. I inherited my coloring and my temper from him. I expected the disappointment. My da and I, the pair of us, can be stubborn, buttin' heads like two goats, but inside, we see things much the same. It was not a surprise when he suggested that I go to live with my married sister until the child came."

"The two of you live with Kiernan, then?"

Her gentle eyes welled. "Nay, the child thinks I am her relation and that Kiernan is her mother. It's what my father thought was best. He said no man would want a woman already with child unless she was a widow."

The things she'd suffered at his expense. Edmund closed his eyes, regretting the time he'd not been there when she needed him. "God in heaven," he whispered. He touched her chin, lifting her face to meet his eyes. "She doesn't know?"

Cara's smile trembled. "I named her Moyran. She acquired my fiery tresses, I'm afraid, but she has her father's beautiful eyes."

"Moyran." Edmund said the name aloud. He looked at Cara with new eyes, seeing a greater resilience in her than he remembered. He pulled her into his embrace. "I should have been there."

She caressed his cheek. "You are here now and that is all that matters."

She hugged him tight, pressing her face against his heart. Outside, the rain had stopped, and thin ribbons of dusky pink sliced across the gray skies. He'd told Gregory when he left that he was going to speak to her family, to see if they had heard from Cara. Despite how he felt, or these new circumstances that further gave cause to his fight, Edmund could not let Gregory marry Cara now. But he had no plan, no help from anyone. He closed his eyes and laid his cheek on her head, his heart crying out to the God of heaven to show him what to do.

"Edmund, there is more I must tell you, and it does my heart no good to be the bearer of such news."

"What is it, Cara?"

"It is about Gregory. I heard firsthand yesterday a conversation between him and his father."

Edmund pulled back, looking at her with a frown. "What need would you have to spy on them, Cara? Have you reason to be concerned for your safety?"

"That was not my intent. I was on my way to tell Gregory to his face that I canna marry him. 'Twas their conversation that stopped me, and I hid in the shadows, my heart fearful at what I heard."

She had his undivided attention.

"They were discussing using the marriage to take my father's land, without causing undue alarm to the rest of the tribes. Once settled, they planned to burn the villages and continue to little by little destroy what is left of our tribes in this area. I believe the way he spoke of it was to 'rid the crown of those Gaelic pains in the asses.'"

Gregory's behavior, his good-natured brother-to-brother act now made perfect sense. Edmund had been invited to the wedding to make it look normal, to show that Normans, like his father, we're in agreement with the union. But Edmund knew there was a personal jab involved, as well. Gregory had always been competitive, in the ways normal boys are, or so Edmund once thought. As Lord DeVerden used Edmund's father, often wielding that puritanical English birth over his Old English one, Gregory was now doing the same. If Edmund suspected correctly, Gregory didn't truly love Cara any more than he would any other daughter of one of the descendents of a Gaelic earl. She was a means to an end and that was all.

Edmund held her by the shoulders. The idea forming in his mind was likely the last act of a desperate man, and its outcome could be the death of them all. "I need you to go to your family. I would do so myself, but I fear that your father would not wait for an explanation, but tie me to a tree before I could open my mouth." He kissed her forehead. "Will he listen to you?"

Cara nodded. "I am his blood, his youngest daughter. Mother to the grandchild that has managed to charm him, even as I suspect I once did. He will listen."

"Then you must go to him, explain what you know. Tell him what you heard between Gregory and his father. I am going to find my father and explain my plan. With any luck he will lend me his help. Meet me at the bridge after the sun sets over the hill—you and as many kinsmen as your father can gather."

Worry lined her face. "What is going on in that head of yours, Edmund Collier?"

He realized then that he was asking her to trust him, to believe that he would not desert her again. "You'll not be rid of me this time. By Beltane, you will be my bride. I swear on my oath."

She nodded and pulled him close. "Aye, see that you don't falter on this, Edmund. Remember how many kin of mine will be waiting on the bridge to meet you."

Edmund's father kept his eyes focused on his clasped hands. He was still processing all that his son had just explained. "I am going to marry her this time, Father, and I intend to expose Gregory's plan."

"It is far too dangerous, Edmund." His mother cast a worried glance at her husband. "Tell him that he must give up this ridiculous notion. It is not worth our lives. If the king heard of it, it will be considered treason. That is what they told us before."

"Hush, woman. Let me think." His father stood and paced the room, as he often did when he was considering his options. "For too long the DeVerdens have held their blue-blooded aristocracy over those of us who have been here longer, keeping an eye on England's port investments. They've used the threat of treason to achieve their every purpose in parliament, and I for one am sick to death of it."

"William, listen to yourself."

"I am listening for once to my gut. Before the statutes, there was no dissention between the Old English and the Gaels. It was when the crown sent in their deputies, and appointed them landlords over us all, that the trouble began. Well, I say it's time they understood that they are not the only English voice in this county."

Edmund listened with pride to his father's words. "We hope to settle this amicably, Father, by asking DeVerden to forfeit his position in lieu of being tried by the entire tribe of Ormond, of the threats against their people."

His father looked at him. "It is true they acted on their own behalf, and not on that of parliament. That could place the entire county in danger of repercussion from the Gaelic tribes. You have the word of this Gaelic woman and one of the castle's maidservants?"

"She speaks the truth. I believe her," Edmund responded. "I have pledged my troth to her."

"They are but women, Edmund. Their word will not hold up in a jury of men."

"I have no intent of making either face any jury, Father." Edmund rose from the table and shrugged into his coat. "Gregory will hang himself by his admission. I only have to have more than one witness to that confession."

"And how will you do that?" his father asked.

"I know Gregory's weakness, Father—his pride. He would stop at nothing to prove how cunning he is. I thought we were once friends, but his friendship was only for what best served him. I know that now. He once held that power over my family, forcing me to make a decision that I did not wish to make. He thinks he has placed me again in a position where I have no choice but to watch him marry the woman I love. And then he'll destroy her people. But I am not going to walk away and let him get by with this a second time, and if you would choose to help me, to be my witness, then be at the castle study in thirty minutes' time. You shall have your proof, and straight from Gregory's lips."

★ ★ ★

Cara ran to Kiernan's house first, and along with Connor, the three gathered the children together and made the journey by cart to their parents' house. Her mother saw to the older children right away, tucking them into bed. Kiernan rocked her youngest in the same chair where their mother had rocked them. Cara's thoughts drifted to how she might look, rocking a child of her own one day.

"Now, give me one good reason, daughter, that I should believe a word that this Englishman has said to you?" Her father's voice, though he tried to control it, boomed within the walls of the small house, bringing Cara out of her reverie.

"Galen, shhh!" her mother cautioned, holding a finger to her lips.

Cara sat at the table across from her da, trying to ignore the sun lowering on the horizon. "Because I love him."

"And isn't that what put you in the mess you are in?"

"Galen," her mother scolded. "Watch your tongue."

"Aye, what's to say that he isn't using this to set a trap? Like sheep being led to the slaughter." He pinned Cara with a wary look.

Cara had not the mind-set of a Gaelic warrior; she did not devise plans on the field of battle, nor understand the politics between tribes or nations. She knew only two things. "He is the father of my child and wants to marry me. He has a plan to help us, Da. His only desire is to live peaceably as we once did, to make it safe for me—" she looked at Moyran, fast asleep on the cot "—and safe for his daughter." She motioned to everyone standing around the table. "Safe for all of us—my family and his."

Her da rubbed his thick red beard and scowled at his daughter. She knew when it came to those he loved, he never made hasty choices. She was the same. Cara knew he was going to agree.

"I will need to meet this young man who thinks he is going to marry my daughter."

Cara jumped up from her chair and rounded the table, hugging her father's neck.

"All right then, we have not much time," he said. "Conner, go fetch your cousin, tell him to ride up to his uncle's place." He took Cara by the hands. "You and the rest of the womenfolk will stay here in the village. I want you out of harm's way."

"Nay, my place is at Edmund's side," Cara pulled her hands from his and fisted them on her hips, prepared if she must to go toe-to-toe with her da.

Galen Ormond cast his wife a long-suffering look.

"She is your daughter, to be sure," she stated.

Cara hugged her mother. "It will be well, you'll see. Edmund can be quite determined."

Her da's shaggy red brow lifted as he looked up at her. "Aye, and haven't we been blessed with the proof of that, daughter? Come on then, we best be going if we're to meet this lad at the bridge."

It took some time and effort to calm down the crowd they'd managed to bring together in a short time. On horseback and on foot they came, rallying as they always did in the name of the tribe.

Cara listened as her da stood atop a tree stump and addressed the restless crowd. "Many of you know that my daughter was to be wed in a few days' time to the son of the duke of Ireland. Unfortunately, we have received news that prevents such a union from occurring."

"She would be better with me anyway, Galen," called a voice from the crowd. The villagers parted as the widower farmer, twice the size of her father, pushed his way through.

"Aye, 'tis probably true, Theron."

"Da!" Cara cried up to him.

Her father looked down at her and shrugged. "However, it is with happy tidings that I announce she will marry, to a man more suited in age. My apologies, Theron, but that is the way of it." The crowd laughed.

"Edmund, my future son-in-law that I've yet to meet, has asked us to gather at the bridge, where we will receive further instruction about his need for us this night." Galen climbed down off his crude platform and grabbed his daughter's hand as they made their way en masse to the bridge. "I do hope, daughter, you know what I am asking of these people."

Cara looked up at the moon, just two days before the full moon of Beltane. She thought of the night when they'd met, and the magic that was theirs in the secret garden. Where love took seed and blossomed, and was rekindled, surviving time and distance. If the gods and goddesses had guided them this far, they would see them through to completion.

11

"AH, I'D BEGUN TO WONDER IF YOU'D BECOME lost, as has my betrothed." Gregory offered a glass of whiskey to Edmund as he entered the study of the castle. It was just where Edmund thought he would be, near a warm fire, his whiskey close by. "We searched every room in the castle and there was no sign of her. You're sure you won't change your mind? It will take the chill off."

Edmund shook his head and made sure that the door to the study was left partially open. "I apologize, milord, that my news isn't more favorable."

Gregory raised his glass. "I commend you, milord. An entire day conversing with those Gaels takes great tenacity."

"There is some good news, however. Ormond indicated he would round up his kinsmen and join in the search." Edmund watched for Gregory's reaction.

The glass paused at his old friend's lips. "How many would you say that is?" he asked, not looking at Edmund.

He shrugged, enjoying watching Gregory squirm at the idea of hundreds of Gaels intruding on Dublin Castle. Even as they spoke, his father led a party notifying several parliament leaders of the unsanctioned plans of Lord De-Verden. Edmund had met with Cara and her father at the bridge, where he'd explained the situation and the hope for an amiable resolution. "You know better than I the numbers. This is not my area of expertise."

Gregory cast him a look and tossed back his drink. "Roughly more than three hundred at last count," he muttered, and poured himself another drink. Edmund waited, letting Gregory find his courage in the bottle.

"That seems to be quite a crowd of Gales, milord. Of course, with that many, they should be able to find your bride in no time." Edmund turned away to hide his smile. "Perhaps she's gone to visit a sick aunt."

Gregory paced the floor, swirling the amber liquid in his glass. "It occurs to me," he stated with some agitation in his voice, "that perhaps I should call off this wedding until the girl decides to show up."

"Or until she is found," Edmund interjected.

"All of our efforts should be focused on finding her." He slammed his glass on a table, picked it up again and refilled it, dismissing Edmund's comment.

"That would be the noble thing to do." He watched Gregory put away his third glass of whiskey.

"What we sure as hell do not need is a pack of unruly Gaels sneaking around Dublin Castle. Bloody sneaky bastards. They've caused more problems for England than I can count."

The corner of Edmund's mouth lifted in a smile. "Tell me something, Gregory. Do you have feelings for Cara? What I mean to say is, do you love her?"

He whirled on Edmund, surprise registered on his face. "Love?" He snorted. "Affection, perhaps, but I'm sure nothing like what you felt for her." He pointed his finger at Edmund, still clutching his glass.

"I guess that was my error, was it not?" Edmund said, baiting him.

Gregory's laugh was caustic. "Your problem, what has always been your problem, is that you are too naive. You see, Edmund, if you wish to succeed in any position of true value, the first rule is the realization that what is important in any relationship is not emotion, but power. Not how it benefits others, but how it benefits you."

He slapped him on the shoulder, and Edmund had to force himself not to swing his fist into his face.

"You see, that's always been the difference between you and me. Your father's like that, too, always looking for the greater good, what is best for all." Gregory tossed him a smirk.

Edmund's jaw ticked as he forced a smile, playing into his former friend's pompous, drunken rant. "Well, it's true you have me there, Gregory. I simply do not understand a word you've said. In fact, I think it's gone over this naive head of mine. Maybe you could put it in terms I will understand?" He held up the whiskey decanter and Gregory eyed him, but held out his glass, anyway.

"Take, for example, this wedding. It was not for love that I had planned to marry your lovely Cara."

"*My* lovely Cara?" Edmund asked quietly. He glanced toward the door, hoping that by now a contingency of witnesses were listening to this conversation. "What do you mean?"

"Don't you see it was a ruse, my dear Edmund? A political game of chess, meant to place the DeVerden dynasty and those who would support it in a better position to gain favor from the crown. Parliament cannot seem to agree on anything without first gnawing the life out of it. I found a way around that, and determined a much quicker means of ridding us of our Gaelic enemies was to first bed them. By marriage, I obtain Cara's dowry—a generous offering of her father's land to begin with, and the rest at his passing. It places us in a position of power. Under their own noses, they have let the enemy in, where it is far easier to find ways to dissolve villages, one by one, until they are no longer a meddlesome burden to England. And do not think that the English king would not reward handsomely whoever accomplished that feat."

"Get rid of those Gaelic pains in the ass to the English crown, eh?" Edmund stated quietly.

"Indeed. There, you do see. I underestimated you." Gregory raised his again-empty glass in salute.

"It is true, my old friend, that I am not as cunning as you are when it comes to politics, nor do we share the same view on relationships. And frankly, I am very proud to be just like my father in that respect." Edmund walked over to the study door and eased it open, inviting Cara, her father and his brother, several parliament members and Edmund's father and mother into the room. All eyes were on Gregory. "You were right about one thing, however. You did underestimate me."

Gregory's eyes darted from one face to another. "Where is my father? Where is Lord DeVerden?"

Edmund's father spoke. "He is being detained in his chambers after being shown mercy, until he can be tried by a just court of his peers."

"You cannot do that. He is the lord deputy of Ireland, appointed by the king."

"Yes, well, he chose to forfeit his title and rights when offered the option of a quick trial by the Ormond tribe waiting just beyond that door." William Collier glanced at Edmund with a smile. "Which leaves me as acting lord deputy until another can be appointed."

Cara moved to Edmund's side, putting her arm around his waist. Confused and angry, Gregory threw his glass at Edmund, who caught it in his hand. Their eyes met as Gregory was ushered from the room by two of the castle guards, now under the new lord deputy. "I fear you will be busy answering too many questions before parliament to attend our wedding, Gregory, but rest assured, we will be thinking of you."

Gregory left, screaming obscenities at the top of his lungs.

Edmund looked down at Cara and kissed her soundly, causing a rousing cheer from the villagers in the outer hall.

Edmund's mother walked over to Cara and took her hands. "As it happens, the abbot is due in tomorrow, and he thinks he is here to marry the lord deputy's son." She glanced at Edmund and raised a brow.

He smiled at his mother and pulled Cara into his embrace. "What say you, milady? It's rather whirlwind, and on the eve of Beltane, true, but would you consent to becoming my wife?"

"Whirlwind, Edmund Collier? I've waited three long years for that proposal. Yes, I will marry ye."

12

One month later

"LOOK AT THE FLOWERS!" MOYRAN CLAPPED her hands with glee.

Cara stepped from the tower stairs into the bright light of midday. She and Moyran had been on a walk, learning the names of flowers. As though by magic, bits of spring had come to the garden. Hidden beneath the brambles and brush, evidence of life had begun to blossom. She smiled, watching her daughter discovering tiny flowers in the grass.

"Time to go, Moyran." Cara felt a quickening inside and covered her stomach with her palm. She smiled, knowing that by winter Moyran would have a playmate. Cara reached up, plucking one of the perfect pink roses from above the gate, and took a last look at the garden where she'd found new life. A soft breeze lifted her hair, as though gently kissing her cheek, and in the wind a voice whispered.

"Thank you, my queen, for your heart that is true. You were my first, which now leaves two."

Cara ushered her daughter through the gate and looked up to see Edmund waving from across the field, where the labyrinth lay beneath the tall grass. The red-haired little girl ran to her father, squealing as he lifted her in his strong arms and twirled her around.

Cara quietly shut the gate, looked over her shoulder and smiled at the Green Man mask, with his laughing hollow eyes and secret smile.

★ ★ ★ ★ ★

PERFUMED PLEASURES
by
Charlotte Featherstone

PROLOGUE

England, 1856

HE WAS SWEATING, THE CRISP SHEETS CLING-
ing to his body as he tossed and turned. Agony rifled
through him, tore at his mind as he thrashed, trying to
free himself from the black web of sleep and nightmares.

With a groan, he fisted the sheets, anchoring himself
for what was to come, vignettes from the war, the ter-
rifying months spent in the trenches. The death that had
surrounded him. He smelled it: war, disease and those who
lay dying. He smelled his own skin, burning from smoke
and heat, mixed with the metallic tang of blood. He felt
the pain as if it were happening all over again, in real time,
and not just in a nightmare.

When would he wake up? When would the visions
and memories end? Or would they? Was he to endure this
nightly—the war? The horrors? The pain of what he had
done to others, and what they had done to him—all in the
name of God, queen and country?

"Give him something, damn you."

The gruff voice called to him from the deep recess of his

mind. He was awake now—but not really, for the memories continued to bombard him like the artillery fire that had once held him hostage in a trench. Mentally, he tried to reach out, to grasp for the owner of that voice, but he was sucked back into the war, with the sound of artillery fire whistling above his head, and the gurgling, rasping breaths of his best friend, who lay dying beside him.

Goddamn it, *no!* He didn't want to relive that memory, or the sound of his friend's last breath, or the way his sightless eyes stared up at him.

Thrashing his head from side to side, he tried to shake away the thoughts, pleading with his mind to purge the memory and spit out another, less painful, recollection of the hell he had endured otherwise known as the Crimean War.

He felt the eyes of the two men standing beside the bed watching him. One detached and clinical, studying the lunatic. One horrified, realizing what his coin had purchased—a ruined body and broken mind.

"If you do not relieve him of this…this pain, then by God, I will."

"He must be awake to take the laudanum, my lord."

"I will not see him this way, goddamn it. *Do something!*"

His uncle, and the only avenging angel he had known since before he had gone off to war. He was here now, in his room, witnessing his weakness. He would see the extent of his wounds. His once fit body withered on the left side. He would know that inside that wasted body was a spirit and mind just as shattered.

He had always admired his uncle. Always sought his approval—his respect and admiration. To be like this now, weak and mewling, and succumbing to a nightmare, was more than humiliating. It was degrading. Impossible. Not for the first time, he cursed the army surgeon who had dragged him from the burning trench.

"Let me die," he had begged the surgeon and his fellow soldiers as they lifted him onto a litter. It had been the pain talking, the pride. He knew the extent of his injuries, felt the agony burning beneath his skin. He hadn't wanted to return to his uncle and Fairfax House a failure.

They hadn't listened, of course, and in the end, he had lived, a fright. A beast, like something out of Mary Shelley's book. A living piece of meat no more alive than a corpse.

"Give him something, Doctor," his uncle growled. "For God's sake, man, have a heart."

If he could weep, he would. But his one good eye no longer would—or could—produce tears. He was no longer in pain—not the physical kind, at least. Laudanum served only to numb his mind and thoughts and subdue the sinister nightmares that always came to him.

Beside him, he was aware of the doctor rummaging through his leather satchel, while outside, the wind howled through the leafless branches, echoing what he himself longed to do. Cry to the sky and God and curse his own injustice.

The winters had been unbearable in the trench, and the sweat on his body immediately cooled, making him shiver, taking him back to those cold, miserable days when his fingers were nearly frostbitten, and his toes utterly numb inside his snow-and-mud-caked boots.

Mercifully, the doctor's thick finger was thrust into his mouth and the bitter taste of opium paste was put under his tongue. It was not long before the images of war—the dead soldiers, the wounded friends, the cries for help—receded.

In his nightmare, he stood whole, unmarked, on the field of Balaklava, a disembodied voyeur, as he watched the last few scenes play out.

And then he saw her, his saving grace. The image that had kept him alive while in the trench. *Catherine.* The lovely girl who had grown up to be everything he desired in a woman. The woman he had loved for years. The woman who was not meant for the nephew of an earl, but for the heir—his cousin.

The February winds gusted once more, rattling the double glazed windows. Spring would be here soon, and so would Catherine Tate. He only prayed that when she arrived, he would be dead, and her memories of Joscelyn Mallory would be the stuff of dreams, not the nightmare he had become.

1

LAMB WAS BEING SERVED FOR DINNER, AND Catherine could not help but think how symbolic it was, for she felt rather like a sacrificial animal. But then, the springs spent with her parents at Fairfax House usually made her feel that way. But never more so than tonight, with Edward's lascivious leer focused on the mounds of her breasts.

Every spring it was much the same. She and her parents spent every May at the estate. Her parents and the earl had picked that month because Edward was home from school then, and they thought it a delightful thing for the two of them to become better acquainted during their month-long sojourn to Fairfax House.

How she loathed these visits. Edward was always hovering by, watching her. This year, they had arrived a fortnight early, and for the past weeks she had been forced to endure her intended's brazen glances and whispered innuendos. After two weeks she was utterly repulsed by him. What it would be like after years of marriage to the man?

Glancing away from Edward and shoving aside her morose thoughts, Catherine gazed out of the window to the garden, which had once thrived with life, but now sat dormant and fallow. She would be mistress of this manor soon. In a week, to be precise. It was her solemn vow to restore the beauty of the garden—and hide in it, far away from her lecherous husband.

"To a long and happy union," Lord Fairfax called, raising his goblet of wine. "We have waited a long time for this year, have we not?"

Catherine's parents—poor, but of noble blood—nodded enthusiastically. Indeed, they had waited for what seemed like forever for their only daughter to grow up and rescue them from genteel poverty.

A realist, Catherine understood the nature of this union. It was a trade of money for bloodlines and beauty. The current Lord Fairfax was only half a generation from the working class. His mother, a blacksmith's daughter, had been fortunate enough to catch the roving eye of the eccentric fifth Lord Fairfax. In a union of lust, Fairfax had married the blacksmith's daughter, and brought shame— and an astonishing amount of common red blood—to the union. As a consequence, the current Lord Fairfax desired true blue blood for his continuing dynasty, choosing his own wife from a noble family. His son, Edward, was to do the same, thus ensuring the future Fairfax lineage and their blacksmith ties would be diluted.

It was her blue, but rather aenemic, blood that would provide the future earls of Fairfax with a credible pedigree. Catherine knew that she was considered pretty and desirable, but her lack of fortune made it difficult to form alliances with suitable lordlings. But Lord Fairfax had "all the blunt in the world" or so her father had claimed, and he had all but purchased her years ago, to be the plaything for his spoiled, cold son.

Edward. How she reviled that she was to become his. She had always been able to spurn him, to be granted however small a pardon from his advances. But those reprieves were lost now. She was to marry Edward, and become the future Lady Fairfax. Her body would belong to him, and she would be forced to endure his attentions, or suffer the very real consequences—debtors prison for her parents.

It was no secret that Lord Fairfax had paid off all her father's debts, both the legitimate ones incurred by the estate they lived in, and the debts of honor that her father had brought upon himself by his incessant gambling.

Catherine knew her role in this bargain. She had been sold to the Fairfax dynasty because she was an aristocrat whose family found themselves down on their luck. As a young girl, she had been told that her beauty and her body were her greatest assets, and that many a man would pay to possess her. She knew then that would be her fate. That some man would purchase her. Unfortunately, it had been Lord Fairfax whose purse opened the widest. And his son could not wait to paw his possession.

Edward had been trying for years to get his hands, and whatever else he desired, up her skirts. The fact had always revolted her. She hadn't wanted Edward, despite the fact that he was handsome and athletic. Her heart belonged to the other male who resided at Fairfax House—Edward's cousin. Joscelyn.

An image of a dark-haired, wild-eyed Joscelyn came to her, and she felt her skin heat and flush with desire. A yearning she tried to keep hidden from those at the table. But Edward, with his steady gaze lingering upon her, noticed immediately. The smile, and the gleam in his eye, told her that he believed her blush to be the product of his undivided attention upon her person—and her breasts, which would not be subdued in the low-cut gown her mother had insisted she wear.

She was not an innocent—not any longer. Once, she had been, but then one night in her bedroom, during those past springtime visits, Joscelyn had awakened her to the delights of being a woman. He had stripped her of her innocence. No woman could ever claim to be innocent after having her body thoroughly kissed and touched. No woman could declare inexperience after allowing a man to explore her sex with his lips and tongue—to have Joscelyn, thick and hard, moving inside her, claiming her body and soul.

Joscelyn had done that. And she had been ruined for anything else. Anyone else. It was only him she desired. That night three years ago, still lived on so vividly in her mind. It was the night before he'd left for the Crimean War. She had been in love—still was—and her virginity was the only thing of value she had to give her lover before he went off to war. It was her gift to give, and Catherine knew she did not want the selfish Edward to be bestowed it. So she had given her body and her maidenhead to Joscelyn, despite the fact that she knew Fairfax had purchased it for his son.

While Joscelyn might have awakened her to the delights of pleasure, Edward made those delights repugnant. His hands were not loving and teasing, but groping and pinching. His breath in her ear was not sweet and stimulating, but panting and sour. And his words…they were not the sensual words Joscelyn had used, but were coarse and guttural. She did not feel adored in Edward's arms. She felt like a doxy he had bought. And when she sat down and truly thought it through, that was what she was.

"What a desolate little copse," her mother exclaimed as

she tracked Catherine's gaze. "I'm quite certain my daughter will have it turned around in no time."

The earl snorted in disbelief. "Cursed, that garden is."

"Nonsense," her mother scoffed.

The earl straightened in his chair. "After all these years, my lady, have you not heard the story of that garden?"

"How could you have missed it?" Edward muttered. "He regales every guest with the morose tale."

Her mother flushed and glanced her way. They knew of the curse, but conversation had lapsed, and there was now an uncomfortable silence, and her mother couldn't bear it. So, to put an end to it, she said, "My lord, won't you tell us the tale. The sunset is upon us and I can't help but think it the saddest little coppice on earth."

The earl turned in his chair and gazed out the window. Behind him, the sun was setting, washing the garden in a palette of brilliant oranges and fuschias—colors so warm, and so different from the cold bracken and tangled brown vines that littered the stone walls.

"Well," he said, clearing his throat. "Fairfax House has been passed down through the family, and it's been said that the garden was once a fine place to have, err, a tryst."

Fairfax's face and jowls immediately reddened. "Begging yer pardon, Lady Tate," he murmured, when Catherine's mother squealed in shock and covered her throat with a pale hand. Edward's leer became more obvious as he picked up his wineglass and peered at Catherine over the rim of the crystal.

"Indeed, I'm quite certain it is," he murmured. "A fine place, indeed."

Balling her fist on her lap beneath the table, Catherine fought to show no outward signs that she was inwardly fuming. Edward always accosted her in her garden. It was there in her secret hideaway that he was particularly beastly. All hands and teeth—and not one concern for her good name, or maidenly pleas that he stop.

"I believe I've heard some talk in the village about it?" her father asked. She noticed how he was settling her mother's nervous, and thoroughly offended, feathers. They may be poor as church mice, but Lady Tate was as proper as any duchess.

Served her right, Catherine thought peevishly, for tempting the earl into conversation.

"Oh, aye, the village story." Fairfax nodded, and began to cut up his lamb. "It is said that this very copse was the scene of the May Queen's fatal demise, and the war between the Winter King and the Green Man. 'Course, that's just the villagers way of explaining the death of winter, and the life that comes with the spring."

"You'll have to excuse Father," Edward drawled. "He is not the most scintillating storyteller."

Fairfax frowned, but did not reprimand his son. For all intents, it was Edward who ran the house and the estate. He was the true earl; the man sitting at the head of the table was just an ornament. What her parents didn't realize yet was that Fairfax was merely a puppet on his son's string.

"The May Queen," Edward began, "was beautiful, but then most May Queens are, are they not? Men, of course, were drawn to her and the bounty of her—" Edward paused, flicked his gaze over Catherine's body, then wet his lips with the tip of his tongue "—overflowing basket, shall we say."

Her mother's face went florid, and Catherine watched as her father wrapped an arm around her shoulder. This was the sort of man her parents were tying her to. This crass, ignorant...

A movement in the shadows drew her gaze, making her forget about her fiancé and how she loathed him. There was no one there when she looked toward the curtains, but the gentle swinging of the tasseled tie told her someone had been there.

"She was to wed the Winter King," Edward continued, "who as you know is the ruler of everything cold and dark. They say she felt some measure of affection for the king, as well as a good dose of desire." Edward met his gaze. "She was a lovely spring maiden, waiting to be plucked by Winter's cold hand."

"And then?" her mother asked.

"Well, the Winter King was well known for his appetites. He was relentless in taking what he wanted to satisfy his needs. But he would not be put off. He had vowed to possess the queen, and nothing would stop him—not even the queen herself."

Catherine knew that Edward was no longer speaking of the fabled Winter King, but himself. And she was the poor queen whose fate hung in the balance.

"Despite his vow, and ardent attentions, the queen remained—" Edward looked at her once more "—aloof, we shall say, afraid of her own passions, and desires for the king. But the king knew just how to unlock the queen's maidenly protest and claim her virtue."

Catherine snorted, and her mother shot her a look of warning.

"There was a man, however, who claimed to be able to coax forth the May Queen's passion. This man who was ruler of all that is warm and light. He took pity on the queen's plight. It was rumored that this man watched her night after night in the secret garden, spying upon the queen and her ardent suitor. Soon, any pity he had turned to lust and jealousy. One night, he gathered the nerve to visit her in her secret hideaway."

"Oh, my," her mother murmured in a breathless whisper. Edward raised his goblet of wine and sipped from it, prolonging the tension, and drawing her mother into the sensual world he was attempting to weave.

"The Green Man, herald of the spring, claimed the king's woman. The queen spurned her king, but the king learned of their affair and cursed their love and the garden where their sin was committed. In a duel, the Winter King imprisoned the Green Man in the garden, forever cursed to watch over the empty, dying place where his betrayal had taken place."

"And the queen?" Catherine could not help but ask. "What of her?"

True to Edward's form, he smiled, showing all his teeth, a predator in a immaculately cut coat and snow-white cravat. "Despondent and ruined, the queen, unable to touch her beloved, ended her life in the garden, taking with her all its beauty and vibrancy. Then the king's retribution was complete, for the Green Man was forced to forever see the death and destruction his wanton passion had wrought."

"You have forgotten the ending."

The voice was deep and velvety, disembodied as it came from the shadows. Catherine's pulse raced, her palms sweating. It was Joscelyn's voice. He was here. Hidden. She'd known he had arrived home from the war that past fall, but she had not seen him, despite the fact that she had been at Fairfax House for the past two weeks.

"Ah, my cousin, the resident ghost here at Fairfax House. Will you not come out and take dinner with us?"

The silence was deafening, the air tainted with menace.

There was an underlying tension between Edward and his cousin, made all the more pronounced by the gloating expression on her fiancé's face.

Why would Joscelyn not come out? Especially after how they had left off? Perhaps he had forgotten their forbidden night of pleasure? Mayhap his affections were engaged elsewhere. The thought made Catherine's heart plummet. If anything, her affections had only grown. She loved him more than ever before, and the thought that he had forgotten her and moved on tore at her. The memories of their shared past and that night of passion were what kept her going in the face of becoming Edward's wife.

"You will forgive my nephew," Lord Fairfax grumbled. "He is recently returned from the Crimean, a—"

"Monster," Edward supplied, at the same time his father provided "wounded soldier." Despite her resolve not to, Catherine gasped, garnering a pointed look from Edward. Joscelyn had been wounded?

"My cousin has failed to tell you the most interesting part of the villagers' tale," Joscelyn continued from his hiding spot. "It is said that though darkness prevails in the garden, the Green Man knows that with the awakening of passion, the fires of love can prevail, burning through the cold darkness at least for a time. It is the Green Man's belief that if he can summon three lovers into his garden—lovers who possess the same passionate intensity that he and his queen once shared—the curse will be broken, and the garden again will flourish, and he and his lover will be reunited in another realm for all eternity. It's said, and believed, that the Green Man will fight his way back, and take his lady love from the vile king."

And then she heard it, as if he had whispered it in her ear, the tale she'd been told as a child about the Green Man and the May Queen. *And each spring on the eve of Beltane, it is said that you can hear his voice on the wind over the garden, singing his song of woe. "I am the wind, softly caressing her hair, the breath near her ear whispering words of passion she yearns to hear..."*

The curtains swished once more, and she saw the back of him—broad and tall—as he moved away. Once more she heard a verse from the Green Man's poem.

*"I am the sigh as she offers me all
and with no reservation I answer her call."*

"Joscelyn," she whispered to herself, "call me into the garden, and I will follow you. I will give you all. Anything you ask."

"The Green Man will not win her," Edward said through clenched teeth. When his gaze fixed on her, there was a warning in his blue eyes. "All this talk of the May Queen is rather fitting, is it not? The Eve of Beltane is a week away." Edward glared at her. "'Tis a perfect time for our nuptials, and perhaps an evening spent toiling in the garden."

She could not tear her eyes from the spot where Joscelyn had disappeared. If she were an innocent maiden, given to fantasy and fairy tales, she might have admitted that the story of the queen and the Winter King and Green Man was a startling parallel to her relationship with Edward and Joscelyn.

But she was not a silly young girl, given to fantasy. She was a realist, and the reality was the Winter King was going to be her husband. But in her dreams, which were hers alone, Joscelyn would be her Green Man. And in the garden, he would awaken her to passion.

2

FROM HIS HIDING SPOT AMONG THE SHADOWS, Joscelyn watched Catherine at the dining table. She smiled at something his uncle said, and she blinded Joscelyn with her radiance and beauty. It was not the first time he had been rendered to such a state by her. No, she had dazzled him before, blinding him to everything but her.

He had thought of her every day and every night. It was memories of her that had kept him alive. After their night together, he had known that he would love her forever, regardless of the fact that she was intended for his cousin. Not the bastard of Fairfax House.

Joscelyn had wondered, during many long sleepless nights, if things would have been different if his mother, the earl's sister, had not run off with a stable hand and gotten herself pregnant. Would it have mattered if his father had married her, or would the stain of his birth not be removed because he was born of a working-class man? Joscelyn didn't think so. Breeding was everything in their world, and he lacked it.

When he had arrived at Fairfax House—an orphan, filthy and starving—he had been but a boy. His uncle, bless his soul, had known that. Had taken him in despite how his mother had disgraced her brother and her family.

The earl of Fairfax had not seen a bastard with hungry gray eyes, but a child. A human being who suffered.

Unfortunately, the earl's humanity was not bequeathed to the son and heir. The man who would possess the woman that Joscelyn wanted above all others was a soulless bastard. Perhaps not in truth, but most definitely in action.

The clanging of silver pulled him from his memories, and he saw an army of servants exit the kitchen, their arms laden with silver dishes and tureens. He ignored the startled glances from the staff who carried in supper. He was used to their stares, their hidden curiosity. When would they become used to his habits of hiding among the shadows? he wondered. Or was he so monstrous that none would find themselves inured to his face?

Turning, he caught a glimpse of himself in the mirror. His right side was cast in blackness, leaving his wounded left side glimmering in the mirror's reflection. Studying the mottled skin, Joscelyn traced the web of melted flesh that ran down his cheek and jaw to his neck. There was little feeling left. Most of the skin was thickened and numb, except for one area on his neck, which was about the size of his thumbprint. That spot was highly sensitive. Strange how his burned flesh had healed that way.

Looking up from the burns, he focused on the eye patch. He half expected to see his dark eyes staring back at him, but he had only one eye now, and it was awash in shadow. Only the black eye patch could be seen. He didn't have the nerve to peel it back and study what lay beneath it. He already knew. His eyelid had been fused shut after the flame had exploded in the trench. His skin had literally melted, blinding him permanently. The flesh around the eye was as puckered and webbed as that on his throat. No, he was a hideous monster, skulking in the darkness.

It had taken him months to accept what he was now. Even longer to come to terms with the fact that he was going to live—with this face and body. Would Catherine accept him, the new Joscelyn Mallory, or would she run screaming from him? Would he see revulsion in her pretty blue eyes, replacing the passion and desire he had once seen shining in them?

As he stared at himself, his mind drifted back to another time, when he had not looked like this. A time when he'd been young and carefree. *Wild. Reckless.* He could almost see her staring at him, and suddenly, the mirror became a portal to the past.

Pale blue eyes, the color of crystals, flashed innocently at him from behind a crimson silk curtain that billowed in the summer breeze. He remembered that day, the first time he had seen her, sitting on the window bench in the conservatory of his uncle's home. He'd been an inexperienced lad then, yet he'd recognized the charged sexual tension coiling in his body the instant his gaze found hers peeking at him from behind the crimson silk. With a glance she had given him life. A reason for existing.

She had been so beautiful, so elegant. So full of ladylike charm.

So bloody out of his reach—and still was, even to this day. But that hadn't stopped him from wanting her, despite what he was—a commoner. A soldier.

Balling his fists, he tried to forget the first time he had touched her. The feel of her beneath his hands had made all the anguish he had ever experienced melt away in a moment that was hallowed and beautiful. The splendor of that first stroke stole his breath, made his fingers tremble as they carefully, reverently, skated along her pale skin, which felt like satin beneath his roughened fingertips. The heat of her still burned. So, too, did the memory of her moist breath against his skin as he traced the contours of her mouth. A mouth that had been designed for carnal pleasures of every kind.

Even now, three years later, his body still ached, still felt hot as he remembered the image of her. In his mind, he had touched her lips, the length of her throat, the curve of her breast.

She had trembled as their gazes met and held, shivered the same way she had when she had been beneath him, and he had been buried deep inside her. In those silent seconds, he had absorbed her into every corner of his being, just as he had that night he'd taken her innocence.

She was still there, in every facet of his existence, in the darkest corner of his soul. She was still his lover in the secrecy of darkness and dreams.

But she belonged to another now.

Turning from the mirror, he studied the guests gathered at the table. He would not sit with them. Would not endure the stares and silent horror. He would not ruin this moment of watching her, undetected.

No, he could not sit at the table, and see her with *him*.

She was his cousin's betrothed. The *titled* cousin, the rightful heir—yet it had been so long since Joscelyn thought of her as Edward's.

Even now, he wanted to brand her, to make her remember what it was like to lie in *his* arms, to feel *his* hands on her body, to remind her of the pleasures they had found in each other.

He could still taste the sweetness of her lips, her breasts

and silken navel, her woman's musk as it covered his mouth. The sound of her coming, the cries of release still filled his ears, and the feel of her body opening, accepting him and molding around him gave him a rush so primal he shook from it.

The memory lingered, and just as he managed to tear his gaze away from her lovely profile, she glanced up to where he stood, concealed in shadows. He moved. She caught the play of his silhouette against the curtain, followed it until the candlelight revealed him. His back was to her, but he allowed himself the illicit pleasure of glancing over his shoulder and looking at her—careful to show her the side of him that had been left untouched by the war.

He knew his uncle had told Catherine and her parents that he had been wounded in war. Edward, ever the callous bastard, had rejoiced in correcting his father. He was not just ruined. He was a monster. He had heard her gasp then. Studied her now, as she watched him.

Was it worry he saw in those crystal blue eyes, or was it desire?

Months ago, he had prayed for death. He hadn't wanted her to see him like this. But now that she was here, male possession began to rule him, to the exclusion of all rational thought. She was his, not Edward's. Joscelyn was still living, albeit a shell of his former self. He existed in darkness and shadow, but he was still breathing. And now that death seemed impossible, he needed her to bring him back to life. She belonged to him, and he would do anything to get her back. And what was more, she wanted him, too. She did not want the heir, she wanted the bastard cousin, and the pleasure she had tasted in his arms.

And he would begin tonight, by luring her to the

garden, where he would touch her, and bring his lips to the expanse of her creamy breasts, which taunted him even now.

"Come into the garden," he murmured, as he took his leave from the shadows, "where our love and passion may be reborn."

It had been years since she had allowed herself to think of *him*. Almost a lifetime since she had permitted herself to recall his face, his voice, his hands traversing her body, awakening her to carnal desires she never could have guessed lurked within her.

After he had left for the Crimea, Catherine was forced to reconcile herself to the fact that there could be nothing between her and Joscelyn. Her parents' precarious financial situation depended upon her marrying Edward, not his cousin. Joscelyn was a soldier, not a titled gentleman. While his income might be enough to keep her, he could not afford to pay her parents' debts. She knew her duty, and was resigned to it.

Yet here she was, recalling him in her mind, naked and godlike; with sculpted muscles and tawny skin that glistened in the sun and moonlight, and felt smooth and enticing beneath her fingertips and lips.

It had been a day much like this very afternoon that had just past, when she saw him for the first time. His black hair had shone in the sunlight, the gentle breeze ruffling through the locks he wore long to his shoulders. The heat of the midsummer's day had been scorching, and having just come from the pond, he had been shirtless. The muscles in his back and shoulders rolled with his gait, capturing her careful scrutiny. The butterflies in her stomach had circled madly as her gaze lowered, settling on his taut buttocks in riding britches.

He hadn't known she was there. But she had hidden behind the curtain in the conservatory more times than she dared admit, just watching him, feeling her body stir to life. She had been innocent, full of curiosity and wonder. The feelings within her when she looked upon him were so strong, a force she could neither endure nor escape.

"I want to kiss you all over. I want to feel you shudder and come...." Joscelyn's whispered words burned in Catherine's belly, filling her with a warmth that curled low in her womb, making it ache until she dropped her arm and pressed her hand to her stomach, trying to stave off the blossoming hunger that began to gnaw at her.

Everyone, including Edward, was busy eating, and thankfully paying her no attention as she stared off at the place where Joscelyn had been. In these stolen moments, Catherine recalled the first tentative touches of Joscelyn's fingers against her skin. Soft and fluttering, like the wings of a butterfly, he had smoothed his fingertips down her throat. She had prayed for more of his hands, for the glimpse of pleasure he had slowly taught her.

He had known what she desired. And he had given it to her.

The heat of his unhurried caresses had wrapped her up in a cloud of sensuality. From her ankles to her calves he had grazed his lips along her skin, whispering endearments as his hand sought her core.

She was warm now, as if he were actually here. Her womb was heavy with anticipation; her breasts felt painfully confined behind her corset and tight bodice, aching to be set free into his waiting palms. Struggling for air, she began to breathe faster, felt her breasts rising and falling as the sensation all but engulfed her. She was breathing too fast. She must stop these memories, but they would not be held back. Suppressed as long as they had been, they now ran unbridled through her thoughts.

His breath against her neck, his lips gliding between the valley of her breasts… She felt her nipples bead beneath her corset. *"Let me take you into my mouth…."* Her womb actually clenched as she remembered the first draw of his mouth on her nipple.

The rhythm of her blood sang in her ears until it was all she could hear. His touch had been dizzying, his allure addicting. She had fallen so hard for his gentle, yet persuasive seduction. Three years later, she could still feel his hands on her body as if she had just risen from his bed.

"Well, then," Fairfax grumbled as he pushed his empty plate aside. "Shall the gentlemen retire to the smoking room?"

Catherine began to rise. "I believe I shall take a turn outside. It's a lovely spring evening, and I'm rather warm."

"Going to the garden then, eh?" Fairfax laughed. "I suppose I shall have to finally see to restoring it. I haven't done so because it seemed a hopeless business. Until you started coming for your visits no one even went beyond the gate. I've always chosen to entertain in the formal gardens, by the orangery. I guess I never saw it as something worthy of investing my money in." Fairfax turned in his chair and gazed once more out the window. "Seemed like such a melancholy place. But if you wish it, my dear, then it is yours. A wedding gift from your father-in-law, and a sizable draft to begin the repairs."

Regardless of her thoughts about Edward, she really did hold some affection for the earl. Fairfax was a generous, kind man, and she smiled—a truly genuine one—and said,

"Thank you, my lord. I will treasure this gift, and the memories of this garden."

Edward scoured her with his eyes from head to toe, but said nothing. Did he know of her memories, or did he assume that the memories she spoke of were of the frenzied pawings he forced upon her? In his arrogant mind, did he believe that she actually enjoyed his attentions? Or did he suspect that she was heading for the garden in search of Joscelyn?

It was dark now, the moon obscured by clouds. She was thankful for that bit of kindness, for neither Edward nor her parents would be able to see her stealing across the grass to the wooden door of the garden. She would be alone there, able to meet with her lover in relative secrecy.

Lifting the gate latch, she let herself slip into the garden, which was dormant and brown. She did not need light to recall its dismal plants and neglected shrubs. Not even the fountain worked anymore. It was filled with moss, and the stone around it was cracked, choked with a twining weed that was the only green present in the garden.

Sitting on the edge of the fountain, Catherine sighed deeply. She had no idea if he would come to her. Would he respect the fact that she was to marry Edward, and keep his distance? He hadn't before, when he had slipped into her room and made love to her. He hadn't cared that she was betrothed to someone else, and neither had she. She had wanted Joscelyn. Still did. In her heart, she belonged to him.

Looking up at the black velvet sky, she indulged in something she hadn't in years—she prayed to God to make it possible for her to have Joscelyn. She pleaded, bargained with her maker. She would never ask for anything else, if he would but grant her this one wish. And then, as if he were listening, she felt something solid and warm press next to her.

The familiar scent of Joscelyn rushed through her body. Spice, and man. The memory of that scent clinging to her skin and bed linen the morning after their lovemaking was still ingrained in her memory. She had smelled her sheets, touched her body, her fingers taking the same path over her curves that his had, as she relived the magic of the night before.

"Cathy." His pet name for her was a cross between a plea and a benediction.

Turning to gaze up at him she could make nothing out in the pitch darkness, just the shape of his shoulders, and the heat of his body so close to hers. "You're alive," she whispered, reaching out to touch him. "I prayed for you every day." She was overcome, her eyes welling with tears. She had never allowed herself to think of him at war. The danger. The possibility he might never return. All her repressed anxieties and fears came rushing through, and she choked on a sob and turned her face away. He was alive, and he was here—with her.

"Alive," he said, cupping her chin in his hand. "Very much alive, and returned to you."

How she wished it could be so. He was alive, and returned, yes. But to her? No, never to her. She was Edward's.

"How lovely you are," Joscelyn murmured. "I watched you at the supper table, marveling at the fact that you have only grown more beautiful." His voice was deeper now, perhaps a bit gruffer, but the sound of it dampened her petticoats, made the petals of her sex throb. "I've wondered what you would look like, all grown into womanhood, and what a delight it is."

Catherine gasped as his hand, warm, rough, pressed

against the exposed flesh of her breasts. "So beautiful, so lush and womanly. Beyond anything I dreamed of those long, lonely nights I spent making love to you in my mind."

"Joscelyn," she cried, and she heard him inhale, felt his body press into hers.

"Cathy." Then he lowered his head to her chest and kissed her breasts. His thumb hooked beneath her bodice and, with a firm tug, her breasts popped free. "I wanted to do that from the moment I saw you leave your room in this gown. I wished it was for me that you had bought this. I wished you had worn it tonight for my pleasure."

"I did," she moaned, raking her fingers through his hair as his mouth, hot and wet, descended between her breasts. Impatient, she cupped one of her breasts, which was heavy with desire, and lifted it to Joscelyn's mouth. The nipple was beaded, aching, and when the tip of his tongue flicked it, she tossed back her head. When his hand replaced hers, and his mouth drew her in deeply, she pulled at his hair, and closed her eyes, allowing herself just to feel. To indulge.

"I have missed the taste of you on my tongue. The sight of you—of these," he groaned as he buried his face in the valley of her breasts. His cheek was rough, arousing, against her soft skin. It reminded her of how masculine he was, and how womanly she was. Where she was soft, he was hard, unyielding, and she took comfort in it, the strength of him.

"I missed this body." His hands were traversing her waist, down to her hips and thighs. "The way it clung to mine, taking my cock in so deep."

Edward said that word, and it always disgusted her. But the way Joscelyn murmured it was heady, evocative. She wanted more of his illicit words in the dark, whispered seductively in her ear, for they were stimulating to her, nearly as much so as his touch.

"Have you thought of it, Cathy, the way my cock and body pleasured you?"

"Every day," she whispered, "Every night as I lay awake in bed and touch myself, wishing it was you."

He claimed her mouth then in a hard, consuming kiss. He stroked her breasts, cupping and squeezing as his tongue searched deeply between her lips. The kiss was not like the ones he had given her before—soft, lulling, enticing. This was a kiss that was commanding. Claiming, and she was powerless against it. She didn't want it to end, only wanted to lie back on the stone, her breasts bared and her body open to him, welcoming him home.

As if he read her mind, he pushed her back, his body, long and fit, pressed overtop hers. His hands, trembling and gruff, pulled at her bodice, tugging it down to her waist, so that her breasts were fully naked and ready for him.

"I can think of no better way to become reacquainted," he whispered to her, "although my body and heart have never forgotten you. A true gentleman, I know, would renew his acquaintance over tea. But it's not tea I want to sip at, it's you, it's the honey between your thighs, and the berries of your nipples."

"Yes." She cupped her breasts in both hands, offering herself up to him. "I need to feel you, to know you're alive and well, and here with me, and not just another dream."

He was looking down upon her, she knew that much. She could sense his wild dark eyes roving over her body, attempting to see her through the darkness. She wished she could see him, could look upon the face she had loved for so long.

Moving to touch him, to cup his face in her palm, she found her wrist shackled, brought up high over her head, and a deep *no* echoed.

She made to protest, but he cut her off as he began suckling her breasts and raising her skirts with impatient hands. Any protest she might have made was lost when she felt the first brush of Joscelyn's fingers against her core.

"Oh, God," he whispered, "you're so wet. I can't think of anything else but getting inside you and reclaiming you for myself."

"I want you. I always have."

"I should be taking my time with you, but I can't. I'm the soldier returned, ready to pillage and conquer."

"Perhaps I am ready for that, Joscelyn. For you."

He slid lower down her body, his long fingers petting her sex. "Then take me, Cathy."

And then she was lost, for Joscelyn's fingers were playing and pulling at her nipples while his tongue parted her sex. He lapped at her, and she moaned. She had loved when he had done this before. He was gifted with his tongue, patient with her and her needs. The rhythm was slow, unhurried, and she touched his shoulders, raked her fingers through his hair, and reveled in the fact that she was here, in her secret garden, with Joscelyn pleasuring her in the most base way.

"Yes," she whispered, lifting her hips to meet his slashing tongue. "Take all of me, Joscelyn." *Pillage. Conquer. Just don't leave me again.*

He didn't think he could wait to slip his cock into her. The noises she was making made him crazed. He'd been too long without a woman. Every woman he had taken while away in the war he'd pretended was Catherine. To be here with her now, to feel her slick folds against his tongue and his ruined cheek, made him feel more alive than he had in years.

She didn't know what he was—scarred and broken. Right now, right here, he was just a man. Her lover. He knew that at some point, the illusion would be shattered. She would soon learn what he was, what mark the war had left upon him. But for tonight, he wanted to be the man she had once known. The one she had allowed to take her virginity.

Christ, she was so sweet, so aroused. There was no shyness in her, no maidenly protests. She was all woman, needing release, desiring pleasure. And her body...good God, she had developed into a stunning, voluptuous woman. He could hardly wait to strip her bare and stare at her, learning her. Seeing in the glow of candlelight the lush breasts he was caressing, and the wet cunt he was tasting.

It was too damn dark to see her, but it was what he needed—what they both needed—for now. The shadows had become his best friend. He knew no other way to come to her.

"Oh, yes," she cried, tugging at his hair. Her stockinged legs wrapped around his shoulders, and he worked harder to bring her release. When she was nearly there, he pushed two fingers into her and she fell apart, her keening cry whispering about them as she bucked beneath his body.

She was breathing heavily, still trembling from her orgasm. Hard, throbbing, he undid his trousers and freed his cock, pumping his hand down the shaft. He was about to fall atop her, to push his cock deep in her body, when he heard the sound of footfalls coming from the house.

"Hurry," he whispered, "someone comes."

With lightning speed, he helped Catherine set herself to

rights, and was disappearing into the shadows before the gate opened.

"Ah, there you are," Edward said. "All alone, I see." He stepped closer until he was standing before Catherine, then he pulled her to the side, to where the moon cast a faint glow on the brown brambles. She was bathed in moonlight, and Joscelyn could see how Edward watched her.

"How beautiful you look tonight," he purred. He touched her, her throat, her décolletage, and Joscelyn wanted to tear his hand from his wrist. The bastard. Touching what was Joscelyn's.

"I've imagined these tits all night. Show me."

"No."

Edward laughed, and Joscelyn stepped closer, though he tried to hold himself back. When Edward gripped a handful of Catherine's hair, Joscelyn saw red.

"You do know that your continued denial only makes me more aroused, don't you?"

Catherine glared up at him. "I am not yet yours to paw."

"You're mine in every way that counts." He tilted her chin up. "Never forget who you belong to."

"Leave her be."

Edward whirled around, his expression turning from lust to hatred. "You," he sneered into the shadows where Joscelyn lurked. "I should have known you'd be out here, sniffing around her skirts like a mongrel."

"The lady said no," Joscelyn growled.

"The *lady,*" Edward mocked, "is none of your concern."

"Be that as it may," Joscelyn said as he emerged from the darkness and reached for Catherine's hand, "the lady is not inclined to indulge you and your amorous pursuits tonight." Careful to keep his left side hidden in darkness, Joscelyn motioned to the garden gate, and Catherine did not hesitate to grasp the bit of freedom that was being granted her.

Both of them watched her retreating figure, and when the scarlet silk of her gown had disappeared behind the gate, Joscelyn turned his murderous gaze upon his cousin.

"If you ever do that to her again, I will kill you."

There must have been something in his expression that made his cousin step back. Certainly, Edward saw that his threat was not an empty one. Joscelyn had killed before. He could kill again, especially this little slug that stood before him. Between him and want he wanted.

"She's mine," Edward sniffed.

"We'll see about that."

The last words from Edward's mouth chilled him to the core. "Just remember this as you're skulking about in the dark, attempting to take her from me—if I can't have her, cousin, then no one will."

3

TOSSING BACK HIS THIRD BRANDY, EDWARD stared into the fire that the comely maid had laid for him. Not even the thought of his voluptuous personal servant, Annie, was enough to stem the anger that was overtaking him.

Goddamn Joscelyn for returning and showing himself to Catherine. Edward would have bet his fortune that his proud cousin would have hidden himself away in his room. After all, he would not wish to have Catherine see him— not after what the war had done to him. Edward had been relieved when his rival had returned home burned and mangled. Joscelyn was a monster. Even the maids shrieked when he caught them off guard, or they found him lurking in the dark. His countenance was the stuff of nightmares. What would the beautiful and luscious Catherine do when she learned her knight in shining armor had become the ugly ogre?

No, Edward had believed that pride and self-pity would keep Joscelyn far away from his future bride. How wrong he'd been. He knew that they had been together in that garden. Felt it. Oh, she looked immaculate and as aloof as ever, but there was something there, a sparkle in her eye, the kind of twinkle that came after a good sound fucking.

He'd kill him if that bastard had taken her. Stupidly, Edward had heeded the wishes of his father by waiting till she was a bit older to claim her. Indeed, she had been young when they were betrothed, only sixteen. But one grew up rather quickly when one was poor. He could have taken her then, or anytime since, but his father had pleaded decorum. Give her time to settle in, to accept the union. Let her grow up. Edward had acquiesced, only to have his bastard cousin come sniffing around her.

He felt desperate, as though time was running out. He must move swiftly if he was to prevent Joscelyn from taking her. He had no doubt about it, his cousin would try to steal her away. And Catherine would go to him, despite knowing her place was with Edward, as his wife and the mother of his children.

The door to his study opened, and in walked the maid. Obedient as always, she was shedding her gown and baring her breasts for him. He liked this one. She was buxom. He'd singled her out because he liked to imagine her as Catherine.

Christ, his obsession with her was appalling. He was a rich, titled gentleman panting after a poor aristocrat's daughter. He could have any number of titled ladies, but Catherine, with her harlot's body and sharp tongue, aroused him. No one else would do. Only Catherine.

He watched as Annie stood naked before him. She was eager to please, and tonight he was in a hell of a mood. His trousers were tented with a formidable erection—but not for the buxom maid. For Catherine, and the way she had looked in the scarlet silk gown—all white décolletage peeking out. Lord, the thoughts that had run through his mind. What he wanted to do to her.

"My lord?" the maid asked, shyly looking down upon him.

Oh, what he wouldn't do to see Catherine this way, humbling herself before him. Perhaps all the amorous thoughts and lusty fantasies he'd had of Catherine while at the supper table could be fulfilled by Annie, and her eagerness.

Settling deep in his chair, he spread his legs wide, capturing her knees with his thighs. He was shirtless, in preparation for their assignation, and she watched as the thick bundle of muscles in his belly flinched and constricted. One day, Catherine would look at him this way.

The maid's eyes widened as he parted the flap of his trousers. His erect phallus throbbed through the opening, and she studied it with a deep hunger, heedless of the fact that she was standing shamelessly naked before him.

She knew what he wanted, what he would ask for as he reached between the parted folds of his trousers and gripped his cock in his hand. He slid his palm up and down the shaft, pleasuring himself slowly, expertly, and she watched him, studying the way he found pleasure with his fingers. It was not so difficult for Edward to pretend she was Catherine. In fact, it was rather naughty to do so, and he found it aroused him, made his cock thicken even more. Annie's eyes widened in appreciation. She always was game for a good hard fuck.

When she lowered her body so that she was kneeling before him, he imagined Catherine doing the same, as if she were a servant set to do his bidding. His hand tightened around his shaft and a muscle jumped and flickered in his jaw as he gritted his teeth, watching her kneel before him, and pretending she was Catherine.

"You know what I want, don't you?"

She nodded and pressed forward, brushing the sides of her breasts against him as she insinuated her body between his thighs.

"Tell me what you think I want you to do to me," he commanded.

She allowed her eyes to slowly trail up his form, taking in every hard contour and muscle, anticipating the moment when he would cover her body with his.

"You want me to suck your cock," she whispered huskily. "And I want to taste you."

His breath rushed out of his chest as she reached for the waistband of his trousers and pulled the black fabric down his hips. He was now naked and magnificently aroused.

"That is what you want, isn't it," she teased, "for me to take you into my mouth?"

"Yes," he half drawled, half groaned, threading his fingers through her hair and cupping the back of her head. "I want you to suck my cock. And I am going to sit back and enjoy watching you do it." *And pretend you're Catherine.*

Annie set her tongue to him and trailed it up his long shaft. She groaned, a husky sound that came from the back of her throat. "I want this," she purred, nuzzling her lips against the throbbing vein that ran the length of him. "I want to feel this pulsating in my mouth."

"Like it pulsates in your cunt?" he growled as he thrust forward, filling her mouth with more than just the head. She sucked him vigorously, allowing the rhythm of his hips to guide her.

Edward felt his thighs tighten around her shoulders, and he nudged her closer so that she could take more of his straining cock into her mouth. She was working it with such enthusiasm that he nearly came seconds later, but closed his eyes and forced himself to find control. He did not want this to end.

Grasping a handful of her hair, he gently tilted her head back so that he could see her pink tongue snaking up and down the length of his thick shaft and curling around the swollen head. His cods tightened, and as if she instinctively knew, she cupped his sac, fondling him in her palms as she made love to his prick with her mouth.

He was content to sit back in his chair, like a pasha being pleasured, watching her, studying the way her mouth looked atop him, and the way her lashes fluttered against her cheeks as her sexual need began to heighten. How bloody powerful it was to take his pleasure this way, to do nothing other than watch and direct her with pressure from his hand. How dominant he felt sprawled out in his chair as she worked his cock with an eager, inexperienced mouth. How fucking satisfying it was going to be when he had Catherine down on her knees, sucking him.

"I am so eager to please you, my lord," the maid murmured between flicks of her tongue.

"How eager? So eager that you would give your body over to me?" She looked up at him through a veil of golden lashes and he saw her pupils dilate, but he did not think it was in fear. Rather curiosity, and perhaps arousal.

"I want you to do everything to me that you have ever thought about."

"Everything?" he asked, brushing her mouth with the tip of his cock, coaxing her to take him between her swollen lips. They trembled, and he saw how she ran a shaking hand down her smooth ivory thigh, and felt himself grow thicker, imagining that hand snaking between her thighs and playing in her plump folds.

"What if I wanted to feel my cock between your breasts? Would you let me?" He'd been thinking of that tonight, with Catherine and her beautiful breasts. He had wanted to take her out to the garden and suck them, coat them.

"Yes, my lord,"

His gaze drifted down the maid's throat and then to her breasts. "Offer them to me."

She did, and the sight of her breasts in her hands, and her fingers stroking her pebbled nipples, was more than he could bear. He brought her forward and gripped his cock, stroking it between the soft valley of her breasts.

"What if I wanted to come on them?" She gasped as he put his hands to her breasts and squeezed them so that they gripped his cock like her sheath. He pressed his mouth to her ear and thrust his hips once more, filling the valley of her breasts with his prick. "What if I want to come in your mouth?"

She didn't have to answer him, for he knew she would bring him to orgasm and keep him inside her mouth until he was limp and spent. And he did that, imagining it was Catherine drinking him down.

She would soon learn her place, he thought, as he began to lose control. Soon, she would know who her lord and master was.

He cried out, finishing off in the maid's mouth. Closing his eyes, he thought of Catherine and his plan, and how absolutely stunning she would look on her knees, sucking him.

When he opened his eyes he saw the ammunition he needed. The one thing that would bind her to him. The only thing Joscelyn could not do for her.

"My lord," Annie purred. "Again?"

He smiled and lifted the maid onto the desk. "All night," he said. "Till you can't stand."

An hour later, Catherine found herself still dressed in the scarlet gown. She had dismissed her maid, her mind a jumble of thoughts, her body quivering with emotion— desire, anger, fear.

Edward had discovered them. What would he do to Joscelyn?

She pressed her head against the windowpane. Whenever she came to visit at Fairfax, she always chose this room because it looked out over the garden—and because she had been able to watch Joscelyn return from riding, or a swim in the pond. When she couldn't sleep, she would rise from her bed and sit on the little window bench and look down at the desolate copse, and feel some sort of comfort. The garden was as isolated as she.

Now, all she could see was the fountain, and she couldn't help imagining how she must have looked with her chest bared and her thighs draped over Joscelyn's shoulders. What must he think of her? They hadn't even spoken or seen one another in three years, and there she was kissing him wildly and parting her thighs for him.

She would have given him more, too, if Edward had not come in search of her. Perhaps it was providence he had. For she surely would have allowed Joscelyn to make love to her, and then where would she be? Even more deeply in love with him, that's where.

The bargain was set. Her role in it firmly outlined. There was no room in her life for Joscelyn, no matter how much she wished it.

The door opened with a nearly inaudible squeak and

Catherine anxiously turned her head toward the sound. The sizzle of moisture against the flickering candle flame sounded above the closing door before the room was snuffed into darkness. Blackness cloaked her and the click of a key turning in a lock sent gooseflesh erupting along every pore of her body.

Oh, God, was it Edward? Had he finally come to take her?

Curling her fingers into her fists, she stemmed the urge to whimper. She was not ready for this. To have Edward in her bed. Her body.

A deep and melodious whisper erupted in the quiet, sending her anxieties scurrying. *Joscelyn.* "I had to come and check on you."

"I'm well." Swallowing hard, Catherine tried to remain cool. Distant. There could be nothing between them. It was best to continue on as she meant to go along—apart from Joscelyn.

"Please, you should leave."

The darkness in the room unnerved her. She wanted to see him. To turn and gaze upon him. She did not want this disembodied voice in the darkness.

He reached out, gathered her up, and though she protested, he ignored her weak objection and snaked his arms around her middle, bringing her flush against his chest, a chest that felt firm and warm beneath his clothing. "You were left aching. Unfinished," he murmured. "I want to remedy that. I want to fulfill your desires."

Joscelyn brought her up against the wall, holding her upright with his thighs pressed against hers. His fingers laced through hers, holding their entwined hands against her side, while his other hand trailed down her throat to her décolletage and down over her breasts. He cupped her and she felt his breath hot beneath her ear, smelled the scent of him, spice and claret, beneath her nose. His thumb slid over her nipple, which hardened painfully beneath her silk gown, and he moaned deep in his throat when she whimpered and squirmed against him.

"You protest this desire, but I can feel it. Your body betrays you," he whispered as his finger slid away from her breast and skated down her belly. "You want to know what it is to feel passion. You want the feel of my hands on you. You want to remember what it is like to have me inside you." His fingers were now at the junction of her thighs, and he was stroking his fingertips against the curls that lay beneath her gown.

Her stomach coiled and tightened and she felt her blood thrum heavily in her veins. She whimpered as he pressed himself against her.

"Do I frighten you with my passion, Catherine?" he asked as he kissed her throat. "Or does it excite you?" She moaned and her legs weakened when he pressed his lips, then his tongue, to her breasts. "It excites you, doesn't it? It is not a shiver of fear, but of desire, a yearning for more. You don't want Edward. You want me."

Despite her resolve not to, she hissed, "Yes," when his fingers expertly reach for the edge of her bodice. Slowly he inched it down until her breasts were nearly spilling out of her gown. "Please," she cried, arching her back when his nails caressed her flesh scant inches from her nipples.

"Are you wet?" he asked, his lips brushing her ear as he whispered the words. His knuckle traced her jaw. She shivered when his fingers touched her skin and his breath caressed her throat. "If I were to touch you, to spread your legs and feel you, would you be ready to come for me?"

She pressed against him, unable to talk or think. How

could she when he was even now lowering her bodice so that her breasts were exposed? With his thumb and fore-finger, he gently rolled her nipple, and automatically she reached for his wrist, knowing she should stop this. But he refused her and instead brought her hand to his trousers and pressed it against the bulge behind the flap.

"Take my cock in your hand, Catherine, and pleasure me."

Her blood quickened when, instead of leaving her to fumble with the buttons, he tore the flap open and she felt his erection spring free. With ruthless determination he curled her fingers around his thickness and pressed himself into her hand.

"Touch me, Catherine," he groaned. "I am quite at your mercy. I always have been."

She did not know what to do, other than to slide her fingers along the satiny skin. She must have been doing an admirable job for he groaned and thrust his hips forward, sliding his erection up the length of her palm. Closing her eyes, she let her head rest against the wall and allowed herself to feel his warmth covering the front of her body. His mouth was everywhere, on her throat, the tops of her breasts, her lips. His hands were roaming the contours of her figure and his fingers cupped and stroked every inch of her burning skin. Her heart was pounding so fast she felt light-headed, and yet she could not stop what was hap-pening even if she desired to. This passion, the feel of him surrounding her, the intimacy of his tongue in her mouth as he possessed her lips, were nothing she'd ever thought she'd experience. It was heaven, bliss, an erotic sensation she could easily find herself addicted to.

In some cognizant part of her mind she tried to recall the fact that this man could not be hers. The knowledge made her desperate to hold him, to clutch at him so that she would never be parted from him. This night must be their last together, and she wanted it never to end.

Fisting her fingers in his silky hair, she brought him closer, seeking his heat and his tongue dancing with hers. He growled and brought his hand up to her throat. His thumb rubbed the pulsating vein in her neck, lulling her into a dreamlike state.

Tearing his mouth from hers, he thrust his hips forward again and she curled her fingers tighter around his erection. Sliding her hand down, then up, she pleasured him, listening to his sucking breaths, feeling the tightening of his body.

He reached between them and placed his hand atop hers, showing her how to hold him and stroke him. When he increased the rhythm, his breathing was a ragged rasp.

Needing to explore the man who held her entranced, she let her fingers slide into his hair and then glide toward his face. With a sharp gasp he pulled away. "The bed," he commanded, reaching for her hand. "I ache with desire to be inside you."

"Why won't you let me touch you?"

He cut off her words by lowering his head to her breast and circling her nipple with the tip of his tongue. "No questions tonight, Catherine. Only pleasure."

Gripping his linen shirt, she felt his heat sear her fingers, his muscles hard and contoured beneath her hands. She sighed when he continued to lave her nipple while he palmed her other breast. Snaking her hands beneath his shirt, she slid her fingers up his smooth skin, kneading the muscles that bunched and tightened. Without warning he shoved himself out of her arms and reached for her hands.

"You don't have to touch me. It is for me to touch and pleasure you."

"I want to feel all of you," she protested, trying to make out his face in the darkness.

"No," he muttered, releasing her hands. She felt him move away from her, then heard his boot scrape against the floor.

For three years he had been waiting for this day. Six months ago he had returned to England. His hunger had only increased, becoming almost an obsession in the ensuing months while he waited for her to arrive at Fairfax House and come to him, so that he could show her everything he felt in his heart. She had kept him waiting until he thought he would go mad with wanting.

And here was his chance. To take her. She was willing, and he was...afraid.

Damn it, he was what he was. Ruined. Burned. Sooner or later she would discover the truth, and then what? *Have this night,* he told himself. *Enjoy her. Don't run away from what she is offering you.*

Stepping closer to her, he curved his fingers around her shoulders, sinking them into her soft skin, and was lost. "I've come for you," he growled before he crushed her mouth with his. "I won't deny myself."

She went slack and crumbled into his embrace, kissing him with an open, searching mouth; clutching his hair in a fierce hold as she struggled to bring him closer while he sucked at her lips and tongue.

Wanton and willing, she told him without words that she was ready for his penetration. Already she was rubbing her pelvis against his, searching for the pleasure she knew he could give her.

Tearing his mouth from hers, he kissed a path across her cheek to her ear. "For three years I lived in that hell, and it was only the thought of you, of coming back to you, that kept me alive. I've had you my dreams, every position, every wicked, depraved act enacted in my mind. You know what I want," he said in a husky whisper as he ran his hands along her hips and started to pull at the silk skirt and the layers of heavy petticoats beneath. "You know what I've come for."

"Joscelyn," she panted, trying to kiss him. But he angled his head so that he could nibble on her jaw and the tender flesh of her throat. He groaned as his hand found the front of her drawers and he discovered, as he flattened his palm against her mound, that she had already dampened the India muslin with her arousal. "You're weeping for it, aren't you?"

"Yes," she said with a frantic, eager moan. "I ache. I burn."

"For any man, or only for me?"

She tipped her head against the wall at her back and looked at him with such honesty that he felt the edge of his anger melt away. His hunger, however, only raged more out of control.

"For you. I have lain awake all these nights thinking of you, dreaming of you. My body would not forget you. My heart could not, either. Joscelyn!"

His name was a soft, startled cry from her lips as he brought her up against the wall and pressed his body to hers. His hands, large and trembling, snaked beneath her gown, rifling among her petticoats until he found the opening of her drawers and slipped his hand inside, cupping her with his palm.

"Slick and wet. I can feel your arousal seeping between

your swollen lips. Tell me you're ready for my tongue and cock."

"Cock," she admitted.

Nearly mindless now, Joscelyn pressed his cock to her hip while he captured her lips with his and began thrusting his tongue in and out of her mouth, an innuendo of what was to come. "I, too, am already wet," he rasped as he tore his mouth from hers and bit gently at her neck with his teeth. "Your body needs what I can give you, and Lord knows that I need—I *must*—feel your quim squeezing me, milking my climax from me."

She was mewling and writhing against him. He could feel the desire emanating from her. He wished he could see it in her eyes, but it was so blasted dark he could see nothing.

He ran his mouth down her throat to suck at the swell of her breast and tongue her nipple, while concentrating on the wetness engulfing his hand. She cried out with a gasping breath and clutched his arms as he lightly passed his finger over her clitoris. "You could come just like this, couldn't you?" he murmured. "You're so hot and aroused that only grazing my finger on your clit would have you falling apart in my arms."

She shoved against him eagerly, searching for his touch. He did not stroke her there, but slowly slid his hand to her opening, tracing the rim of her cunt with his fingertip. He did not penetrate her. He had waited too long for this moment, and the only thing he wanted her to feel was his cock stretching her wide.

The image of thrusting into her tight, hot body fueled his blood, and he felt the front of his trousers dampen with pre-come. Joscelyn finally fully freed himself from his trousers and was reaching for her hand when he felt her fingers curl around his cock.

He groaned and shoved himself into her hand, and she began to run her fingertips up and down his length. It felt so good to at last feel her hand pumping him.

He moved his palm between their bodies and sought her clitoris, which was erect and pulsating beneath the pad of his fingertip. Furiously, he flicked the sensitive flesh, over and over, matching the rhythm of her hand around his shaft as she pleasured him, tossing him off like a skilled whore.

She was panting in little breaths that made his blood pound, and he was so bloody close to spending. But he could not stop until he felt her shudder against him. So he worked her harder, and even when she began to tremble and shake and arch her back, he gave her more, until she shattered in his arms and cried out his name and begged him, a keening plea from deep in her chest.

"I will give it to you hard, because we both yearn for it that way, don't we, Cathy? We both need it like that so that we can exorcise this imprisoned passion that is nearly consuming us."

He pulled out of her hand and thrust his cock deep inside her. She was tight, so bloody tight. He penetrated her in one long stab and she groaned, a beautiful wanton sound, so beautiful that he had to hear it again. So he pulled out and reentered her swiftly, feeling the rush of wetness engulf him as he lodged himself farther inside her.

Without giving her more time, he reached for her hand, raising it above her head so that he clutched it as he thrust up deep inside her. Harder and harder he thrust. Higher and higher she moved against the wall as his cock stabbed her deeper.

"Do you want it, all of me inside you?"

"Yes," she cried, clutching his hand as he drove his hips upward until she could feel all of him pulsing inside. He waited till she was full of him before he began thrusting and breathing against her. Never had anything so wild and unrelenting felt so beautiful and right.

"I'm going to fill you," he said with a hard moan. "And then I'm taking you to the bed, and loving you all over again."

4

NAKED, CATHERINE LAY WITH JOSCELYN, HIS long limbs entwined with hers. It was dark, and despite her requests that he light a candle, or the oil lamp on her dressing table, he refused.

"Just let me hold you, here in the dark."

She did not press the matter, but knew there was a reason that Joscelyn intentionally made it dark in the room. He didn't want to be seen, and it piqued her curiosity. Edward had said at supper that Joscelyn had returned a monster. What did that mean? Was his injury to his face, and did Joscelyn believe her to be so cruel and callow that she would shun him for it?

"You smell so good," he whispered as he pressed his face into her hair. "Even better now that you're marked with my scent."

A jolting sensation crashed through her. It was an odd sentiment, but it struck a chord with her. She was blanketed in his scent. The entire room smelled of him, spice and man—and sex.

"You don't know how many nights I fell asleep dreaming of this, you naked in my arms," he told her.

Cuddling into him, she squeezed him tightly. When her hand began to roam, he put a little distance between them and made certain his left side pressed deeper into the mattress.

"We must have dreamed the same dream, for I thought of the same things. I wished you with me every night."

"Half of me was afraid to return home, fearing that you would already be married to Edward."

Mention of her future husband cooled her. Joscelyn seemed to sense it, and pulled her closer, kissing her cheek, her temple. "That was badly done, wasn't it?"

"No, it wasn't. It's reality."

"Not in this bed, it's not," he said. "The only reality is what has happened between us, the love we've just made. That's reality, Cathy."

"No, it's only fantasy. A make-believe world in the dark. Come morning, we will be faced with the real world. And in that world I am to marry Edward."

"No, you will not. I have the means to keep you comfortable, Cathy. You don't need to give yourself to Edward."

Hope flared in her breast. Joscelyn was the illegitimate child of Lord Fairfax's sister. He'd been brought to Fairfax House as a young boy, after the death of his mother. He'd been penniless, dirty, but Lord Fairfax had treated him as though he were his own. Yet surely Joscelyn did not have the means to care for a wife, and her dependent family— no matter how kind Lord Fairfax had been. Joscelyn could keep a wife, perhaps, but it was not only a wife he would be getting if he intended to have Catherine.

"You doubt that I can provide for you."

"No, of course not." She did not want him to believe

that she was shallow, fickle, concerned with her own comforts. In truth, she would go and live in a little cottage with him, tend his home, the kitchen, launder his clothes and bear his children if she could. But her life was not hers to give away. Love, however much she desired it, was not to be.

"You must understand," she began, wetting her lips. "I am to be married at the end of the week. There is nothing to be done."

"Then we will run away, far, far away where Edward will never find us."

The notion was so tempting. Catherine was ashamed to admit she wanted to accept his offer. They could flee to Scotland or Ireland. Could hide away where no one knew them and build a new life. But her parents…

"Say yes," he whispered, kissing her. "Say you'll be mine. Come to me tomorrow night. The moon is new and the night will be dark. I'll arrange for a horse, and we can make for the border, and Gretna Green, where we can be married."

He didn't wait for her reply and kissed her hard. He had grown thick, aroused, and he easily slipped inside her.

She was panting as he made love to her, her fingers clutching, caressing his back, her face pressed tightly into the smooth contour of his neck. She inhaled his skin, brought him deep into her lungs. She would never forget this night. Never forget him.

When he cried out and poured his seed into her, she prayed that it would be his child she gave birth to, and not Edward's.

Holding Joscelyn close, she told him without words how much she loved him. How she always would.

But come the morning, the fairy tale would end, and cold stark reality would greet her. For tonight, she would pretend hers was a different life. A different ending than the one that had already been written for her.

"You will permit me a turn about the garden?"

Edward's request was not a polite one. It was more a demand. With her parents watching them intently, Catherine gave a slight nod and accepted his arm, placing her fingertips on his sleeve.

"Beg your pardon, Lord Tate, but I am taking your daughter outside for a short stroll. It's lovely and sunny, and we won't be gone long."

"Splendid idea!"

Fruitlessly, Catherine stared at her mother, imploring her with her eyes to put an end to this, but she uneasily glanced away, her mouth pinched in a tight line.

"I trust you don't mind, Lady Tate?" Edward drawled.

"No, of course not," her mother murmured, reaching for her embroidery hoop. Catherine watched as she stabbed the fabric with the tip of her needle. "Don't forget your shawl, dear, for the wind is up today. You won't keep her long, will you, my lord? You would not want an ill bride, I think."

It was the only help she could expect from her mother.

"Of course not, Lady Tate."

With a triumphant smile, Edward led her away from the relative safety of her parents. Of course, Catherine never could rely on upon her parents' prudence. They wanted her wed to the earl's son, and the quicker the better. It didn't matter that Edward had no intention of walking with her. He had something much more sinister planned.

Leading her to the French doors, he ushered her through. When they were out of hearing, he turned to her.

"You slept well, I assume?"

Nodding, she averted her gaze, and instead glanced around their surroundings. Edward had led her out of the salon and down the stone steps to the back garden. In the sunlight, she could see how old the stone wall that surrounded the garden was. And the door, too. It was thick oak, cracked and weathered, and the Green Man knocker, which she assumed had once been glittering gold, was faded and rust covered.

"You are very quiet this morning," Edward observed.

Of course she was. She didn't know what to say, and her usual acerbic tone would not help her. Not this morning. She sensed that Edward was in no mood to be trifled with.

If it were only herself to be concerned about, Catherine would not be so worried. But she had her parents to be troubled over, and now Joscelyn, too. She did not want her lover to come up against Edward, who had never fought fair in his life.

He led her into the garden, motioning to the fountain where he had found her sitting last evening. The memories of Joscelyn came rushing back, and she hid them, hoping she could blame her flushed skin on the sun and the heat of the day—or perhaps even the breeze that occasionally sprung up.

Sitting, she arranged her skirts and watched as Edward paced before her. It was not like him to appear ill at ease. He was always so smooth and calculated. Nothing seemed to bother him. But he was flustered this morning.

Content to sit and wait for him to begin, Catherine used the seconds to study the garden. There was some greenery on the weed that had woven itself over the stone, and a white bloom resembling the blossom on a trumpet vine. There was life in this garden, after all, she mused, as she bent at the waist to pick the bud. She had never once seen anything green in this copse. Never a bloom, not even a bird. But she heard a bird this morning, singing merrily from its perch on the garden wall.

Whatever could be the reason for this sudden transformation?

"About last night." Edward paused. He stopped before her and glared down at her, forcing her to raise her head and meet his stare head-on. "I want you to know that it won't happen again. You will not meet my cousin anywhere, let alone here, out in the garden. Is that thoroughly understood?"

She bristled, hating his commands. But she dared not defy him. She had no difficulty believing that in his present mood her fiancé was capable of anything.

"Do you understand?" he enunciated with cold precision.

Nodding, she let the bloom slip from her fingers and fall to the shell pathway curved around the fountain. "Of course. But you have it all wrong."

"Do I? Do you actually think I believe that? Joscelyn Mallory has been lusting after you since you were sixteen. He wants what is mine. And that is the only reason he's come to you. Because he's jealous. Because he covets my title. My money. My…"

"Possessions?" she suggested.

"Do not tempt me, not today," Edward warned.

He was flushed, his fair complexion blotched and ruddy. He despised being the underdog. Winning was his first concern. Being the best was always first and foremost in his mind. Edward felt he needed to beat Joscelyn, but didn't realize he would never best him. Joscelyn was the better man. Always had been.

Joscelyn did not covet anything of Edward's. He desired Catherine for himself. She was not so naive as to fall for Edward's tricks. What she and Joscelyn had shared last night had been soul shattering. Heartfelt. There was no possible way he had fabricated his feelings in order to take her away from Edward in a fit of pique, and a childish display of jealousy.

"I'm prepared to let last night go, Catherine, if you promise never to even look at him again."

She wanted to fight Edward. To jump up and claw at his eyes, and scream at the injustice of having to marry him. But she remained seated, a paragon of ladylike behavior, suffering under her fiancé's chastisement.

"I am a handsome man, Catherine, with a fit body. I daresay if you spent as much time looking at me as you do *him,* then you would realize that your future husband is not the troll you make him out to be."

Troll, ogre, fiend. He was all those things and more.

"You know how much I desire you."

"I know how much you wish to possess me," she clarified, attempting to lift her chin away when he clasped it in his hand.

"How you tempt me," he said. His voice was tight, and his grip on her chin hurt. "So damn proud, aren't you? You're not even able to see what a gift you've been given."

What she'd eaten for breakfast threatened to come up. She was utterly bilious at Edward's conceit and self-importance.

"Whatever you think of my cousin, Catherine, you must

allow yourself to remember that he is a bastard. He comes to you with nothing, not even a proper name. He certainly hasn't the means to care for you, or for your family."

The reality of that nearly destroyed her. His lineage meant nothing to her, but unfortunately, his lack of wealth did. She could not abandon her parents. Her father and mother had never worked a day in their lives. They would never survive their fate if Catherine did not marry the brute standing before her.

"Joscelyn can give you nothing, I can give you everything. Everything," he said with a leer. "You think you desire my cousin, well, that my dear, is a pale comparison to what you will feel for me once I've bedded you."

"You have an inflated opinion of yourself, my lord."

He smiled, but it was empty of warmth and mirth. "I will enjoy breaking your spirit when you are my wife."

"I'm not yet," she challenged, and winced as he came down beside her again holding her chin in his hand. He was hurting her, but she would be damned if she'd showed it, or her fear.

"Let us have this understood between us. Right now. I am to be your husband. I will be, even if I have to stage your seduction, and arrange for your parents to find us with your legs spread and me pounding into you. Do you understand?"

"How could I not, after the vivid image you have just painted for me?" She was sickened by the thought that he might do something so vile, but she knew he had it in him. He wanted her, and that was all he could think of. In time he would tire of her, and she would be allowed her freedom. Perhaps she might even live here at Fairfax House while Edward frittered away his time in London.

She could only hope he would tire of her soon after their wedding.

"Let me be rightly understood, Catherine. If you or my cousin do anything to prevent our marriage, you and your parents will suffer. I hold their vowels. I could refuse to pay them, or for that crumbling monstrosity you call a home. In fact, I just received another stack of your father's bills in the post. He's back at it, luv, gaming and gambling. If I refuse to pay these new debts, I could ruin him, and it would not take much to do so. And then what, Catherine? Where would they go? The workhouse? Debtors' prison? You haven't any family to take you in, and your parents' friends have all but abandoned them. You and your parents are utterly alone, and dependent upon my mercy."

She swallowed hard, wishing to refute his claims, but knowing she couldn't. The sad fact was that they were completely reliant upon this merciless creature.

"Ah, the lady does understand," he said, as he caressed her cheek. "You are bought and paid for, darling. But if you refuse to come to me, then it will be your parents who will suffer. Think of that when my bastard cousin is whispering naughty little things in your ears. Think of your mother toiling away in the workhouse as he pleads for you to come to him. Your parents' fate is in your hands."

She wanted to cry. Wanted to rail at him, but all she could do was clasp her hands around his wrists as he cupped her cheeks in his palm.

"Now what will it be, Catherine? Me or poverty? My future countess or the ruination of your parents?"

She could hardly speak, her lips were trembling so, and tears were beginning to fall.

"I knew you would see reason, darling. After all, you

always were a most practical female. Hush now," he murmured, "let me take away the pain."

Then he was kissing her and groping her breasts. She clutched at him, trying to push away, until he reminded her that she had made a deal. He was to be her husband, and only then would her parents be safe.

The Green Man ornament slid sideways, scratching the wood and ancient brass, revealing a peephole. He and Edward had discovered that the brass was not merely decoration, but a way to spy on the occupants of the garden.

From his bedroom window, Joscelyn had seen Edward leading Catherine here, and he immediately set out to follow. But instead of opening the garden gate, which squeaked, he chose to spy instead. True, he could not hear them, but he could see them, and he was certain he knew his cousin's intentions for bringing her there.

If Edward thought he would claim her, he was wrong. After last night, and the love they'd made, Joscelyn knew there was no way on earth or in hell that he would give Catherine up. He loved her. Had always loved her, and nothing Edward did would change that.

He saw them sitting on the edge of the stone fountain. Catherine's hands were wrapped around his wrists; Edward was clutching her face. Her eyes were shining, and Joscelyn knew she was crying. What was the bastard saying to her?

And then Edward's lips were upon hers, his hands groping and squeezing her breasts overtop her morning gown. She was struggling, and when Edward broke off the kiss and began tugging at her bodice, Joscelyn began to see red.

When Edward picked her up and placed her on the

ground and fell on top of her, hurriedly pulling up her skirts, Joscelyn reached for the latch, giving little thought to what he was about to do. It was daylight. There were no shadows, no corners to hide in. He would be exposed.

Catherine's cry made those fears evaporate, and he was sprinting into the garden heedless of the fact that Cathy might very well turn from him forever.

"So sweet," Edward panted as he sucked at her neck. His hands were full of her breasts, and his pelvis was grinding into hers. She could feel his arousal sinking between her thighs, despite the fact he was still clothed. She wanted to gag, but instead, she thought of something else—anything else but the man who was on top of her, and what he was about to do.

"Yes," he grunted, as he put space between them and looked down at her. "I knew your tits would be fabulous. A little taste, then."

She cried out as he suckled her hard. There was nothing tender or loving about his embrace. It was overpowering, as he meant it to be. He was showing her that she was in his control, and that she was supposed to submit to his wishes—any wishes. He was the means of her family's salvation, and her body was his payment for saving them.

"Oh, you want it," he whispered into her ear. "I can feel your fingers digging into my shoulders. You want this, don't you?" As if in emphasis, he pressed his engorged shaft against her. "And I'm going to give it to you. Right now."

"No, please, don't!" she cried, struggling beneath his weight. "No," she screamed, pummeling his back with her fists, but Edward only laughed at her pathetic attempts.

"Oh, yes, my little kitten, fight me. It makes me burn hotter."

In the next breath, and with a bloodcurdling roar, Edward was lifted off her, exposing her naked breasts to the air. Unable to move, paralyzed with fear, she darted her eyes to the left, just in time to see Joscelyn toss his cousin to the ground, his head landing a mere inch from the stone base of the fountain.

"I told you I would kill you if you ever hurt her again."

Wiping the blood from his mouth with the cuff of his sleeve, Edward smiled, taunting Joscelyn. "The monster braves the sunlight."

"You would have raped her, and I am the monster?"

"Joscelyn?" Her voice was quiet, weakened with terror. She feared he would not hear her, but he turned to look at her, his face contorted with rage. His gray eye blazed the color black, and it was then that she saw the eye patch, and the scars on his face. Catherine covered her mouth with the back of her hand when she saw the hate in his eyes, the pain etched in his expression.

Oh, what he must have suffered! She could hardly bear it, knowing what he must have endured.

She reached for him, but he turned away from her, focused once more on Edward. "Come near her again, and I will tear you apart, do you understand?"

"You have no authority here, you bastard," Edward challenged. "I can do whatever I wish. She's my fiancée, not yours."

When he reached her, Joscelyn knelt on the ground. There was no warmth, no flicker of passion in his eye, only haunted shadows. "Joscelyn," she whispered, and caught her breath as the breeze swirled around them, lifting his hair and blowing it away from his face. Her hand, trembling, reached for his cheek.

He pushed it away, refusing to allow her to touch him. If possible, his gaze grew more emotionless as he reached for her, bringing her up against his chest and covering her bosom with her dress.

"Joscelyn?"

"Do not look, Catherine." he growled.

He told her not to look at him, but she could do no such thing. How could she not look into the face of her savior?

But he refused to meet her gaze, and instead kept his attention focused straight ahead, while a muscle in his jaw clenched tightly, telling her that the last place he wanted to be was here, with her in his arms.

"Inside!" he commanded. "I will talk with you later."

"Please," she whispered, trying to make him understand that she was not a willing participant in Edward's seduction, but the pain and betrayal she saw in his eye, in the hard lines around his mouth, told her he thought exactly that. He was thinking of last night, of the fantasy they had lived in the darkness, and here it was morning, where cold reality faced them.

"I never wanted to hurt you," she murmured, then fled, running past both men for the safety of the house.

It was better this way, she told herself. If Joscelyn hated her now, he would not seek her out. Not tempt her with his touches and kisses. She would be safe, and so would her parents.

It was what she had wanted all along—for her parents to be free of the choking debt. She no longer wanted to hear her mother weeping at night, or see her father in his study with his head in his hands.

Yes. She had agreed to wed Edward. That was what

she must do. But she had not realized that her heart and body would long for someone else. She had not known how painful it was to love another, and have him turn from her.

5

DAMN IT! SHE'D SEEN HIS FACE AND HER EX-
pression had told him all he needed to know. He disgusted
her, sickened her. He'd heard her gasp. He could still hear
that shocked breath, and Joscelyn could not help but replay
the sound over and over in his mind. He was nothing but
a hideous beast to her. He had been a bloody fool to let
himself believe his foolish dreams.

Three years spent at war, living in a trench, sustained
only by his thoughts and dreams of her. And all for this.
To be cast aside. Pitied. He'd seen the pity in her eyes and
recoiled from it. He wanted her love, her desire, but never
her forbearance.

Was she even now regretting their night of passion? Was
she thinking of the hideous monster rutting atop her? Did
she wish him far away, never to see him again?

With a roar of outrage, he lashed out with his arm,
clearing his dressing table of the metal tins of shaving soap
and the brushes. Then, in an insane movement without
thought, he drew back and punched the mirror, hating the
image it reflected.

"No!" he cried, then punched the shattered glass once more. "No!"

His knuckles were bleeding, and he was spent. Collapsing beside the bed, he leaned his head back against the mattress.

"I will not leave this place without you, Catherine," he vowed to the ceiling. "I will not. Your place is beside me, monster or not."

Moaning, Catherine sank farther into the warm water and rested her neck against the copper tub. Closing her eyes, she allowed the soothing heat and scented water to wash over her skin, taking away the taint of Edward's touch.

"Lean forward and I shall wash your back," Mary, her lady's maid, instructed.

Catherine did as she asked, indulging in the pampering being lavished upon her. Where was Joscelyn? she wanted to ask.

Do not look, Catherine. He hadn't wanted her to see the thick scars that ran the length of his cheek. He most certainly hadn't wanted her to touch him. She had seen fear briefly shine in his black eye, but only too soon it was replaced with a haunting sadness that made her want to hold him. In that moment when he had lifted her from the grass and brought her tight to his chest, she had never seen a man more handsome.

If only he would have allowed her to tell him, to show him that he was wrong, that she was not disgusted by what she had seen. But his pride was pricked, and she knew that Joscelyn had more than his fair share of pride.

The water splashed over her head and trickled down her shoulders. Catherine sighed, wishing Joscelyn would come to her so that she could tell him his scars meant nothing to her, that she still loved him, desired him. But she had the feeling it would take more than mere words to soothe the ache in Joscelyn's soul. She also knew that to reveal her true feelings would give him false hope. There was nothing but more hurt to be gained by such a confession.

"Will you wear the blue gown to supper?" Mary asked.

Catherine only nodded. She didn't particularly care what she wore. She could think only of Joscelyn, and the pain he must be feeling.

"And the sapphires." Mary prattled on. "They go lovely with that gown."

Catherine visibly trembled. Edward had bought them for her, as an engagement gift. They were stunning, but she hated wearing them. They reminded her of what she had sold. Herself.

"You are shivering again," Mary whispered. "Come, let us get you into bed." Standing up, Catherine allowed the maid to help her out of the tub, and stood on shaking legs. "To bed, my lady," Mary ordered, and taking her by the hand, led her there and covered her to her chin with warm blankets. "Now then, drink this."

Catherine reached for the mug Mary handed her, noticing the steam that curled in tendrils. "What is it, tea?"

"Tea, with a mild sleeping tonic." Mary smiled. "Herbs that will make you sleep and dream only peaceful dreams."

"I'd like that. I vow I feel as though I could sleep a week."

"Then sleep," Mary ordered, when Catherine at last finished the tea. "Sleep and dream. You have many hours yet, and I will make your excuses to your parents. Then I will come in and dress you for the evening. You will be so beautiful that your future husband will fall at your feet."

The tea was warm and soothing and the bed so inviting. She hadn't slept last night; instead, she had spent it making love with Joscelyn. Soon her eyes were closing, and she was drifting on a sea of dreams.

After what felt like an eternity, Catherine sat up in bed and looked about the room, disoriented and confused. It was dark outside and someone had lit the candles on the commode. In the hearth a fire blazed, snapping and cracking to life as flame engulfed a log.

Rubbing sleep from her eyes, she looked about the room, realizing that she was very much alone in the chamber. She had a vague, fuzzy memory of Mary coming in and laying out her gown and petticoats.

She had dreamed of Joscelyn, of running away with him. How desperately she wanted to leave her life behind and forge a new one, with him. But that was not to be.

The scene in the garden with Edward replayed itself, and she knew, unequivocally, that Edward would hold to his promise. He would ruin her parents if she decided to see Joscelyn again.

She wondered what had happened after she'd left the garden. Was Edward even now plotting his revenge against her, after Joscelyn had interrupted them?

"There, my lady," Mary said. Standing back, the lady's maid observed with pride the creation she had fashioned. "Your hair looks so lovely coiled like that. And the earrings, they sparkle so nicely in the gaslight."

"Thank you, Mary."

The sapphires were an extravagant indulgence. They were large, cut for maximum sparkle, and with the diamonds edging them they glittered even more. They were stunning, but she would have been just as happy with jet, if it had been given to her by someone she loved, or at the very least cared for.

Looking at her reflection, she saw a woman who radiated purity and innocence. Her artless expression and wide eyes lent her the image of maidenly beauty and virtue. But inside she felt like a whore. She'd been bought, and she had allowed herself to be so.

"Come," Mary murmured. She fixed her fingers on Catherine's bare shoulders. "You will make such an entrance."

Where was Joscelyn? she wondered. Would he be at dinner? She'd seen him, after all, and wasn't that the reason he had used to hide from her? His face? His wounds?

She longed to talk to him, to touch him despite knowing it was utterly hopeless.

Leaving her chamber, she traveled down the stairs, gliding in her heels, the train of her gown trailing behind her. When she reached the first level, she turned past the earl's study and down another hall that led to the dining room and adjoining salon. And that was when she heard it. The scrape of a boot. The sound of male breathing. The feel of him, and the way he had the power to fill up a room with his presence.

"Hello, Catherine."

Stopping abruptly, she whirled around, only to see Joscelyn lounging against the silk-papered hall. One shoulder was propped against the wall, his arms were crossed over his chest. He was looking at her with such scrutiny that she backed away from him.

"Have you no welcome? No kind words for a future family member? No whispered expressions for a lover?"

She couldn't speak, just kept walking backward, unable

to take her gaze off him. He had changed these past years, and not just his scars. There was a hardness about him now, even though he had only grown more handsome. To her, the wounds on his face did not detract from his handsomeness. The patch, worn over his left eye, gave him a rakish, dangerous appearance. Everything about him made her tremble. Made her want.

"Where is your fine gentleman now?" he asked. "The one who you said you would love forever? Gone. Left for dead on the fields. Replaced by this."

The velvet timbre of Joscelyn's voice caressed the length of her body and she tried to run from it, from that reawakening inside her. He captured her before she could dart away, trapping her against the wall with his broad chest and well-muscled thighs.

His gaze flitted over her hair and then down her face. Then his callused finger reached up and traced the contour of her cheek. His eyes lowered to her lips and she felt the rough pad of his finger slide along her cheek to her mouth, the sensation causing ripples of awareness along her nerves as her lips parted beneath his touch.

He peered into her eyes while his thumb caressed her lips, and she stared back, taking everything in, wondering how he had survived. How he had withstood the agony of healing from his wounds.

"It's not the gentleman you want, is it?" he asked darkly, starting a thrilling tension knotting in her belly. He lowered his mouth to hers, all the while watching her with his unreadable, hooded gaze. "What gentleman could make you feel this way? It is the monster that you yearn for."

"Joscelyn, please," she whispered, weakening. She couldn't, absolutely mustn't weaken. Her family. Edward. He could arrive at any time and discover them. And then it would be over. Her father's debts would be called in, and with no means of paying them, they would be forced out into the streets.

"Tell me you want me. Tell me that you're wet, dripping between your thighs."

She was, and if he didn't quit talking like that, she was liable to throw her arms around his neck and kiss him.

"Tell me you want what we had last night. That you still want me after you've seen the horror of my face."

Oh, that was so unfair. How could she admit the truth to him when she planned on turning from him forever? But then, how could she deny him the truth? To leave him with the impression that she was repulsed by what she saw...that was too cruel. Wrong. She could not hurt him. Not that way. Not when she saw the fear, the insecurity shining in his eye.

"Cathy," he whispered, using his pet name for her. "Tell me you're not lost to me."

There was nothing she could do now. She was Edward's. Forever. Steeling herself to be unkind to the only person she had ever loved, Catherine straightened her spine and summoned all her courage to do what must be done—the final betrayal. The act that would take Joscelyn away from her, and protect her family.

"You are misguided, sir," she said, gathering her strength and wits, and evading his impending kiss by ducking beneath his raised arm. "I feel nothing for you—nothing deeper than a base instinct, which you satisfied last night."

He reached for her and spun her around so that she was facing him. He drew her roughly to his chest, which was rising and falling much too fast. "You're a damned liar," he spat, then he brought his lips down to her mouth and kissed her with such mastery that she felt her knees tremble, and she was obliged to take the lapels of his waistcoat between her fingers and grip them to save herself from running her hands through his silky black hair. He groaned, then deepened the kiss, his fingers caressing the column of her throat, and she knew that she was a fool to play into his hands this way. Just as she was about to break the kiss, he moved his mouth away, kissed her chin, tipping her head back and grazed his lips across the skin that crept up above the neckline of her bodice.

"Tell me, Cathy, does he know I had you first?"

She couldn't hide the tiny whimper that escaped. "This isn't right," she said, with a gasp of shock and pleasure as he licked her throat where he knew she was most sensitive.

"And yet you want it."

Her cored bloomed, dampening at the dark, erotic way he had said that. His tongue came out and licked the swells of her breasts that edged the silver lace of her blue gown and the sapphire pendants. Once again she was unable to hide the gasp that escaped. His palm, large and hot, engulfed her breast, and one long finger pulled at the fragile silk in an attempt to expose her nipple, which was erect and waiting to be touched.

"Admit you want it, Catherine," he teased, as his finger circled perilously closer to her nipple. "Admit you want me. To be taken into my arms and fucked until you can't breathe. Until you forget everything but us."

Oh God, yes, she wanted to cry, but she gathered her strength, her resolve. "Desist, sir," she pleaded, shoving herself out his arms. "Or I shall scream and alert the entire household."

His face darkened and he straightened away from her. "You're very good at screaming and having every able-bodied male come to your rescue, are you not? What a fool I was this morning to think you needed rescuing."

There was barely concealed violence in his words, and she stepped back, pained that she was the cause of his anger.

"I would give anything for you. Do anything—" he began.

"Please don't. You know this cannot go any further."

"This is going to go much, much further."

"What more do you want from me?" she demanded.

"Everything you can possibly give me."

"You know I cannot. Edward..." She glanced away, moistened her lips with her tongue. "Edward is to be my husband."

"Because of your parents' debt. Yes, I know. I've always known that is the reason you agreed to marry him, when it was me you wanted."

She could no longer look at him, ashamed that he knew the truth. "Yes," she whispered quietly, "it's true. My parents have all but sold me to Edward to have their debts cleared. And like a harlot, I agreed."

Closing his eye, Joscelyn moved forward, brushed his lips against her forehead. "Many things in life are brought about by necessity, Cathy. This is one of them. I don't think you a harlot, I think you a beautiful, selfless woman who is willing to give up everything in order to see her family safe—a family that cannot be bothered to learn from their past, and cease gambling."

It was the truth, but it wounded her to hear it. Papa had learned nothing from his follies. She was their only child. After she was wed to Edward, there would be no other daughter to barter off. And what if Edward decided to no longer pay their bills? What then?

"At some point, sweetheart, your father will have to become a man and take ownership of his own debts. It is not up to you to pay them for him."

"I—I— You must understand, Joscelyn, the amount he owes…" There was no hope left. "I'm marrying Edward."

"And what of tonight? What of Gretna Green, and our plans to run away?"

She wanted to go. To flee and never look back. How alluring the offer. How tempting he was. How she struggled to do what she must.

"Here," she said, tugging a diamond-and-sapphire ring from her finger. She shoved it at him, waving for him to take it. "This will get you at least a thousand pounds."

"For what, Catherine? My silence? How badly do you want to hide from your betrothed that we've been lovers?"

Her gaze shot to his face. Was he blackmailing her for more? Was it possible? Had he plans to tell Edward that she had slept with him? She thought of her parents, and such panic rose in her breast that she dashed forward, shoving the ring into his hand, then pulling the earbobs from her lobes. "Take them. Everything. Just…don't…"

"Don't say a word?" he asked quietly, as he looked down at the handful of jewels in his palm. "Pretend as though it never happened?"

"Is that enough for your silence?" she asked, afraid to meet his gaze.

"What do you think?" he snapped. "Nothing would be enough to make me forget what we've shared. I spent the past three years wishing for you. Hoping for a future with you, and with one action, you've taken it all from me."

"Joscelyn," she cried, but then stopped. She had been

successful in turning him away. She should let it be. It was, after all, what she needed to do.

"Enjoy your intended," he grumbled. "You deserve one another."

Then he stalked to the door and pulled it open with such force she wondered that the knob did not come loose in his hand. He did not look back, and Catherine was rather glad he didn't. Her thoughts and emotions where still spiraling out of control, and she had no wish to have Joscelyn see the confusion he created within her.

"Ah, there you are," Edward said as he came into the hall from the dining room. "I thought perhaps you were lost."

"No, just delayed."

"Are you well? You're flushed."

"I am very well, thank you."

"Well then, let us go in to supper. And then we might adjourn to the garden, eh?"

Any hunger she felt quickly evaporated. She did not know how she would get through the night, or which excuse she could use to extricate herself from the after-dinner festivities. She only knew she must.

Catherine glanced over her shoulder, only to find Joscelyn in the hall, watching them.

Please don't hate me, she silently asked him. *Please understand why I must do this.*

But with a glare he turned from her, telling her that he did despise her. And with a heavy heart, and the threat of tears, she took her place opposite Edward and tried to forget about what she had done.

6

IT HAD NOT BEEN DIFFICULT AT ALL TO FEIGN illness. Everyone had remarked how pale she was, and she readily admitted that she had the headache. When it was noted that her plate had hardly been touched, Lord Fairfax had offered to send for his physician.

"Just wedding nerves," Edward had said, teasing her. Everyone at the table had laughed.

Oh, God, in less than a week, it would be Beltane. Then their wedding.

What would Joscelyn think of her then?

Roaming her chamber, Catherine could not settle. Every thought came back to her lover. Where was he? What was he thinking? Did he despise her?

Of course he did, she told herself. She'd spent the night with him, loving him, and then come the next day, she'd tossed him away, making him believe it was his wounds—suffered in the war, protecting their country—that made her spurn him. What sane person would not hate her? She detested herself, in fact.

Standing before the looking glass, she gazed at the reflection there. She was wearing a lovely nightrail made of the sheerest silk, and edged in lavish lengths of Honiton lace. It was part of her trousseau, bought, of course, by Edward.

Any woman would be thrilled with something so feminine and beautiful, but she hated it. It reminded her of what she was. A sensual prize in the game of men. Her father, so irresponsible and frivolous with his money, had sold her. Edward, the spoiled aristocrat, wanted to put her on his arm and shower her with clothes and jewels that marked her as his possession. No, she was the pawn of men. What she wanted hadn't mattered.

Her bedroom door creaked, and she glanced up, half expecting it to be Edward. He would not be put off by a mere headache. He had every intention, she knew, of finishing where they left off in the garden. But it was not her fiancé come to ravish her. It was Joscelyn.

With a soft click, he locked the bedroom door and slid the key out of the lock before dropping it into his trouser pocket.

She should have demanded the reason for his presence, should have screamed for help, but she could not, not when he was prowling toward her wearing nothing but an unbuttoned linen shirt and black trousers. Her lips trembled on a soundless word as her gaze slipped along the length of his chiseled chest and flat stomach. Good Lord, had he always looked like this, like a marble statue come to life?

True, he had always been physically fit and wonderfully muscled, but to this extent? Almost helplessly she dropped her gaze to the dark line of hair that disappeared into the waistband of his trousers.

She stood before the mirror, eyes wide, fingers clutching the fabric of her nightgown so hard that her knuckles shone white as he neared her. Finally he stopped behind her, towering above her as he met her eyes in the mirror.

Her knees suddenly betrayed her, and she had to fight to show no outward signs of her body's response to his.

"Am I that frightening that you would swoon?"

"Of course not!" She stared at him in the mirror, saw how his left cheek, chin and chest had been burned. His lips had not been. But his eye... She wondered what was hidden there beneath the patch. "I am no wilting flower," she admonished.

"Obviously," he said, showing his teeth. "You're willing to marry and bed my lecherous cousin. You must be made of stern stuff."

She flushed, angered. It was no less than she deserved, but it hurt all the same. "Why have you come?"

Fire flickered in the depth his eye. "Because you forced my hand. You refused to come out into the gardens after our meeting in the hall. You left me no choice but to follow you here, to your chamber."

"What do you want from me?"

He smiled and she saw that he was no longer looking at her, but at her profile, then the exposed mounds her breasts. "I think we both know what I want."

She trembled. She would not give in to this man, no matter how appealing he might look standing behind her. She just couldn't. It was too dangerous. Edward could walk in at any time. He would not let a locked door stand between them.

"These, I'm afraid," Joscelyn said, reaching into his trouser pocket, "aren't what I want."

She watched as he placed the diamond-and-sapphire earbobs and the ring she had given him on her dressing table.

"Are they not worth enough?" she sniffed indignantly. "Perhaps you wish for our transaction to be in hard currency, is that it?"

The flame in his eye flickered higher. "Baubles and diamonds are not what I'm seeking. I told you, I have money—I've been saving for years by living like a damned monk—all so that I might one day be able to have you."

She did feel like swooning. The notion of what he had done made her want to fling herself into her arms.

"It was always money between us, wasn't it, Cathy. You never cared that I was born a bastard—that never mattered. I know the money doesn't matter to you, but your family—your parents are all you have. Money for their sakes, not your own comforts."

"You don't understand the depth of debt."

"I can still keep you in style, even after paying off your father's most pressing concerns, if that is what you fear."

No, that wasn't what she wanted! Material things meant nothing to her. She wanted to be loved and held.

His fingertips trailed along her collarbone, then over her shoulder. The warmth of his touch burned her through the thin nightgown. "You know what I want, Cathy," he murmured as fingers deftly trailed along the outer curve of her breast. "It's not money I'm after, but something far more precious."

Reaching for her left hand, he lifted it, then slipped the ruby ring Edward had given her as an engagement ring from her finger. With a careless air, he tossed the ring to the carpet, once more finding her eyes in the looking glass.

"You know what they say about marrying in haste," he murmured. "You repent in leisure."

Her eyes flashed angrily at his insinuation. "We mustn't

do this," she gasped. "We must act as though we are little acquainted, for both our sakes."

"Little acquainted?" He chuckled. "I hardly think so, *m'lady.* I'm intimately acquainted with you, or have you forgotten? My cock hasn't forgotten. Even now it's stirring. It's recalling just how familiar we really are."

Her stomach flip-flopped at the reminder. How could she forget him, the feel of him moving inside her? The memory of it was both pleasure and pain.

"Tell me. Have you told my cousin about us?"

Catherine lowered her eyelids so she could watch his lips caress the side of her neck without him knowing.

"Does he know you come to him soiled? Does he know I've had your virgin's blood covering me?"

"What purpose would it serve?"

Irritation flickered in his eyes. "Would he still want you, do you think, knowing you've slept with his bastard cousin?"

She met his gaze in the mirror, holding hers steady. "Are you going to tell him?"

He smiled, lowered his face to her neck again and inhaled the scent of her throat. He did not reply to her question, and soon Catherine was struggling to think and not give in to Joscelyn's skilled lips.

Suddenly he released her and walked around to face her. Brushing her hands away from her nightgown, he forced her sweating palms to her sides.

"What is it you want from me?" she begged, unable to stand the pleasure of his touch. "Just tell me—*please.* And be done with this."

She had asked him that in a quiet, almost wary little voice. It was so easy an answer. Her body. Her love. The heart that was beating so hard in her chest, and the soul that no one ever considered inside the beautiful wrapping that was Catherine.

Joscelyn did not say those words. Instead, he sank to his knees, skimming his lips between her breasts, down the middle of her ribs to the gentle rise of her belly as he did so. Instinctively, her abdomen contracted when his hot breath grazed her sensitive skin beneath the sheer silk gown. His hands captured her hips, stilling her as he flicked his tongue across her navel. When he heard her suck in her breath, he stood and reached for the lace neckline of her gown.

His mouth went dry as he saw the shadows outlining the rounded flesh of her breasts. He wanted to rip the gown from her body, but that would be rash and gauche. This time it was going to be different. This time he knew how to control his urges. This time he would pleasure her like a true, skilled lover—and she would come back to him.

He saw her pink nipples begin to harden through the translucent material. He was standing behind her again, one hand holding the fabric, the other skating up her midriff to rest below her breasts.

Gooseflesh flared to life all over her body and he smiled knowingly as he watched her reaction in the mirror. "Edward's blood might be blue, Catherine, but blue is cold. My blood is red. Hot and lusty. Which man will give you the type of passion you've always craved? The blue blood or me?"

She would not answer him, would not give him the response he needed so desperately to hear. But her body was speaking for her. The words she could not voice, but he heard them anyway, in the shaking breath that escaped her lips, felt them in the way her body trembled.

"What will you tell your husband when he discovers he is not the first? Will you tell him your innocence was taken brutally from you? Or will you admit the truth and tell him how you kissed me, how you let me fondle your breasts, how I coaxed the honey from between your thighs with my mouth? Will you tremble and beg for him, as you did for me?"

Joscelyn brought his finger to his lips and wet the tip, then dragged it across the bud beneath the fabric. The silk was rendered transparent, the fabric molding to the nipple and areole. She gasped as he slid his wet finger over the damp silk, making her nipple curl and tighten as he repeated the action. She gasped again as he lowered the bodice, exposing her breasts for the briefest of seconds before she shielded them with her hands.

Reaching beneath her arms, he cupped the undersides of her breasts, feeling the softness, testing the heavy weight of them. She swallowed hard and closed her eyes, refusing to watch his dark hands as he pried her fingers from her breasts and covered her fully with his.

"Can you not bear it?" he asked, his voice a mixture of need and anger as his thumbs traced circles around her pebbled nipples. "Can you not stand to see my coarse hands covering you? Does it shame you, to have me, a monster, touching you?"

She refused to answer, keeping her eyes tightly shut.

Flicking his tongue up the length of her neck in time to his stroking thumbs, he whispered, "Does seeing my hands on you disgrace you, Catherine, or do you feel mortification because you like it, because you know you should be ashamed to desire the attentions of a bastard commoner who has been burned, beaten, left blind in one eye?"

"You are intentionally being hurtful," she said in a painful whimper.

"Am I? No, only truthful. You're a lady of breeding, and I'm just a mongrel."

"You're brooding for no reason. I've told you the scars mean nothing to me."

"No reason? I'm sulking, Cathy. Do indulge me. It's not easy for a man to spend three years away at war, surrounded by death and despair, his only hope and light the thoughts of a woman he loves. I came home broken, but I have faced my demons—I've shown myself to you. And now you're being a coward."

"A coward?" she gasped.

"Yes, you're either afraid to acknowledge what you feel because you're a coward, or because of me. My scars."

"You're deliberating goading me?"

"Am I? I know you so well, Catherine. How you feel. You're warring with yourself, trying to not yearn, because you know a woman of breeding should not have yearnings for a man who is beneath her. A woman such as you should not be wet and wishing a man such as me would finger her and bring her to ecstasy. Because that is what you want, don't you? My fingers stroking you until you come. "

A small inarticulate sound—from excitement, or from shock?—escaped her parted lips. The rush of her hot breath caressed his flesh. He took satisfaction in the way her hands were clutching the gown, which had fallen to her hips. "It's not you—not how you…look, but how you make me feel. I can't allow myself the pleasure because you will ruin me. How could I ever be with Edward after you? Yes, you're right, I am a coward. Please s-stop, Joscelyn," she stammered, and shivered as he breathed against her. "Stop, *please.*"

"How beautifully you tremble for me." And just to prove it, he took both nipples and rolled them between his thumbs and forefingers, making them stiffen into peaks he wanted desperately to slip between his lips. She shook her head, denying the obvious truth, and he pressed his body closer to hers, brushing his hard cock against the supple flesh of her bottom.

"I could take you like you this, you know. I could make you so needy that you would grant me anything."

"No." The protest came out as a sigh, but he was certain she meant it to be a scathing denial.

He admired her tenacity, but she would not win tonight. He was much too intent on his goal. And his goal was to see everything he had missed out on before. He was here in the light. There were no more secrets between them. He wanted her body—to see it, to touch it, to watch them together.

Skimming his roughened fingertips down the satiny flesh of her abdomen, he rested his index finger at the point where the nightgown dipped teasingly below the small mound of her belly. He captured her gaze and smiled most wickedly. "Now which part will you choose to shield, hmm?"

She was breathing more quickly, and the pulse in her throat throbbed faster. He sensed her desire, the struggle within her to fight what she was feeling. Slowly he pulled the silk from her body, the swishing sound as it slid across her hips erotic in the charged silence. He was about to reveal the thatch of blond curls when she simultaneously lowered one hand to cover her mound, and made to cover her delightful breasts with her other arm and hand. He intervened then, capturing her wrist and holding her still. She made a small sound in her throat when he pulled her hand away from her breasts and brought it up over her head, to rest against his neck.

How damn gorgeous she looked like this, arched, pressed against him.

"We can't…that is…" She swallowed hard. "I don't want this."

"You don't?" Reaching for her other hand, he placed it on his neck, watching in the mirror as her body bowed back. "Let us see how much you don't want this, Cathy."

Her eyes widened when he reached down and hooked her leg over his, exposing the slickness that lay between her thighs. "You're aroused, luv. Admit it. I can see your desire glistening between these plump folds."

She cried out, clung to his hair with her fingers as he parted the swollen lips, exposing pink flesh that gleamed like silk. Her breath left her lungs in a whoosh when he raked one long finger from the bottom of her sex to the crest of curls at the top, then tapped her erect clitoris with the tip of his finger.

"Now that is what I came to see. You completely naked and welcoming me."

He slid his finger deep inside her and watched his tanned flesh disappear into her body. His cock swelled further and he pressed it against her, wishing she would reach around and free him from his trousers. He'd give anything to feel those soft, supple hands on his rigid shaft.

"Joscelyn, please," she cried as she began to ride his hand. "We can't do this. Edward…" She swallowed, gasped and began to cry. "My parents. He'll destroy them if sees me with you."

Joscelyn stopped, released her leg and held her, letting her trembling body mold against his. Looking into her eyes, he swept his fingers down her cheek. "Believe in me,

Catherine. This can work. Trust me to take care of you, and your parents."

She hugged him tightly, shaking her head in denial. "No, it can't, Edward…he's the monster."

"Believe me, Catherine, things are not as desperate as they seem. If you could only see past your fear, you would realize that I can help you. But you've got this notion in your head that you, solely, must bear this burden of protecting your parents. That isn't the case."

"You tempt me, and I want to believe you. But Edward would never agree. Furthermore, he would make our lives hell."

With a sigh, Joscelyn pulled away from her, slowly sliding his hands from her body. "Come into the garden, Catherine. Whenever you want me, I'll be there. Trust me…."

And then he left her. It had been the hardest thing to do, leaving her like that, but Joscelyn knew she needed to come to him of her own free will. It was not only her body he desired, but her trust in him, as well.

7

JOSCELYN CONTEMPLATED THE CONTENTS OF his glass tumbler, which glowed amber in the flickering firelight. He was in a hell of a mood, and brandy seemed just thing. Expect he hadn't done anything to abate the desire and need he still felt swimming inside him.

"Damn chilly tonight," his uncle grumbled with a shiver as he settled into the empty wing chair beside Joscelyn's. Together they watched the crackling logs in comfortable silence.

Fairfax had grown old these past three years. His body was still large and robust, and his skin ruddy, but the exuberance and energy his uncle had once displayed were gone, replaced with a lethargy that comes with age and illness.

"You're well, I trust, uncle."

"Very well, I thank you."

"And your health?"

His uncle shot him a questioning glance, the thicket of his gray brows arching in question. "As hearty as ever. What, may I ask, has led you to question it?"

With a shrug, Joscelyn tipped the tumbler to his lips and

tossed back the contents before placing the empty crystal on the table. "You do not seem in your usual spirits, is all. I thought I might inquire."

The earl's smile was faint, and melted away almost immediately. "As you age, Joscelyn, there is a time in your life when you begin to take stock of what you have done with the years you've been given. You think on achievements and failures, and decisions that you've made—and regrets."

Joscelyn wondered if one such regret was taking in an orphan.

"Sometimes we have the best intentions. Other times, we're quite merciless. Sometimes," he said quietly, "our decisions are based on our beliefs of other people, and sometimes those beliefs turn out to be rather shattering."

"You speak of me."

Fairfax stared at him. "God, no, my boy. Never you. You've far exceeded anything I thought you might become. You're a gentleman through and through. A fine man. And I like to look upon you and think that you were one of my successes."

"Thank you, uncle." He'd seduced Catherine, his cousin's intended, beneath his uncle's roof. No, he was not at all honorable, as his uncle believed. He was a true bastard.

"Edward," Fairfax sighed. "He's the shattered hope I hold. I raised him well, in the same manner as you, and yet he has turned out to be selfish and cruel. I can't fathom it. His mother was an angel, and I believe that I am a fair man. Occasionally I bluster about, but I hope I'm not cruel or callous."

What was this? Joscelyn had never heard his uncle speak of his son in such a manner. What could be the reason for it?

After another deep sigh, Fairfax slid farther into his chair and rested his head against the padded wing. "I knew of the malicious streak in my son when he was but a child. I corrected it numerous times, and hoped he would outgrow his spiteful nature. I believed he had, till…recently."

Joscelyn dearly wanted to ask. But he knew his uncle would say more when he was ready.

"What brings you here tonight?" Fairfax asked suddenly. "You look as pensive as I feel."

Joscelyn had the sudden urge to disabuse his uncle of the notion that he was a gentleman. For some damn reason, he despised knowing that he was misleading the man who had cared him—loved him—like a son.

"I find myself here reflecting on my life. My actions. The consequences. The decisions that have led me here."

With a smile, Fairfax snorted gently, then met Joscelyn's stare. "Catherine Tate, I should think, factors into those contemplations."

For the first time in years Joscelyn found himself blushing. "Indeed, sir."

"I've always known it. There is no need to blush so."

Wiping a hand over his face, Joscelyn closed his eye. "I never meant for it to happen."

"Does any man mean to fall in love?" Fairfax shook his head and stared into the fire. "The heart goes where it wishes, and yours wished for Lady Catherine. That's one of my regrets."

"Which is?"

Fairfax slid him a look. "That I didn't give her to you."

Shocked, Joscelyn sat mute and frozen in the chair. "Sir?"

"I wanted her for the Fairfax dynasty, you see. Penniless they may be, but she and her family come from a long and noble lineage. Their reputations are spotless, despite her father's gambling ways."

"I see."

"I thought she would do very well for Edward. Bring some softness into his life. I...thought, or rather hoped, your interest was a passing fancy that would be soothed and replaced by leaving."

Straightening, Joscelyn felt his body go rigid. "My commission."

His uncle nodded. "You were to be an officer. And you weren't to be near the fighting. I made certain of that. But then everything went wrong, and now...now, damn it, whenever I see you I am filled with such self-loathing and contempt, because it was me, my ambitions, that put you there."

A tempest swirled inside him, and he curled his fingers into fists and strived to calm himself. It was not his uncle's fault. That was much was certain.

"My wounds are not your burden, uncle. A commission was more than a man of my background could expect. I was elated with it. And to be honest, I thought perhaps that my separation from Fairfax House and Catherine would do me well. But it did not work. I've only managed to fall deeper in love with her."

"My son doesn't love her. He wants to make her his possession, and when he tires of her, he'll toss her aside, and I will be forced to watch her, her sadness, her longing for you."

Where was this conversation leading? Joscelyn wondered. Why tell him all this now?

Standing, his uncle made his way to his desk and rifled through the drawers, then returned with a packet of letters. "You are the son I've always wanted, Joscelyn. A man with pride and honor and a sense of duty. You've never asked for a blasted thing since you came here. I…I owe you this."

Joscelyn took the folded paper from his uncle and opened it. After scanning it, he glanced up. "Mother's dowry?"

"Aye. Your father never got his mitts on it, and your mother, God bless her soul, did not live long enough to return for it. By the time I found her, she was dying. I've kept it for you, intending to give it to you when you needed it most. Which I believe might be now."

A packet of bundled missives landed on Joscelyn's lap. "Tate's outstanding debts. Do what you will with them."

As his uncle walked past him, Joscelyn jumped from his chair and faced the man who had been like a father to him. "I—I…" He looked down at the letters in his hand, then back up at his uncle. "I don't know what to make of this."

"Don't you? Do the honorable thing, my boy, and take Catherine away from my son. He will only make her miserable—and you, too."

"If this stems from guilt, uncle, there is no need. I have never blamed you, not in the past, and not even after learning it was your intention to part me from Catherine."

"It's not guilt, Joscelyn. I'm righting a wrong, that is all. A wrong I did to you and Catherine. That woman is gentle and kind. She'll suffer at my son's hands. I may have let Edward rule this estate, and to some extent rule me, but I have eyes, and I see how he treats her. It sickens me that a son of mine could be so cold and uncaring. Catherine does not deserve the fate that I've purchased for her. As I said, do what you may, with my blessing."

"Uncle," Joscelyn began. Then, bereft of words, he

pulled Fairfax into his arms and hugged him tight. "You have given me the greatest gift I could ever ask for."

"Treat her like a treasure. And might I suggest that you take her and leave. Edward has developed a liking for the village pub. Every night he's there. You can have a decent head start on him."

"Thank you, uncle."

"My thanks will come when I see you both happy."

"And Edward, what about him?"

"He'll be placated with the promise of another bride. Desire is fleeting, and that is all he feels for Catherine Tate. Do not worry about Edward, or me."

Joscelyn watched his uncle leave the study, and then sat down to plan his day tomorrow. If the weight of this packet meant anything, his day would be spent discharging Tate's debts.

It was rather fitting, he mused, that his mother, who had been tricked and deceived into eloping with a rogue, was going to save another woman from the same sort of miserable existence that she herself had endured. Joscelyn knew that his mother would wish her dowry to be spent that way.

After discharging Tate's debts, Joscelyn was astonished to realize that there was still a decent amount of money left from his mother's dowry. Combined with some of his savings, he could buy a small cottage, and perhaps take a job as a clerk. He might even return to the army and work in the offices. He could provide for Catherine and any family they had, but there was one thing he could not do: keep paying off Tate's debts. This one time would be all he could do for the man. Catherine would have to accept it if she were to agree to marry him.

Searching the manor for her, he discovered she was not at home, but out in the village with her mother. Slipping into her room, he placed a note on her pillow.

Meet me in the Garden....

Catherine crumpled Joscelyn's letter in her hand. She was sorely tempted, but knew she could not tempt fate once again.

"Shall I dress you for dinner now, miss?"

Turning, she saw her maid rifling through her wardrobe. "No, thank you, Mary. Perhaps you would be so kind as to have supper brought up here. I have a headache, and do not believe I could sit at the table."

"Oh, miss, you do look frightfully pale." With a bob, Mary excused herself. "Let me tell your mother, miss, and then I shall bring up tea and toast."

Grateful for the silence, Catherine made her way to the window and watched the waning sunlight cast shadows over the garden. She saw Joscelyn standing beside the fountain, waiting patiently. Closing the drapes, she blotted out the sight, putting him from her mind. But he would not leave her heart.

The door banged open and she jumped, whirling around to confront the intruder.

"Your maid says you are ill." Edward was standing there, his face red. "What is the matter?"

"A headache."

"Nonsense. You're not missing dinner because of a headache. I've brought a few of my mates around. You'll be at dinner, dressed in the red silk. I want to show my friends what a luscious little piece I've got myself."

Catherine's stomach turned sour. She would not sit there and allow herself to be ogled by his friends.

Edward took impatient steps into her room and grasped her hard about her shoulders. "Do you understand me, damn it? You'll present yourself and entertain my friends, or you will find yourself at the wrong end my hand."

"Edward."

The throaty snarl from the door made him release his hold on her. Catherine saw Lord Fairfax standing in the hall. His expression was dark. "Get your hands off her."

"Or what?" Edward taunted. "Begone, Father."

"The hell you'll dismiss me like that."

Edward's expression turned florid. "What is it you want?"

"You, out of this room. Now."

Like a petulant child, Edward glared at Catherine. "Fine. Stay in this room then, but expect me tonight after I return to the house."

Edward brushed past them. Lord Fairfax watched his son leave, then turned to look at her. "My apologies, Lady Catherine. I assure you, I raised my son better, but he's chosen not to recall the manners he was given."

Rubbing her arms, Catherine nodded. "Of course, my lord. There is no harm done."

"Oh, I doubt that, my dear. But soon it will all be mended. By the by," Fairfax asked, "have you seen my nephew today?"

"No, milord."

"I think you should seek him out. It might very well be worth your while."

Curtsying to him, Catherine watched as her future father-in-law closed her chamber door. What an odd conversation, she thought. Turning, she saw the crumpled missive on the floor and bent to retrieve it.

Edward would be out tonight. Did she dare? Should she risk all and go in search of Joscelyn?

Mary arrived with the dinner tray, and Catherine sat down, contemplating what she should do as she nibbled on a triangle of toast. Was it just her, or had Fairfax been insinuating something when he had suggested that she search out Joscelyn?

There was only way to find out.

8

THREE HOURS HAD PASSED AND STILL CATHER-
ine refused to come to him. He'd spent each of those miserable hours alone in the garden, waiting for her. But he
did not lose hope. It was fear for her family that kept her
away, not fear of him. She did not yet realize what good
fortune had been bestowed upon them. Her uncle had
freed her—had freed him. Now if only he could find her
to tell her. She hadn't been in the house. He could only
hope that she had at last arrived at the garden.

Trudging across the damp grass, he made his way there.
He had no idea what prompted him to do this yet again.
Sleeping on the cold ground, waiting for her, was a pen-
ance, but he could not resist doing so. Maybe tonight she
would come to him.

Lifting the latch, Joscelyn listened to the gate groan on
its rusted hinges. Striding on into the garden, he searched
among the shadows for the fountain.

He hadn't been able to deny himself or stay away.
He had thought about her all day, as he saw to both his
and Tate's affairs. During the long carriage ride, he had
dreamed of what he was going to do to Catherine that

very night. His need for her was so strong, so compelling. He craved feeling her hands on his body, experiencing the satisfaction of plunging his cock inside a wet sheath he had made ache for him. Would she come to him tonight?

It was not a hard rut he was looking for but a tender loving, a melding of bodies and hearts and, God help him, souls.

And there she was, lying on the stone that surrounded the fountain. She was covered by a white cloak, which rippled in the gentle spring breeze as she slept. Like a mirage. He blinked. Blinked again, yet there she was, sleeping before him. She had come to him. Wanted him, and he stood looking down upon her like a fool.

Catherine stirred uncomfortably and the scalloped edges of her gown parted, teasing him with a glimpse of pale flesh rendered white in the soft glow of the moon.

He wanted her, despite his fears, despite not knowing what Catherine truly thought of him. At this moment he didn't give a bloody damn; he only wanted to feel her, to give her pleasure and feel her pleasure him.

Unfastening his breeches, he dropped them to the ground. His cock sprang free, heavy with arousal. Never had anticipation coursed so heavily through him. It was as if he were a virgin again, awaiting his first conquest.

Hearing Catherine sigh and watching her lips part on a soft breath, he felt his body stiffen, and to relieve some of the exquisite ache, he palmed his cock, studying her in the light of the moon. How many times had he pleasured himself imagining this? How many nights had he found release with his hand, wishing it was her body he was pouring himself into? Too damned many.

Carefully, he removed the cloak and laid it on the grass. Then he turned, lifted her gently and placed her on it. She squirmed, and he kissed her, unable to resist sliding his finger across her smooth cheek.

Lying so that he faced her, he propped his head in his hand and trailed his thumb down her throat to where the lace shielded her body from him. It was an erotic piece of clothing, revealing, yet at the same time concealing the places he most desired to see. Her curves were outlined, but he could not see her nipples, only the faintest hint of pink circles beneath the lace design.

Now painfully aroused, he parted the gown with one finger and allowed himself to look his fill. Her breasts, round and full, quivered with each of her breaths. Already her nipples were erect and he could not stop himself from brushing the tip of his finger across them. She moaned and shifted restlessly, and he watched her breasts sway with the movement.

Grasping his cock, he stroked its length, fearing that if he did not do something to assuage his lust he would spread her thighs and sink into her body. Needing to feel her, he parted her gown more to reveal her curls and lush thighs.

He grazed the tip of his cock along her belly, savoring the softness, the wickedness of pleasuring himself while she slept, naked, before him.

"I want you," he whispered in the quiet, unable to stop the words that sprang from the depths of his soul. "Always only you."

"I want you, too," she replied sleepily. He looked up to see her lashes flutter open. She met his gaze and smiled secretly. "Am I dreaming? Have I only wished you here?"

He smiled back. "You came to me, remember?"

"I did. I couldn't pass another night like the last, aching for you. Crying because I wanted you. Joscelyn, I haven't been able to think of anything else but you, and how you must despise me for what I let you believe."

"I never believed you. Edward could convince any woman to do his bidding. But we are together now, and we need not talk of Edward."

"Oh, I hope you aren't just a dream!" she whispered, tracing his mouth with the tip of her finger.

"No," he groaned, reaching for her hand and placing it inside his shirt so that her palm rested against his heart. "I am real."

She smiled, inching closer to him so that her breasts brushed against his shirt and her lips were impossibly near his. When he captured her lips and swept his tongue inside, she mewled softly and brought her hands to his hair, raking her fingers through the length of it. Joscelyn groaned, needing her hands on him, wishing he could be naked in her arms, feeling those soft fingers stroking his scarred flesh.

"I need you, Cathy," he murmured against her mouth. "I need to feel you and taste you."

"I need you, too," she sighed, grasping his hair as he nuzzled the valley between her breasts. "I want you so much, more than you can ever imagine."

He tongued her nipple, listening to her hushed breathing. If he was any sort of gentleman, he would lift her up, carry her to the house and make love to her in a proper bed, not out here in the garden. But he was no gentleman, and the garden on the eve of Beltane was a most fitting place to share their bodies.

Flicking her nipple with his tongue, he smiled when he heard her gasp. He released his cock and flattened his palm on her belly, which quivered beneath his hand. He felt her tremble when he drew her nipple between his lips and sucked.

"My God," she cried, tangling her legs with his and arching her spine.

Her breasts grazed his face, and Joscelyn could not help but push her onto her back so that he could suck at one nipple and tug at the other. She moaned when he rolled it between his thumb and forefinger, and when he tweaked it she gripped his hair. Joscelyn smiled, knowing that if he slipped his fingers between her thighs he would feel the honey seeping from her body.

Her hands were moving now, exploring his shoulders and arms. He felt her fingers pinching his flesh, her nails biting into him through the thin linen of his shirt. Her enthusiasm and heated response encouraged him and he skimmed his fingers down her breasts, past her belly to the damp curls between her thighs.

She whimpered and he captured her cry with his mouth, slipping his tongue deep into hers as he parted her sex and slid his finger up the slick length of her. He circled her clitoris and she bucked against his hand, moaning while she clutched his shirt.

"Yes," she gasped, tearing her lips from his as he slid first one, then a second finger into her.

"Do you need another to fill you?"

She nodded and reached for him, bringing his mouth down atop hers. He growled low in his throat and plunged a third finger deep within her, swallowing her cries.

"God, but I want you," he whispered, nipping her lips while he continued to finger her tight passage. His thumb circled the bud at the crest of her curls and he felt her stiffen, then arch again.

"Beautiful," he rasped, watching Cathy's emotions play across her shadowed face.

Her keening cry echoed along the garden walls as she stiffened and bucked against him, and all the while he drove her on with his fingers until she was panting and writhing and begging for his cock.

"I want to touch you," she gasped, reaching for the tails of his shirt. "I want your skin against mine."

His body froze and his mind went blank when he felt the tentative touch of her fingers on his flanks. "No," he commanded, shoving himself away from her. "No, Catherine, don't touch me, I cannot bear it. I know what you feel."

Catherine lay still on the ground, watching as Joscelyn pushed himself away from her. She couldn't believe he didn't want her touch. He had allowed her to see him, and she had told him that his scars meant nothing to her. Yet still he was afraid.

Letting her eyes skim down his wrinkled shirt, she saw his erection, thick and hard, soaring out of a nest of dark curls. He met her gaze through the shadowed moonlight, but then turned his head, refusing to look at her. She had not missed the haunting loneliness that flickered in his gaze, and she reached for his hand, but he snatched it away.

"Cathy—"

"Shh," she whispered, realizing he was trying to hide his scars. She recalled that his hand had been burned and cut, the same hand she had reached for. He was afraid of her response, and it broke her heart to think he might consider her so shallow. "I want you, the man you are. If that means scars and all, then so be it. Just let me touch you, Joscelyn."

He swallowed hard, and she knew that if she did not say something the moment would be over. She could not let it be, could not go back, after he'd taken her so far. She wanted this, wanted it with him. "You're beautiful to me because you're everything I've ever desired in a man."

Her fingers reached out to his thighs and she tentatively stroked the hard muscle. His jaw clenched and she watched his erection swell further and throb, jutting out from beneath the hem of his shirt. Skimming her hand through his dark curls, she captured his shaft and smoothed her fingers down the length of him. "Please tell me I can touch you like this."

He nodded, and captured her hand in his, curling his fingers around hers, showing her how he liked it.

"I didn't want it this way," he rasped. "I wanted to taste you, to bring you to climax after climax, to have you begging me to fill you."

"I am begging." She met his gaze. "I want you inside me, want you to show me all the things you've dreamed of when you were away, fighting for your life."

"Catherine," he murmured, lying atop her and capturing her breasts in his hands. "I want so desperately to make this right for you."

"You will." She smiled, covering his mouth with her fingers. "It will be perfect."

As she kneaded his bottom, she spread her legs, showing him that she was submitting to him, in essence giving him everything she had left in the world.

"I'll take care of you, Cathy, I swear it."

"I know," she sighed, feeling his beautiful fingers part her, teasing the honey from her once again.

"So wet," he groaned, nudging his shaft between her legs. "It's just for me, isn't it, Cathy?"

"Yes." The unyielding hardness of him slid into her. She was stretched to the limit, and had never felt anything more fascinating than knowing that Joscelyn was inside her, a part of her.

"Cathy," he mumbled against her throat, driving deep. "Tell me you want me, that it's only me you want inside you. I need to hear the words."

Somewhere deep within her she felt his torment, tasted his fear. He wanted to be desired as he was now, and not just what he had been before the war.

"Give me the words."

He was stroking her so hard, so precisely, that she could barely breathe, let alone speak. The exquisite sensation was building again, and Catherine felt herself becoming weightless, floating, waiting for the pleasure to take her.

"Damn it, Catherine, I need to know," he growled. His breath was hot against her skin and she felt perspiration trickle from his forehead onto her cheek. "Please tell me that you feel something."

"I love you," she cried, feeling her body splinter. She clutched him tightly, squeezing him to her as he released his seed deep inside her.

She'd said it. At long last Joscelyn would know how she truly felt. She loved him, and never more than right now, when he was still buried deep inside her.

"Tell me what happened."

Catherine was tracing her fingertips along his chest, tickling his nipple—both nipples. Exquisite pleasure was elicited from the one, and nothing but numbness from the other.

"You don't want to know about that," he said, kissing the top of her head. "Besides, I have something much more important to discuss." She shivered when the breeze blew, caressing their skin, and he held her tight to him, and used his jacket to cover her up.

"Of course I want to know about the war. I want to hear everything."

Closing his eyes, he fought past the images of the conflict. He did not want this moment blackened by his memories.

"Trust me," she whispered, and then rolled over onto him, straddling him, gazing down upon him through a curtain of blond hair. "I will keep you safe," she said, smiling.

He smiled back, filled his hands with her breasts and enjoyed the slick wetness of her quim on his cock. He hardened, let himself go fully erect and waited for her to make the next move.

"Tell me," she moaned as he flicked his tongue over her nipple. "Or I will get off and go back into the house."

He reached for her bottom, gripped her, bit down gently on her nipple until she writhed, moving her sex along his cock. She was such an innocent. She thought to tease him, but what she didn't realize was that he could make her come like this, just with rubbing.

"Joscelyn," she moaned, "tell me."

"That I want to touch you all over? That I want your breasts in my hands, your nipples against my tongue, my cock inching inside you?"

She sighed, a thrilling whisper that escaped through her parted lips when she felt his erection throb beneath her. Instinctively she brushed him, rubbing along him, her lips parting in a silent plea for more.

"I could make you come for me with only words, do you know that?"

She shuddered as he trailed his fingers along the length of her spine.

"Do you want that? To come?"

"Damn you," she moaned, "I want you to tell me what happened."

"I nearly died in a fire that broke out in a trench. I was burned, and I prayed for death. But I'm alive now, Cathy, and I don't want to spend the night with you talking about it. I want to live—with you. Right now."

His lips grazed her shoulder and he kissed her softly. "Make love to me," he whispered. "Show me your love. Your touch. Free me from my prison, Cathy."

Shifting her weight, she straddled him, slid down onto him and listened to his male groan of satisfaction. He was big, and she took him deeply, riding him, uncaring that she was utterly naked in a garden. It was Beltane, after all, and the spring.

Beneath her, Joscelyn moved, raised his legs and shifted her back to rest against his knees. He watched her, caressed her, explored her body. He whispered to her, telling her how she made him feel, how much he loved her. She reached for his hand and brought it to her heart, let him feel it beating against his palm.

"I am so grateful that you came back alive," she said, tears filling her eyes. "I would have died, too, if you hadn't."

He smiled, reached for her and pulled her down to his chest. He gazed at her, revealing so much love in that one, dark, beautiful eye. "I couldn't have gone to meet my maker without experiencing this at least one more time."

Rolling with her in his arms, he positioned her beneath him. Slowly he stroked, loving her, prolonging her pleasure. She was crying out, begging him, and when he couldn't hold back, he came, hot and hard inside her.

Collapsing on top of her, he entwined his fingers with hers. "That was worth any price I had to pay to come back to you, Cathy."

They awoke to the songs of robins and sparrows. The sun was bright, and Joscelyn stirred, feeling Catherine's warm, sated body pressed to his. Cracking open his eye, he glanced around, amazed by the greenery that met his gaze.

"Look," he whispered to Catherine. "The garden has come back to life."

She rose, her breasts bare, and he could not resist touching them. *Eve in her garden,* he mused.

"This is…this is impossible," she gasped. There were the beginnings of buds and blooms. Purple wildflowers carpeted the grass by the fountain, and even the brown weed that had been growing in the cracked and broken stone had turned a lush green. She looked back at him, her eyes full of wonder.

He shrugged and reached for her. "There is something to be said for Beltane magic," he whispered, "and the power of my seed."

She slapped him playfully. "Conceited man."

He sobered, brushed her hair behind her shoulders and captured her face in his hands. "Marry me. Run off, right now, and we will go to Gretna Green. We can be wed by nightfall, and it will be Beltane, and I'll follow you into the woods and make passionate love to you."

When she hesitated, he placed a silencing finger over her lips. "There is no need to worry about your parents. I've settled your father's debts. It is up to him to go on from here. You cannot continue to pay the price of his follies. Marry me, Cathy. I'll make you happy. I'll give you babies, and love, and a garden that you can play in—a garden I'll play with you in."

"Wh…how?" she stammered.

"My uncle," he said. "He gave me my mother's dowry and I used it to pay off your father's debts. It will be the only time, Cathy. Your father is a grown man. It's time he saw to his own debts. But he's starting with a clean slate, and if he resists the follies of his past, he'll be all right."

"Your uncle?"

Joscelyn smiled. "I was as astonished as he was, but it's true. He realized what he had done by saddling you with his son. He wanted you to soften Edward, to make him a better man. But when Fairfax realized his son was a callous brute, he comprehended that what he had done was causing you pain."

"And you."

"Yes. He knew I loved you. He's atoned for his decisions, Cathy. He's given us the freedom to run away and be wed."

Hugging Joscelyn, Catherine cried against his shoulder, and in that one sensitive spot on his neck, where the scars permitted feeling, he felt the warmth of her tears.

"Joscelyn?" called a voice from the other side of the gate. "If you're there, make haste. Edward is home. I've ordered his door locked, but he stirs."

"She hasn't consented yet, uncle," Joscelyn replied, smiling at her.

"Then what is your answer, Lady Catherine? Is my nephew worthy of you? You needn't worry for your parents. There will be no breach of contract suit, and no recriminations from my son. You'll be safe and protected, and allowed to follow where your heart lies."

"Cathy, I love you," Joscelyn whispered. "I always have, and I know I always will. Our lives will be modest, nothing like yours would be if you married Edward—"

"Oh, hush," she sniffed. "Yes, yes, yes, I'll run to the ends of the world if only to be with you."

"Not the ends of the world, my love, just Scotland."

"Prepare the carriage, Lord Fairfax!"

There was a chuckle beyond the gate. "'Tis already done, my dear."

And as Joscelyn rolled her beneath him and kissed her, they heard a whispering in the wind....

"The garden has entwined them with a kiss and an embrace. The young lovers have been set free, but for me, I still seek that magic maiden who will make the number three."

★ ★ ★ ★ ★

RITES OF PASSION
by
Kristi Astor

1

April 1919

IT'S THE GARDEN THEY SAY IS HAUNTED, NOT
the house itself. Those words echoed in Emmaline Gage's mind
as she approached the walled garden in question, one trembling hand reaching toward the latch on the wooden gate.
Pausing, she glanced at the copse of trees just beyond the
gate, then toward the woods in the distance.

I can do this, she assured herself. After all, Emmaline was
a woman of science; she didn't believe in haunts. Such nonsense didn't frighten her, wouldn't send her scurrying away.
Not after everything she'd been through, the horrors she'd
witnessed over the past several years.

Festering wounds and rotted, burned flesh. Amputations
performed without adequate anesthesia. The cries of the suffering, followed by the silence of death.

Indeed, what were restless spirits compared to the horrors
of war?

Emmaline pushed away the memories, refusing to walk
that path in her mind. Instead, she took a deep breath and

forced herself to reach for the latch and slowly, cautiously, ease open the gate and take a step forward.

As soon as the gate closed behind her, a breeze stirred. The hem of her skirt flapped against her calves; a lock of hair blew across one cheek. The leaves rustled noisily while Emmaline scanned the garden, looking for the source of the voice she heard carried on the wind.

Come, sit beside me, it seemed to say. She'd felt the pull toward the garden every day since her arrival at Orchard House a fortnight ago. Until now, she'd ignored it.

Feeling suddenly courageous, she took several steps down the uneven cobbled path that wound through the overgrown shrubs and wild plantings, more brown than green. Hastily, she scanned the rectangular space, but saw no one. Of course not. It was only her imagination. There was no voice, no intruder. There was nothing but the wind whistling over the crumbling stone walls, and through the treetops.

It was an eerie sound, to be sure, but not a supernatural one. She let out her breath in a rush, feeling relief coursing through her veins. And then she allowed herself to look around, walk the full perimeter, her heels clicking against the flagstones beneath her feet.

Despite the garden's current state of neglect, it seemed to fill her with a sense of peace. There was something comforting, almost familiar about the space. Still, the garden needed a skilled hand, and she wasn't certain she was up to the task.

Anticipating this, she'd tried to hire a gardener when she'd first arrived at Orchard House, but everyone in the village of Haverham had sworn there was no point, that in all the years that Mathilde Collins had lived there, no one had been able to make a go of it. The garden was beyond help, they said, and haunted besides—which was all stuff and nonsense. Emmaline shook her head in frustration, hurrying toward a stone bench in a shady corner. She sank onto the seat with a sigh, running her fingers along the face of the Green Man etched into the rough, uneven stone of the bench's back.

The garden was spacious, enclosed by high stone walls on all sides, save the one with the green wooden gate. Though she could still discern the garden's original design, most everything was overgrown and wilted, with several square, fallow beds scattered about. Near the center of the garden stood a stone well, a tin watering pail perched on the rim.

On the far side of the well what looked like neat rows of rose bushes stood wilting in the sun, not a bloom in sight despite the season. Or was there? Squinting against the glare, Emmaline raised one hand to shield her eyes as she attempted to make out a spot of color there at the end of the second row. Rising, she hurried toward it, taking care as she picked her way across the path.

And there it was—one pale pink blossom clinging to a spindly, thorny branch. Her heart swelled with hope at the sight of it, and tears stung her eyes. She retrieved the pair of shears she'd slipped into her pocket, and clipped the bloom, bringing it to her nose to inhale its scent. A single tear slipped down her cheek, and she wiped it away as she made her way back to the bench.

It was a sign. Surely it must be. How else could she explain it? A single flower, no more, and so very familiar.

Her legs trembling, she sank back onto the bench, holding the delicate rose by its stem. She ran one fingertip along the bloom's velvety petals as she allowed the memories to come flooding back.

Oh, Christopher! Why did you leave me all alone? Come August, he would have been gone a year, killed at Amiens. Emmaline had been on the front herself at the time, assigned to a casualty clearing station at Allonville. They'd been celebrating word that the Allied forces had broken through the German lines and advanced nearly twenty kilometers when she'd received the news of her husband's death from Christopher's field commander.

Their marriage had been brief, yet glorious. Emmaline had never expected to fall in love, to marry. She'd been twenty-three—a spinster—when she'd enrolled in the nursing program at Pennsylvania Hospital. When the war broke out in 1917, she'd volunteered to go to Europe, to join the Army Nurse Corps. After all, what was there to keep her in Pennsylvania?

Nothing. No one. Her parents had died of influenza, one right after the other, and her brother—a drunken lout, by all accounts—had long since moved to New York, where he was no doubt getting himself into all kinds of mischief. And so she'd gone to Europe. She'd been stationed in Liverpool, working in an army hospital, when she'd first met Christopher Gage, a dashing young captain in Rawlinson's Fourth Army, who was recuperating from a broken femur sustained in battle.

Captain Gage had long since been released from the hospital, but remained at the base on administrative duty while his leg continued to heal. He'd come to her ward one day to visit an old school chum who'd lost an arm to a German grenade, and it was love at first sight as far as Emmaline was concerned. He'd asked her to dinner that very same day, and began to court her in earnest.

He'd swept her entirely off her feet—figuratively speaking, of course—and they'd married in a quiet ceremony at the base chapel not two months later, with her wearing her dark blue serge street uniform in lieu of a wedding gown, and Christopher as dashing as ever in his khaki uniform. She'd carried a bouquet of pink roses identical to the one she now held, and was attended by Christopher's sister, Maria, who'd traveled up from London for the wedding.

Soon afterward, they'd each managed to secure a week's furlough—seven glorious days—and enjoyed a brief holiday at a nearby inn before Christopher was sent back to the front, fully healed in both spirit and body. Emmaline had gone back to her nursing duties with a renewed zeal. Despite their separation, she'd been deliriously happy. She had hope. A future. And then, with one telegram, she'd lost everything.

Emmaline blinked away the tears that threatened to blur her vision. The past was immutable, entirely unchange-able. There was no point in dwelling on it, in reopening the wound and poking at it with a stick.

Glancing around the garden, at the house looming off in the distance, she reminded herself that this was her future—the future that Christopher had given her. Orchard House, a grand but somewhat crumbling Cotswold estate, Chris-topher's sister had called it when she'd written to offer it to Emmaline. Apparently Christopher's great-aunt Mathilde had lived there most of her life, and had left it to him, her favorite nephew, upon her death. Which meant it was Emmaline's now, and Maria had insisted that she should have it.

Had she any other alternative, she might have refused to take ownership. But she had no family save her wastrel of a brother, no home, and she could not bear to go back to nurs-ing. Not now. She had some money saved—all her earnings, tucked safely away—but even living frugally in London, she was sure to run through it far too quickly, and then where would she be? Back on the wards, she guessed, as she had no other skills, and no prospects.

No, Orchard House was home now. Only, when Maria had called it "crumbling," she had not been exaggerating. Emmaline had spent her first fortnight tidying up, and the house still wasn't cleaned to her satisfaction. Perhaps it was a result of all those years living in hospital dormitories, but she could not countenance a spot of dust on any surface, linens that weren't pristine and crisp, or an untidily made bed.

Thank goodness Mrs. Babbitt—Mathilde's long-time housekeeper—had agreed to stay on, if only a few days a week. Beyond that, Emmaline would have to manage on her own. It wasn't that she was incapable of keeping house; Emmaline and her mother had managed well enough during her youth in Pennsylvania. It was just that Orchard House was so very big. At one time, it had been the grandest house in all of Haverham, and would be still, had it been better maintained throughout the years.

Instead, furniture in various states of disrepair had been piled haphazardly in cobweb-filled rooms, and weeds grew up through cracks in the floorboards. In unused wings, exterior walls had begun to crumble. Only the house's main wing remained fully intact and livable. It would be far too costly to restore Orchard House back to its original state. At best, Emmaline hoped to simply maintain its current condition.

Luckily, the estate encompassed a great deal of land, most of it parceled out to tenants whose rents would help pay the bulk of Emmaline's expenses. She would keep the books herself; she was clever with sums and enjoyed such work. She would do her own cooking, too. She looked forward to it, really—the busywork. It would keep her mind occupied, help stave off the loneliness that had crept into her heart.

She knew she should be grateful for her current situation. There were so many war widows who were worse off than she was. She had a home, an income. Generous neighbors, she mentally added, remembering the basket of blueberry scones that Mrs. Talbot had brought over that morning. And she would always have her memories, she reminded herself.

Nothing, not even the passage of time, could take those brief, beautiful memories away from her. Smiling, she brought the fragrant bloom back to her nose.

If she closed her eyes, she could almost see Christopher's face looking down at her, his lips curved into a smile. She drew a deep breath, remembering his scent—tobacco and soap. Remembering the way the corners of his eyes crinkled when he laughed, his dark eyes filled with merriment.

A shiver worked its way down her spine as she recalled that idyllic week spent tucked away at the inn with her husband. They'd barely left the bed for two full days, and her body had come alive beneath his touch. They'd made love till she ached all over, till she thought she'd die from pure, exquisite bliss. In one week, she'd learned how to satisfy a man, and how to receive pleasure in return. Of course, she'd thought they'd have a lifetime together.

Instead, she was alone.

She'd had no visitors since her arrival at Orchard House save Mrs. Talbot and her husband. Her closest neighbors, they lived in the vicarage at the bottom of the road, and had been quite welcoming, despite the fact that Emmaline was a Catholic and chose not attend services at the picturesque village church over which Mr. Talbot presided. Besides the Talbots and Mrs. Babbitt, her acquaintance was limited to the various shopkeepers whose establishments she'd patronized for food and sundries.

Still, she could not remain a hermit forever. Christopher would want her to get out, to live again. But life would never be the same, now that he'd gone and taken a piece of her heart with him. She'd never feel whole again, like a woman again.

And then, like a whisper on the wind, came the all-too-familiar voice. She'd been hearing it for days now, every time she walked past the garden's walls. Emmaline closed her eyes, knowing full well that her mind was playing tricks on her again, that her self-imposed exile, her loneliness, was making her imagination run wild.

She conjured up Christopher's image once more in her mind's eye—his rugged face, his muscular body, his cock, hard and ready—and she reached between her legs and touched herself.

Her strokes were gentle at first, almost tentative. But as the vision in her mind grew sharper, clearer, she increased the pressure and tempo. The layers of fabric abraded her tender flesh as she continued to stroke her sex, imagining herself with her legs wrapped around Christopher's waist, riding him hard as he whispered her name against her ear.

Her head tipped back, and she could have sworn she heard his voice, his breath warm against her skin. *Come, Emmaline. Come hard for me.*

With a shudder, she climaxed. It took her nearly a full minute to catch her breath, and she remained there, perched on the edge of the bench, her damp thighs pressed tightly together. With her eyes still closed, she traced the Green Man's face etched into the bench with her fingers. Though she could not explain it, she felt a strange kinship with him. It was as if…as if he'd been waiting for her. Watching her. Enjoying it.

Sighing deeply, she opened her eyes, her gaze drawn immediately back to the rose garden. As soon as she was able to focus, she reached for the edge of the bench to steady herself. Either she was imagining things, or the previously spindly, lifeless bush had suddenly sprung to life, its leaves lush and green, its thorny branches supporting perhaps a half-dozen tightly furled buds.

She blinked hard, willing away the improbable sight, but there it remained, as plainly visible as it was impossible. Her heart hammered against her breast, her breath coming in short little puffs. Her vision swam, and her nails dug painfully into the rough stone seat.

A strangled cry escaped her lips as she rose on trembling legs and made her way toward the gate, wanting to get as far away from the garden as possible.

They were right—the garden was haunted. Either that or she'd gone stark raving mad.

2

"DON'T YOU LOOK LOVELY," MRS. TALBOT SAID, patting Emmaline on the shoulder.

"Thank you," Emmaline responded, smoothing her damp palms down the front of her best dress, a mauve linen drop-waist dress with a wide sailor collar. Paired with a cream-colored cardigan and knitted cloche hat, it was the most fashionable ensemble she owned, and she was glad that it met with Mrs. Talbot's approval.

Still, she had to force herself to smile, wondering how she'd ever managed to let Mrs. Talbot talk her into this— attending Haverham's annual Beltane festival. Just thinking about the crowds she'd no doubt encounter there on the village green made her stomach churn uncomfortably. She didn't want to leave Orchard House, didn't want to be paraded around and forced into small talk with strangers.

Oh, she appreciated Mrs. Talbot's efforts, truly she did. The woman only wanted to help, to show the village her approval of its newest resident, despite the fact that Emmaline was an outsider in every way—an American, a Catholic. She liked both Mr. and Mrs. Talbot, found their company pleasant and engaging, even if they *had* been the ones to put the notion in her head that her garden was haunted.

When the roses had seemingly sprung from nowhere, she'd thought perhaps they'd been correct. She'd fled the garden and sworn to never return, to have someone knock down the walls and clear the fields, to remove every last trace of its existence.

And yet the very next day, curiosity had drawn her back again. She hadn't imagined it; the buds remained on the single bush, beginning to unfurl. Only this time she wasn't frightened by them. It was almost as if…as if they were a sign from Christopher.

And so she'd set aside her fears and begun to tend the garden in earnest. She put most of her efforts into the roses, attempting to coax them back to life. And when she wasn't weeding or watering or pruning, she was painting. She'd set up an easel there by the bench, and painted the garden not in its current state, but in full bloom. The place had become her haven, her secret refuge. She felt safe there between those four walls—protected and secure, and somehow closer to Christopher.

But today she was forced to go out where she felt vulnerable and alone amid a sea of strangers. They would surely want to ask her questions that she wasn't yet comfortable answering—about her wartime experience, about her marriage and Christopher's death.

She took a deep, steadying breath, hoping to calm her racing heart, to tamp down her rising panic. Perhaps she should tell Mrs. Talbot that she'd changed her mind, that she felt unwell. Anything to avoid going.

"Come, now, Emmaline." Mrs. Talbot reached for her arm. "Don't look so terrified. I vow, it cannot be as bad as all that. Just a few hours and we'll have you safely home again.

The villagers are so eager to meet you, and you can't hide away here forever."

"I know," she murmured, wiping her damp palms on her skirt. "I...I don't know what's come over me."

"There's Mr. Talbot now," the woman said, raising her voice to be heard over the sputtering motorcar that had pulled up beneath the porte cochere. "He hates the festival, you know," she added with a shake of her head. "Calls it pagan foolishness, especially the pantomime. Which I suppose it is, but it's certainly entertaining foolishness."

"Isn't it just some sort of May Day celebration?" Emmaline asked, still unsure about the festival's origin—and why they would be celebrating a Celtic one in their little English village, besides.

"Exactly that," Mrs. Talbot answered with a nod. "You see, a few generations back, a viscount of great wealth and influence, Lord Brearleigh, lived here at Orchard House. His wife was Scottish, and she insisted that the village's May Day celebration should be a Beltane festival, instead. The young, besotted viscount was happy to humor his wife, and it's been a tradition ever since. Anyway—" she waved one hand in dismissal "—Mr. Talbot only pretends to be scandalized. I've seen him watching the pantomime raptly when he thinks no one is paying him any mind."

Emmaline couldn't help but laugh at that, her fears eased a considerable measure.

Her neighbor rewarded her with a smile, her pale blue eyes full of warmth. "I believe that's the first time I've heard you laugh," she said, then pursed her lips, watching her expectantly. "Dearest Emmaline, the pain will fade eventually. I know it's hard to imagine, but I promise that it will."

"Are you certain?" she asked, her voice a hoarse whisper.

Mrs. Talbot nodded, her eyes filling with tears. "I'm

certain. Mr. Talbot and I had a son, you see. He was a sickly boy, born with a weak heart. When he passed, well...I thought the pain would eat me up inside. But as time went on, the ache in my heart began to fade, little by little. He's still here—" she tapped the spot above her left breast "—but the hurt is eased."

Emmaline reached for Mrs. Talbot's hand and gave it a squeeze. "I'm so very sorry."

The woman nodded. "Just promise me that you won't shut yourself away from the world. You're far too young for that. Now come, we don't want to keep Mr. Talbot waiting. All that pagan fun, remember?"

Almost an hour later, Emmaline relaxed beside Mrs. Talbot on the village green, watching the young maids twirl brightly colored ribbons around the maypole as the setting sun cast wide orange swaths against the sky. Mrs. Talbot had spread out a blanket on the lawn and unpacked a supper hamper, and Emmaline sat with her legs tucked beneath herself, sipping a glass of cool white wine.

"A pagan ritual, I tell you," Mr. Talbot whispered, leaning across the blanket toward her. "I don't know why I allow it."

"Oh, pish-posh," Mrs. Talbot replied airily. "Why don't you leave us be, and go throw horseshoes with Mr. Hackley until the fire-lighting ceremony. Though I know you'll hate to miss the pantomime," she added drily, smiling mischievously at Emmaline.

"Always the same foolish story," he said with a frown before standing and brushing off his trousers. "Perhaps I shall go join Mr. Hackley. If you ladies will excuse me." Ever formal, he tipped his hat in their direction before stalking off.

Emmaline reached for a slice of ham and pressed it

between two halves of a flaky, golden biscuit. "Thank you so much for bringing supper," she said, deciding between two different types of cheese. She chose a soft golden one, and sliced off a chunk.

"Oh, it was my pleasure," Mrs. Talbot replied, reaching for a plate of tarts. "Here, you must try one of these. Sinfully delicious—it's the sweet cream butter, goes right to the hips. But you could use some fattening up, if you don't mind my saying so."

Not the slightest bit offended, Emmaline took two tarts and placed them on her plate, her mouth watering in anticipation. It was true; she'd grown far too thin. Since arriving at Orchard House she'd had to take in the waists of several of her skirts, and her dresses hung too loosely on her frame.

She desperately needed to purchase some new clothing, she realized, glancing around at the fashionable ladies and gentlemen surrounding her on the lawn. She'd bought most of her wardrobe before the war, and styles had changed so dramatically since—hemlines had risen considerably, and lighter colors and fabrics had come into fashion. Perhaps she could buy some pattern books and try her hand at sewing again. She used to be quite handy with a needle and thread, back in her youth.

At the very least, she could raise some of her hems, she decided, fingering the edging of mauve silk that reached near enough to her ankles.

"Ooh, it's time for the pantomime," Mrs. Talbot said with obvious delight, drawing Emmaline from her thoughts as several people in costume took to the makeshift stage before them.

For nearly a half hour, Emmaline watched raptly as villagers recreated the tale of the May Queen, the Winter King and the Green Man. Love, lust, jealousy and greed—it all played out on the stage before them, resulting in the May Queen's humiliation and subsequent death, and the Green Man's imprisonment in the garden cursed by the cruel Winter King. The drama ended with a poem:

I am the wind, softly caressing her hair
the breath near her ear
whispering words of passion she yearns to hear

I am the hand cradling gently her breast
awakening inside what others cannot,
I not so humbly confess

I am the sigh as she offers me all
and with no reservation,
I answer her call

Reborn in her passion, but faced with remorse,
she turns from my arms,
and faces her betrothed

A duel, says he, as I dust off my hands
and comply with his challenge
for her reputation to stand

I am the fire burning bright in my quest
ridding the cold, dark of winter,
winning my May Queen's breast

Yet before Darkness is finished, he utters one final warning,
and to his bride now banished
claims her death come the morning

You shall remain imprisoned in this dead withered place
as atonement for your sins,
and then to me he did face

No one will admire your seductions, kept hidden beneath the
vines
until thrice over you awaken
stone hearts and cause passion to entwine

When the last word faded away, Emmaline let out her breath in a rush. Was it just a coincidence—the withered garden, the voice whispering on the wind? Of course it was, her mind insisted. The story was just that—a legend, told and retold throughout the years. Still, a shiver raced down her spine. Before, she'd thought of the Green Man's image as nothing more than a common garden icon—a symbol of sorts—but now, as she realized how he fit in with the legend, the fact that his image was scattered about her own garden took on new meaning.

She glanced up at the sky, surprised to see that the sun had dipped below the horizon, and the sky was now a dusky lavender hue. The temperature had dropped considerably, and she pulled her cardigan more tightly about her shoulders.

Returning her attention to the stage, she watched as Mr. Talbot, acting as the village's spiritual leader, carried up a brightly lit torch. He said a brief prayer, asking the Lord for bountiful crops and robust livestock, before carrying the torch off the stage and lighting a bonfire in the middle of the village green. Everyone stood, and Emmaline followed suit, joining Mrs. Talbot as they gathered around the blaze.

Several speeches were made, though Emmaline did not hear the words. Instead she found herself gazing at the fire, watching intently as the logs burned orange and red, sending up spurts of bright, fiery ash into the darkening sky.

When she finally dragged her gaze away from the flames, she noticed a man standing directly across the bonfire from her, watching her intently. She blinked hard, focusing her eyes, trying to decide if she'd already made his acquaintance. She couldn't be sure; after all, she'd met so many people before they'd sat down for supper.

Whoever he was, he was a gentleman. That much was evident by his dress and his manner. He stood proudly yet carelessly, a bowler hat resting on one hip. Tall and slender without being gangly, he towered over the men who stood on either side of him. There was no denying that he was handsome, exceedingly so.

Still, his direct stare made her uncomfortable. She dropped her gaze, pretending to examine her black kidskin pumps as if they were the most fascinating things she'd ever seen. Her stomach did a little flip-flop, and she realized that her hands were trembling. And not because the man was staring at her, she decided, but because she'd thought him handsome. It didn't seem right for her to have such a thought—it was too soon.

Feeling as inconstant as the faithless May Queen, she silently chastised herself. And yet she could not help but abandon the sight of her scuffed shoes in favor of the man who still watched her intently from across the fire.

Her cheeks warmed, and a feeling of awareness skittered across her skin. This time, she allowed herself to stare back as the voices around her receded to a faint hum in the background. He was the exact opposite of Christopher, she realized—like the negative of a photograph. Fair where Christopher had been dark. Thin rather than stocky, blond instead of brunet.

But it was his eyes that she found so unsettling. Even across the distance that separated them, she could see something familiar in them, an expression she recognized far too well. He'd seen horrific things—pain and fear and death—just as she had. She could not say how she knew this, but she did.

Inhaling sharply, she dropped her gaze once more. Who was this man, and why was he watching her? Why was he making her think of things best forgotten?

When she looked up again, he was gone. The two men who had stood on either side of him had closed ranks, filling the space the tall, blond man had occupied only moments before. She turned, searching the crowd for him. But it was no use; he had simply disappeared into the night.

Dear God, I am losing my mind. Panic rose in her breast, and her windpipe felt far too tight, too constricted. She needed to get home, back to Orchard House, before she fell apart entirely. It was the press of the crowd, she assured herself, coupled with the heat of the fire.

"...went to get the car," a voice beside her was saying, and she realized with a start that Mrs. Talbot was speaking to her.

"I'm sorry," she said, turning toward the woman. "You were saying?"

Her neighbor reached for her shoulder, as if to steady her. "I asked if you were ready to go, that's all. You look pale—are you feeling unwell?"

Emmaline swallowed hard before speaking. "I think the heat of the fire has made me a bit lightheaded, that's all."

"Come, then. We'll meet Mr. Talbot by the road."

Emmaline nodded, falling into step beside her. "Did...did you see that tall, blond gentleman? The one standing directly across from us during the bonfire?"

"The one in the gray sack suit, carrying a bowler?"

Emmaline's gaze snapped up to meet Mrs. Talbot's. "Yes. That's the one. Who was he?"

Mrs. Talbot shook her head. "I haven't any idea. I've never seen him before. He must be a visitor. A tourist, perhaps. Why do you ask?"

"He just...looked familiar, that's all," she said, the lie slipping easily from her tongue.

"Yes, he was looking at you rather queerly, wasn't he? Perhaps you've met before."

"Perhaps," Emmaline agreed. It was entirely possible, after all. Throughout the war, she'd nursed countless men, their faces nothing but a blur to her. They'd been dirty, most of them. Dirty and bloody and bandaged, and generally unrecognizable after months spent in trenches. But perhaps he remembered *her*.

It was an unsettling thought.

"There's Mr. Talbot," his wife said, hurrying toward the enormous black motorcar, its brass fittings glinting in the moonlight. "Come, let's get you home."

Emmaline just nodded as she climbed inside and settled against the tufted leather seat behind Mrs. Talbot. It was early still and the moon was bright; perhaps she'd take a stroll once she was home, check on the roses, and see that she'd latched the gate securely before she turned in.

What she would *not* do, she assured herself, was continue to think about the handsome stranger.

3

THERE WAS AN AUTOMOBILE COMING UP THE drive. Emmaline set the teakettle back on the stove and wiped her hands on her apron before hurrying to the front door. She wasn't expecting Mrs. Talbot—she'd said she was going into Chipping Norton to visit a friend today—and Mr. Talbot would have no reason to come without her.

Perhaps it was someone she'd met the at the Beltane festival? Unlikely, she decided, as teatime was not a proper hour for paying calls. She opened the door in time to see a red roadster pull up beneath the porte cochere. The driver cut the engine and stepped out, removing his hat and wiping his brow with the back of one hand.

"May I help you?" Emmaline called out, just before the shock of recognition washed over.

The man from the bonfire. Standing right there, in her drive.

He spun toward her. "It's you," he said, his eyes widening with unmasked surprise.

Emmaline shook her head, her mouth suddenly dry. "I'm sorry. Have we met?"

For a moment, he stood there entirely immobile, simply

staring at her. "I don't believe so," he said at last, hurrying up the stairs and extending a hand in her direction. "I'm Jack Wainscott."

"Emmaline Gage," she answered, taking his outstretched hand in her own. His felt warm—*too* warm.

He released her, reaching up to rub one temple. "You'll have to excuse me," he said. "Perhaps it's the heat, but I'm suddenly feeling a bit odd. Anyway, I hope you'll excuse my intrusion, but Mathilde Collins, the previous owner of Orchard House, was my father's cousin. Or rather, was married to my father's cousin."

"Indeed?" Emmaline was taken aback. She supposed this man must be some sort of relation to her late husband, though Christopher had never mentioned any Wainscotts to her. "But what does this have to do with me?"

"Yes," he continued, looking suddenly pale, "I'm getting to that. Orchard House should have come to my father upon old Mr. Collins's death. An entailment, you see. The Collinses had no sons, and my father was the closest living male relative. Make no mistake, my father isn't a generous man by any means, but my mother convinced him to let Mrs. Collins live out her days here. But now that she's gone, my father sent me here to check on the property—to claim it, I suppose. It was only when I arrived in Haverham that I learned that someone had taken up residence here."

Emmaline stepped backward, pressing herself against the front door. "But Mathilde Collins left the property to my husband. My late husband," she corrected, her voice barely above a whisper. Was she going to lose Orchard House, so soon after acquiring it? Now that she'd settled in, now that it felt like home?

He nodded, his hazel eyes meeting hers. They looked feverish, she decided. "I'm afraid the property wasn't legally hers to give," he said, swaying slightly on his feet.

"Would you like to come inside and sit down?" she asked. "I'm a nurse, you see, or *was* a nurse. Army Corps," she added, feeling foolish. She shook her head, hoping to clear it, allowing her nursing instincts, long since abandoned, to return. "Your skin is pale, your face flushed, and I don't like the look in your eyes." She reached for his forehead, wincing when the back of her hand made contact with his skin. "Good heavens, sir, you're burning up!"

Without waiting for his reply, she opened the door and bustled him into the front parlor, leading him toward the sofa. "What did you say your name was?" she asked.

"Jack," he mumbled. "Major Jack Wainscott, Fifth Army, Third Division."

Emmaline reached for his arm just as he slumped to the sofa, his eyes rolling up in his head. "Oh, no, you don't!" she cried, tapping his cheek several times, trying to rouse him.

His eyes snapped open, entirely unfocused. "Major Jack Wainscott," he repeated, his voice slurring. "Fifth Army, Third—"

"Yes, yes, I know, soldier." She reached beneath his arms, tugging him to his feet. "Let's get you to bed, while we still can."

Thankfully, there was a bedroom on the first floor, near the kitchen. It had likely been a servant's room at some point, but it would do just fine. It had a bed, at least, and its proximity to the kitchen would prove useful. She'd cleaned it and made the bed with fresh linens just last week.

A quarter hour later, she had him settled in bed, his jacket and necktie removed, along with his shoes. He was unconscious, feverish and flushed, his entire body trembling. She unbuttoned his shirt, looking for signs of a rash, or of any sort of wound that might be infected. She saw nothing that would explain his current state.

Reaching for his wrist, she checked his pulse. It was far too rapid and thready. Influenza, perhaps? If so, it seemed a particularly virulent strain, considering how quickly he had deteriorated. After setting a cool cloth on the man's forehead, she hurried back to the front hall to ring up Mrs. Talbot and ask her to send the doctor at once.

Jack struggled to open his eyes, feeling as if weights were pressing against them. He managed to open them a fraction, and then tried to turn his head. In the dim lighting, he could barely make out the shape of a woman with dark hair standing near the door. Beside her stood a man with gray whiskers and a low, gravelly voice. Their heads were bent together, the two deep in conversation.

No longer able to bear the weight of his eyelids, he allowed them to close, but tried to remain focused on the voices, trying to make out what they were saying. He caught only snippets, a few phrases here and there.

"Influenza…nothing we can do but wait it out…dangerous strain, one we've not seen in these parts…highly contagious…suggest we have him moved."

"I've already been exposed…experienced nurse…he must stay here."

"Quarantine…no visitors…at least a fortnight."

"Thank you…yes, on the chest of drawers…will call you if there's any change. Tell Mrs. Talbot…"

Jack swallowed hard, his throat dry and scratchy. He ached all over, and he hadn't any idea how he'd gotten into this unfamiliar bed. Where was he? And who were these people? He was tired, so very tired. He just wanted to sleep. If only someone would bring him a glass of water…

★ ★ ★

Her patient was not doing well. Emmaline sat by helplessly, watching him toss and turn, his face deathly pale. Every once in a while his glassy eyes would open, staring unseeing at the ceiling, and she would wipe his forehead with a cool cloth while she whispered soothing words to him.

It didn't matter what she said—he couldn't hear her. He was entirely delirious, his fever raging out of control. More than once his breathing had grown so labored that she'd feared she was losing him.

When that happened, she stripped him down to his drawers and bathed him with rubbing alcohol, cooling his head with ice packs while she said a little prayer.

By the fourth day, he seemed to stabilize a bit, though he remained in a deep sleep. She sat by his side now, working on a needlepoint sampler while he slept on, his limbs occasionally jerking as if he were dreaming.

"Water," he croaked, startling her from her work. She tossed down the sampler and hurried to fill a glass, pressing it to his lips. He tried to drink, but most of the water dribbled down his chin, soaking his thin cotton undershirt.

For the briefest of moments, his eyes fluttered open, fully focused this time. "Emmaline?" he murmured.

"Yes, I'm here," she answered, surprised that he remembered her name. He'd heard it only once, just before he'd collapsed. She bent over him, examining his pupils. They were almost fully dilated, the hazel ring barely visible now despite the lamp beside his bed.

She reached for his hand and clutched it tightly in her own, willing him to fight the fever. If only there was something she could do! She hated to watch this strong, handsome man waste away like this. It didn't seem fair. He'd beaten death once; he didn't deserve to go like this. No one did.

"Fight, Mr. Wainscott," she urged as his eyes fluttered shut again. "You must fight this! I can't do it for you. You mustn't give in. I'm sure there's someone, somewhere, who needs you. Who loves you. Fight for her, whoever she is."

His legs twitched, and Emmaline dropped her chin to her chest in despair. His breathing was shallow now, rasping and dangerously fast. She laid a hand on his burning cheek, caressing it, willing him once more to fight.

Almost immediately, his breathing improved. "That's it, Mr. Wainscott," she murmured. He seemed to enjoy her touch—it appeared to calm him, somehow. She moved closer, perching on the side of his bed.

"You just need to know that someone is here, that's all. I'm not going anywhere," she promised. Smiling down at his prone form, she ran her fingers through his damp hair, marveling at its softness as she combed it back from his forehead.

"See? Just sleep," she whispered, as his breathing quieted, becoming more regular now. "Tomorrow it will be better."

She only hoped she was right.

She was there beside him, his angel of mercy. He could hear her even breathing, somewhere near his left elbow. He hadn't any idea who she was, but she'd been there beside him all night. He'd woken several times from a dreamless sleep, and each and every time she'd wiped his brow with a cool, damp cloth, and then held a glass of water to his lips, murmuring encouragement as he drank. He'd wanted to ask her name, but he hadn't been able to muster the strength to do so. Instead, he'd simply fallen back against the pillows each time, listening as she bustled about the room. Eventually, she'd return to her spot beside the bed—a cot, perhaps? He wasn't sure, but it seemed as if she never left his side.

Just how long had she been tending him? He had no idea; he'd entirely lost his sense of time. He tried to sit, doing his best to remain silent so that he did not wake her. Eventually he managed to pull himself up to a seated position, where he could finally take stock of his surroundings.

It was nearly morning, he realized; the room bathed in the dim, hazy light of dawn. The space was small and sparsely furnished, with only the narrow iron bed he currently occupied, a single chest of drawers, a nightstand, and a small cot pushed against the wall. There wasn't room for much else.

On the cot, the woman lay sleeping on her side, facing him, a quilt pulled up to her chin. She looked peaceful, with one hand tucked beneath her chin, her rosy lips parted slightly. He watched as her chest rose and fell in perfect rhythm. Her dark hair was fanned out on the pillow, a single stray lock falling across one cheek. His fingers itched to brush back that errant strand, but of course he could not.

Who was she? He vaguely remembered driving over to Orchard House, intent on speaking to the woman who had taken possession of the estate, but beyond that he had no firm memories. Right now, the only thing he could recall was her gentle touch, her soothing voice as she tended him.

Growing tired, he collapsed back against the pillow. He would shut his eyes for a few moments, perhaps allow himself to doze as he waited for her to awaken.

And then he'd find out who she was, and thank her.

"You're awake," Emmaline said, watching with surprise as Mr. Wainscott's eyes fluttered open. Wiping her hands on her apron, she hurried to his side and reached up to feel his forehead. It was cool and slightly clammy, and she let out a sigh of relief. "And your fever has broken. How do you feel?" She reached for his wrist, lifting it off the bed and placing her fingers across his pulse. It was strong and steady, a marked improvement.

"Thirsty," he croaked. "Hungry, too."

Emmaline nodded, smiling down at the man. "That's a good sign. You have *no* idea what a fright you gave me."

"How long have I been here?" he asked, his voice hoarse.

"It's been five days since you took ill. You were lucky you were here when you collapsed. If you'd been out somewhere, alone…" She shook her head. "Anyway, drink this." She held a glass of water to his lips.

"I've got it," he said, taking the glass in one shaky hand.

Her brow knitted. "Are you sure? I vow, you're still as weak as a kitten."

He looked determined—male pride, she supposed. With a nod, Emmaline released the glass and watched as he brought it to his mouth and drank deeply.

"Better?" she asked as she took the empty tumbler and set it down beside the pitcher on the nightstand.

"Much," he said with a nod, then reached for her wrist, startling her. "Thank you."

"It's only water." She glanced down at his fingers, still wrapped around her wrist. They were long and elegant, like an artist's.

"Not for the water," he said, shaking his head. He finally released her. "Though, yes, I suppose I should thank you for that, too. But I meant for everything. I can only imagine the inconvenience I've caused you, the trouble you've gone to. I do hope you've had some help."

She shook her head. "The doctor wanted you quarantined. Since I was already exposed, I did not see the need to have you moved."

"You mean to say that you've been here alone with me, all this time? Five days?" he asked, his voice rising.

"Five days is not so very long, Mr. Wainscott. Besides, I'm a nurse, remember? Or at least I was, before I came here. I'm perfectly equipped to handle situations like this one. I promise you were never in any danger—"

"You misunderstand," he interrupted. "I'm certain I had the best care possible, thanks to you, Miss…" He trailed off. "You'll have to pardon me, but I cannot recall your name."

"Mrs. Gage," she supplied. "Emmaline." She had no idea what had prompted her to provide her given name. She'd certainly never allowed such familiarity with any of her previous patients.

"Emmaline," he repeated. "Of course. And you must call me Jack."

"Very well, Jack." She reached down to straighten the bedcovers—a habit, she supposed.

He looked toward the window. "What time is it?"

Emmaline turned toward the window. "Nearly noon. It looks like rain, doesn't it? Anyway, if you'll excuse me, I'll go prepare you some broth. If that goes well, perhaps you can have some toast later."

"I suppose beggars can't be choosers," he said with a sigh.

A quarter hour later, Emmaline returned with a steaming bowl of broth and set it down beside the bed. "I suppose you're going to insist on doing this yourself, too?"

"You know me too well," he joked.

She set a tray across his lap. "I know your type," she corrected. "After all, bravado was a common wartime trait."

He straightened his spine, readjusting the tray. "Did you serve on the front?"

Emmaline nodded, placing the bowl and spoon on the tray before him. "First at a clearing station at Passchendaele, then Allonville."

His eyes seemed to darken. "When were you at Allonville?"

She swallowed hard before replying. "The last year of the war. Why?"

"I came through that clearing station," he said, his voice suddenly dull. "In 1918. Just after the attack on the twenty-first of March."

"You were at Saint Quentin? In March of 1918? Good God, you were Fifth Army, weren't you?"

His eyes met hers, his gaze unflinching. "Fifth Army, Third Division."

She nodded, sinking to the cot beside his bed. "You said as much the night you arrived here."

How on earth had he survived it? She'd heard that the Fifth Army had been all but decimated. They'd been at the very front, and had taken the brunt of the German attack. Trench mortars, mustard gas, chlorine gas, smoke canisters— the casualties had been horrific. There had been very little for them to do at the clearing station afterward; most of the wounded had perished right there in the trenches before regimental medical officers had even been able to get to them.

She watched as he spooned the broth into his mouth, his hand trembling as he did so. One bite. Two. Torturously slow. And then he let the spoon clatter back to the tray. Taking a deep breath, he turned toward her. "My entire unit was destroyed that day," he said, his voice flat. "Fathers, brothers, sons—gone, nearly all of them. I've never quite understood why I managed to survive. Me, with no wife, no children. No one back at home who cared whether I lived or died, save my mother and sister."

Emmaline's throat felt tight, her windpipe constricted. She swallowed hard, willing the tears to remain at bay. "I'm sorry" was all she managed in reply.

"So am I," Jack said, sounding utterly defeated.

"I should leave you," Emmaline said, rising from the cot. "Let you finish your broth in peace."

"Please stay." Jack's voice broke ever so slightly.

Emmaline nodded, reaching for the spoon on his tray. "But only if you'll let me help you."

4

EMMALINE PEERED AT JACK OVER THE TOP EDGE of the book she held in her hands. He looked tired, though he'd never admit it, stubborn man. "Shall I stop there for the night?"

"No, keep going," he answered, opening his eyes. "I'm finding this all...quite illuminating."

She was reading aloud from Forster's *A Room with a View*. She'd found it in the library, and Jack had asked her to read it to him. It was clear that the novel wasn't to his taste, and yet he was indulging her, pretending to enjoy the romance between Lucy Honeychurch and George Emerson.

"In fact," he continued, "can you reread that last bit? You know, the part where she was gazing at him longingly?"

"Oh, do shut up!" Emmaline cried, smacking his arm with the book.

"Well, you must admit it's a bit overwrought," he said with a shrug.

She shook her head. "I won't admit to any such thing. It's beautiful and romantic, the writing so very vivid. Why, I can almost see the streets of Florence, just as Mr. Forster has described them."

"I suppose." He sounded unconvinced. "What does Lucy possibly see in George, anyway? He's a rather sullen chap, wouldn't you say?"

"Not at all. His manners are just not as refined, that's all. Anyway, it's all about escaping society's constraints, and George represents that escape, along with an escape from sexual repression. Lucy is a truly brave heroine."

He shook his head. "You got all that from the text? Why, it's just a love story. And a rather dull one, if I might say so."

"Oh, never mind. Perhaps I should find a more titillating passage—would that make you happy?" she teased.

"I should have my sister send over some of her earlier works, and have you read those aloud," he said with a chuckle.

"Is that so?" Emmaline had learned that his sister, Aisling, was a novelist, married to a botanist and living in Cambridge. Jack spoke fondly of her and her husband, even though their marriage had caused a terrible scandal back home, as the groom's father was unknown, and his mother a washerwoman. Jack loved to talk about Aisling—it was clear that they shared a very close bond.

"Did I ever mention that her first publication credits were short stories in the *Boudoir?* Published under a pen name, of course."

Emmaline just shrugged. She'd never heard of the *Boudoir,* though it *did* sound rather racy.

"Yes, indeed," he continued. "My sister got her start writing naughty stories. *Very* naughty."

"You're teasing me," Emmaline said with a sigh, marking the page in the book with a square of needlepoint. "It isn't nice, you know—teasing one's nurse."

Jack's eyes danced with mischief. "Actually, I'm not teasing at all. They're scandalous stories, I tell you. Trust me, I've read every last one of them. I'm the one who took them to London and sold them to the *Boudoir.*"

Emmaline raised one brow. "I presume I'm to find this shocking?"

He shook his head, a shock of blond hair falling carelessly across his forehead. "No? Oh, right. I forgot, you're an American. It's much harder to shock an American, isn't it?"

She resisted the urge to stand and brush back the lock of hair from his forehead. "What, precisely, are you trying to say about Americans, Mr. Wainscott?" she asked instead, allowing herself to enjoy the banter.

"I've no idea, really." He shrugged. "It's all balderdash. But it made you smile, and you've a beautiful smile. Your entire face lights up. And there you have it, my ulterior motive. I've *always* got a motive. Just ask my sister."

Emmaline's heart fluttered at the compliment. "I imagine you do," she murmured, her cheeks growing warm. "Always have a motive, that is."

"Speaking of which," he said, "do you think we could take a turn outside? In the garden, perhaps? It's far too stuffy in here tonight."

Emmaline shook her head in frustration. "No. No turns outside, no leaving this bed. I let you overtax yourself this afternoon, and you need your rest."

He'd insisted on ambling about the house before tea, and he'd nearly collapsed from exhaustion. She'd let him out of bed against her better judgment, and he'd proved that he wasn't quite ready. The influenza had taken a far greater toll on his body than he realized. She'd never met such a stubborn man.

"I know what we'll do," she said, suddenly having an idea. "We'll give you a shave. I don't know why I didn't think of it sooner. I found some shaving supplies in one of the washrooms when I first arrived. Surely there must be a usable blade among them."

He reached up to rub one heavily whiskered cheek. "I suppose you're right. I would hate to forfeit my claim on being a dandy. I take great pride in it, after all. It's not much, but it's all I've got."

"You're incorrigible," she said with a shake of her head. "I'll be right back. You're *not* to get out of that bed while I'm gone, do you hear me?"

"I wouldn't dream of it," he replied. "You're quite bossy, you know."

Emmaline folded her arms across her chest. "You do realize I'm going to be holding a blade to your throat in a few moments, don't you?"

"I like you," he quipped. "Very much, to tell you the truth. Surely you wouldn't harm a man who holds you in such high esteem? Even if I am lying here rather helplessly."

Her pulse leaped. Dear Lord, the man had no idea how his careless words affected her. "You're far too charming for your own good," she said, trying to sound disapproving.

"Perhaps I used to be, before the war. Now I'm just a bore. Like Cecil Vyse," he added, tipping his head toward the book. "The poor bloke."

She rolled her eyes. "Have you been listening to yourself? I vow, you could charm the skin off a snake."

For the briefest of moments, he looked thoughtful, serious even. "It's been…years since I've laughed the way I have today," he said, somber now.

"I'm glad," she said. "You've made me laugh, too. It's been…" She trailed off, realizing that she'd almost said *fun*— which was ridiculous, really. She was only nursing the man back to health, not enjoying a house party. "I'm enjoying your company," she said instead. "Now if you'll excuse me for one moment, I'll go gather the shaving supplies." She hurried out before the telltale rise of color in her cheeks gave her away.

Not ten minutes later she was back, carrying a bowl, shaving soap, a brush and a blade. "Here we are," she said, setting it all down on the nightstand.

He'd unbuttoned several buttons on his shirt while she'd been gone, exposing a fair amount of his chest. The skin was smooth, slightly tanned, the muscles sharply defined. Despite his illness, he looked healthy. Virile, even.

She dragged her attention away from his chest and concentrated on the soap instead, mixing it to a thick, rich lather. "Shall I tuck a towel around your neck?" she offered.

He shook his head. "Would you mind if I took off my shirt instead? That way we won't risk soiling this one."

The doctor had retrieved Jack's traveling case from the hotel, and it now sat on a stand in the room's far corner. Of course, Jack had meant to stay in Haverham only for a night or two, so he'd brought very little. Emmaline had been laundering his clothes with her own. At present, one freshly pressed shirt hung in the kitchen.

"Very well," she said, relenting. "Do you need help?"

He undid the few remaining buttons and began to shrug out of it. "I think I can manage," he said with a wince. "Damn, I hate being an invalid."

Emmaline waited as he finished the task, his face an inscrutable mask. Clearly, he hated displaying any sign of weakness—as if she would hold it against him. "There's nothing to be ashamed of," she said softly. "You were gravely ill. You'll have to be patient, that's all."

"I only wish...well, that we'd met under different circumstances," he said, barely able to meet her gaze. "Do you have any idea how emasculating this is? Being tended like a child?"

She took a step toward him, dipping the brush into the lather as she did so. "I'm a nurse, Jack. It's what I do."

"And that's how you see me, isn't it? As a patient, and nothing more?"

She met his gaze. "How else should I see you?" she asked, her voice barely above a whisper. *Like a man,* she silently answered. A ridiculously handsome, funny and altogether irresistible man. A man who had begun to haunt her dreams, to fill her with a sense of longing—of desire—that she hadn't felt since Christopher. She shook her head, as if to clear it. This was madness. It was too soon.

"Never mind," Jack said with a sigh, then lifted his chin. "Go on. Don't worry, I promise to sit very still and behave myself."

"Very well." Emmaline moved closer, leaning over him as she lathered him up. Once she was done, she set aside the brush and reached for the blade. She made one swipe across his left cheek, then another.

"This angle is awkward," she said, shaking her head. "Would you mind if I sat on the edge of bed beside you?"

"Of course not," he answered with a shrug, moving over to make room for her.

She felt his entire body tense as she leaned across him. She tried to ignore the heat that had coiled in her belly, instead focusing on the blade as she dragged it across his skin. *Be professional,* she reminded herself. *He's your patient, nothing more.*

Jack could barely stand it. Damn it, but her breast brushed across his chest with every stroke of the blade. He could have sworn that he felt the hardened peak of one nipple through the fabric of her blouse, pressing up against him. Thank God he was impotent, because otherwise he'd surely be suffering from an embarrassing cockstand that would no doubt send her scurrying from the room.

Because she didn't think of him as a man, but a patient—a weak, helpless patient who could barely wipe his own ass at present, for fuck's sake. He choked back the bitter gall of self-loathing.

The night of the Beltane festival, he'd spied her across the bonfire and had been immediately intrigued. Smitten, even. He wasn't foolish enough to believe in love at first sight, but it had felt like a lighting bolt from the sky, the moment he'd laid eyes on her. She was so very beautiful, fragile looking and ethereal. He'd been struck with a burning, almost primal desire to protect her, to take care of her.

Instead, he was lying in bed like a weakling, allowing *her* to take care of *him*. When he'd first seen her, he'd only thought how nice it might be to take her to bed. In the three days since he'd awakened, he'd come to know her, to admire her strength and humor and kindness. Now, he wanted to fuck her *and* spend the rest of his days by her side, her devoted slave. Pure and utter madness.

"Tip your chin up," she said, moving the blade to his neck. "And do be still. I'm dangerously close to your carotid."

Several moments passed in silence save the sound of the blade scraping against his skin.

"There you are," she said at last, sitting back and wiping his face with a towel. "Now you look more like a baronet's son."

She had shaving soap on her cheek. He wanted to wipe it away, but knew that touching her would place him in dangerous territory. "You've got soap—right there," he said, pointing to her face.

"Where?" she asked, reaching to her chin.

"There." He indicated the general direction with a wave of one hand.

She swiped at her cheek, and missed it entirely.

Taking a deep breath, he reached for her. She leaned toward him, and he could smell her now-familiar scent—rosewater and lemon, clean and fresh and sweet. He brushed away the soap, allowing his fingers to linger, to move down toward her mouth, toward her chin. Before he knew what he was doing, he found himself cupping her face, moving his mouth toward hers.

"Emmaline," he groaned, just as his mouth came down on hers, hard and hungry.

In a flash, her arms were around his neck, drawing him closer as she rose up on her knees. He heard her whisper his name against his lips, felt her tongue trace his bottom lip.

He reached around her, cupping her ass as he dragged her closer, till she was nearly sitting on his lap. Devil take it, but his cock had stiffened, pressing against his trousers. *What the hell?*

The shock of it made him gasp, and Emmaline pulled away. Her gaze met his, her dark eyes wild.

"Did I hurt you?" she asked.

He just shook his head, unable to utter a single syllable in reply.

"Jack?" she whispered, and it sounded almost like a plea. He wasted no time answering it, but dragged her mouth back to his. Her lips were soft and pliant, her breath as sweet as honey. His tongue skated across her teeth, begging for entry.

In the front hall, the telephone rang—once, twice.

"Please don't stop," Emmaline said breathlessly. She was pressed against him now, her mouth opened against his, her tongue touching his, teasing and then retreating, driving him wild. She was like one of his wildest erotic fantasies come true.

God help him, it had been so long... If she kept this up, he was going to come right now. Her bottom was pressing against his hardened cock, providing him proof that he was no longer damaged—that he was a man again.

And she was a woman—a willing woman, in his bed. He'd never wanted anyone like this, with a mind-numbing, burning desire that overrode all sensibility and good intentions.

He plucked her blouse from the band of her skirt, pushing up the fabric, trying to free her breasts from whatever undergarment she wore beneath. Sensing his struggle, she pulled away, drawing the blouse over her head in one fluid motion. Seconds later, she'd rid herself of the undergarment, and was entirely bare to the waist, straddling his hips.

Lowering his head, he ran his tongue across one rose-colored nipple. Her head tipped back, a low moan escaping her lips. God, how he needed this—needed her. Taking the now-pebbled peak in his mouth, he suckled gently while his hands reached beneath her skirt, searching for her knickers.

Just as he found them and hooked his fingers inside the waistband, Emmaline moved off him, groping for his trousers' fastenings. "Are you sure?" he asked her, reaching for her wrists. "Emmaline?" he prodded. "Christ, I want you so badly, but only if you're completely sure. I haven't anything...no protection with me." Why would he have brought condoms with him to Haverham? He certainly hadn't had any use for them lately. He hadn't been able to get it up since the war. This was a completely unexpected development.

"I'm sure, Jack. Entirely sure," she added, looking him square in the eye. Her pupils were dilated, her lids heavy with desire. He nodded, releasing her wrists and pushing down his trousers, freeing his eager cock. Holy hell, but he hoped his erection lasted, hoped he could perform.

Reaching under her skirt, Emmaline slid her knickers down, removing them before she straddled him again, fitting herself over his tip. Unable to bear it a moment longer, he raised his hips, sheathing himself inside her. She cried out, and he stilled at once, terrified that he'd hurt her.

Bloody hell, what had he done?

But then she began to move, rocking against him, her breath coming faster and faster as she rode him. He wanted to meet her thrusts, but weak as he was, he found he couldn't. He couldn't do anything but lie there, watching her, feeling the pleasure well to a crescendo inside him. Any moment now, any moment and he—

"Jack!" she cried out. "Oh, God, now!"

He felt her come, felt her cunt tighten around him, and it pushed him right over the edge. He cried her name between clenched teeth, his entire body taut and rigid beneath her as his seed pumped into her. The orgasm seemed endless, their bodies in perfect unison. Finally, she collapsed against his chest.

It took him longer than her to catch his breath. He was still panting when she raised her head and looked at him, her brow knitted with concern. "Oh, Jack, what have I done? I'm such a fool—you're not even well."

"Trust me, darling, I haven't felt this well in ages," he quipped, willing his breathing to slow to normal.

He saw tears gather in the corner of her eyes as she rolled off him. "If I've hurt you, if I've harmed you in any way—"

"Stop," he said, unable to bear it. He reached for her shoulder and drew her back to his chest. "Stay with me tonight. Please?"

Relief washed over him when she nodded. "Let me turn out the lamp, and I'll move to the cot," she said.

"Oh, no, you don't." He held her tight, bending down to kiss the top of her head. "Though you might consider losing this," he added, tugging on her skirt.

"It goes against all my nursing instincts," she murmured, her breath warm against his neck while she wriggled out of her skirt.

"That was by far the best nursing care I've ever received. Hell, I don't know what I did to deserve it, but you won't hear me complaining."

She sat up and leaned toward the nightstand to turn out the lamp. "Go to sleep, Jack. Nurse's orders."

Lying there in the dark, with a naked Emmaline pressed against him, Jack just smiled. As ill and weak as he was, this might very well have been the best day of his life.

5

EMMALINE AWAKENED WITH A START, CONFUSED by the weight across her chest. It was an arm, she realized, blinking at the sight. A man's arm, dusted with fine, dark blond hair. Confused, she sat up abruptly before she remembered where she was and what she'd done.

Good God, she was in Jack's bed! Her patient, a man she barely knew, a man so weak that he hadn't been able to take more than a dozen steps yesterday. She'd chastised him for pushing himself too hard, and then she'd gone and slept with him? Whatever had she been thinking? Bloody hell, she might very well have killed him.

Panic rising, she looked over at him, watching for the rise and fall of his chest, for some sign of life—anything. She almost wept with relief when he turned on his side, reaching for her.

"Emmaline?" he mumbled sleepily.

She swallowed hard before replying. "I'm here, Jack."

"Thank the devil," he said, opening one eye. "I thought I might have dreamed it."

"Apparently not," she said, reaching for the blanket to cover herself.

Both eyes open now, he dragged himself up to a seated position beside her. "Please don't tell me you regret it, Emmaline. Hell, even if you *do* regret it, do me a favor and lie to me, because that was perhaps the most wonderful night of my entire pitiful existence. You would not take that from me, would you?"

What was the point in denying it? "Of course I don't regret it."

His mouth curved into a smile. "Good. Anything else would surely be an act of cruelty. Have you any idea how lovely you are when you first wake up?

She shook her head. "I'm sure I'm a fright." She reached up to her lips, which felt tender and swollen. Between her legs felt tender, too. It had been so very long since someone had made love to her. Her body was simply not used to it.

And, she realized, it was the first time someone had made love to her without protection. Wartime had not been a time to take chances—not when both she and Christopher had been on their way to the front. They had always used a condom. But this time…this time there had been nothing between her and Jack, no barriers. Just flesh against flesh, and it had been exquisite.

She pushed aside the feeling of disloyalty that was nagging at her heart. Christopher was gone—he was not coming back to her. And Jack, well…Jack was *here*. Now.

"You look so faraway," Jack said, brushing the back of one hand across her cheek. His touch was so very soft, so gentle.

"I should get you some breakfast," she said, glancing at the window. The sun was high in the sky; it must be close to noon. "Some toast, perhaps, and some tea."

"Not yet," he said, dipping his head toward her neck. His lips were cool against her skin, drawing gooseflesh in their wake.

"Perhaps it can wait," she murmured.

In the distance, a door slammed. "Yoo-hoo! Emmaline, dear!"

Dear Lord, it was Mrs. Talbot! Emmaline's heart began to race as she leaped from bed, frantically searching for her skirt and blouse.

"Emmaline?" Mrs. Talbot shouted once more. "Are you around, dear? I don't want to come any farther than the front hall. The doctor made me swear I'd wait another week, but I just couldn't bear it."

"I'll be right there," she called out, shooting Jack a panicked look. "Just give me a moment." He retrieved her knickers and skirt from the bedclothes and tossed them to her.

Whatever was she going to do? Surely Mrs. Talbot would be suspicious when she saw the rumpled state of her clothing, the tangled mess of her hair. Pulling on her blouse, she hurried to look in the mirror above the chest of drawers. She groaned aloud when she saw the deep purple mark that Jack's mouth had left on her throat. However was she going to hide that?

Moving as quickly as she could, she stepped into her skirt and fastened it, deciding not to worry about her knickers. Instead, she kicked them under the bed.

"Emmaline?" Mrs. Talbot called out again. "Have I come at a bad time? I tried to ring you last night, and got no answer."

"I'm…I'm just taking Mr. Wainscott's temperature right now," she lied. It would buy her a minute or two.

"Very well, dear. I'll wait."

Emmaline attempted to tidy her hair, but without a brush, it was no use. It fell past her shoulders in tumbling waves, and for once she wished she'd cut it into a more fashionable bob. She tried to arrange it so that it covered the mark on her throat, then smoothed down her clothes as best she could.

She glanced back at Jack, who sat watching her with a boyish smile on his face, clearly enjoying this. "At least put your shirt on," she whispered. "Just in case!"

And then she hurried out, forcing her features into a placid, professional mask. "I'm so sorry to keep you waiting, Mrs. Talbot."

"Good heavens, look at you!" the woman cried out as soon as Emmaline stepped into the front hall. "You're a mess— you look as if you haven't slept in days. I knew this was too much to ask of you. I told Dr. Hayward so, but the man just wouldn't listen."

Emmaline attempted a smile. "Oh, it's nothing, really. You must excuse my appearance. I'm afraid I fell asleep in my clothes last night, and then I overslept. I was just now checking on Mr. Wainscott, but I assure you I'm perfectly well and rested."

Mrs. Talbot's eyes narrowed suspiciously. "Are you certain?"

"Of course. It's all going very well, and my patient is recovering nicely."

Still looking unconvinced, Mrs. Talbot held out a basket. "I brought you some scones and muffins. I was afraid you wouldn't have any time to bake for yourself."

Emmaline took the basket, her heart swelling with gratitude. "That was so kind of you, Mrs. Talbot. They smell delicious. But you really should go—the entire house is supposed to be under quarantine. I'd never forgive myself if you were to take ill."

"Oh, I'll be fine. I'm a tough old bird, as they say. Anyway, I just couldn't bear the thought of you alone all this time with that strange man. Why, you don't know him from Adam!"

"Well, he's one of Mrs. Collins's relations. A cousin of some sort, I think he said."

"Mathilde never mentioned any Wainscotts." She tipped her head to one side, her mouth pursed. "Except maybe an Aisling Wainscott. An authoress of some note, I believe. Some sort of distant relation, she said."

"Yes," Emmaline said, "that's Jack's—Mr. Wainscott's sister."

"Is that so? Well, I still don't understand what he was doing out here when he took ill. He must have known that Mrs. Collins passed."

"Mrs. Gage?" Jack called out, and Emmaline glanced over her shoulder in surprise. "If I might trouble you for some water."

Emmaline bit her lower lip, trying not to smile.

"I should let you get back to your patient," Mrs. Talbot said. "Please don't tell Dr. Hayward that I came by. I vow, I'll never hear the end of it if you do." Her eyes narrowed a fraction. "What's that there on your neck?"

Emmaline reached up to cover it with her palm. "Oh, it's nothing. Just a scrape. I was just…ahem, that is to say—"

"Mrs. Gage?" Jack called again, clearly trying to sound particularly pathetic.

"I'll be right there, Mr. Wainscott," she replied. "Thank you again, Mrs. Talbot. I'm so grateful for the baked goods. I know Mr. Wainscott will be, too, as soon as he's well enough to enjoy them."

The woman nodded, leaning toward her and whispering conspiratorially. "Just don't let him run you ragged, dear. Let him know who's in charge, that's all."

"Of course." Emmaline walked her to the door and saw her out, one hand still covering the mark on her neck. "Good day, Mrs. Talbot!" she said, then shut the door and turned the key in the lock. If only she'd thought to lock it before now.

Letting her breath out in a rush, she picked up the basket of sweets and hurried back to Jack's side.

"So, this is your garden," Jack said, releasing Emmaline's arm as he sank to the bench. "I must say, from your description, I was expecting far worse."

She shook her head, glancing around the walled space with an expression of wonder on her face. "I've totally neglected it since your arrival, and yet it looks much improved. I can't imagine how, as we've had so little rain."

"Curious, isn't it? I say, whoever designed this garden was inordinately fond of the Green Man's image, weren't they? His face is everywhere." An odd sensation prickled Jack's skin. "I almost feel as if we're being watched."

"I feel it, too," Emmaline agreed. "As if this is the garden of legend, the one where the Green Man was imprisoned by the Winter King."

"You saw the pantomime?" Jack asked.

"Yes. I didn't realize *you* did."

He shrugged. "I confess I found it a bit melodramatic."

"Of course you would," Emmaline said with a laugh. "Anyway, you sit and rest for a bit. I'm going to pull some weeds and trim the roses."

He nodded gratefully. He'd never admit it, of course, but he was exhausted. The walk from the house to the garden had near enough done him in. His traitorous legs felt entirely weak, and his heart was beating like a rabbit's. Blasted influenza. He wanted to save every last ounce of energy he had for more entertaining forms of physical exertion.

His mouth went dry as he watched Emmaline make her

way across the flagstones toward the roses. Devil take it, but she was beautiful. She would never believe it, of course. He'd never met anyone quite like her. He couldn't put his finger on it, but there was something far more natural— more earthy, perhaps—than the ladies with whom he was acquainted.

He watched as she cranked the handle on the well and filled the watering tin, marveling at the grace with which she moved. There was something so very feminine about her, so soft and gentle, despite her waiflike appearance.

She was nothing like Claire—the polar opposite, really. Oh, Claire was beautiful, too, there was no denying that. But there was a hardness to her features, an angularity to her slim, boyish frame. Jack had sometimes thought that every-thing Claire said or did was carefully calculated, meant to craft and hone an image rather than express true sentiment. He'd never known exactly what was going on in that sharp mind of hers; never truly understood what she'd felt or cared about. In all the years he'd known her, she'd been mostly a mystery to him—an intriguing puzzle to be solved.

Of course, hadn't he done the same thing? Cultivated the image he wanted to project to the world, that of an uncom-plicated, carefree country gentleman. That image was far better than the real Jack, the one who fretted over his future, who hated his father for the callous way he treated his wife, who felt things far too deeply than he ought.

Perhaps he and Claire Lennox were perfectly suited, after all. He'd loved her enough to want to marry her, and *would* have married her if the war hadn't left him impotent, broken in both body and spirit. Breaking off their engagement had seemed the only fair thing to do. She deserved more. She hadn't been happy with his decision, despite the fact that he'd been unable to make love to her—an embarrassing debacle if ever there was one. Twice he'd tried, and twice he'd failed, his cock lying limp despite her valiant efforts to seduce him.

What had happened here at Orchard House to change that? How had Emmaline, a woman he barely knew, managed to cure him? Especially considering his physical state at present? He shook his head in amazement, feeling his cock begin to swell even now as he watched Emmaline bend over the roses, her perfect backside presented to him like a gift. The sun was behind her, and he could clearly make out the shape of her legs beneath her calf-length skirt. God, he wanted her. But he'd wanted Claire, too. Every man had wanted Claire— blonde, beautiful Claire with her cornflower-blue eyes and perfect little bow of a mouth, a cigarette dangling from her lips while she batted her lashes provocatively.

He had to tell Emmaline about Claire, about his broken engagement. It was only fair. After all, it had only been, what? Three, four weeks since he'd called off the wedding? He wasn't sure. But Emmaline had been entirely forthcoming about her own past, and he knew he should do the same.

There was no doubt that she had loved Christopher Gage with all her heart. Not that Jack was surprised. He'd met her late husband on more than one occasion—they were distant relations, some sort of cousins-in-law. Chris had been an attractive man, the kind who turned every woman's head with his dark good looks and easy charm. He was smooth where Jack was awkward, confident where Jack was insecure. There was an intensity about him that women seemed to find irresistible. Of course Emmaline had fallen for him, and why not? As much as Jack hated to admit it, Chris Gage had been a damned good man, generous and intelligent to a fault.

How could anyone live up to that? Why would anyone even try? Gripping the stone bench on which he sat, Jack traced the outline of the Green's Man's face with a finger.

Devil take it, but he wanted to try. He couldn't *help* but try. He wanted her that badly.

"What are you thinking about over there?" Emmaline called out, startling him. "You look far too serious."

"Do I?" he asked, struggling to add some jocularity to his voice. "Perhaps you should come over here, and I'll show you exactly what I'm thinking about."

"Should I, now?" Her mouth curved into a smile. "And what about these poor roses? You would have me abandon them in their time of need?"

"What about *my* time of need?" he teased, loving the bloom that had sprung to her cheeks.

She shrugged, setting aside the watering pail. "You look quite well to me. Far better than yesterday. I think the fresh air is doing wonders for your health."

"I think *you're* doing wonders for my health," he corrected. "Come here," he ordered, feeling emboldened. Perhaps he wasn't a confident man, but he could pretend to be one. He'd certainly read enough of Aisling's scandalous stories to know how a sexually assertive male was supposed to act.

Still, he hadn't expected Emmaline to obey. And yet she was doing just that, wordlessly crossing the flagstones that separated them, a mysterious smile playing on her lips. As if on cue, his cock sprang to attention.

Yes, she had cured him. Of that he was certain.

6

EMMALINE PAUSED DIRECTLY IN FRONT OF JACK, who sat there watching her, openmouthed, as she begun to unbutton her blouse. She hadn't the slightest idea what had possessed her, what had made her so bold and brassy. She only knew that she wanted him beyond reason.

She wasn't herself, hadn't been for days now. And yet this somehow felt *right*. Perhaps it was just that Jack was nearly a stranger, that he didn't know the sensible, predictable Emmaline, but the impulsive, sensual Emmaline instead. She wanted to be that woman, if only temporarily.

Her trembling fingers fumbled with the final button on her blouse, and then the thin voile fabric parted, revealing the lacy camisole she wore beneath it. She took a deep breath, her gaze locking with Jack's heated one.

"You're sure?" he asked, reaching for her hands and drawing her closer.

She nodded. "Entirely so."

A warm breeze stirred, fluttering the hem of her blouse and raising gooseflesh on her skin. Above them, the leaves rustled. A bird dipped toward them, chattering gaily. The sun warmed her skin as Jack pulled her down onto his lap. The garden seemed somehow...pleased.

Emmaline closed her eyes, inhaling sharply. The air was redolent with the scents of earth, of grass and sunshine—and Jack.

"Your hair," he said, his voice rough. "I want it down."

Emmaline nodded. Only a handful of pins secured the bun at the nape of her neck. One by one she removed them, placing them in her skirt pocket. Jack loosened the coils with his fingers, gently combing through her hair until the loose waves fell across her shoulders. A shiver worked its way down her spine as his lips replaced his hands on her hair, his mouth moving toward her neck, toward the sensitive skin beneath her ear where her pulse beat like butterfly wings.

A sigh escaped her lips as she melted against him. His erection pressed firmly against her bottom, proof of his desire. She couldn't help but squirm against the length of him, suddenly desperate to feel him inside her again.

"Please," she murmured, unable to stand it a moment longer. "Jack, now—"

He silenced her with his mouth, hot against hers. It was a demanding kiss, and Emmaline relented at once, her lips parting as his tongue sought entry. *Yes,* her mind screamed as he deepened the kiss. *Yes, just like this.* She wanted to be taken hard.

But then his mouth moved away. As if she were as light as a feather, he lifted her from his lap and set her gently on the bench beside him. Again his mouth slanted toward hers. The kiss seemed to go on forever, their tongues searching, exploring. Finally, his lips moved from hers once more. Her head tipped back as he trailed hot kisses down her throat, across her collarbone. Roughly pushing down her camisole, he continued lower still. Emmaline felt the delicate fabric give, heard a ripping sound, and then his mouth was on her nipple, his teeth scraping against the puckered skin. All her nerve endings seemed to come alive at once, her skin hot and flushed and seemingly electrified as he flicked his tongue across the sensitive peak, again and again.

Her hands fisted in his hair as she pressed him to her breast, wanting more. When he began to suckle her, she thought she'd go mad with wanting.

"Now, Jack," she said again, wriggling against him. "Please."

"Now what, Emmaline my sweet? Say it. Say it now," he ordered hoarsely.

What did he want her to say?

And then somehow she knew—knew exactly what words to say to set him over the edge, to make him give her exactly what she wanted. "Fuck me now. Now, Jack."

She heard his sharp intake of breath, saw his pupils dilate, and her heart soared with victory. Next thing she knew, he'd dragged her to her feet and bent her over the bench, her skirt somehow gathered around her waist. Glancing over one shoulder, she watched as he hastily unfastened his trousers and reached inside his drawers to free his erection.

She let out her breath in a rush of anticipation, gripping the back of the bench so tightly that her knuckles turned white. She arched her back, gasping softly when she felt his fingers tug down her knickers, baring her entirely to his sight.

"Dear God, Emmaline," he said with a sigh, his movements slower now. She felt a finger slide down her cleft, parting her. She was already wet and ready for him, aching to feel him inside her.

Instead, he stroked her, teasing her clitoris while he slipped one finger into her sex. "You're so very beautiful," he said, his voice thick with desire.

It was as if everything around them ceased to exist—the garden, the cloudless sky, the chirruping birds. It was just the two of them there, in some other plane of existence where nothing mattered but their pleasure. Her legs grew weak, her breath coming far too fast now as he continued to stroke her, pushing her closer and closer to release. Just when she thought she couldn't stand the exquisite sensations another second, he stopped, withdrawing his wicked fingers.

A moment later, she felt the tip of him pressing against her slick entrance. With one thrust, he buried himself fully inside her. Instinctively, she arched further, taking him in even more deeply, wanting nothing more than to be filled by him. His fingers dug into her hips as he clutched her to him, her name a whisper on his lips.

In the distance, a motorcar rumbled down the road. A horn sounded, perhaps in greeting. She didn't know, didn't care. All that mattered was Jack pressing against her backside, pumping into her now with a steady rhythm that made ripples of pleasure begin to radiate from her core.

The force of her orgasm caught her entirely off guard, making her knees buckle slightly as she leaned into the bench for support. Behind her, Jack groaned, finding his own release just in time to make hers even more intense than she'd thought possible.

His head dropped to her shoulder, his lips pressing against her as he murmured her name, over and over again. It was only when his body began to tremble against hers that she remembered his weakened state. Alarm shot through her at once, and she moved away from him, wincing as he slipped out of her, leaving her cold and empty.

"Good heavens, Jack," she cried, quickly pulling up her

knickers and smoothing down her skirt. "You must sit down. Here." She guided him back to the seat, her breath catching as he slumped down with a sigh.

"I'm fine," he said, smiling drowsily as he fastened his trousers. "More than fine, really. Honest to God."

She shook her head. "I think we should get you back inside. You've had enough excitement for one day."

His eyes danced with mischief. "That *was* rather exciting, wasn't it?"

"Perhaps it was," she said, rather annoyed with herself for risking his health yet again. "But now I'm ordering you back to bed."

"Bed, you say? Please tell me you'll be joining me there."

She glanced over at the roses she'd neglected. "I've still some work to do here in the garden. You should get some rest, and I'll wake you in time for tea." She needed to get away from him, to rid herself of the distraction, or she'd never get anything accomplished.

"Oh, very well," he grumbled.

Emmaline couldn't help but smile. It was easy to imagine what he must have been like as a boy. "That's the spirit," she said cheerfully. "Why, we'll have you better in no time."

But as soon as the words left her lips, she wished she could take them back. Her smile disappeared at once. Because as soon as he was well, he'd be leaving her—leaving Orchard House, and Haverham. Or worse still, making *her* leave Orchard House. That was why he'd come, after all. To put her out.

Reluctantly, she dragged her gaze to meet his. All the mischief and merriment had completely fled his features. Was he thinking the same thing she was? Likely so, she realized. There was no getting around it—they were on borrowed time, and every step he took toward recovery meant a step away from her.

Tears burned behind her eyelids, but she would not let them fall. Soon enough, she'd be alone again. And then she'd have all the time in the world for tears.

Jack heard a gasp, felt a movement beside him in the dark. In the distance, thunder rumbled. He heard a whimper, realized it was Emmaline. Rubbing the sleep from his eyes, he sat up and reached for her just as a flash of lightning illuminated the room. "Emma?" he whispered, touching her shoulder. "Emmaline?"

She didn't respond. A crash of thunder rattled the windowpane beside the bed. He heard Emmaline's sharp intake of breath, felt her body trembling.

Because of the storm?

It didn't make sense. Emmaline was strong, perhaps the strongest woman he'd ever met. What was a storm, compared to the war and its horrors?

When the next flash of lightning lit the sky, he saw that her hands were pressed against her ears, her eyes squeezed shut. "Emmaline?" He shook her shoulder this time, leaning over her prone form.

"Stay down," she murmured. "Trench mortars. Nerve gas…" Her voice trailed off as she rolled to her side, her legs drawn up to her belly.

"No, no, it's just thunder. A storm." He cupped her cheek with his palm, surprised to find it damp. "Emmaline?"

Another crash of thunder shook the glass, and she sat up with a gasp. "What…what happened?" she stammered. "Where am I?"

She'd been sleeping, he realized. Dreaming.

"Home, love. At Orchard House." He drew her against his chest. Her heart was beating wildly.

"Jack?" Her fingers dug into his flesh.

"I'm here," he answered, pressing a kiss against her temple.

She let out her breath in a rush. "Dear God, Jack. I had a dream, a terrible nightmare. I was back at the front, and you were there. You and Christopher. There were mortars going off everywhere, and I was trying to get to both of you at once, trying to…" She trailed off, shaking her head. "I could not save you, not both of you."

"Shh," he murmured against her hair. "It was just a dream, probably triggered by the thunder. But you're safe, everyone's safe." Except Chris, of course, who was beyond being saved. Jack wondered whom she'd chosen in her dream, but didn't dare ask.

She began to cry, hot tears scalding his chest. "I'm so sorry, Jack."

Perhaps that was his answer?

"Don't cry, Emmaline." He couldn't bear to watch a woman cry, particularly if he'd played a part in it. And it seemed he had—at least, in her dream.

At once, rain began to pelt the glass. Lightning flashed, thunder boomed as the storm reached its climax. He held her tight, murmuring soothing words as she continued to sob. By the time the storm subsided, her tears were reduced to sniffles and she lay against his shoulder, spent.

"I hope you'll forgive me," she said at last. "I've no idea what came over me. The dream…it was so very real. I could hear the mortars, smell the smoke in the air, and I was help-less to do anything. It was like losing Christopher all over again. And you—" she shook her head "—I didn't want to lose you, too."

He didn't know what to say in reply, didn't know what she wanted to hear. He'd hoped beyond reason that there was a future for them, but had feared that she wasn't quite ready, that this had only been an interlude of sorts, as far as she was concerned.

"Oh, I know I've no claim on you," she continued. "It's just that the thought of you leaving, of finding myself all alone again—"

"I'm not going anywhere, Emmaline," he interjected, buying time. "Not just yet. The quarantine, remember?"

"Yes, yes, of course. The quarantine." Raising up on one elbow, she peered down at him sharply. "You must tell me, Jack—is there someone at home, waiting for you? Someone who…well, who would not be happy to know what we've done here?"

He swallowed hard before replying. He had to tell her the truth—there was no other way. "I was engaged until very recently," he said simply.

"What happened?"

He should have known it would not be that easy. "I called off the wedding. Despite my assurances to the contrary, she is not convinced that I won't change my mind, given time."

"Do you love her?" Emmaline asked.

The pain in her voice slashed through his heart. "I did love her once. Perhaps I still do," he answered truthfully. "But whatever I felt with her, it's nothing compared to what I feel with you. I know it sounds trite, but damn it, Emmaline, it's the truth."

She nodded, biting her lower lip. For a moment, she said nothing, and Jack let out a sigh of relief. But then came the question he'd hoped she wouldn't ask. "How long? Since you broke off the engagement, I mean."

This was where it would get dicey. What would she think of him if he told her the truth? That it had only been a matter of weeks? After all, her husband had been dead for nearly a year, and her feelings for him still lingered. Yet he could not possibly lie to her, not if he wanted a future with her. And he *did* want a future with her, goddamn it.

"It was recent, wasn't it?" she asked when he remained silent. "I thought as much."

There was nothing to do but say it. "Three, maybe four weeks." And now she'd think that he'd used her, an easy fuck to help him get past the heartache.

She reached a still-trembling hand up to his cheek. "It's all right, Jack. Perhaps…perhaps we both needed this. To forget the past, to move on with our lives."

No, he wanted to yell. No. It was more than that. He squeezed his eyes shut, resisting the urge to push her on the matter, to try and make her see the truth. Because upon closer inspection, the truth seemed mad—that he'd somehow managed to entirely forget the woman that he'd loved for several years, the woman he'd planned to marry, and fallen in love with *her* instead, in less than a fortnight, and with him barely conscious a good portion of that time.

Why would any sane person believe that? It was far easier to believe that he'd been using her—and worse still, she made it sound as if she'd been using him, too.

"I'll cherish this time we had together," she murmured, her breath warm against his ear. "Always."

Just like that, she'd dismissed him.

Yet when she rolled atop him, he did not push her away. If she wanted to use him yet again, then by God, weak and desperate fool that he was, he would let her.

7

"WHAT'S THIS?" EMMALINE ASKED, REACHING for the ragged leather book that Jack held in his hands. The cover was battered and scarred, some sort of Celtic symbol etched in gold leaf that was crumbling away.

Jack readjusted the wire-rimmed spectacles he wore when reading. "Funny you should ask—it's quite curious, really. I found it tucked in a drawer, over behind the shelves in the back. It appears to be a book of legends, and there was a note card tucked into this spot, here." He held the open book out to her. Around the margins, someone had scribbled notes in red ink.

"Well, what does it say?" she asked, her curiosity piqued.

"It's the same story as the pantomime. You know, the one acted out at the Beltane festival, about the May Queen and her husband, the Winter King. And look—" he flipped the page over "—here's a plate depicting the cuckolding Green Man, just like the etching on the bench in the garden."

She shrugged. "It's a fairly common image, Jack. There's one carved in the gate, too—did you notice? Just above the peephole?"

"Ah, yes, the peephole." He flipped several pages. "There's

something here about that, too. According to the legend, that's how the Winter King learned of the May Queen's infidelity. He spied her in the arms of Green Man through the peephole."

Emmaline couldn't help but smile. "It's not the same peephole, of course. This is just a story, a fancy bit of make-believe. It's not about the garden here at Orchard House."

"Why do you suppose there's a peephole in a garden gate, anyway? What does one do in a garden that would require such a thing?" His hazel eyes were dancing with mischief behind the smudged lenses of his spectacles.

Emmaline felt the heat rise in her cheeks as she remembered just what she and Jack had done in the garden not two days past. "I'm sure it's just for decoration," she murmured. It hadn't occurred to her that someone might have spied on them, but now that the idea was planted in her mind, she'd never be able to dismiss the possibility. Good God!

"Anyway, whoever wrote these notes in the margin noticed the same similarities I did. Look, there's even a well mentioned!" He'd become quite animated, Emmaline realized. The color was beginning to return to his cheeks, and his jaw suddenly looked less hollow.

She smiled, taking in the length of his legs stretched out from the leather chair where he sprawled. "It's just a coincidence, Jack. Surely you realize that."

He tapped the page with his finger. "And here the author talks about how the fruit shriveled up on the trees once the Green Man was banished to the garden. You've an orchard."

"Yes, *outside* the garden walls. Come now, Jack, you're just being silly."

"Haven't you ever felt...I don't know, somewhat lusty out there?" he asked.

"What, in the garden?" she hedged, remembering the times she'd pleasured herself there, before Jack had arrived. She *had* felt somewhat lusty there, though she could not explain why. She'd only thought herself lonely at the time, missing a man's touch.

"I wonder if there are any standing stones nearby," he mused, turning the book sideways to read a note scribbled in the corner of one page.

Emmaline shook her head. "I haven't seen any. I could ask Mrs. Talbot, I suppose."

"We have a circle of standing stones at home," he said distractedly. "My sister used to like to go there to write. She said she felt some sort of energy there, or some nonsense like that."

"Your home is in Dorset?" she asked curiously. He'd mentioned Dorset before, but nothing more specific than that.

"Yes, in Bedlington. A quiet little village if ever there was one. Aisling was always desperate to get away. I quite enjoy it, myself. More so when my father's away," he added cryptically.

"You don't get along with your father?"

Jack's eyes darkened at once. "Oh, we get along well enough, the bloody bastard. It's my mother he torments. Keeps a mistress in London, you see. Which wouldn't be so terrible, I suppose, if my mother didn't love him so desperately." Jack's voice had taken on a hard edge.

"I didn't mean to pry," Emmaline said.

"Don't apologize." He closed the book and set it on the chair's arm. "Anyway, it's not a secret. I suppose I should be grateful that he spends nearly all his time in town. Running the estate keeps me occupied, after all. It's only too bad that Aisling inherited the head for figures instead of me."

"You love your sister very much, don't you?" Emmaline

asked, noting the way the tension in his jaw seemed to disappear each time he mentioned her.

His mouth curved into a smile. "She's a bloody brat, but yes. By God, you should hear the way she curses! Always having the last word, and trust me, her words are colorful. Perhaps sometime...never mind." He waved one hand in dismissal.

What had he meant to say?

"Anyway," he continued, "it's a good thing she managed to overcome her snobbery in time to realize what a good chap Will Cooper is. Took a bit of maneuvering on my part, but she played right into my hands," he said with a laugh.

"Was her husband in the war?"

"Yes, and he managed to come through unscathed but for the loss of hearing in one ear. A mortar explosion," he explained. "I lost my hearing entirely for a fortnight after Saint Quentin, but eventually it returned to normal. Seems like a small price to pay, considering the fate of the rest of my unit." His face grew taut, his mouth pinched. At once, the appearance of vim and vigor that she'd admired only moments before abandoned him.

Emmaline lifted the book from the chair's arm and perched there beside him, laying a gentle hand on his shoulder. "If you'd like to talk about it, Jack, go ahead. I know I can't erase the memories, but perhaps I can share the burden. I was there on the front. I know how dreadful it was. And before that, I lost both my parents to influenza, one right after the other. I'm no stranger to loss."

He reached up to cover her hand with his. "I'm sorry, Emmaline. Listen to me, going on, when your losses were all far more personal than mine. You must think me a terrible coward."

She didn't think anything of the sort. She knew what

war did to people, knew the lasting effects of witnessing such horror on a daily basis. "Of course I don't think you a coward," she said, leaning into him.

For several moments they sat like that in silence, their breathing in perfect unison. An energy seemed to course between them, leaching away the sensation of loss and replacing it with a peacefulness that Emmaline hadn't felt in ages. He must have felt it, too, because he seemed to relax against her.

"Go on," she prodded, far too comfortable to move a muscle. "Tell me what else your battered little book says about the garden."

And so he did.

"Amazing," Dr. Hayward said, removing the stethoscope from his ears and draping it around his neck. "A remarkable recovery." He turned toward Emmaline, smiling broadly. "Perhaps you should consider coming to work for me, Mrs. Gage. I could use a good nurse. Regular office hours, and all that."

Emmaline shook her head. "I'm afraid that managing Orchard House is a full-time occupation at present," she said, then realized her mistake. Jack hadn't yet said what he meant to do with the property. She'd considered asking him if there was any way she could rent the house, but knew she could never afford to do so.

She glanced over to where he sat, buttoning up his shirt. His face was an unreadable mask. She wondered at his sudden glumness. They'd had a pleasant morning, after all, poring over old photographs she'd found in the attic. It was only when the doctor appeared that the smile had seemed to vanish from Jack's face, taking his good mood along with it.

"As for you," the doctor said, turning his attention back

to Jack, "I'm afraid you're not quite well enough to risk the drive back to Dorset. Not yet, at least."

"No?" Jack asked. There was something in his voice—disappointment, perhaps? She couldn't be sure.

The doctor shook his head. "No. You're in far better shape than I expected, but still too weak to safely take the wheel, particularly all alone and in a roadster, where you'd be exposed to the elements." He stroked his whiskers, looking pensive. "I suppose you could return to the hotel, but I'm inclined to say that it's not prudent to do so. I'd rather we continued the quarantine till the end of the week, unless Mrs. Gage objects."

Emmaline was caught off guard. "No, I…he can remain here at Orchard House as long as necessary. I've no objection. Unless Mr. Wainscott does, that is."

"Of course not," he said, though he did not meet her gaze.

Dr. Hayward nodded his approval. "Good, good. And what of your health, Mrs. Gage? Have you shown any symptoms since your exposure?"

"No, nothing at all," Emmaline said. "I've been quite well. I must have already been exposed to this particular strain at the hospital in London."

"Likely so," the doctor agreed. "We've had no other cases here in Haverham, so it looks as if we've dodged the proverbial bullet. Well, I suppose I should get back to the office." He busied himself returning his things to his black leather case. "Oh—" he held up an envelope "—I nearly forgot. Mrs. Talbot asked me to give you this. It must have gotten mixed up with her post."

Emmaline took the envelope from him, recognizing the familiar script. "It's from my husband's sister," she said with a smile. It had been ages since she'd received a letter from

Maria and hoped she was well. "Thank you, Doctor. Here, let me show you out." She led him out of Jack's room, toward the front hall. Jack remained perched on the edge of the bed where they'd left him.

"I'll stop by again at the end of the week to check on him one last time," Dr. Hayward offered as he tipped his hat onto his head. "He seems a bit distracted. Hope he's not giving you too much trouble. I know this is terribly irregular—Mrs. Talbot is ready to have me drawn and quartered for putting you in this situation. Thank heavens her husband is a man of the cloth!"

"Mr. Wainscott has been a perfect gentleman," Emmaline said, "and an easy patient, Doctor. And tending him, well… perhaps it's reminded me why I became a nurse in the first place." She liked to be needed, she realized. Useful.

"Perhaps you'll reconsider my offer, then. Once you're better settled here at Orchard House, that is."

Emmaline just nodded, her entire future far too uncertain to commit to anything at present.

The doctor smiled at her warmly. "Well, good day, Mrs. Gage." With a bow, he took his leave.

As soon as Emmaline shut the door, she glanced down at the envelope still clutched in one clammy hand. Maria's letter. She would see that Jack was settled back in bed, and then perhaps she'd go out to the garden to read it. While she was there, she could water the roses and check on the lavender that had begun to bloom behind the bench. Each day seemed to bring something new to the garden, the brown slowly gaining a more verdant hue, spots of color appearing where there had been none. She could not explain it, but since Jack's arrival, life had begun to return to the barren plot.

Much like her own bleak existence, she realized. What would become of them both, once they'd parted?

With a shake of her head, she forced away the unpleasant thought and hurried back to his bedside. She found him reclining against the pillows, his eyes closed, his chest rising and falling in a slow, steady rhythm.

"Jack?" she whispered, pulling a blanket up to his waist.

"Hmm?" he murmured. He opened his eyes, his gaze at last meeting hers. There was something there that she hadn't seen before, something so raw, so hungry, that Emmaline's breath caught in her throat. For a moment she was rendered entirely mute, her heart thumping against her ribs.

He took a deep breath, a muscle in his jaw twitching as he did so. "Emmaline, I—" He abruptly cut himself off, closing his eyes, shuttering them from her. "Never mind. I'm a bit tired. Would you mind if I rested?"

"Of course not," she murmured, tucking the blanket more tightly about his hips. "I'm going out to the garden for a bit. I'll check on you when I return." She reached for one of his hands as she leaned over to kiss his forehead. *Still cool.* Beneath her fingertips, his pulse felt strong, perhaps a bit fast. She made a mental note to check it again later.

"I won't stay gone long," she promised. Later, she would attempt to lift his spirits. Perhaps they could do a jigsaw puzzle, she decided. She'd seen several in the library.

She glanced back down at the letter, anxious to learn what news it contained.

8

EMMALINE WAS THERE IN THE GARDEN, SITTING
on the stone bench, just as Jack expected. He closed the gate
and took several steps toward her, waiting for her to acknowledge his presence. She must have heard the latch open, must
have sensed his approach.

And yet she sat unmoving, her head bowed, her hands
folded in her lap atop a creamy white envelope. The sky
had turned a dusty lavender. Tea time had come and gone,
and Emmaline had never come to wake him as she'd promised. Instead, he'd awoken on his own, a bit disoriented and
groggy after such a long nap.

And then he'd remembered the letter—from her husband's
sister, she'd said. It was clear that, in her heart, she and Christopher Gage were still joined. There was no room for him,
never would be. Jack had realized it the moment the words
had left her lips. It had been a sobering thought, an arrow
shot through the sail of his confidence. There was no point
in declaring his love, not now. At best, he hoped they could
part friends.

Still, he grew alarmed when she continued to sit there, as
still as a statue. As he drew closer, he could see that she had

been crying. Her nose was red, her eyes wet and swollen. "Did you receive some bad news?" he asked, unable to curb his curiosity.

She started, as if she'd been oblivious to his approach. "What? Oh, no." She swiped at her nose with one wrist.

Her dark eyes looked slightly wild, he realized. Panicked, perhaps. What the hell was in that letter?

"You've been crying," he said, feeling foolish for stating the obvious, but he hadn't any idea what else to say. "You've been sitting out here for hours."

At last she turned to face him. Her pain was palpable, a living, breathing thing that seemed to suck all the goodness right out of the garden. "This letter is from my sister-in-law," she said at last, her voice breaking. "She's written me all these lovely things about how much Christopher loved Orchard House, about how happy he was visiting his aunt Mathilde here, how glad she is that I'm here. She says…she says she hopes that I can feel his presence here, keeping me company, watching over me." Her voice tore on a sob. "But I haven't felt that at all, Jack. Not since you arrived, at least. What kind of woman am I, what kind of wife, to have forgotten him like that? To have moved on so quickly, so easily?"

He knelt before her, taking one of her trembling hands in his. "It's been a year, Emmaline. What kind of woman would sit here, day after day, pining away for a husband who's been gone so long? I'll tell you what kind—a lonely one," he answered when she said nothing. "The kind who buries herself right alongside her husband. You've every right to get on with your life."

Her eyes narrowed, and she snatched back her hand. "That's easy for you to say, considering you were engaged to marry someone else only a few short weeks ago. How easy it must seem to you."

"That's not fair," he protested. "You've no idea how hard it was for me, how much I hated hurting Claire like that. But this is different—Christopher's gone, Emmaline. He's gone, and he's not coming back. Your continued suffering doesn't change that."

"You think I don't know that?" she snapped.

"Then why punish yourself for moving on with your life? Do you honestly think if Chris were here with you in spirit, watching you, that he'd want to see you sad and lonely? Wouldn't he want you to be happy instead? To be loved?"

"Loved?" she choked out. "Who said anything about love?"

Jack took a deep, fortifying breath. "I am. I'm saying it now. I love you, Emmaline Gage."

Her eyes widened, her mouth forming an *O* of surprise.

Jack continued on, needing to get it all out in the open. "I realize it seems rash, that I sound fickle and inconstant. And perhaps I am, but damn it all, I *do* love you. I'd planned to tell you so, right up until the moment I realized that you're still in love with your husband. Your *late* husband," he corrected.

"But…but you said you were still in love with your fiancée," Emmaline sputtered. "Just yesterday, you told me so."

"I said that perhaps I still loved her, not that I was still *in* love with her. There's an enormous difference, you know."

Emmaline shook her head. "No, I don't know. You either love someone or you don't."

He raked a hand through his hair. "It's not that simple, Emmaline. I've known Claire for many years. We were friends long before we were lovers. I can't just turn off my feelings for her like a switch."

"Of course not," Emmaline said with a shake of her head. "It's just that...that...oh, never mind!" She rose, her gaze darting around wildly, as if looking for an escape.

Jack stood and reached for her wrist. "Just listen to—"

"If you'll excuse me," she interrupted, her voice cold and detached. She tried to tug her wrist from his grasp. "Tea will be ready shortly. I apologize for the delay."

Damn it. A sharp pain tore through his gut. He'd done this badly, and now he was going to lose her. He had to do something—*say* something—to make her understand, before it was too late. "Don't do this, Emmaline. Don't shut me out. I know I may seem like a man without much depth, but damn it, this cuts like a knife, straight through my heart."

A single tear slipped down her cheek. Still, she remained unmoved. "I can't do this right now, Jack. I can't have this conversation. Please release me—*now.*"

It felt as if the air had been knocked from his lungs in a single blow. Stunned, he complied, flexing his hand as he released hers.

Without another word, Emmaline turned and briskly walked away from him. Jack didn't turn and watch her go—he simply stood motionless, staring at the spot where she'd stood only moments before, his hand now clenched into a fist.

As soon as the gate clattered shut, he cursed loudly. Almost as if on cue, the sky seemed to darken. The wind picked up, sounding eerily like a wail of despair as it blew over the garden walls. One fat raindrop splashed onto Jack's bare head, then another. He knew he should hurry inside, knew that it was pure folly to remain outside in a downpour in his weakened state, but he didn't give a fuck.

Call it pride, call it stubborn foolishness, but if she wanted him to keep his distance from her, then he damn well would, whatever the cost.

With a groan, he sank to the stone bench and dropped his head into his hands. When the rain came, it came hard, pounding Jack's shoulders with a ferocity that matched his frustration.

For the first time in nearly a fortnight, Emmaline slept in her own bed. After she'd cleaned up from tea, she'd climbed the stairs to her own bedroom without so much as telling Jack good-night. She hadn't a choice; she could not face him, could not bear to see the hurt and betrayal there in his eyes.

He'd told her he loved her, and she'd entirely dismissed him. What else could she have done? She'd been overcome with guilt after reading Maria's letter, and not yet recovered from the shock of the news of Jack's recently ended engagement. It was all too much.

As it was, she was grappling with her own feelings for him, unable to believe that she could fall in love with Jack so quickly, even though she'd fallen for Christopher in an equally short space of time. Still, that had been wartimes, and everything moved at a quicker pace when life seemed so precarious.

And yet…she and Jack understood each other. She knew exactly why he got that haunted look on his face when he talked about Saint Quentin, and he understood why the sound of thunder could turn her dreams into nightmares. They seemed kindred spirits, two lost souls who were meant to find one another, somehow.

And they had, in the oddest of circumstances. Surely it was fate. At least, she wanted to believe that it was. But the rational part of her mind told her that it was nothing more than circumstance—two people from different worlds, thrown together at a time when both were vulnerable. After all, Jack was a baronet's son. She knew enough of England and its social classes to realize that the heir to a baronetcy didn't usually consort with women like her. In fact, under normal circumstances they would not have ever crossed paths.

She was sure that his fiancée was a woman of good breeding, a socialite who would not do a day's work. The very idea of changing a dressing or bedpan would make her cringe in horror. She was a beauty, no doubt, her clothing and hair the height of fashion. How could Emmaline ever compete with that?

As it was, she'd been lucky enough to catch the eye of a man like Christopher Gage, who'd been handsome and charming and kind. He hadn't been titled, or even particularly rich, but he'd come from a good family, and truly, he'd been far more than she'd deserved.

That sort of luck happened only once in a lifetime, and she'd be a fool to think that anything could come from her affair with Jack, even if he did claim to love her.

Even if she loved him, too. And she *did* love him—oh, how she did. There was no sense in denying it. He was funny and gentle and kind and sweet, not to mention undeniably handsome. He set her blood afire, made her entire body ache with need.

She rolled over onto her back, staring up at the ceiling in the darkened room. Was he doing the same, downstairs in his own bed? She could barely stand it, being apart from him. However would she survive it, once he was gone?

Heaven help her, but just thinking about him made her damp between her legs, made her want to touch herself. Resisting the urge, she turned back to her side, clutching a pillow to her chest. She wanted to believe that Jack was right,

that Christopher would want to see her happy and loved—
that he'd want her to marry again, have children. Of course
he would. Christopher had loved her, after all.

Unable to stand it a moment longer, she sat up in bed.
Even if they weren't meant to be together, she couldn't bear
to spend what time they had left away from his side. If that
made her faithless and inconstant, then so be it. She was not
perfect; she'd never claimed to be. But Jack deserved to know
how she felt, even if she could not risk her heart by saying
the words aloud.

Her resolve firmly in place, she threw off the bedclothes
and slipped from the bed. Moving silently through the dark
house, she made her way downstairs, tiptoeing across the hall
toward the room where Jack slept. The door was ajar, and she
paused just outside, listening for his soft snores, but she heard
nothing. Reaching out, she pushed the door open, peering
inside to where the moonlight cast silvery stripes across the
narrow bed.

It was empty.

"Looking for me?" a voice called out behind her, and Emmaline gasped as she spun around.

"Good heavens, Jack! You nearly scared me half to
death."

"Sorry about that." He took a step toward her, glass clink-
ing. Peering more closely, she saw that he carried a tumbler
in one hand and a bottle in the other.

"Brandy," he said, holding out the bottle. "Found it in
the study. Hope you don't mind." His voice was uneven, his
speech slightly slurred, Emmaline realized.

"Are you drunk?" she asked, wrinkling her nose as the
smell of liquor wafted toward her.

"Not even close," he answered, swaying toward her. With a clunk, he set the bottle down on the sideboard against the wall behind her. "Though I'd like to be."

He was clearly drunk, despite his protests. She glanced down at her nightdress, suddenly wishing she'd put on her robe.

"So, you must have a purpose. This little nighttime visit, I mean." He waved the hand carrying the glass, and Emmaline felt a slosh of liquid on her bare feet.

"Give me that," she snapped, taking it from him and setting it on the sideboard beside the bottle. "Just how much have you had to drink?"

"I say, not nearly enough." He reached for the glass, but Emmaline swatted away his hand.

"You're ill, you know. You shouldn't be drinking hard liquor—it's only going to set back your recovery." Which wasn't entirely true, of course. It *was* just brandy, which was often considered medicinal.

"No, you wouldn't like that, would you?" he slurred. "The sooner I'm well and out of your hair, the better, right?"

She sighed heavily. "Just go to bed, Jack. It's late, and you're drunk."

"I'm not drunk," he protested, sounding almost sober all of a sudden. "Not in the slightest. I can hold my liquor quite well, believe it or not."

"Come now." She reached for his elbow. "You're going to regret this in the morning when your head is spinning and your stomach lurching."

"The only thing I'll regret in the morning is not doing this," he said, reaching for her and tugging her against his chest. His mouth came down hard on hers, hot and demanding, tasting of brandy.

Caught entirely off balance, Emmaline clutched at his chest, trying to steady herself. His fingers bit into her shoulders as he pulled her closer still.

He kissed her deeply, and Emmaline realized she could not fight it; she had no desire to fight it. A soft moan escaped her lips as she opened her mouth against his.

And then, almost as suddenly as he'd grabbed her, he released her. "Why were you creeping around down here? Were you looking for me? Tell me the truth," he demanded.

"I—I just wanted to check on you," she stammered, afraid to admit the truth. That she wanted him. Needed him. Couldn't go a single night without having him, not with him under the same roof.

"Liar," he spat. "You're a damned poor liar. You owe me the truth, at least. You wanted *this,* didn't you?" He turned her, pressing her back to the wall, grinding his pelvis into her. He caged her with his arms, his palms pressed against the wall behind her. She couldn't have escaped, had she wanted to. He was bigger and stronger than she was, even now. "You don't love me, won't have me, but you'll fuck me all right, won't you?"

His mouth moved toward hers and she turned her head, avoiding his kiss. She was trapped, cornered, and instinct took over. "Get away from me," she said coldly, tamping down the hysteria that was rising in her breast. "You've no idea what I want. What I feel."

"Then tell me, Emmaline. Damn it, tell me what you feel. Tell me what you want from me."

Tears stung her eyes. She couldn't speak, couldn't possibly say the words she wanted to.

"I laid my heart bare to you," he continued, his voice hard, "and you flayed it. And now you come down here, looking for a fuck. That's all it is to you, isn't it? Do you pretend I'm your husband while you—"

Her hand flew out and struck him hard across his cheek.

They stood there glaring at one another for what felt like an eternity, not saying a single word. He rubbed his cheek with the palm of one hand, the other still pressed against the wall by her ear. There were no other sounds save their breathing, coming fast.

Finally, Jack broke the silence. "Goddamn it, Emmaline, I'm sorry. I—"

She silenced him with her mouth, rising up on tiptoe to press her lips against his. Without breaking the kiss, she reached down, fumbling with his trousers, desperate to have him—*now*. Only her fingers were trembling so badly she couldn't work the fastenings, and Jack grew impatient. Pushing aside her useless hands, he accomplished the task in a fraction of a second, then reached under her nightgown and dragged down her knickers, nearly ripping them in the process.

And then he was inside her, pressing her up against the wall as he buried his cock deep, rocking his hips against hers. "Jack," she whimpered against his neck, her teeth scraping against his skin. "More."

Understanding her need, he reached down and lifted her off her feet, allowing her to wrap her legs around his waist, her back still pressed to the wall as he drove into her—harder and faster, till she was panting.

"Oh, God, Emma," he exclaimed, his voice ragged. "I can't…I won't last…come for me." He reached down to where their bodies were joined, pressing his thumb against her clit, stroking her hard while she cried out his name, over and over again.

In seconds, she climaxed, wave after wave of pleasure

making her entire body vibrate. She felt him stiffen just as his head tipped back, the cords in his neck standing out in stark relief. Quickly, he pulled out of her, allowing her feet to return to the floor as his seed spurted hotly against her belly.

Emmaline leaned into his chest as she caught her breath, inhaling his scent, wanting to remember it forever.

9

JACK EYED EMMALINE ACROSS THE BREAKFAST table, desperate to read something in her expression that would indicate how he should proceed where she was concerned. Her face had remained a polite mask throughout the interminable meal. She smiled as she passed him a plate of toast or poured his coffee, made small talk about the weather and her plans for the day. Indeed, she'd been pleasant enough, in a detached sort of way, ever since she'd woken up naked beside him.

But what did it mean? That she'd forgiven his brutish behavior? That she was willing to forget the fact that he'd all but taken her unwillingly, up against the wall? Or that she simply wanted to pretend it hadn't happened? The last thing he wanted to do was misstep somehow, but damn it, he needed to know what was going on in that head of hers.

"I thought I might turn the beds in the far corner, over by the juniper bushes," she was saying as she smeared strawberry jam on her toast. "They seem to get a fair amount of afternoon sun. Maybe I'll try to replant the bluebells over there, along with the lilacs. What do you think?"

"Perhaps," he replied, trying to catch her eye, but failing

miserably. When she reached for the coffeepot, he caught her wrist, holding it firmly in his hand. "Emmaline, we need to talk. About last night..." He trailed off, hoping that she would say something first to lead him in the right direction.

She shook her head. "There's nothing to say, really."

"There's plenty to say," he countered. "If you'll just listen."

Her dark eyes filled with tears. "I'm sorry, Jack."

"*You're* sorry?" he asked. He could feel her hand trembling beneath his. "I'm the one who should be apologizing. I never should have been so rough, so violent—"

"Don't," she interrupted, meeting his gaze. The color had risen in her cheeks, staining them pink. "Please, don't apologize. I acted foolishly yesterday, in the garden. You were right, and—"

The doorbell rang. Emmaline bolted from her seat, nearly spilling her juice in the process.

And what?

"Are you expecting someone?" he asked, rising from his seat and reaching for her shoulder to steady her.

She shook her head. "No, not at all. Dr. Hayward said he wasn't coming back till the end of the week. Perhaps it's Mrs. Talbot."

Again the bell sounded. Emmaline glanced over her shoulder, toward the front hall. "I'd better go see who it is. You sit—" she gestured toward the chair he'd occupied only moments before "—and finish your breakfast."

But Jack remained standing, watching as Emmaline hurried out. Moments later, he heard the front door open.

"Hullo," said a crisp, feminine voice—far too familiar. "I'm looking for Jack Wainscott. They told me at the hotel that I might find him here. Are you Mrs. Gage?"

"I am," Emmaline answered. "I've been tending him since he took ill. You must be his sister, Aisling."

No. Oh, no.

"I'm his fiancée," she replied sharply. "Claire Lennox."

Without wasting another second, Jack strode toward the front hall, hoping to salvage the situation as best as possible.

"What are you doing here?" he called out, stepping up beside Emmaline, who stood goggling at Claire. Why the hell had she called herself his fiancée?

"What do you mean, what am I doing here?" Claire asked, looking from Jack to Emmaline, and back to Jack again. "Your mother said you were only to be gone a few days. It's been more than a fortnight, and no one's heard a word from you. Everyone was worried."

"I fell ill with influenza," he explained, slightly flummoxed. It wasn't like his mother to keep track of his whereabouts. "I was nearly unconscious for five days straight."

"And there isn't a hospital here you could be taken to? If you were so very ill, that is?" Claire's eyes were cold as she regarded him with unconcealed suspicion.

"It was a potentially lethal strain, Miss Lennox," Emmaline offered. "The doctor hoped to keep him under quarantine. Since I'm a trained nurse, it seemed best to leave him here."

"I see." Claire bit out the words. "Still, it seems as if you could have telephoned. Unless, of course, you've been otherwise occupied." Her look was accusing, and Jack's annoyance rose a notch. What right did she have, barging in like this and making Emmaline uncomfortable? It wasn't any of Claire's business where he'd been, or what he'd been doing.

He took a protective step toward Emmaline, his arm brushing against her shoulder. "I think you should go—"

"Won't you come in?" Emmaline said at precisely the same

time. "We were just finishing breakfast. I can offer you some coffee and toast, if you're hungry."

Claire swept inside, looking as regal and haughty as ever. "I breakfasted already, at the hotel. But thank you, I will come in."

For a moment, the three of them simply stood there awkwardly.

"Might I have a word with you in private, Jack?" Claire said at last. "If you don't mind, that is, Mrs. Gage." Claire offered Emmaline a tight smile, one that did not reach her eyes.

"Of course not." Emmaline's forehead was creased with a frown. "Here, use the front parlor. I'll go out to the garden for a bit and give you some privacy."

"Emmaline," Jack said, reaching for her elbow. "I'll only be a few minutes."

She wouldn't meet his eyes. "No," she murmured, looking at her shoes, the doorway—anywhere but at him. "Take all the time you need. If you'll both excuse me."

"Well, isn't this cozy," Claire said, as soon as Emmaline left them. "I suppose *this* is the real reason you broke off our engagement?"

"Whatever are you talking about, Claire? I only just met Emma—Mrs. Gage," he corrected.

She raised one perfectly arched blond brow. "And where, pray tell, is Mr. Gage?"

"Dead," he answered simply. "A casualty of the war."

Her mouth curved into an ugly smile. "Well, then. Aren't you two a match made in heaven?"

"Look, Claire," he said, clenching his hands into fists by his sides. "I have no idea what you're doing here, what game you're playing at. But I made it quite clear before I left Bedlington that we were done. You've no right to come here and start making accusations—"

"Are you denying that you're playing house with her, then? Your little war widow?"

"It's none of your damn business."

"I suppose that's my answer, then," she said with a sneer. "What's happened to you, Jack?" She shook her head. "Running off and abandoning Wainscott House in favor of your latest piece of ass is your father's style, not yours."

"Get out," he said, barely able to control his rage. If she didn't leave immediately, he would be sorely tempted to do or say something that he'd no doubt regret later on.

And then her face crumpled, tears filling her eyes. "I'm sorry, Jack. I shouldn't have said that. But you must understand, your mother was frantic. Something…something happened at Wainscott House—a burst pipe of some sort, I can't say exactly. Some rooms were flooded, the carpet ruined. Your father's in London, of course, and you were nowhere to be found. You know how your mother is, and so I said I'd come find you. And then when I heard that you were here, alone with some woman…" The tears ran freely down her cheeks now, and she wiped them away with the back of one hand. "Did I mean so very little to you, Jack? I gave you five years of my life—five years! And this is what I get for it?"

He raked a hand through his hair, his stomach lurching uncomfortably. "I'm sorry, Claire. Honestly. I don't what else to say."

"I waited for you, all those years," she continued.

He shook his head. "I never asked you to wait. I was glad that you did, but I never expected that you would."

"And I didn't even care that you couldn't…well, you know, when you came home from the war. If you'd only given it time, perhaps tried a bit harder—"

"Tried harder?" God, talk about emasculating. He *had* tried. Perhaps he just hadn't wanted it enough, hadn't wanted *her* enough. But he'd never say that, not to her. It would be far too cruel.

"Have you been able to...you know...with *her?*" she asked, so well bred that she couldn't bear to say the words aloud.

He would not lie to her. "Yes" was all he said in reply.

Claire nodded. He saw her swallow hard as she straightened her spine, digesting the truth. And then she laid a hand on his sleeve. "Come home, Jack," she said, earnest now. "To Dorset. You've got responsibilities there, a life there." She glanced around, as if seeing her surroundings for the first time, and shuddered. "This...this isn't you. It near enough broke your mother's heart when Aisling married Will Cooper. How do you think she'll take it if you throw everything away for...well, for this woman, whoever she is? She's not like you, Jack. Like *us.*"

He held up one hand in warning. "Don't say another word."

"Don't run out on your responsibilities like your father does," she pushed, going for broke. "You're far better than that—I know you are."

Perhaps I'm not, after all. He shook his head, trying to clear it. "I don't owe anyone anything. My responsibility is to Wainscott House alone, and I will see to those responsibilities. You may tell my mother that I'll be home by the end of the week. Beyond that, where I go or what I do is no one's business but my own. I'm sorry that I've hurt you. Truly, I am. But we're done, Claire. *Done.* And now I'll ask that you leave."

She raised her chin in the air, as proud as ever. "I'm staying at the hotel in town till the day after tomorrow. When you come to your senses, you can find me there."

"Goodbye, Claire," he said, hoping she understood the finality of his words.

"Goodbye, Jack," she answered, and then she was gone.

Jack slumped to the sofa with a groan. Devil take it, but he suddenly felt like the villain that Claire had made him out to be. How was he going to explain it all to Emmaline now? Claire was staying in Haverham, for fuck's sake. She was no longer the faceless ex-fiancée who Jack claimed to be done with, but the very real woman who was just up the road, waiting for him. Things had just gone from bad to worse, and there wasn't a damn thing he could do about it.

At once bone tired and weary, he rose and strode out, headed to the garden to learn his fate.

10

EMMALINE HEARD THE CAR DRIVE AWAY, KNEW that Jack would come looking for her any minute now. She continued turning the soil in the bed, digging into the rich, loamy earth with her spade. She knew what she had to do, and what she would tell him. It had become crystal clear, the moment she'd opened the door and seen Claire Lennox standing there.

The woman was even more beautiful than she'd imagined, like a perfect little china doll. She exuded wealth and breeding and fashionable taste—everything that Emmaline so sorely lacked. Emmaline was a poor country girl from Pennsylvania, after all, one who'd spent the majority of her adult years on hospital wards. If there had ever been a youthful bloom to her cheeks, it was long gone now, taken from her by the war, by widowhood.

Jack belonged with a woman like Claire; she had been raised to marry a gentleman like him, to run his household and raise his children. She would entertain his guests with practiced ease, delighting everyone with her wit and charm. She would be intimately acquainted with his family and friends, an integral part of his social circle.

Emmaline could do none of these things, could *be* none of those things. She would always be an outsider, awkward and unsure of herself when away from the wards. After all, the hospital was the one place where she felt competent and self-assured. She was a good nurse. An *excellent* nurse, she corrected.

Besides, working with a village doctor in his Cotswold office would be a far cry from the army hospitals in which she'd toiled. Children with sniffles, women in childbirth, broken bones to be set—these were the concerns of a country nurse. There would be no wards, no nurses' dormitories, nothing to remind her of the life she'd left behind. She would take a room in the boardinghouse beside the grocery, perhaps even begin to attend services at the little stone church over which Mr. Talbot presided. Yes, Mrs. Talbot would like that, she thought with a smile.

A bead of perspiration ran down her forehead, and she swiped at it with the back of her forearm, hoping she hadn't trailed soil across her skin in the process. It was warm for May, the sun bright and strong in the clear blue sky.

The hinge on the gate creaked, and Emmaline let out her breath in a rush. It was time—time to send Jack home, back where he belonged.

"There you are," he called out, striding over to where she knelt. He looked drawn, tired. But he was well, far more so than she'd been willing to admit. It might take him some time to regain his strength, but there was no real danger in sending him home with Claire.

Setting down her spade, she peeled off her gloves and tossed them to the cobbles. Standing, she reached for Jack's hand. "Come, let's sit."

Silently, he nodded, following her to the stone bench and taking a seat beside her.

"I *do* love you, Jack," she began tentatively. "I want you to know that, first and foremost. Perhaps it's rash, perhaps we've both lost our wits, perhaps this garden really is enchanted," she said, attempting to smile. "Who knows? But whatever the case, I love you."

Jack raked a hand through his hair, mussing it. There was a look of defeat, of resignation in his hazel eyes that made Emmaline's heart hurt. "Then, Christ, Emma, why does it sound as if you're about to break my heart?"

She took a deep breath before answering. "Because I have to set things right. This time we've spent together—it's been wonderful, magical even. A healing time for us both. But don't you see? We've been shuttered away, removed from the rest of the world, living a dream. It can't go on like this forever."

"And you've decided this in the space of time that I was inside, talking to Claire? And I've no say in the matter?"

"Oh, Jack, you were so very ill. I'm not certain you realize how grave it was when you first collapsed. These were extraordinary circumstances. Had we met some other, more ordinary way, there's no telling what might have happened. But this…this isn't real."

"I know what I felt when I first saw you there across the bonfire—the instant attraction, the desire to know you. Are you saying that wasn't real, either?"

"That hardly counts. We hadn't met, hadn't spoken a single word to each other."

"But I knew, even then—"

"Oh, Jack," she interrupted with a sigh. "That's easy for you to say now, but if your business hadn't brought you here to Orchard House, we never would have met at all."

"But my business *did* bring me here. To you," he added, squeezing her hand. "I see that as fate intervening."

She shook her head. "You may not realize it now, but you need to be with someone who doesn't hear mortar explosions in every crack of thunder, who doesn't share your memories of the stink of mustard gas, of flesh wounds left too long untreated. You need someone to bring light into your life, not sustain the dark memories of war. Someone like Claire, Jack. You used to love her—you said so yourself. You were going to marry her, and if not her, then someone like her. You were thrown off your path, that's all. I'm just putting you back on that path. Someday you'll thank me for it."

A muscle in his jaw twitched. "If you think that's true, then you don't know me at all."

"And there you have it, Jack. I *don't* know you. It's only been a fortnight, and none of it spent in the real world. This was a lovely interlude, but that's all it can ever be—a wonderful memory that I will treasure forever."

"And there's no changing your mind?" he asked. "Nothing I can say or do to convince you otherwise?"

She shook her head, her eyes damp now. He nearly groaned aloud—not one but *two* crying women in a single day. Lovely.

"You should go to her, Jack. Find her, before she leaves town, and allow her to see you home safely. You can come back later for your car—it'll be safe enough here. I'll have my things out of Orchard House by the end of the week. I've decided to rent a room in town, and accept Dr. Hayward's offer of employment."

"You're not leaving Orchard House," he said, his voice flat. "This is your home now. I'll speak to my father and explain the situation—he won't turn you out. I damn well won't let him."

She was startled by his outburst. "It's rightfully his, Jack. You were quite clear on that when you arrived here. I have no legal claim besides Maria's word, and I'm sure she had no knowledge of the situation besides what it said in her aunt Mathilde's will."

"And I'm my father's heir, which means the property will rightfully be mine someday. And I'm saying that it's yours."

She swallowed hard. "You can't do that."

He rose, releasing her hand. "Of course I can. If you'd feel better about it, I'll talk to my solicitor and have some papers drawn up. An agreement of sorts, whereby you lease the property from me for a pound a year, or some such nonsense."

"It doesn't seem right," she said, though her heart swelled with hope. "What will your family say?"

"As if I give a damn what my family says," he sneered. "My father spends a small fortune to keep his mistress in style in London. Let him think whatever he wants. It's of no consequence to me."

"But…but what will Claire think? Your wife might not be so—"

"I'm not marrying Claire," he said coldly. "I decided so when I broke off our engagement last month, and nothing has changed on that count. If anything, her appearance here has only made it clear just how ill suited we were to begin with. Your doing this—forcing me from your life—accomplishes nothing, Emmaline. *Nothing*," he repeated. "Now if you'll excuse me, I'll go inside and pack my things."

With that, he turned and strode angrily away.

Emmaline just sat there, watching him go as her heart broke into a million little pieces.

Emmaline sat back on her heels, staring at the flower beds in frustration. Why, there had been buds on these plantings a fortnight ago. And now...now they were a brown, withered mess, despite her efforts. Blast it!

Must she fail at everything? She'd poured her heart and soul into this garden, and yet it refused to flourish. Oh, things had begun well enough. Before Jack had left it seemed as if she was going to succeed where no one else had, at least according to Mrs. Talbot. First the roses, then the lavender. Bit by bit, things had begun to show signs of life. She'd gotten ambitious, replanting beds based on color schemes— blues and lavenders in one, reds and pinks in another.

They'd seemed fine at first, the blooms just beginning to bud in several sunny spots. And then...nothing. She'd watered, she'd fertilized, she'd even spoken to them daily, trying to coax them to life. And still they refused to cooperate.

She let out a sigh of frustration. Perhaps she should take Mrs. Talbot's advice and give up. After all, giving up what was she did best. However had she let Jack walk out that door, convinced it was for the best? *I'm nothing but a coward,* she thought bitterly, wishing for the millionth time since he'd gone that she'd taken more time to consider her decision before acting so rashly.

It had been two full weeks since he'd left, and Emmaline hadn't set foot once in the downstairs bedroom he'd occupied, not even to strip the bed and change the linens. She couldn't do it, couldn't bring herself to go inside and touch the things he'd touched, afraid the scent of him would linger, afraid the memories would be too much to bear.

But Mrs. Babbitt was set to return to her housekeeping duties in the morning, and would no doubt wonder why the room sat untouched. *I'm going to have to do it myself,* Emmaline realized. *Tonight.* Once and for all, she would enter the room and face the memories head-on. There was no other way.

She rose, glancing toward the house in the distance.

Orchard House was officially hers now, at least according to the letter that arrived in yesterday's post from Jack's solicitor in London. He certainly hadn't wasted any time. She knew she should be grateful. He'd provided her with a home, after all, when he had every right to take it away from her. But it all seemed so final, especially since he'd already sent someone to retrieve his sporty red roadster and drive it back to Dorset.

He wasn't coming back. She'd driven him away, and now he was gone forever. Her shoulders sagging, she picked her way across the flagstones and headed back inside, determined to tackle the downstairs bedroom now, while she still had the courage.

A quarter hour later, she pushed open the door and stepped inside the room in question. She inhaled deeply, expecting to smell his scent, but it was gone. The room smelled slightly musty, nothing more. An unexpected wave of disappointment washed over her, and she found herself moving toward the bed, reaching for the pillow on which he'd slept so many nights.

Picking it up, she pressed it against her nose, closing her eyes as she imagined him there, his golden head lying on the soft cotton pillowcase. *Nothing.* There was nothing, no lingering scent.

Feeling almost frantic now, she dropped the pillow back to the bed and began to search the room, looking for something—anything—to prove that he had been there. A button, perhaps, or a misplaced sock. In his haste to leave, he must have forgotten some little thing, something worthless and yet priceless, all at once. She pulled back the bedclothes, nearly ripping them from the bed.

And then she found it. Tears stung her eyes as she reached for the crumpled undershirt. She remembered pulling it over his head the last night they'd spent together, right after he'd made love to her in the hallway, half-drunk and a little wild.

Once they'd reached the bedroom, she'd removed his clothing, piece by piece, till he'd been entirely naked. And then she'd stood there in the light of moon and stripped off her nightgown, completely unabashed and unashamed before him. They'd made love twice more before the sun had come up, before they'd fallen into a deep, satisfied sleep.

And when she'd awakened, she'd allowed herself a measure of hope. It had been a glorious feeling, no matter how uncertain. Perhaps they *could* have a future together, despite the unorthodox way they'd met, despite their differences. She'd allowed herself to actually believe it possible.

Right up until Claire Lennox had shown up and shattered that illusion. Damn the woman! If not for her intrusion, they would have had several days more to figure it all out, to sort through the uncertainties and reassure themselves that fate *had* meant for them to find each other.

Crumpling the undershirt into a ball, she held it close as she sank to the bed. Still fully clothed, she lay down, her knees tucked into her chest, the shirt pressed to her face. If she breathed deeply enough, she could still make out his scent, however faint. She could almost imagine his warmth, curled up there beside her.

When the tears came, she did not hold them back. She let them flow freely, let the sobs tear from her throat unchecked.

11

"YOU SIT, DEAR. I'LL POUR." MRS. TALBOT REACHED for the ceramic teapot. It was Emmaline's favorite, a pale rose-colored floral design that she'd found tucked away in a box in the attic. The petals had been hand-painted in raised enamel, the detail particularly impressive. Why it had been put away so unceremoniously would remain a mystery, considering its pristine condition.

"Thank you, Mrs. Talbot," she said, watching as the steaming, caramel-colored liquid filled her dainty cup. "But truly, I'm fine. You needn't trouble yourself on my account."

"It's no trouble at all." Mrs. Talbot set down the teapot and patted Emmaline gently on one cheek. "Besides, isn't it obvious that I'm buttering you up? I vow, I'm going to convince you to tell me what's troubling you before the day's out."

Emmaline spooned two lumps of sugar into her cup, avoiding the woman's prying gaze as she did so. "What makes you think something's troubling me?"

"Well, dear, it's as plain as the nose on your face. You haven't been yourself for weeks now. At first I assumed it was simply exhaustion from tending that man all on your own.

But if that were the case, then you should be well recovered by now. He's been gone, what? Nearly two months?"

"Nearly," Emmaline murmured, bringing the cup to her lips. It had been fifty-four days, to be precise. Each day just as bleak as the one before it.

"Then I can only assume it's something to do with your job. Is Dr. Hayward working you too hard? I can speak with him, if you'd like."

Emmaline set down her cup too hard, sloshing tea onto the saucer. "No, of course not. I'm enjoying my work with the doctor. It's quite rewarding, actually."

Which was the truth, particularly her work with the village's children. Perhaps she'd found her true calling in pediatrics.

Mrs. Talbot eyed her sharply. "Well, then, what is it that's taken the bloom from your cheeks? The light from your eyes? Don't get me wrong—you were a bit melancholy when you first arrived here in Haverham. But now…" She trailed off, shaking her head. "You should be getting better, not worse. Mrs. Babbitt says that when you're not working, you spend most of your time sitting in garden—"

"She told you that?"

Mrs. Talbot waved one hand in dismissal. "Oh, don't be cross with her. She's worried about you, that's all."

"I *like* the garden," Emmaline said with a shrug.

Mrs. Talbot shook her head, her mouth pursed in disbelief. "It's a wasteland, Emmaline, in case you did not notice. I would have expected you to give up by now. I don't know what it is…bad soil, perhaps? Something to do with acidity or something like that. Whatever the case, Mathilde Collins couldn't make a go of it, and neither will you be able to. And then there's the rumors of it being haunted—"

"It's not haunted," Emmaline interrupted impatiently. She'd long since dismissed such notions.

Mrs. Talbot laid a hand atop hers. "I'm a good listener, you know. Whatever it is, you can tell me."

"I—I don't know what you mean," she stammered, the heat rising in her cheeks. Mrs. Talbot was far too perceptive. Perhaps it came from being a minister's wife?

Her neighbor just smiled, patting her hand. "Of course you do, dear. And I'm not leaving here until you tell me."

Emmaline swallowed hard, feeling cornered.

"A burden is always best shared," Mrs. Talbot pushed.

"Is that from the gospels?" she hedged.

"Yes, the gospel according to Clara Talbot. Go on."

"Oh, very well." Emmaline let out her breath in a rush. Perhaps she *would* feel better if she unburdened herself. Either way, it was tell the truth or come up with a convincing lie— and she'd never been a good liar. "If you must know, it's to do with Mr. Wainscott," she blurted out before she had time to think better of it.

Mrs. Talbot's eyes narrowed at once. "I knew it. Taking care of him has exhausted you, hasn't it? Are you ill? Have you spoken to Dr. Hayward about it?"

She sighed, dropping her gaze to the napkin in her lap. "I'm not ill, Mrs. Talbot. I'm…heartsick."

She chanced a glance up, and saw Mrs. Talbot's faded eyes widen with surprise. "Ohhh," she murmured. "I see. You're suffering from a bit of…of unrequited feelings?"

"No." She cleared her throat uncomfortably. "My feelings…they were…requited." Good God, she'd never been so humiliated in all her life.

Mrs. Talbot's brows knitted. "I don't understand. Are you saying that you…that he…"

Emmaline nodded. "We fell in love. I know it was fast—I

realize how utterly mad it must seem, considering how ill
he was. Still, there's no denying what I felt. Some women
are lucky to find a perfect love just once in their lives. I was
lucky twice."

"Did you—that is to say, were you…"

"Yes, we were intimate." Emmaline's cheeks were burning
now, her shame complete.

"And then he *left* you?" Mrs. Talbot sputtered indignantly.
"But wait, wasn't that woman who came to town, the one he
left with…wasn't that his fiancée?"

"His ex-fiancée," she corrected. "He'd broken off the engagement before he came here to Haverham. Apparently she
was having a hard time accepting it as fact."

Mrs. Talbot looked entirely flummoxed. "I still don't understand. If the two of you were in love, then why did he
leave with her?"

How could Emmaline explain, when she barely understood it herself? "He left with her because I told him to,
because I felt guilty and frightened and confused, all at once.
I told him we could not have a future together. At the time,
I believed it to be true. But now…now I'm not so sure."

"Oh, dear. There must be something you can do. Have
you telephoned him?"

She shook her head, cupping her hands around her now
cold teacup. "It's not that simple."

"Of course it is," Mrs. Talbot said with a shrug. "You
ended the relationship—so un-end it."

She sighed heavily. "I'm afraid there's no undoing it. I
made my decision, and he readily accepted it. I cannot blame
him—I was firm on the matter, and I left him no room for
argument. Still…so much time has passed, and he has not
made a single effort to contact me. I can only assume that

that means he has moved on. Perhaps he's married Miss Lennox, after all. I told him that he should."

"I can't believe you would give up so easily. If you truly love him, that is," Mrs. Talbot said. "And I would guess that you do, considering how miserable you've looked these past two months. Oh, dear God—" she clutched at Emmaline's wrist, her gaze drawn directly to her midsection "—you're not…that's to say, he didn't…are you certain…"

"No, I'm not with child, if that's what you're asking." It was only after Jack left that she'd realized she very well might be. She'd actually cried when her menses came a week later, and to this day she wasn't sure if they were tears of relief or disappointment.

Mrs. Talbot let out a sigh of relief. "Thank heavens for that."

The sound of a car's motor in the drive drew their attention toward the front hall.

"Oh, that'll be Mr. Talbot," Mrs. Talbot cried, rising from her seat. "Bother that. What terrible timing the man has! How can I leave you now?"

"I'll be fine, Mrs. Talbot. Truly. And you were right—I do feel much better for having told you. How can I ever thank you for listening and not judging?"

Mrs. Talbot smiled weakly. "Just promise me that you won't give up, that you'll try to set things right with him. If you think he's deserving of your affection, that is."

"He's a lovely man," she said softly, realizing that she meant it with all her heart. "I only wish you'd had the chance to get to know him."

"Well, perhaps I will someday." A horn sounded, making Mrs. Talbot jump. "Oh, dear. I really must go. But don't fret, I have a feeling this isn't quite over yet."

If only she was correct! The trouble was, Emmaline was

nearly certain she wasn't. She'd wasted too much time as it was, waiting, hoping, biding her time. It was time to get on with her life, once and for all.

And that meant life *without* Jack Wainscott.

"Oh, don't laugh. I can try if I want." Emmaline filled the watering pail from the well, then carried it toward the roses—or the barren rosebushes, as was the case.

This is what I'm reduced to, she thought to herself—talking to the image of the Green Man etched into the bench while she gardened. Anyone watching through the peephole in the gate, listening to her as she went about her business, would think she'd lost her wits. And perhaps she had. She smiled to herself as she bent over the most promising of the bushes and doused it with water. This was the same bush that had produced the pink blooms in early May. Even now, she could see the beginnings of a few buds, though they never seemed to progress any more than that before withering away.

It was growing late in the season for roses, anyway. Perhaps she should turn her attention to something else, something that might bloom well into autumn. She knew she ought to give it up, that it was just an exercise in frustration, but she took pleasure in going through the motions. She'd come to enjoy the physical exertion. As long as she considered gardening a pleasant activity in which to indulge rather than a means to an end, there was no risk of disappointment.

Much like the letter she'd written to Jack just last week. She wasn't expecting a reply, but it had felt good to put the words on paper, to open up her heart and let the sentiments pour out. Mostly, she'd apologized—for doubting him, for pushing him away, for underestimating the strength of her feelings.

She'd managed to get his address from the hotel. It had

taken a bit of finagling on her part; she'd claimed that he'd left behind an expensive personal article that she'd only just found. And so she'd learned that he resided at Wainscott House in Bedlington, Dorset. Apparently that was all the direction needed. Emmaline had gathered her courage and posted her letter, with no expectations whatsoever of a reply.

At least, that's what she kept telling herself.

With a shrug, she set down the watering pail by the well and turned to survey the day's work. Beds were dug, dead stems were trimmed away, everything was watered and clipped. Not that there was much to show for it.

She turned toward the Green Man's image. "I'm wasting my time, aren't I?" she asked with a laugh. "Go on and say it—I'm a stubborn, pigheaded woman who simply doesn't know when to give up."

"You're a stubborn, pigheaded woman who simply doesn't know when to give up," stated a deep, decidedly male voice behind her.

It couldn't be....

With a gasp, Emmaline turned toward the voice, her heart beating so fast she feared it might burst.

Dear God, it was him! Standing just inside the gate, his bowler hat in his hands, the late afternoon sun turning his fair hair to burnished gold. He looked like a vision, the most beautiful vision in all of England.

"Jack!" she called out, launching herself toward him. But she stopped short when she reached his side, suddenly afraid. What if she'd misinterpreted his presence there? What if he'd only come to deliver some papers regarding their lease agreement? Or worse, what if he'd changed his mind about allowing her to stay?

"I got your letter," he said, reaching inside his jacket and removing the folded page in question. He held it out, its edges frayed and worn. "I read it, over and over again."

She nodded, her mouth dry. "I see that."

"I hadn't allowed myself to hope, and yet your words... well, I had to read them several times before I could believe them." He paused, staring down at the page, turning it over in his hands. "I hadn't expected this."

Oh, God, it was too late! He'd gone and married Claire Lennox. Emmaline's stomach clenched into a knot, and she feared she might begin to retch.

He just continued to stare at the letter, saying nothing.

"Please, Jack," she whispered hoarsely, unable to bear it a moment more. "Don't torment me so. Just answer me this— is it too late? Did you...are you and Claire—"

"No!" he interjected, his hazel eyes widening. "Good Lord, no. Is that what you thought? I would have waited for you forever." His mouth curved into a smile, making her pulse leap.

Emmaline shook her head. "I should not have made you wait a single day. Will you ever forgive me?"

"There's nothing to forgive," he said. "If you'll have me, that is."

Her heart soared and her blood thrummed hotly through her veins. "How long were you planning to stay?"

He shrugged. "I was thinking perhaps forever. Unless, of course, you have other plans."

"But your home is in Dorset. However will we manage—"

"My father's home is in Dorset," he corrected. "Mine is wherever you are. I say, you've a spot of dirt, there on your nose."

Emmaline laughed, reaching up to swipe at it. Only Jack

could finish off a romantic declaration in such a fashion! "There, is that better?"

"Come here," he said, voice breaking slightly on the last syllable.

She didn't waste a moment complying. Tears of relief flooded her eyes as he wrapped his arms around her. She could hear his heart hammering against his ribs, matching the rhythm of her own. She felt his lips against her hair, sending a shiver of delight down her spine.

"So, did he answer you?" Jack murmured against her ear.

Emmaline pulled away, looking up into Jack's amused eyes. Heavens, but she'd almost forgotten that such a lovely shade of hazel existed. "Did who answer me?"

"Why, the Green Man, I suppose. Isn't that who you were speaking with when I arrived?"

"Oh, *do* shut up!" she said, playfully punching his arm. "Besides, it's not polite to spy on someone unawares."

"Then why is there a peephole in the gate?"

"A fine question, indeed." The breeze stirred, warm and sultry against her cheeks. Soon it picked up momentum, making that odd sound that happened when it blew over the garden's stone walls. Emmaline reached up to brush a stray lock of hair from her eyes.

"It almost sounds like laughter, doesn't it?" Jack asked, glancing around. "I think we've pleased him."

Emmaline rolled her eyes. "Pleased *who?* I vow, you speak in riddles!"

"Why, your Green Man, of course. I've an idea," Jack said, grinning now.

Emmaline decided to play along. "Oh?"

"Let's give him a show," he suggested. "One he won't soon forget. If he's to be imprisoned here forever, we might as well entertain him, don't you think?"

"He's not imprisoned forever," she corrected. "Just until three couples find true love in his enchanted garden. Wasn't that how the legend went?"

He shook his head. "I've forgotten. Maybe it was 'unleash their passion.' Something like that, I suppose."

"Perhaps *we're* the third," she said. "Wouldn't that be grand?"

Jack's grin grew wicked. "Let's show him, then."

"Here?" She glanced around, watching as the wind blew a twig across the flagstones behind him.

"I can't wait a moment more, Emmaline." Jack's voice was hoarse, laced with desire.

She nodded. "Nor can I."

12

EMMALINE'S FINGERS FLEW OVER HER BUTTONS. Jack stood back and watched, barely able to believe that this was happening—his wildest dream come true. He let out his breath in a rush as her blouse parted, revealing the creamy skin above her chemise.

"Come," she said, crooking one finger, then turned and led him farther into the garden, toward her favorite stone bench. He'd pictured her there so many times in the past two hellish months that the image was burned into his brain. Now she looked like Eve herself, removing her clothing bit by bit as she made her way across the flagstones. By the time they reached the bench, nothing remained but her chemise and lacy knickers.

He quirked one eyebrow. "My turn?" he asked, his fingers already hovering over his jacket buttons, his cock hard and straining against his trousers.

"It's only fair, don't you think?" she asked, sitting on the bench and primly crossing her legs.

He glanced back over his shoulder before returning his attention to a near-naked Emmaline. In seconds, he'd doffed his coat and unbuttoned his shirt. "You're not expecting Mrs.

Talbot, are you?" he asked, pulling his shirttails from the band of his trousers. "She does have a knack for arriving at inopportune moments. And there *is* a peephole, as we've discussed."

"Are you afraid of being caught in a compromising situation, Jack Wainscott?" A smile danced on Emmaline's lips, lighting up her entire face.

He unbuttoned his trousers and stepped out of them, tossing them to the bench beside her. "Well, she *is* the vicar's wife. We would not want to shock her too horribly with our scandalous behavior. I haven't yet made an honest woman of you, after all."

"Oh, had you planned to?" she asked, reaching for the hem of her chemise and pulling it over her head, baring her breasts to his hungry gaze.

He stifled a groan, nearly shaking with anticipation now. "Dear God, Emmaline," he groaned, barely able to keep his hands off her. "Just as soon as you'll let me. Tomorrow, if possible."

She laughed, rising to stand before him. Her fingers hooked into the waistband of her knickers, and he held his breath as she slowly slid them down, past her hips, to her ankles. Graceful as ever, she stepped out of them, entirely bare now.

His gaze skimmed down her body, from her face to her rose-tipped breasts, to the tantalizing dark triangle where her thighs joined, to her shapely calves down to her toes, and back up again. He saw her shiver in response, her skin flushed pink, her dark eyes burning with unconcealed desire.

"You are so very beautiful," he said in awe, amazed as ever that she was real, that she was there, that she was his.

"Tomorrow's a bit soon, don't you think?" she asked, taking two steps toward him. Her fingertips skimmed down his chest, drawing gooseflesh in their wake. "After all, I'm not going anywhere. And if you're here to stay…" Her fingers pushed past the waistband of his drawers, moving toward his cock.

"I'm here to stay," he answered breathlessly, watching incredulously as she lowered herself to the bench, her dark head bent toward him as she pushed down his drawers, till his erection sprang free. Devil take it, if she did what he thought she was going to—

A groan caught in the back of his throat as Emmaline's lips closed over his cock. Slowly, she eased him deeper into her mouth, until the tip pressed against the back of her throat. Her lips tightened against his shaft, increasing the pressure as she drew him out again. Instinctively, he reached out to cup the back of her head, resisting the urge to close his eyes.

No, he wanted to see her, wanted to watch as her tongue darted out to lick the drop of moisture from the tip of his cock, her fingers closed around his ballocks now. Holy hell and damnation, he wasn't going to last another second—he was going to come right here and now, before he'd even had the chance to pleasure *her*.

He tugged her to her feet, swinging her around so that she faced the bench now. In a matter of seconds, he'd managed to free himself of his drawers and pull her down atop him, straddling him, ready for her to ride him.

Their coupling was quick—hurried and frantic. With each stroke, he pulled her down harder, wanting to fill her entirely, wanting to make her writhe against him and cry out his name as she came.

Only when she began to do just that, her cunt pulsating against his shaft, did he find his own release.

Emmaline laid her head against his shoulder, her breathing slowing as they sat there, their bodies one as they listened to the songbirds calling gaily to one another, to the breeze ruffling the leaves, to an automobile horn off in the distance.

Jack could have sat like that forever, his heart thumping against hers, their bare skin warmed by the sun. A sense of peace filled him, and he bent to kiss her fragrant neck.

"That should do nicely," she murmured, sounding entirely sated.

He raised one brow. "Oh?"

"To convince the Green Man that we've found true love, I meant. Though if you'd like to try again…"

"Give me ten minutes," he said with a laugh.

She nodded, her tongue tracing lazy circles on his shoulder. "I would say five, but I've been ill, remember?"

She sat up, her gaze meeting his. "Thank God for the influenza. Otherwise, who's to say what might have happened?"

"Regardless, I would have preferred a more…well, *masculine* way of getting acquainted."

She brushed back a lock of his hair that had fallen across his forehead. "You were charming, even unconscious."

"How many days was I out again?"

"Nearly five. You talk, you know. In your sleep," she clarified, grinning at him. "Even when unconscious."

His brow furrowed. "Should I be worried?"

She shook her head. "You called out my name, more than once. Even though you'd only learned it moments before you collapsed."

He shifted her in his lap. "When I first awoke, I had no memory of you—of your name. Odd, isn't it?"

"Your subconscious must have remembered, that's all." She shivered against him. "It's getting cool. We should go inside."

He rubbed his hands down her arms, trying to warm her. "I suppose we should. As much as I'd love to stay here, just like this, forever." Though in truth, the rough stones beneath him were starting to feel abrasive. Amazing how he hadn't even noticed before.

She disentangled herself and stood, reaching for her discarded clothing. "Let's go in and I'll give you a full examination, to make certain you've recovered fully," she offered, and he wasn't sure if she was teasing or not.

"No examinations! I'm no longer your patient." Dear God, the humiliation of it all.

"Well, then, perhaps you'd like to examine *me,* instead?" she teased.

"I say, now that's a fine idea." He nodded, excited by the possibilities.

She reached down and plucked his drawers from the stones, her eyes dancing with mischief. "Catch me, then," she called out, dashing toward the garden gate.

He wasted no time at all in complying.

As the gate latched shut behind the pair of lovers, a voice on the wind could be heard, laughing in delight.

Then there were three, it seemed to say.

And now…I am free.

Two weeks later…

"But—but it's impossible," Emmaline stammered, turning in a slow circle.

Jack shrugged. "It would seem so. And yet…just look."

Emmaline could barely believe her eyes. She was standing amid a sea of color. Green, blue, purple, pink, yellow…color, everywhere. The garden was a veritable Eden.

The roses, well past their season, were in full bloom. Bluebells, violets, lilies, irises, hollyhocks…they all blossomed in a lush profusion of color and scent, creating a multicolored palette that filled the entire walled-in space.

Emmaline blinked rapidly, thinking that perhaps her eyes were playing tricks on her, but the view remained the same.

The well still stood in the center, and the bench remained in the shady corner. That much hadn't changed.

Only the garden had come to life around them.

"Amazing, isn't it?" Mrs. Talbot asked. "I declare, I simply did not think it possible."

"Nor did I," said Jack, the fading sun turning his hair a dull copper.

Emmaline planted her hands on her hips. "I don't see how anyone could have thought it possible."

Mrs. Talbot nodded, her eyes shining brightly. "I should bring Mr. Talbot here to see this. It's almost like...like a miracle."

"Or something like that," Jack said, holding up the tattered leather book he'd retrieved from the library just before they'd stepped outside.

"You don't think..." Emmaline trailed off, unwilling to voice her thoughts aloud in front of Mrs. Talbot.

Jack strode purposely toward the stone bench, tapping the Green Man's image while grinning at Emmaline. His look seemed to say *I told you so.*

Emmaline grinned back at him.

"Shall we go inside for dinner?" he asked, reaching for her hand.

"Indeed. I'm famished," said Mrs. Talbot.

Emmaline nodded, allowing Jack to thread his fingers through hers. She glanced up at him—her Beltane miracle—and smiled, saying a silent thanks to whoever had brought them together.

And then, no longer alone, she fell into step between them—Jack and Mrs. Talbot—and headed toward home.

★ ★ ★ ★ ★

The first book in the tantalizing new *Sins and Virtues* series by

CHARLOTTE FEATHERSTONE

The Unseelie Court will perish unless one of its princes can win a woman's love—honestly, without coercion— and love her wholly in return.

Noblewoman Chastity Lennox is purity incarnate—a sensual prize well worth winning. But Thane's carnal quest proves more challenging than he ever dreamed.

No other has ever been able—or willing—to resist his erotic charms. Chastity's resolve is maddening...and intriguing. It makes him want her all the more. But how best to seduce one who truly seems above temptation? Discover her greatest weakness and become the intoxicating essence of her deepest, most forbidden desires....

"Featherstone has what it takes to write keeper-worthy, full-scale historicals"
—*RT Book Reviews*

www.Spice-Books.com

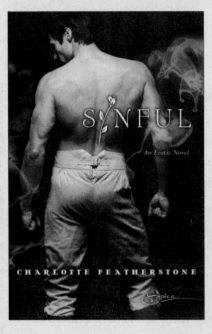

Bestselling author

AMANDA McINTYRE

Ensnared in the untamed Dark Ages of north England, Sierra understands all too well what it takes to survive—the ability to numb the soul. She has learned this lesson the hard way, watching her mother die at the hands of the king's henchmen, seeing her brother cast out into the cold to perish and discovering that the treacherous, leering king holds a crucial secret about her past.

But when he grants Sierra her life, she discovers the pardon is perhaps worse than death. Sierra is made executioner's apprentice, forced to witness unspeakable suffering while encouraged to explore her own sexual power.

Brainwashed and exhausted, Sierra feels her heart slowly growing cold—until Dryston of Hereford is brought to the dungeon as a traitor and spy. Using her sexual allure to extract the warrior's secrets, Sierra finds herself torn between duty and desire. Soon Sierra is craving the only man who can help set her battered soul free and give her a chance for revenge....

Tortured

Available now wherever books are sold!

www.Spice-Books.com

SAM533TR